Missing!

Neive Denis

The third book in the Sonoma Whittington series.

Copyright

First published in 2016
Copyright © Neive Denis 2016

National Library of Australia
Cataloguing-in-publication data
Creator: Denis, Neive, author.
Title: Missing! / Neive Denis.
ISBN: 9780975028728 (paperback)
Subjects: Australian fiction.
 Detective and mystery stories.
Dewey Number: A823.4
-

ISBN:978-0-9750287-2-8 (paperback)
ISBN: 978-0-9750287-3-5 (eBook)

Dedication

To Michelle –

for your valued support and friendship

Contents

Other Books by the Author

An Ancient Solution
A public Service

CHAPTER 1

"Excuse me, Miss. Excuse me."

"Oh, sorry, were you talking to me?"

"You're a private investigator aren't you? My friend… she's a friend of Emily's… she said you were, and that you were staying with Emily for a few days."

"Yes that's correct, I am a Private Investigator and I am staying with Emily for a few days, so what does that …?"

"We have a problem …er… well, we think we *might* have a problem."

"Who is 'we'… does this involve Emily?"

"No, I mean my husband and me. We don't know what to do and we're just about going out of our minds. It's about our daughter…"

"Is this something that maybe you should be talking to the police about? It depends on what it is that's worrying you about your daughter whether I might be able to help you or not."

"We tried talking to the police. They didn't want to know; said we were being overprotective and making a fuss about nothing. Look, can you at least hear me out? Let me tell you why we think something is wrong."

"Y-e-s, but I don't promise there is anything I can do. I am only here for a couple of days."

"Please… Our daughter often goes away – sometimes on her own, sometimes with her best mate. She rings us regularly, not every day but maybe every second day. She has a blog -- or whatever you call those things that are like an electronic diary. The only other people who can read it are my husband and me: her parents. Every night she writes up what she did for the day."

"That must be useful to you, but it doesn't tell me why you think there is a problem."

"She hasn't rung since soon after she arrived and hasn't updated her diary."

"If she's young and got caught up in what she was doing, that wouldn't be unusual. It doesn't mean anything is wrong. It probably means she is enjoying herself."

"If you would just hear me out; there's a coffee shop over the road. Perhaps I could buy us a cup of coffee and tell you the story."

"Okay, I was thinking of getting a coffee anyway. I do need to tell you, however, that I'm not sure what I can …" I didn't get a chance to finish what I wanted to say as she cut in quickly.

"Don't jump to any conclusions, please, not until you've heard what I have to say."

I don't want to give her any false hope that I might be able to perform some sort of miracle for her. My expectation is for another mother's story about a daughter she thinks has fallen in with bad company, or has gone off the rails in some other way. It's not that I don't want the business, or that I don't care. The agency is doing very well and I am kept busy, but it's not good policy to turn down potential clients in my line of work because one never knows when the next job – or if the next job – will come along.

If this were a Millhaven parent, it wouldn't be too hard to find out what the daughter was doing. However, when I am staying with Emily in Moxton for only a couple of days, there doesn't seem much point in getting the woman's hopes up. Anyway, it might be that I can't help her. Whichever way it goes, I need to let her down in a way that doesn't hurt too much… and possibly create a whole truckload of damaging word of mouth comment.

As we crossed the road to the coffee shop, I cast my mind over my current workload. If there is something in what this woman has to say, do I have time for even a superficial look at it? Some reassurance that things weren't as bad as they were beginning to think might be enough to ease her mind and avoid getting me a bad review. Could I fit it in with the current work I had scheduled? Not enough information yet to make decisions. We entered the coffee shop and selected a table. I concentrated on maintaining an open mind on the subject and took care of some basics while we waited for someone to take our order. "Maybe we should introduce ourselves while we wait. I'm Sonny Whittington, and you are…? She looked a bit shocked by the question. I pushed a business card across the table to her.

"Geez, what must you be thinking. I didn't even introduce myself. I'm Maggie Sinclair. My husband is Tony, and our daughter is Sarah. It's Sarah I need to talk to you about."

A young woman with too much make-up and hair dyed as black as coal, but without the sheen, came to take our order, successfully halting conversation for a few moments.

"Okay, why do you think there is a problem with Sarah? Where is she? What has she done to make you so concerned?"

"She's missing."

Brevity is not going to get us anywhere. I hoped she would be a bit more expansive with the rest of the story. After a couple of moments, without further prompting, Maggie offered another morsel of information.

"The Police said we didn't have anything to suggest she was missing. We were just fussing about our only child being away from home. They wouldn't listen when I tried to explain. We *know* something is wrong. Sarah is often away from home. It's not the first time she's been away… but it is the first time she hasn't contacted us regularly while she was away."

"You say she often goes away; perhaps, if you give me some background to Sarah, where she goes and what she does, I'll be able to get a better picture of your daughter and will be better able to understand what you tell me." The coffees arrived causing another brief pause in proceedings.

"She's twenty-two and works out here at the mine like the rest of us. She has a fantastic job and works with her best mate, Gillian… no, sorry, used to work with Gillian. They worked a strange roster: four weeks of twelve-hour days and then two weeks off. They're paid buckets of money and they both like to get away from the place when they have their time off. What they've always done is save up like fury then, as there is nowhere much to spend it out here, they would head off to somewhere when they were rostered off. Their travel has been to all sorts of places: Tasmania, New Zealand, Japan, Bali, Broome -- just to name a few."

"So these trips are for about two weeks? It seems they travelled together, but did they go on escorted tours or make their own arrangements?"

"Sometimes on escorted tours but, a lot of the time, they make their own arrangements because they say it often works out cheaper and they can spend their time doing exactly whatever they like. They don't always go for two weeks at a time. For instance, when they went to Broome, they only spent a week there."

"What's the story with Gillian? You said Sarah used to work with Gillian. I'm assuming something happened to that arrangement."

"Like all the mines right now, this place is letting people go. Gillian worked in a slightly different section of the same department as Sarah, and she heard rumours the work in her area was being outsourced. She started applying for other jobs and landed one overseas almost straight away. The two girls wanted to keep their friendship alive and planned they would still travel around together once they worked out what Gillian's schedule was."

"Was Gillian with her on this occasion?"

"No, Gillian's been gone a couple of months or more now, but only in her new job for about a month. She took some leave before she started the new job and now has to work for a while before she gets any time off. It is about three months since the girls last went anywhere. Sarah decided it was time she had some time away from the place, so she went off on her own this time."

"Where did she go, and how did she go? Was she part of a tour or was she doing her own thing?"

"She thought about going overseas somewhere but decided against it. That alternative lifestyle community over the border holds these fantastic festivals – or markets, or whatever they call them. The girls always spoke about going to one of them. These events take place over long weekends. Anyway, there was a long weekend coming up, so Sarah decided to go and arranged everything herself. She did say that, if she liked the look of the area, she might hire a car and have a look around the district."

"So, that long weekend was last weekend – a week ago now?" Maggie nodded. "When did she leave and how did she travel?" This was becoming exhausting. I was willing Maggie to just launch into the story and tell me how it all happened. "Maggie, suppose you tell me everything that happened from just prior to when Sarah left."

"Uhmm, yes okay; she packed and was ready to go when she finished work on the Friday – a week ago today. We were both on night shift last week so, as soon as she finished work, I drove her to the airport. She had to change planes and all that, but she was due to book into her accommodation that afternoon. All that went okay."

"She booked in as arrange on Friday afternoon?"

"Yes, she rang Friday night to say she had arrived. I checked with the place and they confirm she checked-in on Friday as planned. They don't remember seeing her about after that, but they didn't expect to. People spend their time out and about the place on those weekends, not hanging around their motel."

"When did you check with the motel?"

"I rang them on Monday morning because we hadn't heard from Sarah since Friday night. Apart from anything else, I needed to know if she was coming home after the weekend. I needed to know if I was to collect her from the airport on Tuesday, or if she was going to stay and look around for a few days. Anyway, they hadn't seen anything of her. She hadn't changed her booking and was still expected to book out on Tuesday morning."

"Why didn't you ring Sarah?"

"We did but she didn't answer. I rang the motel again on Monday night and asked to be put through to her room. She wasn't there, so I left a message for her to ring me urgently. I needed to find out what her plans were before she left the motel. I think something was wrong with her mobile phone. We rang several times and left messages but she didn't ring back. Once she left the motel, I wouldn't know where or how to contact her."

"Did you hear from Sarah – or the motel after that?"

"When I hadn't heard from her by Monday night, I was going to ring the motel as soon as it got to be a civilised hour on Tuesday morning. Then, I was busy at work and didn't have a chance to ring until lunchtime. There were missed calls. The motel had been trying to get in touch with me. They tried ringing Sarah when she didn't check out on Tuesday morning as planned."

"So they hadn't seen anything to suggest there was a problem until she didn't checkout as planned?"

"No, they hadn't seen anything of her but didn't worry until then. When they couldn't reach Sarah, they tried ringing me at home. Of course, there was no one at home because my husband and I were both at work. The motel's housekeeping staff had Sarah's room listed as vacated on Tuesday morning and went in to clean. They reported that all Sarah's stuff was still in the room. The motel was very obliging and said they will hold Sarah's belongings and, if she suddenly turns up again, she would have no problem getting a room as they had vacancies after the weekend."

"Is that when you went to the Police?"

"Yes, as soon as I finished work, I went to see them about what to do. They dismissed the whole thing as a case of my being overprotective. I was worried sick. I looked up what I worked out was the police station nearest to where Sarah was staying and I rang them. They weren't interested either. They assured me young ones have a good time at these festivals, don't worry too much about letting their parents know what they are up to, and often forget to go home as planned."

This sounded like the Police's standard response to parents after one of these festivals. I had developed a mental picture of what such a festival could be like for the younger generation. If that picture was anything like reality, I could appreciate why the Police would trot out such a well-worn response to a worried parent.

After a couple of sips of her coffee, Maggie continued. "I know they were suggesting that drugs and/or booze probably were involved and that offspring who indulged too much sometimes tried to 'sort themselves out' before they returned home. I tried ringing them again first thing this morning. They were even more dismissive this time -- quite rude in fact. However, I got the clear message that they were not interested and not going to do anything."

"I know this is going to upset you but, is it likely Sarah might have gotten involved in something like that?" I wasn't completely surprised when the question upset her and drew an angry outburst that lasted a few moments. I let her rant. She slowly regained her composure and we returned to cordial discourse.

"No! Gillian's brother died a couple of years ago from a drug related situation. Sarah was sweet on him and they had just started going out together. She was devastated. His death had a lasting impact. She never could stand drugs and didn't know he was a user. Gillian said he wasn't a user, but for some reason chose to experiment – with fatal outcome – while on an overseas holiday."

Maggie had destroyed the paper napkin she picked up early in our conversation. Now tears began tumbling down her cheeks. I fished a pocket packet of tissues out of my bag and slid them across to her. The girl with the dyed hair was making her way to our table. I waved her away. Maggie did not need an audience right now.

My head and heart were in conflict. My heart went out to Maggie, but my head kept telling me to leave it alone … or, at best, to have another quick word to the police, then hand it over to them. For the moment, my heart was winning the battle.

"It's only fair I tell you up front that I don't normally work outside Queensland, and that I already have a heavy case load to deal with. I planned to spend only a few days in Moxton before returning home to Millhaven on the weekend."

"Doesn't your license allow you to work outside this state?"

"I am licensed to work elsewhere, but you can't carry out an investigation by staying at home and playing on Google. You do have to go to where the case leads you. It helps if you are familiar with the area you're going to work in. If I want to give my clients the best service for their money, I work in the state I know best. However, having said that, if you can put together everything you know about Sarah's trip – every possible detail – I'll have a look at it. I'm not making any promises. I'll take a look at what you give me, and I'll let you know if there is anything I can do."

She wasn't exactly impressed with my offer, but admitted it was the most anyone offered to do so far. The arrangement was that she would put everything together tonight and drop it off at Emily's place early tomorrow morning when she was on her way to work.

We left the coffee shop and went our separate ways. As we parted company on the footpath, I thought of something else and called her back.

"Has Sarah updated her electronic diary at all since she left home?"

"She added a bit on the Friday while she was travelling, but nothing more since."

CHAPTER 2

As I had walked into town, I had time to mull over all Maggie had told me – which wasn't much -- as I walked the short distance back to Emily's house. Created to provide the basic facilities for an intended mining camp, Moxton, like Topsy grew and grew as more mines opened in the same general area.

Although the town itself became something more than a mining camp, the town centre never really matched the growth. Now, it remained small and had a forlorn and tired look. The only additions to acknowledge the community's growth were the coffee shop and a large community hall in a back street that sometimes doubled as a movie theatre. At some point, the local authority created a couple of grassy areas in the town centre and planted a few shrubs. Water is precious out here, with mining operations having priority over its use. Nobody questioned that but, consequently, the authority's attempts at beautifying the town suffered. Grass and shrubs struggled to survive from day one. The unusually long dry spell ended their struggle. Dead grass and shrubs in almost the same condition did nothing to improve the dry, dusty town centre.

It was early afternoon when I arrived back. I missed lunch but wasn't hungry. Emily was still at work and her mother, Sandra, had taken herself off for an afternoon nap. You can't help good luck. The house was quiet. With the place virtually to myself, I decided to spend the time doing some preliminary research until whatever time one or the other of the women appeared. I booted up my computer and got busy.

First task: find a map of the festival town and expand it to street level. I don't know what that will prove but at least it will give me some idea of the layout of the town and its facilities. Then I went in search of any festival advertising material. There were two sites offering information and, between them, provided a reasonably comprehensive overview of the location and the weekend's program.

The festival venue was a field not too far from the town's motels strip. If Sarah stayed at one of those motels, she could walk to the festival. It wasn't a long walk and the simplest and shortest way would be the country lane running along behind the motels. I imagine it was better to walk than drive, and then have to find somewhere to park the hire car – if she had hired one. Note to self: check whether Sarah hired a car from any firms in the vicinity.

That gave me my next task: look up all the local car hire firms and note their contact details. It didn't take long. There were only three located within the town itself or close by. I took my phone out onto the back deck to call them. The first place I rang was hesitant from the outset and reluctant to talk to me. I went into persuasive mode but still didn't have much success until I delivered my 'killer shot'.

"Look, I know you don't normally give out information about your clients. However, my client is now desperate about her missing daughter. We are about to turn the whole matter over to the police in the morning. I thought it might help the police make quicker progress if I could give them as much information as possible to begin with. It also would avoid having them front up to your door with a warrant to search your records for any information that might shed some light on what has happened to her. It appears I was mistaken, so I will have to let the police handle their investigation in their own way."

It seems the information could be available if I didn't mind waiting a few moments while she looked it up for me. Of course, I didn't mind waiting for her to look it up, if it wasn't too much trouble… How simpering I can be when it suits. The woman came back to me after only a minute or so.

"Uhmm, yes, a Sarah Sinclair from Moxton hired a small four-door sedan last Saturday. It's due for return tomorrow … oh, but there's an additional note. It says she wasn't sure how long she would need it and might return it on Tuesday morning if she decided to go home early. Well, that didn't happen. That's last Tuesday I'm talking about so, presumably, she'll return it tomorrow."

I felt my stomach tighten. After thanking her and telling her I would check on the car again car tomorrow, I ended the call and sat idly watching magpies fighting over a lizard one of them caught. Too early and insufficient evidence to jump to conclusions, but my gut didn't agree. It didn't like the way things were shaping up. At last, I stirred myself. People would descend upon me shortly. Was there something else I could do before then? I didn't have the name of the motel Sarah stayed at, so I couldn't annoy them. I doubted there was anything they could tell me anyway.

Another idea came to me. I didn't think it would help find Sarah, but it might shed some light on anything that happened during the festival. I brought my computer out onto the back deck and searched the internet for any media reports on the festival. The town was too small to have its own local newspaper. There was a monthly newsletter by some local community group but the last edition was prior to the festival and wasn't helpful. A weekly newspaper produced in the neighbouring town offered some titbits from the festival, but nothing of any use.

I pondered what else I might search while still connected to the internet and idly skimming the rest of the latest edition of the newspaper. I wasn't really reading anything. It was all just drifting past me. Then my subconscious screamed at me. I sat up, focused on the screen, and carefully backtracked over the previous couple of pages. Ah-hah, there it was: the thing that jolted my subconscious to life. I read the article, and then I read it again -- more slowly.

It was about a young woman – almost 17 years old and still a schoolgirl – who it alleged disappeared sometime early on the Saturday night of the long weekend. The girl and her father travel around the circuit with their stall selling hand-made leather handbags. They camped in their caravan in an area off to one side of the festival site set aside for that purpose for stallholders. The father and some of his colleagues from the circuit had a night on the town after the festival closed down on Saturday night, after which the father and a female colleague spent the night together in a motel.

When they arrived back at the festival grounds late on Sunday morning, the man found his daughter wasn't at their stall. What did she think she was playing at? Why did she think he brought her along with him? Her job was to operate the stall any time he wasn't there. A string of bad language trailed in his wake as he stormed off to check the caravan and anywhere else she might be. There was no sign of her. The paper went on to report that she did not return to the festival and there has been no contact from the girl.

The article concluded with reference to something of a similar nature that occurred prior to the start of the festival. There was no mistaking the newspaper's negative view of such festivals, particularly when they occurred in its district. While much of its criticism probably was true, I suspect the editor holds something of a Puritan view of life. Reference to the earlier article sent me off in search of it. There didn't appear to be any logic in the paper's layout, so it took a fair amount of painstaking searching to find the relevant story.

It related to an incident that occurred during the various activities involved with setting up the site for the festival. The alleged abduction of a young woman occurred on the Thursday evening before the festival.

She worked alone stacking stock in the small tent from which she would sell her hand-made jewellery. Robbery didn't appear to be the motive. An elderly man walking his dog heard screams and saw what he believed was a woman being bundled into a dark coloured van.

Sandra wandered out onto the deck and announced she was going for a walk. "I need to do something to wake myself up. I was only going to have a nap but slept soundly for so long, I can't seem to wake up properly. Do you want to join me for a stroll around the town?"

"No thanks; I walked this morning and I doubt anything has changed around town since then. I thought I might catch up on some work this afternoon." She waved as she went back inside. A moment later, I heard the front door close.

I didn't think there was anything else I could do today except type up notes on what little I'd discovered this afternoon. After that, I sat pondering the worrying stories of the two women who went missing at the time of the festival. Was Sarah the third one to go missing? My gut instinct told me there was no good news associated with Sarah's lack of contact. The sound of Emily's car on the gravel driveway brought me back to reality. I closed my computer and went to meet Emily as she came into the house.

"Get glasses and the white wine out of the fridge and I'll join you on the deck as soon as I've changed," she said as she made her way through to her room.

I did as instructed and used the few moments before she joined me to cast my mind back over the week's events. A former work mate invited me to her wedding, which took place in Brisbane over the long weekend. We were reasonably close when we worked together, but our relationship gradually reduced to long emails for birthdays and Christmas, and the occasional short message in between.

The wedding invitation came as a surprise. My initial reaction was to renege on attending. We weren't that close anymore. After giving it some thought, I decided to go. It was an opportunity to catch up with a couple of other people I hadn't seen for a while, and I wanted to see a show that would soon end its Brisbane run. I flew down late on Saturday, did the wedding thing on Sunday, took in the show and saw a couple of people on Monday, and caught up with a couple of coppers I'd worked with in the past on Tuesday. Then, everything in Brisbane done, I flew to Moxton on Wednesday to stay with Emily for a couple of days.

Emily and I stayed in contact after she worked with me on a case a while back, and she kept harping about getting together again sometime. Her mother, Sandra, and I had been friends for years. After Sandra's husband ended up in jail for his involvement in a drugs trafficking network, she remained in Millhaven but spent increasing amounts of time with her daughters, one in Brisbane, whom I didn't know well, and Emily at Moxton. I caved into pressure to visit Moxton on my way back to Millhaven after the wedding. …And so, here I am, and I'm supposed to drive back to Millhaven with Sandra sometime over the coming weekend. That arrangement might have to change if I take on the job of finding Sarah Sinclair.

I poured the wine as Emily joined me on the deck. Now wearing shorts and a loose top, her hair, damp from her quick shower, piled up haphazardly on top of her head. She heaved an exaggerated sigh as she plonked herself on a chair.

"Bad day?" I asked after we took our first sips.

"Yeah… no, just long, busy and boring. Have you been working?" she asked and nodded towards my computer.

"Sort of; I had an interesting trip to town today. You don't happen to know Sarah Sinclair do you?"

"Yeah, I know Sarah and her mother, Maggie, but I don't think I know her father other than to look at. Why do you ask?"

"It seems she has gone missing… at least that's what her parents believe."

"That doesn't sound like Sarah. She's level headed and quite capable of looking after herself. I know she and her mate, Gillian, did a fair bit of travelling together. She was a bit down for a while when Gillian left here. What's the story about her going missing?"

As succinctly as possible, I explained about Sarah's solo trip to the festival and how her parents had no contact with her since after she arrived in the town last Friday night. Without applying too much thought, I added my concerns about her welfare after reading the articles about the two females whose disappearances seem linked to the same festival. Emily came to life immediately. She sensed intrigue and mystery, her excitement visible all over her face. I tried to defuse her interest, saying how I hadn't accepted the job and didn't know if I would. It was to no avail. She was off and running, posing all sorts of hypotheses about what might've happened to Sarah.

"Whoa, hang on a minute. I don't know that anything has happened to Sarah. The whole thing is just a bit out of keeping with normal practice and her parents – probably with some justification – are worried about what might be going on."

"Yeah, yeah, I hear you; but, as you said, it's out of keeping for Sarah to remain incommunicado for so long. From what I know of her, she's very close to her parents. She would be aware of how concerned they would be and would not willingly create that sort of worry for them. So, what's your next move?"

"I don't know that there is a next move… yet. I've only spoken to her mother over a cup of coffee, so I don't have all the facts. Maggie is supposed to drop some stuff around me tomorrow morning early. Maybe after that, I'll have a better idea of the whole story and be in a position to make a decision about whether I want to get involved or not. If she really has gone missing, it will be a matter for the police rather than something I can do much about."

I gazed out across the back yard as I spoke. While the words were for Emily's benefit, in reality, they probably were an attempt to convince myself that was the truth of the matter. As I finished speaking, I glanced over at Emily. She was struggling to hide a grin.

"What's so funny? I can't see anything humorous in the story so far."

"Who were you trying to convince with that dialogue? You know you're going to take the job. There's just too much mystery – intrigue – involved for you to walk away from it… that, and your very natural concern for Sarah's well-being, of course."

The sarcasm in her final comment hit its mark. She was right. In spite of the little I know about it, Sarah's disappearance has grabbed me by the collar and is tugging me into its web of intrigue. … And yes, I am concerned for her well-being, but I'm also concerned about what happened to those other two females. Emily's curiosity was rampant, but there was no opportunity for further discussion. Sandra arrived home from her walk.

CHAPTER 3

True to her word, Maggie rang the doorbell around seven o'clock this morning. I had just puffed my way the last few metres back to the house from a jog around the neighbourhood and felt obliged to apologise for my appearance. The morning already was sultry, the humidity level stifling. After the run, my T-shirt was wet and sticking to me. A few strands of my unruly brown curls that I had pulled up loosely into a ponytail escaped and now plastered themselves to my face.

I noted the slightly startled look from Maggie as she eyed me up and down. She was ringing the doorbell as I ran up onto the back deck. I kept running, across the deck, in through the back door and down the hallway to open the front door to Maggie. She looked down at the large manila envelope in her hand and gradually extended her arm to offer it to me.

"There's still no word from her," she said quietly with downcast eyes. "I don't know how useful any of that will be to you." She gestured to the envelope. "Everything we have or know is in there. It doesn't look like much now I've put it all together, but it is everything."

I simply nodded. "Have you put your contact details in there somewhere? I'll go through it all as soon as I've had a shower. Can I contact you somewhere today if I have any questions or need to speak to you about any of it?"

"Yes, I put all my contact details in there. Please, if you want to know anything, just give me a call. I just wondered… I know you haven't read anything yet, but do you think you can… uhhm… you *might* be able to have a look into it for us?" She stammered. I focused on the envelope, the pleading look on her face more than I could bear.

"You're right, I'll need to go through all of this before I can tell you anything definite, but I'll probably be able to make a few inquiries. We'll see what happens after that."

"Do you need a -- what's it called? -- a retainer or something to get started? Do you take personal cheques, or how do we pay you? I could give you a cheque now, if you like."

"Let's just take it slowly, shall we. Let me read this stuff first and maybe make a couple of phone calls, and then I'll get back to you. After that, hopefully, I will have a better idea of what might have happened."

Maggie left and I headed for a shower. Then, feeling and looking a bit more presentable, I made coffee and toast and took it and Maggie's envelope out onto the back deck. It was Saturday morning. Emily and her mother believe weekends are for long sleep-ins. I was thankful. Their absence allowed me to breakfast and read the envelope's contents in peaceful solitude. After a quick look at everything in the envelope, I fetched a notebook and started making notes and lists of questions that needed answers.

There wasn't a lot of new information in Maggie's material. It did provide the names of the motel Sarah stayed at and the Police station Maggie rang. First entries on the list of things to do today were to ring the motel and to check the location of the Police station Maggie mentioned. Later today, I must check with the hire car place to see if Sarah returned her hire car. It would be useful to know about usage of Sarah's credit cards during the week. Were there any other transactions apart from the motel's imprint of the card and the hire the car? It didn't seem likely I would get access to that information, and it was equally unlikely her parents would be able to access it either. However, it was worth asking Maggie. I added it to the list of things to do.

The household was stirring. I returned everything to the envelope and took it to my room. On my way back to the kitchen, Emily, heading in the same direction, joined me. A couple of minutes later, Sandra arrived in the kitchen. She was dressed in her walking gear and announced she would go for a walk before breakfasting later. Emily made cereal and juice for herself while I made another coffee, and we carried it through to the back deck. I don't think we wasted time even on 'good mornings' before she launched into it.

"So, what's our agenda for today? What do we tackle first?"

"What are you on about? It's the weekend. What do you normally do on the weekend?"

"No, I mean about Sarah. How are we going to tackle this case? Oh, you said Maggie was going to drop off some information. What time is she coming?"

"She's been already… and yes, she gave me some stuff. It's not a lot to go on but now I know a bit more than I did before. I want to make a couple of phone calls and then I'll talk to Maggie again. By the way, before you go off getting all excited about 'the case', I haven't agreed to take it yet. I won't make a decision about that until I've looked into a few things first.

Regardless of whether I take it on or not, what makes you think you might be involved in anything?"

"We worked well together before remember: Therese's death. I thought you might want to use my fine deductive powers – not to mention my local knowledge – to help solve this case as well." She finished with a wide-eyed impish grin. I just knew she would use her help in investigating my former boss' death as a lever to get involved in the potential Sarah Sinclair case.

I'm wishing I had even enough for me to work with, let alone something for Emily to do. We heard Sandra return from her walk. Emily went through to the kitchen to help make Sandra's breakfast. It was too early yet to start ringing people, and it was Saturday, so I booted up my computer and searched for Police stations in the area surrounding the festival's location. As I waited for the information to load, it occurred to me that I didn't know much about that festival that enticed Sarah away for those few days.

When it loaded, the Police Stations information wasn't particularly helpful. The one Maggie contacted probably would not be my first choice. There were several in the area surrounding the festival location, but none stood out as being linked to the place. After pondering that for a few moments, I decided to check the online local phone book. It took me a while to figure out that Minden Hill, the location for the festival, was actually an area within the Forestdale district.

No phone book for Minden Hill. I tried for one for Forestdale. Success… well, a kind of success. I found the phone book but it listed all the Police Stations within the district's boundaries without identifying them as belonging to any particular area. Okay, I know when to give up. I parked the police station question to one side in favour of finding out more about the festival.

It seems Minden Hill is populated by lots of craft-producing people enjoying an alternative lifestyle… and the place is into festivals in a big way. Any excuse will do: solstices, winter moon, Easter, Christmas, and even 'it's a while since we had one' seem reason enough. Some are touted as music festivals that have an art, craft and produce market on the side. Others advertised as markets have musical entertainment as an adjunct. The festivals (as opposed to the markets) are primarily about music and reputedly attract musicians from 'near and far'. A check of entertainers at festivals over the last couple of years showed a wide range of musicians. Some were what I assumed to be 'local' performers, but the number of well-known 'big name' entertainers was surprising. I also discovered the event Sarah went to was a 'festival' and not a market occasion.

More notes to myself, and prioritising things to do occupied the rest of the available time alone before Emily and her mother joined me on the deck. Emily plopped down on the chair opposite me. I saw her look up at me excitedly and knew what was coming. She was about to launch into a stream of questions about what she already had decided was *our* Sarah Sinclair case. I shot her a hard look accompanied by a slight shake of my head. It worked. It staved off any discussion of Sarah's disappearance. Emily's face fell, her disappointment obvious. She lowered her eyes to her coffee mug and spent the next few moments driving it in circles on the table in front of her. I will need to square off to her later.

Sandra announced she was going to shower and then go into town to see if she could find something 'nice' for lunch. Emily protested that there was no need. "There is plenty in the fridge to make lunch. You don't have to go into town." Sandra insisted she wanted to go into town for a couple of other reasons as well. "In that case, take your car. You've already had one walk today, and the day is warming up," Emily said. Sandra gave her daughter an indulgent smile, collected her breakfast things and disappeared into the kitchen.

Time to make amends with Emily. "Sorry about the look before. I knew you were going to start discussing Sarah Sinclair. I don't particularly want it discussed in front of your mother at this stage. It really isn't a case yet. If I decide to look into it, I will need to tell her about it as I won't be travelling home with her." Emily nodded her understanding but continued to look glum. I let her be. She would either get over it, or not.

"Mum planned on leaving for home tomorrow at the latest. I think that's what the 'something nice for lunch' was all about… part of getting into farewell mode. If you aren't going with her tomorrow, she most likely will opt to stay here longer. She doesn't have any reason to go home right now, but she knew you would want to get back to Millhaven – and she counted on a long chatty drive back with you. I don't really mind her staying; she's no trouble. It's just that her presence does seem to make demands on my time."

"It's nice to have friends – and family – stay over now and then, but it does tend to cramp your style while they are there. Routines end up right out of whack. It's something of a relief when they are the sort that knows when it's time to leave… and that includes me."

"You may stay as long as you like… and I have plenty of flex days I could take to help you." Her grin wasn't exactly evil, but I got the message that, if I was staying in Moxton with her, she would be 'helping'. After thinking for a few moments, Emily stood and announced, "I think I'll go into town with Mum. There are a couple of things I can take care of, that way, I won't have to worry about them later on when we get busy." She dropped me a knowing nod, then turned and walked off.

About ten minutes later, after a chorus of 'back soon, see you later' from the vicinity of the front door, I heard the car drive off, and I was alone to get on with things again. A phone call to the relevant Police Station remained at the top of my list of things to do. Problem was: which Police Station? I didn't know which one to ring. Oh well, what are friends for if not to be there when you need them? When you don't know the answer, phone a friend… so I did. At least, that's what I thought I did. Ben Richards was a long-time friend whom I had known from years ago when he was a young police officer in Millhaven and just starting to climb the rankings ladder. We worked together a year or so ago when a case involving the death of my former boss brought me to Ralston. Ben was head of Ralston's Homicide and Special Unit at the time.

Emily and her mother had third party involvement in the early stages of that case, and Emily's help as the case progressed proved invaluable. It was also the case that saw Geoff Inneston, Sandra's husband, end up in jail for his involvement in a drug trafficking network. Emily seemed to accept her father's fate well, but I was cautious around Sandra for a while after that. However, I soon learned that she too accepted it as her husband's just come-uppance.

Those recollections flitted through my mind as I keyed in Ben Richard's number and listened to it dialling. I was about to hang up. It was Saturday. Anyone who didn't need to be at work would be at home. With Ben's work number still ringing, I flicked through my contacts list for Ben's home number. As I was about to end the call and try his home number, someone picked up the phone. "Ben, it's me, Sonny. Long time since we last spoke…"

"Hello, who did you want?" a gruff voice demanded.

I couldn't remember what rank Ben held the last time we spoke or, for that matter, what rank he might hold now. Best not to mention a rank and risk getting it wrong, I decided. "I was after Ben Richards," I said. "Have I rung the right number?"

"Hang on a minute…" Whoever had answered wasn't happy about being disturbed on a Saturday. A brief period of silence filled my ear, but I thought I could hear sounds in the background, followed by the deafening rattle of the phone being picked up.

"Who did you want to speak to and why?" Another gruff but somehow familiar voice demanded.

"Ben Richards; I'm a friend and need to contact him." I thought I heard a faint chuckle.

"Can't be much of a friend if you don't know he is no longer at Ralston."

"Oh, I see. I'm sorry I bothered you. I don't suppose you can tell me where he is stationed now, could you?" I asked ever so sweetly.

"For God's sake, Sonny, what mess have you got yourself into now? Since you've ruined my morning as it is, you might as well tell me about it."

"Pete?" I recognise that voice! "Pete Messell! How are you and what has happened to Ben?" There was that rumbling laugh I knew so well from over our many years of friendship. I first met Pete when he was a sergeant at Millhaven station. He was Ben's second in command when I worked on that Ralston case.

"I'm well, thank you for asking." I detected a touch of the trademark Messell sarcasm. "Ben is currently on leave prior to taking up his new position so, effectively, he's no longer attached to Ralston."

"I assume he is still climbing the ladder. So, where is he off to this time?"

"Millhaven… as officer in charge of that district." He left the statement dangling in mid-air, knowing it would take me a moment to realise its implication. Ben and I had come close to being more than friends a couple of times in the past, and now he was coming back to Millhaven. Was that a twinge of excitement I felt?

"O-o-h, I see. Uhmm, so who is taking his place at Ralston now?"

"That would be me… so, how about you tell me what's on your mind."

"Good to see I still have friends in the right place. Now, the reason I called…" Pete cut me off.

"That will depend on what you ask me to do – whether you still have a friend here, that is."

As succinctly as possible, I told Pete of my unexpected *possible* case that came out of a couple of days break spent at Moxton. "So why are you ringing here instead of talking to the local coppers?"

"Good point, but the local plod dismissed the mother as being overprotective. It seemed clear to her they weren't interested and were not about to do anything to help."

"You've never let anything like that slow you down before."

"Maybe not, but I only received all the details this morning. The local station apparently is one of those small ones not manned on weekends and at various other times. I did ring. Got a recorded message that the place was unmanned and to ring a different number in case of an emergency. I didn't hold out too much hope of doing any good with the locals, and I couldn't see much point in wasting time and effort ringing another number for the same result."

"Okay, point taken. What exactly did you want them to do – the local blokes, I mean?"

"Well, in the first instance, it would have been good for them show some interest in what I had to say about a missing young woman. I suppose that was expecting too much. I would have settled for some information on which police station services the Minden Hill area of the Forestdale district."

"Where are you now and is this a good number to call you back?"

"Moxton… and yes, it is my mobile number." The call ended with Pete saying he would call me back when he had something to tell me.

I decided to risk a quick call to the hire car company while I waited to hear back from Pete. It was still early they told me. Sarah had until 2.00pm to return the car. They promised to ring after that time to let me know what had happened. I wasn't at all confident they would, and I needed as much information as possible to pass on to Pete. It took a bit of coaxing and mention of the Police getting involved, but they eventually were forthcoming with the car's colour, make, model and registration number..

After recording everything gained from that call, I sat staring into space for a few moments as I pondered what else to do – apart from making another cup of coffee. Deciding there was nothing more I could do without more information, I headed for the kitchen. Not a great believer in telepathy, I have to admit to sending Pete Messell strong mental messages to ring me – now please. I didn't know how long it would be before the others returned, and I knew it would be almost impossible to avoid questions from Emily and Sandra if they were around when Pete called.

Coffee drunk, I was pacing the back deck when Pete's call came. The main Forestdale Station serviced the Minden Hill area. He gave me their number, and I gave him details of Sarah's hire car. Pete didn't seem too sure about the reception I could expect from the Forestdale coppers but, after giving them the few details he had, he warned them to expect a call from me. I wouldn't want to disappoint anyone, so I rang the Forestdale number. Pete's anticipated less than warm reception was right on the money. Nevertheless, I got on with outlining the sequence of events leading up to Sarah's disappearance.

The call lasted about twenty minutes. I gave them the facts as I knew them, they asked questions, and I felt relations thawing as we progressed. Towards the end of the call, I heard Sandra's car pull up in the driveway. The others had returned. A few moments later, Emily came bounding out the back door onto the deck. I held up my hand to stop her and waved her back inside. She hesitated briefly but complied, but not before shooting me a hostile look.

I could hear Emily and Sandra in the kitchen. No doubt, I had ruffled Emily's feathers and this resulted in sentencing me to solitary confinement on the deck for a while. I took advantage of the solitude to write up my notes from the Forestdale call. By the end of the call, I felt there was a positive tone to their response. They said they would begin investigations and keep me informed. That sounded good but it was Saturday and I doubted anything would happen before Monday… and, I didn't place too much faith in their promise to keep me informed.

Time to smooth ruffled feathers, and to tell Sandra I wouldn't be heading back home tomorrow. After stirring things up all over the place, I could hardly abandon everything and hare back to Millhaven. Somewhere along the way, I subconsciously made the decision to hang around for another couple of days or so to see what developed. However, I wouldn't tell Maggie I had taken the case until after that. I closed my computer, took a deep breath and headed for the kitchen.

Lunch was almost ready. I hadn't realised how late it was. After a few quiet conciliatory words to Emily, I pitched in to help with setting the table and transporting food from kitchen to table. I broke the news to Sandra about my staying on for a couple of extra days, and watched Emily's eyes light up.

"I was looking forward to the two of us having a long catch-up time driving back to Millhaven, but it wouldn't be like that anyway. Did you know Gwen Whitehouse when she was in Millhaven?" Sandra's question drew a blank with me and I shook my head. Emily did likewise. Sandra went on to explain.

"Our husbands worked together on some project in Brisbane years ago and she and I became friends. We renewed our friendship when they moved to Millhaven a few years after we did, but then they moved to Moxton about four years ago. I ran into her in town soon after I arrived here and suggested she come and stay with me for a few days to catch up with all her Millhaven friends. She told me this morning she has decided to drive back with me tomorrow."

"I'm relieved to hear that," I said. "I was concerned about letting you down and having you drive back to Millhaven on your own."

"It wouldn't have been a problem. If I hadn't arranged with Gwen to go back with me, I would have stayed on here until you were ready to leave." I slid a sideways glance in Emily's direction. She was finding her empty plate and cutlery quite absorbing -- apparently.

Once all trace of lunch disappeared, Sandra took herself off for her customary afternoon nap. Emily somehow managed to contain herself until her mother was out of earshot. "Okay, we're alone now, so what happened this morning, and who were you talking to when I came home?"

"Let's take another glass of wine through to the sitting room where we can discuss things in comfort." My suggestion met with no argument, and I was soon giving Emily an abridged version of this morning's progress.

I kept it simple, only sharing selected aspects. It wasn't a question of Emily's confidentiality. Too much still sketchy information would only have her rushing around developing outlandish possible scenarios of what happened to Sarah. I didn't need anyone adding to the confusion I already felt. Even so, after a few sips of wine, she began making suggestion – not only about what might have happened but also about how she might start helping me with the case.

Two o'clock came and went without a call from the hire car company. I weakened and rang them at around five o'clock: no sign of Sarah and they were giving her until Monday morning to return the car before reporting it as stolen. After my call to them earlier today, that probably wouldn't come as a surprise to the Forestdale coppers, but I didn't bother to share that thought.

Nothing else of any consequence to the case happened. Dinner was lovely but a bit subdued in light of Sandra's impending departure the next morning. In a move to give her and Emily time together before she left, I disappeared off to my room soon after dinner and fell asleep after reading only a couple of pages of the novel I had been trying to read since leaving home a week ago.

CHAPTER 4

After seeing Sandra off back to Millhaven, Emily and I wandered back to the kitchen to make breakfast. As Sandra and Gwen were treating themselves to breakfast at a McDonalds on their way out of town, the kitchen was devoid of activity so far this morning. Halfway through setting up the coffee machine, Emily announced she was going for a run and would leave breakfast until afterwards. She went off to change. Not feeling at all inclined towards anything athletic this morning, I made toast and coffee and retreated to the back deck.

Despatch of toast and coffee does not require anyone's full attention. I booted up my laptop – out of force of habit rather than with any definite intent. In the time it took to load, I thought of something to look up. What happened to those other two missing females? I hadn't explored the wider realms of the news media world, only the Forestdale area newspapers. Perhaps the Saturday editions of those local papers might have an update on the girls' fates.

Three papers were 'local' to the Forestdale area. I scanned each of them from the time of the first disappearance through to the latest editions. Nothing new found, and no further mention in any of them. Searching state-based newspapers presents as something of a daunting task so early in the morning, but this might be the only quiet time I have until Emily goes to work tomorrow. To simplify the process, I checked my notes for the name of the first woman who disappeared, typed it in and sent Google off to search for anything and everything to do with that name. Wise move; Google returned quite a few sites. I began working through the list, beginning with the most recent.

The first item referred to the television broadcast of a plea by the family for information on the whereabouts of the first woman who disappeared while setting up her stall prior to the start of the festival. It carried an image scanned from a photograph of the woman – attractive looking. The accompanying text described her as having shoulder length red hair, hazel eyes and fair complexion. No age given – how politically correct of them!

It was hard to tell from the grainy image, but her age looked about thirty, maybe somewhere in the range of mid-twenties to thirty. I downloaded the article including the image.

I looked at each of the other entries listed. They went back to the day after the woman's disappearance but provided no new information for my files. Nothing more of interest there, I moved on and checked for anything on the other young girl who disappeared sometime during the first night of the festival. Google produced about the same number of entries again. The most recent article again carried an image of the girl, this time scanned from what might have been a class photo. It showed her in her school uniform. Other similar uniforms appeared to surround the girl.

In the photo, there was a long braid hanging over the girl's left shoulder, and she appeared to be in the front row of the class photo, suggesting she was among the shortest in the class. I scanned the article for a physical description and found it in the penultimate paragraph: seventeen years old, 160 centimetres tall, long blonde hair, blue eyes, fair complexion and stocky build. Another look at the image confirmed much of that description. She was quite pretty and likely to develop into an attractive young woman, but there was nothing in the image to suggest she was of stocky build.

Were the two disappearances linked? Apart from the time of their disappearances (at the same festival), there was nothing to link the two females. It was possible – even probable –they knew each other. They both worked on market stalls and probably attended many of the same festivals and markets, but there was nothing to suggest they might be anything other than acquaintances at best. I looked at my printouts of the images of the two girls, searching for any similarities. Both had fair colouring and were a bit on the short side, although the older of the two was the taller at 170 centimetres. What did I know about Sarah Sinclair?

A recent photo of the lass was amongst the material Maggie gave me. I lined Sarah's photo up on the table beside the two printouts. She also was fair with longish copper coloured hair. At 165 centimetres, her height was halfway between those of the other two, and she was a slim gorgeous looking girl. I sat back for a while and studied the images laid out on the table, but it didn't spark any bright ideas on how to proceed. The only thing that came to me was that, if the same people were responsible for the disappearances, it seems they had an aversion to brunettes.

I hadn't read the article relating to the schoolgirl's disappearance, having only skimmed down to details of her physical appearance. A quick read revealed two things: the journalist responsible was both sceptical and devoid of any sensitivity in relation to the situation. Her – the name suggested the writer was female – hypothesis was that the girl took advantage of parental absence to run off with a boyfriend – probably one who did not meet with her parents' approval. I noticed a retraction and an apology by the editor in the next edition of that paper. The paper likely was in the market for a new sub-editor after that bit of poor editing.

Sundays were not great for progressing investigations. I felt restless and frustrated by my lack of progress. With only one other avenue I can follow up today, I rang Maggie. It was only just a civilised hour to be ringing someone, but she answered on the second ring. After the appropriate apology for disturbing her Sunday morning, I explained my call. "I was hoping you might be able to give me details of Sarah's bank and what credit cards she might have."

There was a slight pause before Maggie answered and I was about to check if we were still connected when she replied. "I could have put that information in with the other stuff I gave you but I didn't realise you would need it. Why do you need it?" I explained that any activity on her bank account or credit cards would help track where Sarah had been – and where she might be now. It seems the request increased Maggie's anxiety level but, once I explained, there was no reluctance to name the bank for the account and credit cards.

"Thanks, Maggie. They will check bank information as a last resort because of all the rigmarole involved in getting access to that information. The police would avoid going down that track if they can, but sometimes there is no other way anyone can access those accounts to get that information."

"…But that's not necessary. I can access all of Sarah's bank information. We set it up a couple of years ago so that I can look after things when she is away travelling or whatever. Many travellers were having problems at the time with credit card skimming when they were overseas. Sarah set it up so I could check all her accounts so that, if something a bit fishy appeared, I could alert her and the bank about it straight away."

"Have you been checking while she is away this time?"

"Well no, I haven't looked at anything since she left. She was only going for the weekend. I didn't see any need to check anything and it hasn't occurred to me to look when she didn't return as expected. I can have a look now…"

"A-a-h yes, it would be great if you could do that but… would you mind very much if I was there when you did it? I could come over straight away." She gave me her address and I looked it up on the map of Moxton town I bought when I first arrived. Damn! I wish I had my car here. The Sinclair home was a bit further away than I expected. It would take me a while to walk there.

I picked up my phone to ring Maggie to tell her about the delay in my arrival. As I was halfway through keying in her number, another idea occurred to me. Was I bold enough to go with it? Yes I was. Desperation does that to you. I keyed in Emily's mobile number – hoping like hell she had it with her. She answered after the fifth ring. Fate is kind today! "What's up?" she gasped into her phone.

"Look, I hate doing this, but I wondered whether you might lend me your car for a half hour or so. I promise not to bend it and I wouldn't be taking it out of town."

"Yeah, that's not a problem… but it comes with a proviso. You have to tell me what you are up to that you need a car." I agreed. "Okay, you know where I keep the keys in the office. I'll let myself in with the spare key if you're not there when I get home." Brief but profuse thanks delivered. Then I was out of the house and on my way to the other side of town.

Maggie had the coffee machine cranked up and morning tea on the table by the time arrived. Although it was obvious she didn't want to waste time on niceties, she insisted on morning tea before we looked at Sarah's financials. I was happy to play along. I too was much more interested in the financials than coffee and cake… but the cake was delicious.

We started with Sarah's main credit card… no transactions recorded since just after she arrived at Minden Hill. Her other credit card account was the same. Next, Maggie logged onto Sarah's savings account. It showed no activity since before Sarah left for the festival. The whole exercise produced no good news. "Now what…?" Maggie asked quietly.

I swallowed hard and tried to put a positive spin on things. "I'll tell the police what we found. That's one more thing crossed off the list of possible things to do when someone goes missing." I wasn't feeling brave enough to tell her that a lack of activity on all of Sarah's accounts was not a good sign. However, Maggie didn't strike me as a fool. If she hadn't already done so, it wouldn't take her long to work that out for herself. There was no point in lingering, so I was soon on my way back to Emily's house.

Emily, already back from her run, emerged from her shower as I let myself in. No mistaking her anticipation, she bounded down the hall to greet me and followed me into the office as I returned the car key to its rightful place. "Well, come on, where have you been and what happened? Don't keep me in suspense. Uh-oh … I'm not sure I want to know. You don't look very happy, so I'm guessing it is all bad news."

She made herself a coffee – I settled for water – and we adjourned to the back deck. In a few short sentences, I told her about Maggie's running a check on Sarah's financials and the worrying outcome. She looked away from me and asked, "You don't think she is still alive, do you?"

I shrugged but avoided her eyes as she turned back to look at me. "That's a possibility – one of several maybe. On its own, it's not enough to draw that conclusion."

"What happens next … what are you going to do?"

"I'll let the Forestdale police know – and probably Pete Messell as well -- about today's check on Sarah's accounts. Apart from that, I haven't anything else that I can go on with right now. I'll wait until after I speak to the Forestdale coppers tomorrow, but it's beginning to look like I need to go to Minden Hill if I'm to make any progress."

The only other thing I managed today in relation to this case is organising all the information – such as it is – into one coherent file. It didn't progress the case in any way, but it did take me a step closer to being ready to leave when the time came to depart for Minden Hill.

CHAPTER 5

Monday morning saw the wet weather everyone expected for Easter finally arrive. I awoke to leaden skies and puddles everywhere from overnight rain. Until at least eight o'clock, there was nothing I could do. That's when people I needed to talk to start arriving at work. A jog around the neighbourhood would help to fill in part of the next couple of hours and might help relieve some of my building frustration. I dressed and quietly let myself out the front door. As soon as I left Emily's front yard, it started to drizzle.

Overcoming the temptation to turn around and go back inside, heavy-footed, I set off on what would be a somewhat shortened route. After about two blocks of unpleasant going, the rain worsened. It bucketed down to create a heavy curtain over most of the town. My phone vibrated. With my back to the rain and hunched over to shield my phone as much as possible, I answered it expecting to hear Emily asking where I was. Pete Messell's booming voice was a surprise.

"Pete, can I call you back in a couple of seconds?" He said 'okay' and disconnected. Still clutching my phone, I started running flat out to a bus shelter about fifty metres further along the street. Everything was wet – my clothes, shoes, my phone and me. I looked for something dry to wipe my phone. The only relatively dry thing around was the part of my bra under my boobs. With my back turned to the street, and hoping any passers-by would think I was admiring the graffiti on the rear wall of the shelter, I made the best of what I had. After removing some of the water from the phone, I returned Pete's call.

"I was going to call you when it reached a more respectable hour."

"You were going to tell me the girl had arrived home?"

"Chance would be a fine thing. No, Sarah's mother has access to all her daughter's financials and yesterday I asked her to check them all. There's been no activity on any of the accounts since before Sarah left home. I'll ring Forestdale later this morning to tell them as well."

"This is not looking good."

"I know what it suggests. I'm hoping there is some amazing explanation that doesn't involve tragedy. I didn't share my concerns with her mother."

"I'll let Forestdale know and I'll ask them to ring you. By the way, where are you staying?" I told him. "Ah yes, I remember her. What's her address and how long are you planning to stay there?" It seemed like a strange question but I gave him Emily's address and explained that it looked as though I might need to go to Minden Hill to make any progress. He didn't comment, and our call ended a few moments later.

The rain dropped back to a drizzle again, so I left the bus shelter and headed back to the house by the shortest route possible. A brisk breeze came up about half an hour ago making life miserable by blowing what rain there was parallel to the ground and straight into my face. The temperature also dropped a few degrees and I now felt chilled to the bone. By the time I reached the house, I was less than enchanted with the day so far, and devoid of any sense of humour. Emily almost fell about laughing at the state I was in when I arrived back. It did nothing to improve my mood.

Showered and caffeine level topped up, I pondered what to do next. There didn't appear to be anything else I could do from Moxton. I decided to give the Forestdale coppers another hour or so to ring me (in accordance with Pete's request to them) before I weakened, and I rang them. Although I knew what the outcome of follow-up calls would be, I rang the motel Sarah stayed at and the car hire mob. Neither had anything new to report and, yes, the hire car lot this morning were going to report her car as stolen.

No point in sitting around doing nothing any longer; I opened my laptop and looked for flights that would get me as close as possible to Minden Hill. It was disappointing but predictable, but there was no avoiding having to change planes in Brisbane. A flight to Brisbane left Moxton at one o'clock today and a second flight that would take me as close as possible to Forestdale left Brisbane at three o'clock. I could make the connection without hanging around in the Brisbane terminal for too long. All things going to schedule, I would be on the ground and collecting a hire car by about four o'clock.

While dithering about whether to book flights at this stage or not, my phone rang and I answered it absentmindedly without checking the caller ID. The familiar voice tore my attention away from the flights schedules I had up on my screen. Pete Messell. "It's not often you get to talk to me twice in the one day, not lately anyway."

"This is true. To what do I owe the honour?"

"They found your missing car." He now had my undivided attention.

"That was quick. Where did they find it?" Before he could answer, I continued. "… and does it tell us anything?"

"I don't know that it tells us anything yet. There was no one in it if that's what you're asking. It's just been found. They are still arranging to bring it in for forensics to have a go at it. Oh, in answer to the other part of the question, it has been sitting in one of those multi-storey carparks for a week… in Brisbane."

"Brisbane! No, that can't be right. Are they sure it is the right car?"

"No question about it. They are trying to locate CCTV footage of when it arrived in the carpark. I'll update you as I get anything new." The call ended and I sat staring at my phone and trying to take on board Pete's news. Brisbane! … Why Brisbane? If they find the CCTV footage, I'll bet it won't show Sarah at the wheel. Pete's call hadn't helped, and only added more confusion to the mix. However, it did help sort out something else: *I was going to Minden Hill today*. First, a quick call to see if the Forestdale police had anything interesting to share, and then book flights for this afternoon -- and, in the meantime, hope seats are still available.

The Forestdale mob had nothing new to offer, and were not too impressed by my intended arrival on their patch. "Why on earth would you want to do that?" the officer I had been dealing with asked. "What could you do that we haven't already done?" Good question and one I chose to treat as rhetorical rather than try to answer it.

I sensed Forestdale was lining up to rid themselves the whole Sarah Sinclair issue. They were too quick to the opinion that finding the car somewhere else moved the whole 'disappearance problem' to that somewhere else: onto someone else's patch, and away from Forestdale. From experience, I knew trying to acquaint a copper with the error in his assumption would only waste time and emotional energy. Instead, after reiterating that I would be in Minden Hill tonight, I ended the call… and began the tedious process of booking flights online.

Does Moxton run to something as exotic as a taxi service, I wondered. A noise from somewhere in the bowels of the house startled me as I sat mulling over how I might get to the Moxton airport in the absence of such a service. I went in search of the noise. Emily was doing her laundry. "Isn't it Monday today?" I asked. "And weren't you supposed to start your next roster today?"

"I was supposed to have a day off on the Thursday before Good Friday but I worked a colleague's shift that day so she could get away early for Easter. It's supposed to be her day off today, but she is paying me back by working my shift for me. …So, what are we going to do today towards solving your new case?"

"Ah well, I do have something for you to do. You can drive me to the airport around lunchtime." That required an explanation of where I was going and what I planned to do when I got there.

She looked troubled. "It's too short notice for me to go with you today, but I could join you tomorrow. I'll ring work now to organise time off from tomorrow. How long do you think I'll need to be away?"

"Whoa, you are not taking any time off. You're not invited on this trip." Emily looked as though I had slapped her hard. I jumped in to ease the situation. "It's not that I don't want your help. It's quite possible I will once I work out what's going on, but it would be a waste of your time to come with me yet. There is plenty of preliminary investigation required before I'll be able to work out how to proceed. When I get that sorted out, there might be cause to call on your assistance." My attempt at peacemaking seemed to ease things a bit, but Emily still wasn't happy about not joining me at Minden Hill.

Most of the remainder of the morning was occupied with organising everything I needed to take with me, typing up last minute file notes, and making lists of things I needed to do and prioritising it. We grabbed a sandwich for an early lunch on our way through town before Emily dropped me at the airport. My flight left on time and a strong tailwind had us on the ground in Brisbane about ten minutes ahead of schedule.

After checking all was okay with my connecting flight, I found a café/bar that doubled as a bookshop. Parked at a small table against the back wall, I sipped my coffee as I skimmed a newspaper left behind by a previous customer. My phone rang alerting me to the fact that I hadn't turned it off at Moxton before boarding my flight. I checked the caller ID. Did my heart just flutter? Maybe it missed a couple of beats.

Damn, Ben Richards still could cause that response every time we made contact. An image of the tall, hunk of man-mountain with incredible blue eyes flashed through my mind as I answered my phone. "How's the idle life going?" I asked by way of greeting. "I hear you are on leave right now, preparing yourself for the next big step up the ladder." That so familiar deep-throated laugh rumbled across the ether.

"Our old mate, Pete Messell, called about something to do with work and mentioned how you were harassing them again. What have you gotten yourself into this time?" I gave him a summary of the case thus far. "Pete said you were on leave. Where are you? I take it you are not spending your leave in Ralston."

"I spent a few days in Brisbane free-loading off old friends I caught up with before slipping over the border for a couple of weeks of R&R on the northern New South Wales coast. Why are you heading to Forestdale? Pete said the car involved was found in Brisbane."

"Yeah, but it doesn't make any sense at this stage. Maybe Sarah did drive back to Brisbane. It's possible, but I need to start at Forestdale to see if there is any sort of trail that leads back to Brisbane… and to try to get a feel for what might have happened."

"Hmm, might be a good move. Anyway, we won't be too far from each other while you are down here. I'm staying at Byron Bay. Let's see if we can catch up some time. Minden Hill is only a bit over an hour away from where I am."

I agreed catching-up would be good. Then, I heard my flight called and I hurriedly ended the call with a promise to ring him again after I knew what I was doing at Minden Hill… possibly tomorrow night."

About an hour later, we were taxiing to the terminal at Ballina airport. Not too many passengers meant only a short wait for luggage to be unloaded. Next step: find the hire car office located somewhere in the terminal. That proved surprisingly easy and I realised as I made my way to its counter that this was the same place as where Sarah had hired her vehicle.

A hard-faced woman trying to convince someone (probably herself) she was younger than she was came to the counter. She would have been mid-fifties and her face showed – to quote a phrase oft used by Ben Richards – she had done a lot of miles. Make-up applied too thickly caked in cracks and crevices of her face. Her bright fire engine red lipstick, although following current trends, made an already too wide mouth look grotesquely large. All this she topped off with unnaturally black hair plastered in place with so much product that a Force 4 gale wouldn't ruffle it.

Unsure what sort of reception I might receive, I introduced myself and handed across one of my business cards. My card in her hand, she turned and took a couple of steps across to what I assumed to be her desk. The woman's outfit suggested she must not own a full-length mirror. When she stood at the counter, I could see only down to the top button of her skin-tight white blouse. The blouse, open a little too low, displayed a touch more creased and spotted décolletage than I need to see. Now she had moved away, I could see she teamed the blouse with an equally tight, short black skirt that ended a good distance above the knees of her sturdy legs. Visible bulges a short distance from the tops of her thighs indicated where some form of control undergarment ended. No question about it, she must be devoid of any sort of decent mirror.

She picked up a pair of spectacles lying on the desk and slapped them on her nose. There was an audible sniff as she read my card. "I've told you all I know, Miss Whittington. What more do you hope to achieve by coming here to harass us?"

"I didn't come to harass you. I want to hire a car. Can we get on with it, please? A small four door sedan will do, and I might need it for three or four days."

"I hope this isn't going to result in another lost vehicle," she said as she made her way back to the counter. "We are only a small branch. Someone making off with one of our vehicles places us in a difficult operational position – not to mention the expense involved." She flapped her hand dismissively as if brushing aside the thought of it all.

"My interest is not in your missing vehicle… which they have located, by the way. I'm only interested in the missing young woman who hired it, and possibly the other two women who went missing." A dark haired young woman poked her head out from behind her computer screen.

"We haven't heard any more about them, have we?" she asked.

"About who…?" her boss demanded.

"The other two girls that are missing…"

"They haven't hired our vehicles as well have they?" the boss asked and looked horrified. The young woman shook her head. "How do you know about them?" the boss demanded.

"It was in all the media when they disappeared, and then the family of the young one did that thing on TV asking the public for help; real tear-jerker stuff. Don't you read the papers or watch TV?"

I cleared my throat loudly. "I would like to be on my way. Can we get the paperwork done so I can get to where I need to be sometime before dark?" I was never going to make her Christmas card list. She vented her displeasure on the keyboard of the computer mounted on the counter. As she typed, I filled in time reading various brochures and signs on the counter. A small sign at the other end of the counter caught my eye. I was tempted to turn it around the other way so that it faced the woman. I smiled at its bold announcement: *We are dedicated to providing courteous service*. Perhaps today was a rest day from such demands.

It was a tick after 4.30pm but, at last, I was on the road and heading for Minden Hill about an hour and ten minutes away – or so the seductive voice of the navigation system assured me.

CHAPTER 6

The *Wisteria Inn* looked pleasant enough as I drove in and parked outside reception. I hadn't made a booking, but I suspected getting a room wouldn't be a problem. It wasn't. After parking in the gated guests' carpark at the rear of the motel, I trundled my suitcase through the rear entrance and down the corridor to my room.

It was an L-shaped building, with its long side running parallel to the street and ending at the boundary fence that separated it from the next motel. The short 'arm', containing only what appeared to be a single large room. It right-angled off the main part of the building and ran along the boundary fence almost to the footpath. This arrangement provided a wide covered colonnade running the full length of the motel. While all the guest accommodation was on the ground floor, a partial upper storey occupied the area above reception and the restaurant. I assumed this was the manager's residence. A magnificent wisteria with a glorious display of pendulous blooms, the source of the motel's name, adorned the front wall of the reception area and continued its way up to the second storey.

After another trip to the car to retrieve computer bag and other sundry bits and pieces, it took no time to settle in and set up. That done, I decided a priority should be to check out the security arrangements for late entry to the building. Dusk was falling when I pushed through the rear entrance doors and wandered into the guests' carpark. A high metal fence similar to pool safety fencing surrounded the carpark area. It included a substantial looking gate across the entrance driveway.

Closer inspection revealed two sensor systems. One mounted high on a pole just inside the fence would open the gate in response to a signal from the small gadget they gave me to place on the dashboard of my vehicle. The other sensor, mounted adjacent to the lock on the gate itself, was a swipe card affair. I checked my room key – no electronic door keycards here. The large plastic card that served as a key tag identified the motel and the room number to which it belonged, but it also carried a magnetic strip of some sort on its reverse side. Small print above the strip informed me it was to be used to unlock the gate if returning to the motel after ten o'clock at night.

Best I test the card reader security system while there is still some daylight left. A small button on the lock inside the gate opened it, so leaving the motel on foot late at night was not a problem. I pushed the button. The gate slid back with almost no sound and I walked through. Once on the outside, I checked how easy it might be to reach through the gate and push the button on the other side. It wasn't. Steel plate surrounding the locking mechanism ensured even someone with a large hand could not reach the button to open the gate from the outside. I swiped my key tag through the card reader. Nothing happened. Okay, try all options before going to reception for help. With the card turned around so the magnetic strip faced the other way, I swiped it again. The gate slid open smoothly with no more noise than before.

I stepped into the gateway and held the gate open while I inspected the locking mechanism and the surround area for any CCTV cameras. No obvious cameras -- but I could see what I thought might be sensors… sensors that perhaps might trigger an alarm if the gate didn't close properly. This triggered a vague thought about how someone might circumvent the system to enter the motel illegally after hours. Once inside the carpark, there were no other security devices to contend with, and entry through the backdoor only required walking within range of the automatic door sensor. I made mental note of the size and depth of the opening of the housing into which the lock on the gate fitted. It wouldn't take much to fool this system.

As I turned to walk back inside, a flock of rainbow lorikeets rose out of the bush and swooped towards me. I watch them come, a mass of raucous flashing colours that passed overhead and rose up and over the motel. It was as my eyes followed their flight that I saw it. From high on the rear wall of the building, a floodlight pointed down over the carpark. Well concealed in the light's mounting bracket was a camera lens. Ah-hah, so there is a camera of sorts out here. As I walked back inside and made my way to reception, I wondered about its range and focus. Reception was busy. A couple of people waited while a third completed registration. Sometime tomorrow, when things are quiet will be a better time for what I have in mind.

After freshening up, I found my way to the in-house restaurant. There was only one couple at a corner table. I climbed onto a stool at the bar and ordered a white wine. With the young bloke behind the bar not run off his feet at the time, it seemed an opportunity to do the 'first time tourist' thing. He was up for a chat. After asking a couple of general questions about the Minden Hill area, I raised the subject of the festival. "Am I right in thinking there was a music festival or something here over the last long weekend?"

"Yeah, there is one every year at Easter. It's getting bigger every year and they are managing to pull in some big name entertainers now."

"Is there just music or are there other attractions, or other things happening as well to interest patrons?"

"No, it's not just about music. There are circus acts and poets providing other entertainment… and there are the market stalls, of course. Those stalls always attract another group of people who aren't interested in coming for the music or entertainment on offer."

"I did a bit of reading up on this place before I arrived. I'm just passing through but thought it worth stopping for a couple of days for a look around. I seem to remember reading about some woman disappearing during the festival. Is that right?"

"Yeah, bit of a mystery that. I think there was more than one disappeared." I gave him my most surprised look and leaned closer as I encouraged him to tell me more. "One of them was staying here. I wasn't on duty the night she disappeared so I don't know too much about it."

"I take it she was here for the festival though, and not just passing through."

"She booked in for the weekend, I think. I sort of remember seeing her but I don't think I ever served her."

"You were lucky getting a night off over Easter. With the festival and everything, I imagine the place was booked out and you would be busy every night."

"I worked Friday and Saturday nights and someone else worked Sunday and Monday nights. Like you said, it was Easter, so they wanted to give us all some nights off."

"So which night is she supposed to have disappeared?"

"I don't think anyone is real sure but they think it might have been Sunday night when the big final night show was on. I haven't heard any more but I don't think they found her."

"It won't do Minden Hill's reputation much good if people go missing when they stop here. Anyway, it's been nice chatting but I think I had better go and do something about ordering dinner. I see more people coming this way. It will get busy. I'll have to wait for my food, and I'm starving."

I took my wine to a table along the back wall of the restaurant and scanned the menu. It wasn't too adventurous but there were enough interesting dishes to keep me undecided for a few minutes. After ordering the braised lamb shanks, I sat idly sipping my wine and observing the other guests arriving. They were mainly an elderly lot, most of whom looked weary as if they had a long day's travel behind them. There were a couple of younger unattached males amongst them -- possibly company sales representatives. I wondered whether any of tonight's wait staff were on duty the night Sarah disappeared or if they remembered her at all.

Most of the diners ate and left, not lingering any longer than necessary at their tables. By dawdling over my meal and another glass of wine, and then deciding I would have a coffee, I managed to outstay all the others. My 'friend' from behind the bar disappeared soon after the last of the other diners.

A young lass who cleared away after the diners was now setting up the tables with fresh linen and cutlery in readiness for the next day. She didn't seem to be in any particular hurry, so I thought I'd try a chat. "I was talking to the guy behind the bar before about the girl who disappeared during the festival. It occurred to me that her disappearing like that must have stirred things up around here for a while. She was staying here I believe. Did you know her at all?"

"Yes, I think I spoke to her once or twice. I don't remember her coming into the restaurant, but I help on reception sometime and I think I spoke to her there. There are quite a few ethnic food stalls at the festivals and markets, as well as stalls selling the usual Aussie fast food. Some guests don't come into the restaurant, except maybe for breakfast. They choose to sample the various foods on offer at the festival."

"I'm holding you up by sitting here chatting. I'll let you get on with it. Goodnight." If nothing else, I gained the distinct impression tonight that catching up with all the staff, especially any that spoke to Sarah, would be a protracted process. All I gained so far was that they think Sarah disappeared on the Sunday night of the festival. If that was the case, why isn't her hire car still in the motel's carpark? My understanding is that the festival site is only a short walk from the motel. It seemed unlikely Sarah would drive there.

Emily rang as I was unlocking my door. I juggled key and phone, as I battled one of those doors that won't stay open unless you lean on it with all your weight. After throwing the key onto the table and letting the door bang closed behind me, I plopped onto the end of the bed in readiness for what I knew would be a long inquisitive call. "How was your trip? I take it you are at the same motel as Sarah stayed in. What's it like? Have you had a chance to speak to anyone about her disappearance yet? What..."

"Whoa, whoa; ease up on the questions. I can't even remember what your first question was, let alone answer all the others. Let's see, there was nothing out of the ordinary about the trip. I arrived on time and hired a car. Wisteria Inn is the motel where Sarah stayed. I didn't arrive until this evening, so there hasn't been time to look around or talk to anyone. I think that just about covers it." Not strictly true, I know, but it's easier to tell her that than face the interrogation that would follow if I said I spoke to a couple of the staff. …And I wasn't going to mention I spoke to Ben Richards and that we might catch up while I was down here.

As I didn't have anything exciting to tell her about the case, she went on to other subjects. Her mother arrived home safely and she and Gwen already had arranged to meet up for coffee with some of their mutual Millhaven friends. Her next topic was more interesting. Maggie Sinclair rang Emily this evening. She enquired about any progress on the case, but also told Emily that, all of a sudden, the local police were interested in Sarah's disappearance. Good on you Pete, I thought but kept that to myself. The call did eventually end and, after a quick shower, I fell into bed feeling exhausted after having done not much all day.

Sleep wasn't going to come just yet. My eyes were drooping heavily when my phone rang. It was Ben checking up that I arrived okay and wanting to know where I was staying. We didn't chat for long, probably because I kept punctuating the conversation with yawns. The next thing I remember was my body clock telling me it was time to get up.

First thing on my list of things to do today is a visit to the Forestdale police station. I am not expecting a warm fuzzy welcome but I'm hoping someone will at least talk to me. In the interest of not lugging too much stuff around with me, I placed the file containing all the information gathered to date on Sarah's disappearance in a tote bag along with a notebook, a couple of pens, a digital recorder, my phone and my purse. It seemed like a civilised hour to call on people so, making sure the door locked behind me, I made my way to the carpark.

A flock of birds twittering in a magnificent Camphor Laurel tree just outside the perimeter fence greeted me. They all took to the air when I reached my car parked close to the overhanging branches of the tree. The size of the tree suggests it is very old and, being something of a landmark saved it from removal like the rest of its counterparts from the narrow strip of ground between the rear perimeter of the blocks and the back lane.

Tall and stately, the tree sported a pronounced asymmetrical look. Although they trimmed the lower branches evenly all round initially, they now trimmed those on the lane side to a greater height. This ensured clearance for high vehicles using the lane. On the motel side, they stopped removing branches once the lower ones cleared the perimeter security fence. The branches extending over the fence provided partial shade for a couple of the parking bays, but anything parked there was at the mercy of falling leaves and the birds.

After wasting a couple of minutes admiring the tree, I drove towards the entrance gate. The gadget on the dashboard did its thing and the gate slid back smoothly. Once outside the carpark, I did a quick check of the map to refresh my memory and then headed off to talk to the local coppers. Not too many cars about, which was a good thing as the route to the police station twisted and turned as it wound through suburbia. Note to self: look at the map again later; there has to be a more direct route.

My assumption was correct: no warm welcome. In fact, it felt more like icicles hanging off it. Seems my fame preceded me! However, with perseverance and little concern about making friends, I eventually reached the officer I spoke to on the phone. He wasn't exactly thrilled to see me but did manage to be civil. We went through to a small room (probably what passed for an interrogation room at this station) and sat opposite each other at a grey Formica topped table. With the initial niceties out of the way, we were down to business and I soon found myself sharing the contents of my file. As we went through my file, a distinct thaw set in across the table. By the time he suggested we get coffee, we were old mates.

Back at the table and sipping our coffees, I felt the *détente cordiale* that now existed would allow me to ask the questions I hesitated to ask while we established a relationship. "My research about the festival turned up a couple of newspaper articles about two other females reported missing around the same time. Are the Police working on the assumption there is a connection between all three disappearances?" For a moment, I didn't think he was going to answer. When he did, he chose his words carefully.

"The first alleged disappearance is a concern. That one…"

"The first one, she was the older red-headed woman who disappeared before the festival started?"

"Yes, she arrived early – on the Thursday – while most of the other stallholders didn't arrive until sometime on the Friday."

"You say 'alleged'; surely she either disappeared or she didn't. What doubt can there be about it?"

"Her caravan was on site and she had started putting up her stall, but she never appeared during the festival. She never finished setting up and her stall never opened for business. A group of stallholders follow the festivals and markets. They all know each other and, although they don't necessarily become friends, they do seem to keep an eye out for each other. Other stallholders reported her disappearance to us."

"Wasn't there a family member concerned when they hadn't heard from her?"

"A brother contacted us yesterday. He spoke to her soon after she arrived at Minden Hill. His new daughter's christening was last Sunday and the woman had agreed to be the child's godmother. The phone call to his sister confirmed the christening arrangements and that she would be back in time to attend."

"Right, so her non-attendance raised his concerns and he contacted you, unaware that she went missing more than a week ago."

"Correct. She is divorced, lives alone and spends most of her time travelling around by herself. There is no family other than the brother. If it weren't for the christening, even the brother wouldn't know anything was amiss."

"…So, you're telling me that you hadn't started investigating her disappearance before her brother called?"

"Y-e-s, but we had no evidence she had disappeared. As reported to us, her behaviour seemed unusual but any one of a number of explanations could apply. The circumstances surrounding this one were different from the second incident that…"

"Am I correct in assuming the second incident refers to the disappearance of the young girl?"

He nodded and drove his empty coffee cup around in circles on the table a few times before answering. "Her father reported her missing the next morning. Young seventeen year old left alone at night…" he shook his head in disgust. "Someone spoke to her as she was leaving the site a bit before eight o'clock. She told them that, instead of cooking dinner for herself, she decided to go to McDonalds. No one saw her return."

"She walked along that track through the bush to McDonalds?" He nodded in reply. "I take it nobody heard or saw anything useful to the investigation?"

"No. Oh, there's been plenty of *speculation* about what happened. Most people tend to favour the notion that she ran off with some bloke."

"I imagine that can't be dismissed out of hand any more than some of the other ideas the locals have come up with. If memory serves me correctly, there was something in the newspaper about someone seeing the first woman being bundled into a car. What was the outcome of that?"

"Ah yes, a concerned citizen did come forward. If you haven't been along the track, you won't be aware there are a number of shacks in the bush off the side of the track. In fact, if you go looking for them, you wouldn't know they were there. A bloke from one of those shacks reported seeing what he thought was a woman being bundled into a dark coloured van."

"You don't seem convinced about that information."

"The residents of those shacks are renowned for seeing things; anything from aliens to pixies, depending what they were on at the time. It is not unknown for them to seek attention for their own purposes – whatever they might be."

"If I might recap for a moment, there is no evidence gathered so far that progresses your investigations into the disappearance of those first two women. That's not hard to understand given the circumstances. My interest is in the disappearance of Sarah Sinclair, but I don't discount there might be connection with those other two incidents. Have you uncovered any evidence relating to Sarah's disappearance? ...And, in case you're wondering, I do believe it is a genuine disappearance and not something that can be explained in some other way."

"I have nothing on Sarah Sinclair's disappearance to date. Until Ralston police contacted me, I wasn't aware of her disappearance... perhaps I should say, *alleged* disappearance. Your file is compelling and makes a strong case for a disappearance but, at our end, we have found nothing to substantiate that assumption or to refute it."

"To summarise what I am hearing, you have nothing to indicate Sarah was abducted or disappeared by other means and aren't about to devote too many resources to proving – or disproving – that assumption. Would you agree that was a fair assessment?"

"Look, I know that's not what you hoped for but, like most stations these days, we are understaffed and have a backlog of incidents to investigate, including the three disappearances. I am dealing with the disappearances myself in between everything else I have to do, so progress is slow... and yes, you could argue it is non-existent. I am doing the best I can and I will help you with your enquiries if I can wherever I can. I would like us to keep in touch and that, if you do come across anything interesting, you will share it with me."

While I agreed to keep in touch and share whatever I found, I left Forestdale Police Station with no great expectation of any good news emanating from there any time soon.

CHAPTER 7

It was close enough to lunchtime when I left the Police Station for my thoughts to have turned to food. A short stroll up the street brought me to a coffee shop offering both indoor and outdoor dining. I ordered a salad wrap and mineral water and sat outside under the shop's brightly coloured shade sail. A casual survey of the immediate area carried out while waiting for my food suggested this was a small compact shopping precinct. All the usual amenities – banks, supermarket, department store, hairdresser, etc. were there. There seemed to be a whole host of small specialty stores sprinkled in between, including one selling women's fashions and a shoe shop nestled side by side.

Time to move; I had an investigation to get on with but I didn't quite know what to do next. I need to interview motel staff but there is unlikely to be anyone much about until later in the day. As a last resort and in a bid to get me up and moving again, I decided to drive to the festival site. This would provide me with the perspective a stallholder arriving at the site would have. Later, I will walk the track to see if I can track down the bloke who claimed to see a woman being bundled into a car.

From where the road entered the festival site, directly across the field I could see where the bush track ended. Also across the field and further along from the track, a now dreary looking sign indicated *stallholders' caravan sites*. I sat with the engine idling for a few minutes while I surveyed the area. Surrounded virtually all the way around by dense bush, the field lay at the centre of a virtual natural amphitheatre. The cooler weather in this part of the country meant the grass hadn't grown too much since the festival, and the indentations left by the tents, stage and other structures association with the festival remained clearly visible. I slid the car into gear and eased my way onto the field.

Although I intended to drive all the way around the perimeter of the field to the caravan area, a deep drainage ditch some distance from the sites brought me to a halt. Oh well, I need the exercise, so a walk will do me good. The grass was long, ankle deep for much of the way. It seemed prudent to tread carefully to avoid stepping in a hole and wrecking an ankle. A strange hush hung over the place. The only sound was the whisper of the breeze through the surrounding bush. I felt an involuntary shiver. It was cool on the field, but it wasn't so cold that I should shiver. Get a grip, Sonny, I told myself. you'll be jumping at shadows next.

After all this time, I didn't expect to find any exciting piece of evidence lying in the grass. My walking the site was more about getting a feel for the place and gaining an understanding of how it looked during the festival. Maybe there is a subconscious hope that my being here might rouse festival ghosts to help with the case.

An intrusive sound brought me back to the real world and I spun around in search of its origin. No ghosts, just a leering youth who emerged from the bush and swaggered across the field towards me. With his jeans in danger of giving up their remaining grip on his skinny hips and a torn flannelette shirt flapping in the breeze, this was more like a mother's nightmare than a ghost. While still some distance away, he called out. "You're too late for the festival, Darlin', but you can still be entertained. No point wastin' a trip to this here field is there now?"

Wonderful, just what I need! …Or maybe it is. Is this a clue to what happened to the other females? Somehow, I doubt it, but a second young lad's appearance from out of the bush made me focus on the present. Two of them together created a bit of a worry, but they were both quite skinny, full of bravado rather than muscle. The first lad, close enough now for me to see him clearly, was a member of the great unwashed youth of the place. I let him come towards me without answering his taunt. He kept coming but his pace slowed and I saw a shadow of doubt cross his face and lose itself in the three-day stubble it found there. When he was about three metres away, he stopped. His mate, a few metres behind him, also deciding to give in to uncertainty, stopped.

There were a couple of obscene suggestions about the pleasures they could give me before the nearest one rushed at me. I saw his mate start running as well. Here we go, any moment now this could get interesting, I told myself. While hoping I looked terrified, I stood my ground. The first one, now believing he was close enough, swung a right hook at me. I stepped aside, raising my arm to block the blow as I did so. No cause for alarm after all. As it turns out, he wasn't close enough to make contact and only succeeded in swinging himself off his feet to land in a scrambled heap on the ground about a metre from me.

Good, he's okay for the moment; now what about his mate, I thought as the first would-be hero hit the dirt. A scream split the air as I looked up to see what was happening with the other bloke. He was rolling on the ground, grasping his ankle and turning the air blue with his language.

It didn't take much to work out he had fallen in a hole of some sort. His painful ankle totally obliterated any previous bravado and ardour.

With that one out of action, I returned my attention to the one who fell at my feet. As he hit the ground, I firmly wedged my knee in his back. He seemed a bit groggy, probably banged his head when he hit the ground, but now he started to stir. I reefed his arm up hard behind his back, got up off him, and hauled him up onto his feet. There was little resistance. He was so light there was nothing of him. It made getting him to his feet easy, but there were consequences.

Once he was on his feet, his jeans gave up their tenuous grip on his hips. They slid gracefully to his ankles, effectively hobbling him. It's probably true that he hadn't planned on this happening or he wouldn't have chosen today to go commando. He made a vain attempt to retrieve his trousers. My grip on him rendered it futile. I couldn't help myself. I cast a disparaging look in the direction of his tackle and shook my head in disgust.

"Is that what was on offer? Not much pleasure likely from something that size. Best you hide it again before it dies of shame." In spite of his pain, his mate with the damaged ankle managed a grin… or was it a grimace at my poor attempt at spontaneous ridicule?

His jeans still around his ankles, I roughly shuffled him over to his mate. After giving his arm behind his back a hard upwards yank to provide him with a bit of pain to occupy his mind, I pushed him down to join his mate on the ground. He managed to drag his jeans back up without leaving the ground, and tightened his belt a couple of notches. That's a relief. I don't want to see that sight again today.

Two dejected specimens sitting on the ground avoided eye contact with me. No longer the swaggering duo I first encountered. Good, they seem docile enough now to ask questions about what they were up to in the bush, and if they knew anything about missing females. I could suggest I believed they were involved with the disappearances. That should shake them up enough to loosen their tongues – that is, if they do have anything of interest to tell me. I took a step back in case one of them tried for hero status by lashing out with his leg.

"Right, now before we begin you should be aware that I am pretty pissed off about having my day disrupted by you two useless louts… and when I am that way I am prone to becoming very unpleasant. Is there anything there that you don't understand?" Neither responded but one did give a slight shake of his head. "No. Good, let's move on then shall we? I'll ask questions and, if you have any sense at all, you will answer them. If you're thinking of trying your luck and messing me about, I wouldn't recommend it."

They both continued to avoid eye contact with me but their body language suggested they understood their situation and that I had their attention. "Okay, first question: it's an easy one, what were you up to in the bush before I arrived?" They exchanged glances, then focused on the ground and didn't answer. "Not answering has upped my anger level a bit more and I think I need to start working it down again. …So, which one of you wants to be first to help me with this?"

The one with the wrecked ankle jerked his head up and there was fear across his pimply face. "No, it's okay. I'll tell you." I gave him one of those 'get on with it' kinds of looks. "We weren't up to anything. We were skiving off and came down here so no one would know."

"Skiving off from what? …and what were you going to do, sit in the bush and twiddle your fingers all day?"

"We are apprentices and we are supposed to be at block training all this week, but we decided to give today a miss.

"…And do what?"

"He had some weed and I had a six-pack. We bought a couple of pies on our way here so we had ourselves set up for a good day."

"Why come and annoy me when I arrived?"

"…Thought you might have come to round us up and… well, you were only a bit of a female on your own. We thought we might as well have some fun while we were here."

"I'm not sure I buy that, but I'll let it go for now. You seem to know this bush well. Well enough to hide in there and grab unsuspecting females as they used the track?"

"We didn't grab no females. What are you on about?" The question caught the attention of the bloke with the jeans problem. "Who says we done females?"

"I ask the questions. You provide the answers. Three women disappeared during the festival here last Easter. What do you know about that? You had all sorts of interesting suggestions about what you were going to do to me. Is that what you did to the others?"

The question and answer session went nowhere for a while but, as I continued to push the point that it shouldn't be too hard to fit them up for involvement in the disappearance of at least one of the women, things slowly improved. After a few minutes of playing cat and mouse, the breakthrough came.

'Skinny hips' became rattled and blurted out what he probably tried to avoid from the start. "We done nuffin' wrong. We never touched any of them females – none of 'em – but I reckon we know somethin' about it.

Don't we, mate? We saw somethin' important goin' on out there – in the dark out there on the track. We saw it a couple a times didn't we, mate."

"What were you doing and where were you to be able to see whatever you saw?" That question brought a long pause. 'Mate' with the busted ankle took the initiative.

"Look, if we tell you, it can't go any further, right?" I flapped my hand to indicate maybe yes or maybe no. "Okay, it's like this. We snuck off to a bit of a hideout place we use in the bush along there. We were up for a bit of experimenting, if you know what I mean." I shook my head to indicate I had no idea what 'experimenting' meant. I had a fair idea but I wasn't about to let him know that.

"We got hold of some stuff and we were going to experiment with it. You know, try it."

"You mean drugs? You were going to try using some form of drugs?"

"Yeah, but our parents would kill us if they found out. Mine would anyway, but his would give him a hard time as well."

"Why would yours react worse than his?" Then it became interesting. The kid with the busted ankle was the son of the detective inspector I had been dealing with about Sarah, the one I spent a slab of time talking to and having coffee with this morning. "I see. I was talking to your father this morning and it's likely I'll be speaking with him quite often over the next few days. If you want your 'experimenting' to remain a secret, I suggest you tell what your mate here was talking about when he said you saw something happen on the track."

"We finished work early on the Thursday before Easter and met up with this bloke he (points to his mate) knows to do a bit of business. When the oldies parked in front of TV, we sneaked out to our hideout in the bush. There were noises in the field, so we crept up close for a look. A couple of caravans had arrived early."

"So, there were two caravans on site already?"

"Yes, there were two of them. Anyway, while we were crouched there right at the edge of the bush, this woman walks past us and starts off down the track."

"You actually saw a woman leave one of the caravans and start walking along the track? What did she look like?"

"I dunno. She looked like a woman. She wasn't too young, I don't think… and… yeah, and she had red hair."

"So what happened after you saw her start down the track?"

"We decided it was safe and headed back to our hideout. Before we got there, we heard a car somewhere on the track. Vehicles don't use that track. We got a bit twitchy and decided we should check it out before we got down to business. A van had backed into a bit of a clearing off the side of the track, and parked there not far from our hideout. The noise we heard was his engine start up. Then, it drove back onto the track and crept along it back towards the woman. When it came close to the woman, it stopped but the engine kept running. A bloke got out and went over to the woman. We thought it must be one of those… what do you call them… assignations. He probably had a wife, or maybe she had a husband, they didn't want to know about their meeting."

"What side of the van did the man get out from?"

"I dunno. What do you mean?"

"Did he get out of the driver's side or the passenger's side of the vehicle?"

"Oh, uhmm… the passenger's side, I think. It was the passenger's side, wasn't it?" he asked 'skinny hips' who remained strangely silent throughout the discussion. 'Skinny Hips' thought about it for a moment before agreeing it was the passenger's side.

"Okay, a man gets out of the passenger's side of the van and goes to meet the woman. Did they look as though they knew each other, and what happened after that?" This process was like drawing teeth. I am beginning to wonder if I'll ever get to the end of the story.

"Eh? N-o-o, I don't think they knew each other. They didn't rush into each other's arms, if that means anything. Anyway, then the man walks right up to her. I thought he was putting his arm around her, but then we heard a sort of muffled scream – or a yelp or something. That's when this other bloke gets out of the van – yes, out of the driver's side – and runs around and opens the back doors on the van. Then he goes over and helps the first bloke who is dragging this woman towards the van. She is kicking and struggling and it took the two of them to drag her to the van and bundle her into the back. She started to scream. One of the blokes, I don't know which one, slugged her one and she went quiet."

"All right, you saw the woman loaded into the van and silenced. I assume the van drove off after that."

"Yeah, they slammed the rear doors shut and jumped back in the van. I thought they would drive off towards the field because the van faced that way, but they didn't. They backed and filled about a dozen times to turn around on that narrow track before heading off the other way; back towards town."

"That's good work. Have you told anyone about what you saw… like the Police, for example."

"Not bloody likely; we can't do that, like you know, without having to explain what we were doing out here."

"I see your point. Did you happen to see anything else happen on the track over the festival weekend?"

"Uhmm, well, yeah; we did. We tried our luck and snuck out again the next two nights, but there was too much happening at the festival and we didn't feel safe. We did see that van again. It parked in that same clearing on the next two nights."

"…Anything happen on the track on those nights?"

"Yeah, we had this sort of routine. When we went to the bush, before we went to our hideout, we would sneak through to the edge of the field to see what was happen there first. The next night…"

"That would be Good Friday night, was it?"

"Yes, Good Friday; anyway, that night we managed to sneak out early – maybe around seven o'clock. We went straight over to check out the field, and thought we had been sprung by this young girl who walked past at the wrong time."

"What was she like?"

"Hmm, young, bit fat, blonde – good looking though-- don't remember much else. Anyway, she didn't see us and she heads to the track the same as the other one. That all rang a bit of a bell for us, so we crept back to where we could keep an eye on the van. It was much the same as the previous night, but different – if you know what I mean." No, I didn't know what he meant.

"Well, this time, they let the girl walk a bit past the parked van before they started the engine. Then they raced towards her. She moved over to the side of the track when she heard them coming and they drove up beside her. They stopped just a bit ahead of her, and it was the same. A bloke got out of the passenger's side, ran back to the girl and grabbed her. The bloke on the driver's side got out straight away, opened the rear doors and helped the other bloke bundle the girl into the back of the van."

"Did she scream, call out, or anything?"

"No, nothing at all and, by the time they dragged her to the van, she wasn't struggling or anything. She was just sort of limp and floppy. It was like the first bloke knocked her out or something. This time, they didn't have to turn around. The van faced the right direction, and they drove off towards town."

"Did you see the colour of the van?"

"It was night and the van was a dark colour; dark blue, I think."

"Did you go back there for the third night, the night after the young girl was taken away in the van?"

Uhmm, yeah, we were planning to have another go at… well, you know what we wanted to do. We checked out that clearing first thing and, when we saw the van there again, we legged it. I don't know what happened to those girls, but I don't think it was too good for them. We got a bit nervous. The blokes in that van were real bad buggers. We didn't want to run the risk of getting tangled up with them."

"How big was the van, was it something like a Transit van or something smaller? You don't happen to know what make it was?"

"Nah, don't know about the make, but it was only one of those small models."

"It would be good if you could show me that clearing where the van parked – not now but in the next day or so. By the way, how's the ankle?"

"Bloody sore!"

"Will you be able to walk home or do you need a lift?"

"I can walk. It's going to be difficult enough explaining how this happened without you driving me home."

"What about you, Sunshine, have you got those jeans under control now?" He shrugged – not very talkative is 'Skinny Hips'. I turned my attention back to the walking wounded. "What's your mobile number…?" I sensed resistance. "…So I can ring you to arrange a time for you to show me that clearing where the van parked, and in case I think of anything else I need to check with you."

"I'm not giving you my number. I don't want you ringing me. We've probably said more than we should already. I don't much fancy those blokes in the van coming back to deal with us for blabbing. That's part of why we didn't say anything before now."

Skinny Hips chimed in. "Who has been shooting their mouth off? *We* didn't say nuffin', it was *you* spillin' ya guts to this bit of skirt. I said nuffin'."

"That's all right. Don't worry about giving me your phone number, I'll ask your father for it the next time I'm talking to him." That did the trick, he recited his number and I keyed it into my phone. I handed him one of my business cards. "My number is on there. Call me if you think of anything else, or if you have some spare time to show me that clearing."

Everything came to a natural end. I didn't have any more to say and the two lads looked at a bit of a loss as to what to do next. "Well, come on you pair, off you go. You might also want to think about that 'experimentation' that you were keen to have a go at. This is the fourth time you've tried, and someone or something always stopped it happening. Perhaps the Gods are sending you a message. Maybe you should forget about it. Quit while you are still alive."

The two lads struggled to their feet and staggered off – Skinny Hips supporting Busted Ankle for a few paces. It didn't take him long to realise that, with his ankle well supported in his high-top trainers, it wasn't too painful to limp along under his own steam. They started slowly, casting an occasional glance over their shoulders at me, but soon picked up pace. After only a short distance, they veered off into the bush and didn't continue around the perimeter of the field to the end of the track as I expected.

I stood watching for a few moments before returning to my car. It had taken a while to get a little information but it was good information. I leant on the open car door and tried to make sense of what happened. It produced a cold dark feeling in the deepest recesses of my mind. It was late, and I needed to get back to the motel to write up my notes on everything I'd been told. I turned the vehicle and headed back the way I came. The motel wasn't far away – by line of sight – but the route back meandered through suburbia and an area of small acreages.

CHAPTER 8

By the time I arrived back at the motel, it was much later than I expected. A press of the button on the dashboard gadget had the security gate sliding silently open. No new cars in the parking area suggest it is a quiet time for the motel. I went directly to my room and drank a couple of glasses of water. It had been a long dry afternoon. Then it was down to work to record all the information collected during the day while it was still fresh in my memory.

Not much to worry about from my visit to Forestdale Police, happy to take copies of material in my file, they were not in any hurry to share their information with me. That assessment might be a little unfair, as I don't think they had much. After all, they only decided to take an interest in the case yesterday. It will be interesting to see how things progress from here on.

The information from my new friend with the busted ankle had more to offer and took longer to write up. If nothing else, his comments made mockery of (his father) the detective's comment about the old bloke who claimed to see a woman being bundled into a car. Whether high or not at the time, there is a fair chance that is what he saw. With everything recorded, I made a coffee and sat back to mull over the new information. While it was frustrating that the boys hadn't hung around on the third night to see what happen out there on the track, I would almost be prepared to bet Sarah met with the same fate as the previous two females. Time to examine that track; with any luck, I might locate the only other person who claimed to have seen anything.

After checking that my camera, notebook and a small torch were in my bag, I marched out the back door and into the carpark… and came to a dead stop. Twilight already had closed in. My watch suggested that, at just after six o'clock, it was supposed to be this dark. So much for going to have a look at the track, it was now too late and too dark. While I dithered about coming to that conclusion, I wandered unintentionally towards the security gate. A voice from the shadows startled me.

I spun around searching for the source of the voice. In the deep shadows at the gate-end of the rear wall of the motel, one of the restaurant staff enjoyed a quiet smoke. He looked relaxed as he leant with his back to the wall, so I wandered over to chat to him. As I got closer, I recognised him as one of the wait staff from the previous night – the wine waiter, I think. "You not dining in tonight?" he asked.

"Yes, I am. I didn't realise it was so late and I came out thinking I would take a stroll down that track through the bush. Did you work over the Easter weekend when the festival was on?"

"Yeah, I worked the whole weekend. I don't have anyone at home – no wife or family or anything – so I worked and let the others take some time off to be with theirs."

A quick scratch around in my bag, and I was showing him Sarah's photo. "Do you remember this woman at all from that weekend?" He studied the photo for a few moments in the poor light then nodded. "Did you talk to her or see her around much?"

"Nah, but we don't usually see guests much when they are here for the festivals. They are out there doing what they came to do: enjoy the festival. I did talk to her a couple of times though." My pulse rate stepped up a couple of notches.

"Do you remember when or what you spoke about?"

"Hey, what's with all the questions? Are you the Police or something?"

"No nothing like that, it's just that she went missing while she was here and her parents asked me, while I was here, to see if I could find out anything about what happened to her. She seems to have just vanished. Anything she said, although it might seem unimportant, could offer a clue about her disappearance. We don't know how or why it happened; only that she went missing from here while she was at the festival." He stared off into the distance through his cigarette smoke for a few moments. I held my breath, afraid he might elect not to say anything more. At last he swivelled his eyes back to me.

"So she's the one that disappeared. I overheard a few whispers around the middle of last week about some woman who hadn't come back to checked out but all her gear was still in her room. Christ, that's a shame. She seemed nice from what little I had to do with her. I spoke to her in the restaurant one night. We only had a couple of diners that night. I think it might have been her first night here."

"What did you talk about?"

"It wasn't anything important. Because we weren't busy, I was the only one waiting tables and doing the drinks that night. The other couple of diners left early. She was the only one left in the restaurant when I was clearing tables and setting up for the next day. She asked if I would get to see any of the festival, and she said she was surprised there weren't more people booked into the motel. I explained that we were booked out for the weekend but they all would arrive the next day. That was it. She finished her drink, said goodnight and left."

"You said you spoke to her a couple of times. When was the next time you spoke to her?"

"Uhmm, let's see. It must have been the Sunday night. Yes, it was the Sunday night. That was the night they had the big music show to wrap up the festival before all the musicians and stallholders started packing up and moving out the next day. It happened a bit like us now. I was out here having a smoke before I started work when she came out and had a bit of trouble getting the gate to open. I went to see what the problem was. The button was sticking and you had to be a bit firm with it. We had a bit of a chat and I asked her, the same as I asked you, if she wasn't going to be dining in the restaurant that night. You see, we were booked out. It was getting late and, if she was just going for a walk before dinner, by the time she got back she might have trouble getting a table."

"Was she planning on dining in?"

"No. No, she said she wasn't hungry. She had sampled the different foods all day but, if she got hungry later on, she would get something from one of the food stalls that she hadn't tried yet. There wasn't much else, just that she was impressed with that night's program and was looking forward to enjoying the music."

"Did you see her or speak to her again – later that night perhaps?"

"The restaurant was busy and we worked until nearly midnight. I didn't see anything outside the restaurant. Unless I was outside or out in the hallways, I wouldn't see her come back anyway. I better go; I'll be in trouble again for starting late."

He threw his cigarette onto the bitumen and ground it out with his shoe before hurrying inside. I looked around. Night had fallen while we chatted. The carpark security lights created an area of glaring brightness in the surrounding velvety blackness. As there was no point in trying to check out the track now, I followed my recent acquaintance and made my way to the restaurant. There were a couple of extras dining in tonight but we were so few that there were several unoccupied tables between each of the occupied ones. My fellow diners already had ordered and their food started arriving while I sipped my pre-dinner drink and waited for my taste buds to indicate what they liked on the menu.

It seems tonight is 'Roast Night', with a choice of roast beef, lamb or pork dominating the menu and only a couple of other pasta dishes available for those with a preference for something other than roast meat. I chose the roast pork – with crackling and apple sauce of course – and sat back to reflect on the day. The arrival of my meal returned me to the here and now. As I started to eat, the last of the other diners left the restaurant. Not a particularly social animal at the best of times, I welcomed the solitude. It didn't last long.

On her way to clear another table, the young dark-haired girl who had served me since my arrival stopped at my table on her way past. "Excuse me, Miss, but Gary…" She jerked her head in the direction of the bloke I talked to earlier outside. "…Gary said you were asking about the girl that disappeared." I nodded and laid my knife and fork down.

"Did you talk to her at all while she was here?"

"We are not supposed to talk about it; give the place a bad name if word gets out that someone disappeared from here." She shrugged, glanced over her shoulder towards the kitchen, and continued. "Around the time she was supposed to check out, I was near the back door when I saw a man getting into one of the cars parked out the back. Nothing unusual about that I suppose, except he was a stranger. He wasn't one of our guests and I hadn't seen him around at all."

"Did you check him out or anything?"

"I was fairly sure I knew whose car it was. That's why it caught my attention. Anyway, I memorised the number plate, and went and checked it out at reception. I looked up that Sinclair woman's registration form. That's whose car I thought it was. The plate on the car the bloke drove off in was the same as the one on her registration form."

"Did you say anything to anyone about it?"

"That old dragon of a receptionist came in while I was checking it out and got all bent out of shape about what I was doing. I explained why I was checking the records. All I got was a lecture about how the records and that woman were none of my concern, blah, blah, blah. I asked her if she knew someone had come to collect the woman's car. The old girl looked a bit taken aback by that, but told me it was none of my business."

"So, it appears someone – that bloke – had the car key, or you would have noticed him messing about trying to hot wire it."

"Yes; he just walked up to it, unlocked it with the remote, got in and drove off. I sometimes do a shift on reception so, the next time I was on duty there, I checked that Sinclair woman's details. Her gate remote – that thing you put on your dashboard – is still outstanding, and so is her room key."

"That fits. I don't think she was planning on disappearing so those things wouldn't be handed in."

"Then... I think it was last Friday. Yes, it was last Friday. I opened up the office because the dragon was ill and didn't come in until later that day. I was booting up the computer ready for the morning's checkouts, but I hadn't opened the door yet. The next thing, I heard a key rattle through the after-hours check out slot. I raced over to get it in case someone was trying to check out without paying. It was the key to room five, the one she had. I sneaked down before I opened up to have a look. Everything was still in her room."

"What did you do about it... who did you tell?"

"Nothing and no one; there was something funny going on about that woman and I'd already been in trouble for snooping. When I'm in reception, I'm only supposed to do registrations and checkouts – nothing else – and definitely no snooping. ...So, I opened up and dropped the room key through the slot again. There's a clear plastic box at the office end of the slot, so you can see if keys are there. I didn't say anything to anyone about it, and I haven't heard anyone talking about it."

"Didn't the manager say anything... talk to the staff about the disappearance at all?"

"The manager... we don't never see 'im down here. He has some other business – or so I hear tell – that he runs from upstairs. I don't know what it is, but it must keep him busy. We never see him down here."

"...So, he is the manager but he doesn't spend any time in the motel?"

"Well, it's one of those 'Mister and Missus' management teams. She – his wife – she comes down here some days ... most days I suppose. Only spends a bit of time down here making sure everything is okay and then disappears again."

"Well, who runs the place if the management aren't spending any time on the premises?"

"Oh, they spend time here – but upstairs and not down here. The old dragon on reception runs the place for them. I think she might be some sort of relative. I better get on and get finished before someone starts asking questions." She cast a nervous glance in the direction of the kitchen.

"Thank you, you've been very helpful."

"You won't tell them (a jerk of her head towards the kitchen) I said anything, will you?" I shook my head and she hesitated for a moment before speaking again. "I hope you don't mind me asking, but what's your connection with all this? Are you a copper?"

"I'll make a bargain with you: I won't tell anyone about what you told me, if you don't tell anyone about me. Bargain...?" She nodded enthusiastically. "I'm a private investigator Sarah Sinclair's parents hired to look into her disappearance. The Police wouldn't take them seriously, but I think they do now. They might start coming around asking questions. It will be up to you -- and Gary – whether you tell the Police what you have told me, or not. Only you will know whether you might be risking your jobs if you do."

On my way back to my room, I pondered the 'cone of silence' motel management had placed over Sarah's disappearance. I can understand them wanting to protect the motel's reputation from gossip and speculation but, in so doing, they were obstructing the investigation of Sarah's disappearance – and her possible rescue. My gut was telling me something else was going on here, but it didn't give me any clues about what that might be.

More notes to record from tonight's two informants, and a shower to have, and then I would be ready for a good night's sleep. I fell into bed about ten o'clock but sleep didn't come. After tossing and turning for some time, I got up and opened Sarah's file. Something in the back of my mind kept nagging me. It wouldn't come forward, so I decided to draw up a timeline in the hope that it might produce some glaring anomaly that I had missed.

The timeline didn't take long. So far, I didn't have much to put on it. I started it at Good Friday when Sarah left home, but soon realised I needed to extend the front end of the line to accommodate the disappearance of the first woman on the Thursday night. With Thursday added to the line, I wrote beneath it 'redhead disappeared'. Then, above the line, I added everything I knew so far about anything to do with Sarah. Oops, I need to backtrack again to Good Friday and add below the line 'blonde girl disappeared'. It was a pathetic looking timeline… and I still didn't feel I needed to go back to bed.

I gazed at the timeline for a few moments. There wasn't anything else to add to it. At last, my brain decided to kick in. What happened on the Saturday night? It didn't appear that anyone disappeared on that night, so what was different about it? …Or, perhaps someone did disappear, but I – and maybe the Police – didn't know about it. That question occupied my mind for a few minutes while I gazed at a garish abstract painting on the opposite wall. If someone did go missing and no one reported it, how can I find out about it? Nothing enlightening came to me, so I noted the question to ponder at some other time, and returned my attention to the timeline.

My focus settled on the more recent end of the line; the entries for the car and the room key. A return to Brisbane to find Sarah's trail there now seemed unlikely. Sarah didn't drive that car to Brisbane, of that I now was sure. Such a trip would require her to buy fuel at least a couple of times. No such transactions appeared on any of her bank accounts. The other blindingly obvious fact was that she would not have returned her room key without first collecting all her gear from the room. There was only one logical conclusion.

The man seen taking off in the car drove it to Brisbane and then, by other means, made his way back to Minden Hill to return the room key. That would account for the couple of days' gap between the two events: driving to Brisbane and returning. If I accept that premise, then Sarah might still be in this area. An alternative scenario that I didn't want to dwell on was that they took her with them and dumped her either in Brisbane or somewhere along the way.

Neither scenario was particularly comforting. A dark cold feeling of dread surged through me. For someone else to have the car key and the motel key, they must have taken them from Sarah. She would take her room key with her so she could get back into the motel after the festival ended for the night, but why would she take her car key when she wasn't driving anywhere? Ah-hah, perhaps… yes, she would have a bag with her, or a purse of some sort. She would need money – or maybe cards – to buy food or anything else from the stalls. She would put her room key in the bag to avoid dropping it, and the car key might be there from the last time she used it. If she put the room key and cash in her pocket, she would not pick up the car key as well since she wasn't intending to drive anywhere that night.

I tried to block it out, but my mind kept showing me a picture of Sarah being bundled into the back of a dark blue van. This was not good news. Up until now, the disappearances of the other two women -- and probably Sarah -- remained a story without an end. It was the thought of what that ending might be that worried me. I climbed back into bed and lay there going over what I knew so far, what I should do next, and what I might find at the end of it all.

CHAPTER 9

Sometime after I went back to bed, I managed to fall asleep and ended up sleeping late this morning. As a result, Wednesday morning got off to a slow start and remained sluggish until well after breakfast. Somewhere in the midst of my deliberations before I fell asleep, I decided to explore the bush track today and to try to talk to the residents who supposedly live in shacks in the bush beside it.

By about half nine, I felt a bit more alive and, with much of last night's dew dried by this morning's warm sun, I couldn't procrastinate any longer. I roused myself and headed for the track. After only a few strides down the track, I became aware of the damp chill pervading the place. The width of the track would make it difficult to drive even a small vehicle along it without scratching the vehicle and tearing pieces from the trees. No sunlight penetrated the dense canopy of the bush that surrounded the track and extended right to the very edge of it. I peered into the gloom that extended for as far as I could see of the track.

Maybe with the sun directly overhead, the track would become more welcoming if some light managed to filter through the foliage. No sunlight dried anything here. Last night's dew still clung to leaves and branches, and gathered in large drops on spiders' webs. This didn't make for a pleasant stroll. It didn't improve matters when birds in the trees, startled by my presence took flight, showering me with dew. I'm wondering whether I do want to talk to the residents of any shacks along the way. It will mean trudging through the very wet bush to knock on their doors.

I walked past the first shack without noticing, but something made me turn back. My subconscious must have noticed something off in the bush and now called me back. Well-hidden by the intervening growth, something just visible some distance off the track made me backtrack. A faint path led off the track towards the shack. Too much to expect it to take a straight line to the front door, I trudged along a narrow damp path that meandered around trees and, eventually, through well-tended plots of vegetables.

'Shack' is the most apt description of the residence. Construction appears to be from anything the local tip could provide. It sat in the centre of a substantial area that once sported natural undergrowth. Now cleared of what nature had intended, it supported horticulture. Vegetables and some fruits thrived in the well laid out cleared area. Something of a dilemma confronted me when I reached the shack. How do you knock on the front door when there is no obvious door? As I wandered around the side of the shack, I came across an opening that was probably the entrance. For want of something better, I knocked on the rusting sheet of corrugated iron that edged one side of the opening.

A bleary eyed and scruffy-looking elderly woman demanded to know what I wanted. On closer inspection, maybe she isn't so elderly; perhaps she's just well worn. None too pleased at being disturbed at whatever she was doing, she wasted no time in acquainting me with her displeasure. There was nothing to do but wait until she finished her rant before I tried to explain why I came. Her vitriol finally spent, she stood hands on hips effectively blocking the opening. I took it as my cue to answer her earlier demand about what I was doing there. In the hope that it might smooth the way somewhat, I opened with an apology before getting to the crux of my visit.

"I'm sorry I disturbed you, but I was wondering if you might have heard or seen anything unusual happen along the track over the weekend of the Easter festival." That drew a blank look, so I tried a bit more persuasion. "I believe a couple of women went missing from around here over that weekend and there's been suggestion that it might have happened out there on the track. I'm only interested because a friend of mine went missing from here on that same weekend and her parents are just about beside themselves worrying about what might've happened to her."

She stood there still defiant, but I thought I detected a softening in her face. "I heard about it; bad business that. They think it happened out on the track, eh? Don't know why they would think that. I don't know anything about it, but I mind my own business like, and don't take much interest in what else is going on around the place. Sorry, can't help you, dear. Now, if you don't mind, I'll get back to what I was doing… and I'll thank you to push off and leave me to get on with it."

Okay, that was interesting – if unproductive – but I'm concerned that's going to be the tone I'll encounter from all the residents along the track. Back on the track, I trudged only a short distance further on before coming to a small clearing off the left-hand side of the track. Although it was more than a week ago, I wondered if there might be some remnant tyre tracks in the clearing to indicate this is where the van parked to wait for its victims.

A quick stir of the contents of my backpack located my small torch. I stood on the track and played the torch beam over the ground in the clearing. Nothing jumped out at me to suggest anything might've parked here. If I wanted to be sure, the clearing needed closer investigation. A quick look in both directions up and down the track confirmed I wasn't sharing the area with anyone else, so I stepped off the track and carefully made my way into the clearing.

Damaged lower branches on some of the surrounding trees caught my attention. The ends of some branches, though broken, still had their ends hanging by a sliver of bark, while others, more severely damaged, littered the ground below them with their broken bits. I couldn't tell when the damage occurred. It would take someone with specialised knowledge to determine how recent it was. A thick blanket of leaf litter covered the entire area, obliterating all evidence of what lay beneath it. I walked carefully around the perimeter of the clearing, eyes glued to the ground for any sign of recent activity. While quite large areas of leaves looked crushed, there was nothing to suggest what caused the damage.

So far, I had nothing conclusive, but I was convinced I had found the clearing where the blue van parked. I found myself back on the track and moved to stand on the edge of the track in the centre of the entrance to the clearing. I tried imagining myself as the blue van parked here waiting for its victim. My recent acquaintance with the busted ankle said that on the first night –the Thursday night – the van drove out of the clearing and went left along the track. It drove only a short distance before catching up with the redheaded woman. The big question: how far is a 'short distance'? Was it as little as five metres or perhaps forty metres or more?

I stepped back onto the track and peered into the gloom that filled the distance in the direction the van went. With the track being so narrow, it would require considerable backing and filling for a vehicle to turn around on the track. In fact, it probably would run off the edge of the track in the process. If that were the case, there should be clear evidence of where it happened – provided it did happen as my new 'friend' said. There was nothing else to do but take a walk and have a look. I strode off down the track, counting strides as I went and metalling convert the number of strides to metres. After what I calculated to be about forty metres, and with nothing to show for it, my frustration level registered in the red zone.

"How much further can a 'short distance be?" I said aloud to the empty track, and then quickly checked around me to make sure I was alone on the track and I didn't have any curious spectators. Indecision parked itself on my shoulder.

Should I keep going? About fifty metres ahead of where I now stood, the track disappeared around a curve. I stood in the middle of the track dithering about whether to carry on or return to the clearing. The problem with walking the track with my eyes fixed firmly on the ground was that I wasn't looking for any other shacks tucked away in the bush. If I returned to the clearing, I could walk the same stretch of track again, this time scouring the surrounding bush for shacks. Indecision ruled. Swinging my head from right to left several times, I looked both ways along the track in the hope inspiration on how to proceed might descend upon me. As I looked along the track to my left again, something off the edge of the track some distance ahead caught my eye. Decision made and, with excitement building, I picked up my pace and continued in the same direction along the track.

Plenty of action happened here. The track itself showed little evidence of what went on. However, the softer ground on either shoulder of the track told another story. A confusion of tyre ruts remained visible, identifying the spot where the abduction occurred. Elation replaced frustration – for maybe a couple of heartbeats. So, I had found the spot. That only posed another question. If the comment in the newspaper article is believable, the bloke who reputedly saw the woman bundled into the van lives around here somewhere. The question is where and how close.

It is possible the man took an evening stroll and happened to be in the right place at the right time. Thinking about the man recalled something else: The offhand response to my mention of it at the Forestdale Police Station. I needed to find that man and, apart from anything else, assess his credibility for myself. I peered into the bush alongside the track where I stood. No sign of a shack. Maybe, if I go a little further along, I might find a path or see a shack. Sure enough, after about another five metres, I spotted a lightly defined path leading off the track into the bush. Of course, it didn't head off in a straight line. Even from the middle of the track, I could see that it took off at a wide angle from the track. A couple of metres further along the track beyond the path provided a glimpse of a shack set well back and almost completely hidden by scrubby growth.

This proved a different trek from the one I made to its neighbouring shack. No neat vegetable plots to negotiate this time as I trod the damp path. By the time I reached the cleared area around the shack, the bottom of my jeans and my trainers were soaked. No problems finding the door this time, a wild looking bloke wearing nothing more than a sarong came out to meet me. His welcome suggested an invitation to tea and scones wasn't about to be forthcoming. "Wha'cha want?" he demanded.

I used the same line I used before about looking for my missing friend and trying to find out what happened to her and the other two women who disappeared. He didn't buy it. With his head cocked to one side, he glared at me sceptically. I took his reaction as an invitation to explain further. "I wondered if you might have seen or heard anything out there on the track during that festival over the Easter weekend."

"I minds me own business… and I expect other people to mind theirs." Okay, more persuasion needed, and I don't think batting my eyelashes – if I knew how to do it – would work.

"That's a sound policy but, it's such a quiet isolated spot you have here, that anything unusual, like a car out on the track at night, might catch your attention. I don't imagine many, if any, vehicles use that track."

"No, you's right there, very rare for a vehicle to be on that track – especially at night. But, that don't mean I pay particular attention to what's happening down there."

"No, of course you wouldn't, and you wouldn't walk all the way out to the track to investigate some strange going on, even if it sounded like a car messing about out there. I just thought that, maybe while you were going about your normal routine, you might have heard something but paid it no attention. Maybe you were already in bed and it woke you up, for instance."

"Naw, I weren't in bed; I were out and about at the time…"

"You weren't at home when there was an incident on the track, is that what you're telling me?"

"Oh, I was at home all right, but I was out and about outside. I was indulging in my nightly ritual, I was."

"That sounds intriguing, what does that nightly ritual involve?"

"Pissing on her next door's pumpkins."

"Okay, you've got me intrigued. Tell me about it."

"That fat cow next-door just keeps clearing more ground and planting more vegetables and stuff. She's been making her way towards my place. If I don't do something, soon I'll have her bloody pumpkins growing under me window. I've had enough, so I'm taking action. Pumpkins don't like getting their leaves wet see. You have to water them at ground level. They get some sort of mould if their leaves get too wet and it kills them."

"That is interesting. I didn't know that." I also didn't know he had a window.

"No, I suppose you wouldn't. You don't look like much of a gardener. …But, what I tell you is true, and it also applies to those zucchini things she grows. So, at night just before I go to bed, I wander outside to see if there's any lights lit at her place. If her place is in darkness, I piss on her pumpkins. I have a plan. I just do a few plants at a time along the edge closest to my place. The next night, the next few plants get the treatment and so on to the end of her plantings. After I come to the end of the pumpkins, there are a few zucchinis to deal with as well."

"I assume the goal is to kill her pumpkins. Is it working, and what happens when you get to the end of the zucchinis?"

"It is slow, I'll give you that, but it does work. Quite a few of her vines have turned their toes up. Of course, just one watering is not enough to do the trick so, when I reached the end of the zucchinis, I come back up here and start again."

"Were you taking care of her pumpkins on the Thursday night before Easter? That's the night, according to a newspaper article, that somebody claimed he saw a woman being bundled into a vehicle." He giggled mischievously.

"Ay, I did happen to be down there looking after the zucchinis when this van started up. It sounded too close, so I wandered down towards the track to see if it was where it shouldn't be, or if it were the wind just drifting the sound this way from somewhere else."

"You went down towards the track and realised there was a vehicle there. Then what happened?" Geez this is hard work. He seems to be enjoying stringing out the story for as long as possible. Still, if I want to know what happened, I have to play along.

"This van came roaring along the track and stopped suddenly – just back there a bit." He gestured towards a point back along the track. I said nothing but mentally urged him to continue. "Yeah, then it comes to a stop, all sudden like, but the motor kept running. There was a fair ruckus going on – grunting and a few words like a fight might be happening. I shifted a bit closer for a better view. As I moved to a better position, I heard this funny sound… sort of like a muffled scream. From my new position, I saw three people struggling down there on the track. Two of them dragged the third one around to the back of the van. That third person was a woman, a woman with long red hair."

"If it was dark, how could you tell her hair was red? It must have been difficult enough to work out it was a woman."

"The back doors on the van were open and the little light in the… in the cabin, I suppose you call it… provided just enough light to make out a few details – like her red hair. Anyway, she was having none of it. She wasn't getting into that van – and she was putting up a good fight. Then, one of the blokes delivers a haymaker… Mohammed Ali would've been proud of it. It all went quiet. She stopped struggling – out to it I guess after the belt she got – and between them, the two men bundled her into the back of the van and drove off. Silly buggers, they should have driven out the way they were facing but, no, they spent ages trying to turn that bloody van around on that narrow track."

"Did you tell the Police what you saw?"

"Nobody came asking, well, not for a few days anyway. I tried telling that big-knob detective what I saw but he didn't want to know. Said he was too busy to listen to me making up stories and got one of his lackeys to get rid of me." That fits with my impression of him.

"Did you tell anyone else?"

"Not right then, but a bit later after the cops had gone. There was this reporter hanging about – nothing more than a slip of a girl she was. The coppers wouldn't let her anywhere near the place, but she saw me trying to talk to them. After the coppers left, she caught up with me and we had a chat. I told her what I saw, but I don't know what she did about it."

"I can tell you what she did. She included in her article the fact that a man said her saw the woman being bundled into a vehicle. One way or another, the Police would have found out about it, even if they didn't do anything about it. It's probably a good thing you weren't tempted to go down and do something heroic like trying to save the woman. God knows what they might have done to you if they weren't too worried about knocking her out cold."

"I thought so too. Besides, I couldn't really go down there. I had my pyjamas on at the time."

"I don't think what you were wearing would have bothered them."

"No, maybe not, but it would have been uncomfortable for me." How mid-Victorian of the old boy to worry about such things at a time like that. He sensed my confusion and chuckled. "You see, you're never likely to see my pyjamas hanging on a clothes line. They don't come off." It took me a couple of seconds to compute that last comment. Then it dawned on me. Yes, he would have felt a tad vulnerable sallying forth to rescue her stark naked as he was.

He walked me down the path and showed me the vantage point from which he viewed the abduction. Then I took him out onto the track and showed him the tyre impressions left by the turning van. We walked back up to his shack together chatting as we went. He hadn't seen or heard anything further unusual over the following few nights, and was just glad to see the festival over and an end to the music filtering through the trees to disturb his peace.

It turned out to be a productive morning after all, and I had new respect for my friend with the busted ankle. The truth of his story about that first abduction now confirmed by probably its only other witness. I felt less confident about the value of his father, the Forestdale detective who seemed to be handling the case. Before heading off to walk the remainder of the track to the field, I resolved to ring Ben when I got back to the motel. There wasn't much further to go to reach the field, but I kept an eye out for any other shacks tucked away in the bush. I saw only one more and met its resident as she stepped off her path and onto the track. She was like the three wise monkeys: saw nothing, heard nothing and basically said nothing.

Once I reached the field, I resisted the temptation to wander around on it. That could wait until another day if I thought it necessary. I found myself with only one option, turn around and head back the way I came to the motel. By the time I reached the town end of the track, it was lunchtime. After retrieving my purse from my room, I wandered along the street to a small coffee shop. At the door, I hesitated about going inside. It wasn't impressive looking. Nevertheless, I was hungry and I didn't want to waste time on looking for somewhere to eat when I had notes to type up and a call to make to Ben.

A salad and a mineral water don't take long to despatch. The shop was empty, service prompt, and I found myself back on the street about twenty minutes after I entered the shop. My intention was to head back to the motel and get on with things I had to do but, after only a few metres along the street, I felt the hairs on the back of my neck starting to prickle. Instinct said someone was watching me. I slowed my pace and ambled along idly looking in shop windows as I passed. A shop selling women's fashion seemed a good place to linger a little longer.

This store's windows were not square onto the footpath as was the case with most of the other shops on the street. They had a mock bow window look and, their sparkling clean glass combined with the shop's dark interior provided an excellent place to check for anyone following me. After checking the street from all angles in the shop windows, I moved off again towards the motel. The feeling of being watched persisted. I moved out to the middle of the footpath and stood there looking around as if trying to make up my mind what to do next. The ruse worked; I think I tagged my tail.

The man seemed familiar and I thought about where I might have seen him as I crossed the road and began window-shopping along the other side of the street. Ah, yes; now I remember. I caught a glimpse of that man further down the street as I entered the coffee shop. It was possible he had legitimate reason to be wandering around the street at the same time as I was, but somehow I didn't think that was the case.

After scrutinising the windows of a few shops, I came to an amazing shoe shop. This tiny Aladdin's Cave displayed the bootmaker owner's own handmade creations. I stood in front of the window drooling over the exotic shoes and boots displayed, and had to remind myself that I was supposed to be using the window to check for a tail. My 'companion' appeared to be loitering on the other side of the street but keeping up with my progress. Gee, now I had a real excuse to go into the shoe shop. Filled with the most amazing creations, temptation made it hard for me to focus on the real task.

I caught sight of the man disappearing into a cafe on the other side of the street. No doubt, he intended waiting in the cafe while I browsed in the shoe shop. Temptation won out. I purchased a pair of soft suede ankle boots. A pair of shoes in the window appeared made from an unusual type of leather. I dragged the owner out onto the street to show him the shoes and ask about the materials used in them. "Yeah, it's unusual isn't it? It's stingray skin tanned into leather. You won't believe how soft it is. Come back inside and I'll take them out of the window so you can feel it." We went back inside and I cooed over the feel of the shoes while keeping one eye on the café across the street.

There was nothing else to do in the shop, but I hadn't come up with a plan of how to leave unseen and get back to the motel without my tail. I had reached the door on the way out when a bus drove down the street and pulled up across from the shoe shop, effectively blocking my view the cafe from which my tail watched me. If I couldn't see him, he probably couldn't see me. Using the bus as cover, I dashed back across the street, crossed the footpath, and continued straight into the open door of the shop in front of me… and almost gagged.

An overpowering combination of perfumes met me. The place sold scented candles, handmade soaps, votive oils and oil burners, potpourri and probably every other perfumed item imaginable. On the plus side, the only light in the shop came from a couple of low wattage wall sconces and the flickering tea lights under a couple of oil burners. Its window offered a good view of the street. Soon after I entered the shop, the bus drove off and, a few seconds later, my tail trotted past my vantage point, swivelling his head from side to side, searching the footpath in front of him and the other side of the street as he went. I waited a couple of minutes to see what might eventuate.

Just how much time can you spend smelling various coloured handmade soaps without raising the shopkeeper's suspicions? I contemplated buying a bar of the stuff to justify lingering over the display of soaps for so long. To my relief, I saw my tail jog back past the window and continue towards the café he occupied earlier. The phone behind the counter rang and the shopkeeper answered it. I grabbed a jar of the 'natural organic' hand lotion that was on special today, slapped the requisite five dollar note on the counter, waved away the bag offered one-handed by the shopkeeper as she continued her phone conversation, and made my way to the door.

At the door, I hesitated, checked the street, and stepped back inside when I caught sight of my tail crossing the street. He crossed the street at an angle, travelled a short distance along the opposite footpath and disappeared down a side street. I stepped back inside and, for a few moments, feigned great interest in a display of scented notepaper near the door. A car came out of the side street and roared past at a bit more than the legal speed. There was only a fleeting glimpse of the driver as the car flew past, but I recognised my tail behind the wheel. With no further interest in the notepaper, I stepped out onto the footpath and looked up the street to see the car disappearing into the distance away from the direction of my motel.

There are times when you don't waste time thinking things over and just act. That's what I did. Somehow managing the urge to run because of the attention that might attract, I headed back to the motel at a pace only slightly slower than double-time.

CHAPTER 10

A startled receptionist looked up as I barrelled through the front door of the Wisteria Inn and made a beeline for the wall opposite her desk. A rack attached to the wall and another revolving display stand held maps, tourist brochures and 'what's on in town' type information. After several minutes of paying close attention to this material and watching the street at the same time, and with no sign of that car again, I went to my room.

In response to my first instinct on entering my room, I checked out every bag, cupboard and drawer looking for any sign of intrusion during my absence. Relieved to find nothing disturbed, I took out my phone, sat on the bed and called Ben. It came as a surprise when he answered immediately. I expected him to be surfing or out doing whatever it is that holidaymakers do. "No surfing happening at the moment," he told me. "…Couple of sharks creating a bit of bother so the beaches are closed. Anyway, I'm glad you rang. I'm thinking I might drive out to Minden Hill to join you. But, you rang me, so what did you want to tell me – or what do you want me to do?"

"I was going to give you an update on what I've found so far. However, that was my thinking before I went for lunch. Now there is something else I want to talk to you about." It turned into a long conversation. I told Ben about the two lads I met at the field and the information they provided, about my morning sleuthing along the bush track and chatting up the residents. He seemed impressed. That changed when I voiced my concerns about the local detective I had dealt with, and how something about him didn't smell kosher. That bit impressed him less so. Then it was time to tell him about my after-lunch game of hide-and-seek with the bloke following me. This last piece of the story clinched it. "That's it; I am coming to Minden Hill. I'll see you this evening."

There was something reassuring about Ben being at Wisteria Inn. I didn't want him to get involved in my case – he had no jurisdiction this side of the border anyway – but, if needed, he could take care of my tail for me while I got on with other things. It took me an hour or so to type up my notes, and then I stopped to make a coffee before going back to read over them. On my way back to my computer, coffee in hand, a random thought brought me to a standstill. Instead of going to my computer, I retrieved my phone from the bed where I dropped it after talking to Ben. I keyed in Ben's number again.

He was driving and expected to be at the motel in less than half an hour. I told him of my idea in an echo-ridden hands-free conversation while he drove. "I think there might be some merit in people here not realising we know each other. I don't know why I think this, but my gut tells me it the right thing to do. When you check in, you should ask for Room 6. I'm in Room 7 and it has an adjoining door with Room 7. That could be handy if we want to talk without being seen together."

"Y-e-s, I see you point, but how am I supposed to ask for Room 6 without getting asked why I want that room?"

"I don't know. Tell them you're superstitious, or that you're into numerology and six is your lucky number. Think of something. Anything will do."

"The adjoining door will be locked. It would only be unlocked if a family occupied both rooms or for some other similar situation."

"Yes, it is locked now, but I wouldn't have thought that a problem for two skilful and innovative people like us. If we do things this way, we will be two single strangers passing through the place. Of course, we could happen to meet and get chatting at the bar, and maybe even end up dining together."

"Does this fantasy of yours extend beyond dinner?" His chuckle rumbled through my phone. I made some appropriate – but unprintable – remark and our conversation ended.

I read over my notes, amended and added as necessary and then packed them away. After fetching a bottle of mineral water from my bar fridge, I opened the sliding glass door and took my drink outside to the colonnaded area. A small round wrought iron table and two matching chairs were against the wall. Their placement suggested they were for use by guests in Room 6 or Room 7. I sat on one chair, put my fee up on the other, leaned back and pondered what to do next as I sipped my mineral water. As I sat there mulling over my case, time slipped my, and it wasn't until a car pulling up in front of the reception area caught my attention that I returned to reality. I watched the driver climb – unroll more like – out of the car. Ben had arrived.

There was registration to complete and then the business of taking his car around to the guests' carpark, so it was some time before I heard noises coming from Room 6. I stayed at the table and, a few moments later, I saw the corner of the curtain in Room 6 flick back for a moment. Ben knew where I was. After procrastinating for a few minutes longer, I wandered back inside as my phone started ringing: Ben making contact. The short call lasted long enough for us to arrange for 'two strangers to meet' at seven o'clock at the bar in the restaurant. I filled in time going over my case file until it was time to shower and dress for dinner – that is, if you call jeans and a clean tee shirt dressing for dinner.

At about five minutes past the appointed hour, I strolled up to the bar and perched on a stool, leaving an unoccupied stool between Ben and me. He already had a drink. I ordered a white wine, and an excellent portrayal of a casual meeting of two strangers followed. We chatted amicably -- where are you from, what do you do for a living (some good inventiveness there) and a pile of other 'nothings' – before agreeing that maybe we should share a table for dinner. Although there were few other diners, we chose a table in the furthest corner of the room, and interspersed our serious discussion with lots of laughing in a bid to create the impression it was something different.

Dinner over, it was time to go back to our rooms. I departed first, leaving Ben at the table finishing his drink. A couple of minutes after I was back in my room, I heard his gentle tap on my door. I let him in. "There's no one around and I managed to bump the CCTV camera a little to one side. I'm hoping its focus now just misses the doors on this side of the hallway."

"Okay, now you're here, let's attack that adjoining door to see if we can work some magic on that lock."

It took nearly ten minutes with the pair of us simultaneously using my lock picks and a credit card to get the stubborn lock to yield. Once we unlocked the door, the normal, easy-going working relationship Ben and I shared returned. He sat at my small table with my case file while I made us mugs of the terrible free instant coffee provided in the rooms. When I slid the mugs onto the table, Ben was studying the photo of Sarah. "Pretty young thing isn't she? She would attract attention – or worse."

"Yeah; it would be good to have photos of the other two women who went missing. I don't know what for; maybe it's just to satisfy my curiosity, but I have a feeling they might be useful."

"The other two women aren't your concern though. Their disappearances are not your case. What's your next move? What are you going to do tomorrow?"

"My thinking was to track down that reporter who reported the old bloke seeing the first woman bundled into a vehicle. She might not know any more than what's in her article but I think she is worth following up.

If nothing else, it would be good to know what drew her to the track in the first place." Ben agreed it might amount to nothing but was worth a look.

I flicked through my file to retrieve the printout of the newspaper article and put it to one side. It had her name on it and I would take the printout with me tomorrow when I went to see her. "Ben, there is something else that's nagging me. I might be looking for something that's not there – and has a perfectly acceptable reason for not being there – but I can't help wondering if there were only three women went missing that weekend."

"If someone did go missing, they wouldn't have anything to do with your case either." Ben heaved a theatrical heavy sigh. "Come on, let's get it out there. Tell me what's behind that concern. Why do you think there might be more? Surely, if there were others, alarms would have been raised by now."

"It's a bit hard to put into words. It is probable people associated with the festival used that track on Friday, Saturday and Sunday nights. Few – possibly only one – used it on the Thursday night and there would be very few, if any, using it on the Monday night. These disappearances seem to be a serial thing -- following a pattern even – so, why didn't someone else go missing on Sunday night, or even Monday night if anyone was still around?"

"Could be any explanation but, as I said before, somebody would be looking for them by now."

"I don't know that I agree with that. Sarah was missing for a few days before her parents became anxious – and then nobody took them seriously until I stirred things up more than a week later. It was much the same for the first victim. Nobody knew she was missing until she didn't show up for a family event and her brother couldn't contact her. The only one who caused any immediate action was the young girl who disappeared on the Friday night. That was because she was travelling with her father who missed her the next morning."

"Hmm, there might be something in it, but I think you should park it to one side for the moment and get on with your case. I accept that, while finding out what happened to Sarah is your objective, the two earlier disappearances might be relevant to Sarah's disappearance. However, nothing else that happened is relevant now. It could become so later on, but that will be the time to worry about it."

"What are your plans for tomorrow now you are staying in beautiful Minden Hill?"

"Ah well, I have big plans: sleep late, go for a wander up that bush track, nose around on the festival site, and drive around generally taking in the sights of the area." I warned him about getting involved in my case or doing anything that could link him with me or my case. I wanted Ben completely detached, and felt a need for him to remain something of a hidden emergency safety device. I didn't share that last thought with him. I could imagine his reaction to it, and I didn't need it.

We spent another hour or so discussing what mutual acquaintances had been up to since the last time we talked, of his new posting to Millhaven and Pete Messell's elevation to head Ralston's homicide squad. I tried to stifle a couple of yawns without much success along the way. Ben got the message. "I can see my presence here is secondary to your need for sleep. We'll catch up sometime tomorrow. Keep your eyes open for your tail. Whatever his intent was, I doubt he's given up on it yet." With that, he disappeared through the adjoining door to his room.

In spite of the yawns, I knew sleep wasn't going to be easy to come by, so I cleared away evidence of our earlier coffee and turned on TV. The most entertaining program was a late night doom-and-gloom world news broadcast. I gave up, crawled into bed -- and tossed and turned for what seemed like half the night before sleep finally came.

CHAPTER 11

It was a restless night haunted by strange dreams. Although I couldn't remember details of them this morning, they left me feeling unsettled. I tried to dismiss them as nothing more than residuals of my discovering I had a tail yesterday. That ploy was only partially successful, and I was something less than my sparkling best as I made my way to what passed as the 'local' newspaper office.

The paper wasn't local to Minden Hill, as I discovered before leaving Moxton. It served as the whole district's local paper. The drive to the larger neighbouring centre took me past dozens of pleasant small acreages sporting either vegetable crops or small numbers of various livestock. Half an hour after leaving the outskirts of Minden Hill, I was looking for a parking spot near the newspaper's building. When I did find one, it was a block and a half away and, by then, the sun was hot.

My arrival met with disdain from the receptionist, whose self-manicure I interrupted. I asked for the reporter by name and promptly encountered the third degree about why I wanted to talk to her and about what. When she ran out of questions, with some obvious reluctance, she keyed in a number before turning her chair 180 degrees to present her back to me as she spoke to whoever was on the other end of the call. The call ended, she turned back to face me and removed her headset. "She's busy. If she gets a moment in the next half hour or so, she'll come out to see you." With that, she left her chair and the reception desk and disappeared through a door into the interior of the building.

An interesting game is happening here, and it seems to be at my expense. After examining the array of posters and framed photos around the wall of the reception area, I decided to take more direct action. There was no sign of the receptionist's returning and nobody else associated with the place wandered through the area while I waited. When the receptionist keyed in the reporter's extension number earlier, I watched and memorised the number. I wandered over to a large poster dominating the front wall of the reception area. It extolled the ideals held by this newspaper and provided contact details in a bottom corner.

I pulled out my phone, keyed in the first part of the number on the poster and substituted for the last four digits the extension number the receptionist used. It was a gamble. It might reach anyone and not the reporter I wanted. Perhaps the gamble hadn't paid off. The number rang for quite a while. About to cancel the call, a voice on the other end surprised me. It was male, and not the person I wanted. Instinct jumped in before I could ask for the reporter. It insisted my request should not be too formal. Okay, it's worth a try, I thought. "Oh hi; is Dani around at the moment? I just wanted a quick word if she's free."

The hesitation lasted several heartbeats. I was beginning to think I'd blown it when he answered. "Uhmm… ah yes, here she comes now; looks like she was getting coffee."

Then a female voice announced, "Danielle McLeod…"

"Danielle, I was hoping you might have a couple of minutes to talk to me about one of your earlier articles that I'm interested in."

"Yair, it's quiet at the moment. I'll be right out." Surprise, surprise; she is not busy. I do hope that receptionist comes back while I am still here. I have the sharp edge of my tongue to share with her.

A slim young woman came into the reception area through a side door. About my height, with olive skin, dark hair and eyes to match, she was drop-dead gorgeous. She announced herself. "Danielle McLeod…. You wanted to see me?"

"Thanks for seeing me. I am interested in an article you wrote after the Easter weekend festival at Minden Hill, about a woman who went missing."

"Oh yes, I know the one. What's your interest? If you are looking for more information, I don't know that I can help you. It has gone quiet and there hasn't been anything more since I wrote that article. I don't know if she ever turned up again."

"There is a lot more to the story and I think it's not going to be quiet for much longer. If you have a few minutes, I would like to have a chat about your observations while you were on that bush track the day the police were there, and about your interview with one of the residents whom you quoted in the article."

"You're suggesting that there's… Would you mind telling me who you are and what your interest is in the story?"

"I'm Sonoma Whittington -- but Sonny, please." While she read the business card I gave her, I explained. "As it says on the card, I'm a Private Investigator. I've been engaged to look into the disappearance of a young woman from that festival." She looked at me for a few moments without saying anything. I suspect she was weighing up the implications of what I told her.

"Correct me if I'm wrong, but is sounds as though you are talking about a different young woman from the one I wrote about. Did another young woman go missing?" I nodded. "Now it's my turn to ask if you have time to talk." I nodded enthusiastically. "Let's go somewhere quiet to talk. Do you feel like a coffee?"

We walked to the end of the next block and entered a bookshop. Why a bookshop, I thought as I followed her through the store and down a short flight of stairs. "Best coffee in town," she informed me as we pulled our chairs out from a small round table towards the back of the place. There were no other customers. The place was cool with low lighting, deathly quiet and a bit reminiscent of a long dark cave. It seems Dani is a regular here. The beaming barista who came to take our orders greeted her by name. She was right about the coffee. It was good.

"Okay, so tell me about this other girl you are looking for."

"Here's the deal: everything is off the record for the moment, but you can have an exclusive when I have unravelled a bit more of the story." As I expected, she tried manoeuvring around that arrangement, but I refused to budge. "If anything ends up in print now, it could jeopardise my case – and possible the girl's life as well as mine. I am a target already, and that's without them knowing who I am or what I'm doing here. I think we can work together on this in a way that benefits both of us, but I can't afford a maverick – or some sort of lone wolf – involved. There's too much at stake."

She walloped me with a barrage of questions about how our 'arrangement' might operate but, by the time we were ordering a second coffee, we had shaken hands on the deal. Refuelled with caffeine, she opened her notebook. "Right, if we are going to do this, before we go any further, you should tell me what I've gotten myself into."

I pictured Ben Richards shaking his head and groaning in despair at my actions as I launched into the story of not one missing woman, but three. Dani took pages of notes as I spoke. I can read things upside down, but Dani's own breed of shorthand stumped me. She might be writing a shopping list for all I knew. The last of the information delivered, I sat back and looked across the table at her. She still sat with pen poised above the page as if expecting more.

"That's it. That's as much as I've managed to piece together so far," I told her, but she didn't move. Her lack of response was confusing and I felt wrong-footed. Had I just committed a major error of judgement in talking to this reporter? Then, she slowly closed her notebook and looked across the table at me. The intensity in that look told she understood and my concern was unnecessary.

"I remember some fuss about a teenager going missing but I thought it turned out to be nothing more than the girl running off with some bloke. The third one you told me about is all news to me. There haven't been any whispers around the traps about it. I understand your sentiments about that detective. It has long been my belief that he had an aversion to investigating – or any other form of activity that looked like work."

"Not much point in being a detective if you don't like investigative work."

"True, but his approach seems to me to follow a set pattern: find some piece of evidence, conjure up a story around it and then pin the crime on somebody or, failing that, have it declared an unsolved case. That's my assessment of how he operates. He just wants to get rid of a case so he can go back to sitting at his desk, drinking coffee and reading the paper. Oh, and he is not a close acquaintance of the truth."

"That last bit I had already worked out for myself."

Our meeting stretched well beyond the few minutes I anticipated. By the time it ended – because Dani had to dash off to another appointment – we had put a couple of moves in place and agreed a couple of strategies. As we emerged into the bright sunlight on the footpath, a discomforting thought occurred to me. "Dani, please take care. I picked up a tail yesterday. Although I didn't see him this morning, doesn't mean he isn't around. I don't know what his game is yet, but I don't think he's a talent scout for some mega TV show. You had better get a move on. I'll do some window shopping on my way back to my car."

I chuckled to myself as I drove back to Minden Hill. Towards the end of my meeting with Dani, I decided to tell her about Ben. I replayed that part of our conversation. "Look there is a guy at the Wisteria Inn maybe I should tell you about in case something comes up and you can't get hold of me. His name is Ben Richards, big hunk of a guy with incredible blue eyes. Ben and I worked together a bit in the past and he was on holidays in the area. So, while we know each other, as far as everyone is concerned, we don't know each other – if you get my drift."

"Is there something more than 'we worked together' I should know about? You know, in case an opportunity arises – if you get *my* drift."

"What…? No, nothing more; feel free to go for it."

"O-k-a-y, so it is hands off then. I get the message."

"What message? I said go for it."

"Ah yes, but when it is said like that, I can see the big 'reserved' tag on him from here."

"No… No, that's not the case. I don't know where you got that idea from."

"You've forgotten how to play the dating game?"

"I don't think I ever played it. If I did, it was so long ago, I don't remember it, or how to do it."

"Rubbish; it's like riding a bike. You get a bit rusty but you don't forget how to do it."

It doesn't matter how many times I replay that particular snippet of conversation, I can't for the life of me see where she got the idea there was anything between Ben and me. There almost was on a couple of occasions, but it never quite managed to happen. With Ben soon to take up his new post at Millhaven, I wonder if there will be a third 'almost'. How would it work …*if*…we managed to move to the next level when he came back to Millhaven? That's something I don't think I want to contemplate right now.

With my mind so engrossed in what I did or didn't say to Danielle McLeod, I neglected to check for any tails, and was about halfway back to the motel before I thought to look. Careless of me, I chided myself, and proceeded to check almost constantly for the rest of the trip. Ben's car was not in the motel's carpark when I drove in. For a moment or two, I wondered where he had gone … or, more correctly, I wondered what he was up to and whether it involved my case.

Although my kidneys were awash with coffee, it was now lunchtime and I felt peckish. After considering the situation for a few moments, I decided to risk a walk to the nearest food place. On my way through the lobby, I decided a quick check of the street might be in order before venturing out. There were small local maps in the brochure rack on the wall. With the map held so it was clearly visible to anyone outside interested in what I was doing, I hoped I gave the impression of studying the map as I cast furtive glances at the world outside.

No sign of any bodies or strange cars lurking in close proximity. Still holding the map in front of me, I sauntered out onto the footpath and headed for the shops – and lunch, I hoped. The first block or so proved quiet, but pedestrian traffic increased as I neared the shopping area. Rather than get something to eat from the first food place I came to, it seemed prudent to walk a bit further through town. Not because I was looking for anything special to eat, but because it provided greater opportunity to flush out anyone interested in me. I stopped to peer in every shop window as I passed and wandered back and forth across the street. No one took any notice of me.

Confident I didn't have a tail, I took advantage of a group of young girls who spilled out of a wine bar onto the footpath. They were celebrating one of their number's forthcoming wedding. The ridiculous veil and headpiece one of them wore was a dead give-away about who was the bride-to-be. All well primed, the tight group occupied almost the whole width of the footpath as they romped along the street. I slipped to the inside edge of the group -- closest to the shop fronts -- and attached myself to them.

At one point, they had to bunch up close to the shop fronts to allow a couple of women pushing prams to pass by. Not slowed by their new configurations, they continued in this way past three shops before spreading out once more to occupy the full width of the footpath. The third shop was a coffee shop. As the group rolled on past it, I darted into the coffee shop.

Soft lighting and expensive prices accompanied mouth-watering aromas. With one eye fixed on the world outside the plate glass windows, I sipped iced water and dallied as long as possible over the menu before ordering. The food seemed to take an eternity to arrive. Under other circumstances, I would entertain rude thoughts about the quality of service, but today, the delay suited me fine. By the time the food arrived, I was becoming self-conscious of my rumbling stomach.

Although the price was enough to cause indigestion, the food was good, and so was the coffee – even the second cup. I took my time and, while I savoured my meal, I thought about what my next move might be. By the time I paid the bill, I had decided to take a walk along that bush track this evening. I wanted to see first-hand what conditions were like there after dark. This meant leaving it until sometime after seven o'clock, and perhaps closer to eight o'clock. Mental note to self: let Ben know what I'm doing so he won't hang around in the motel's restaurant waiting for me for dinner.

My route back to the motel again meandered through the shopping precinct without producing any unwanted interest in me. I hesitated in the lobby on the pretext of returning the map I had taken earlier to the wall rack. In spite of the fact that I clocked no one following me, I felt some relief, but not enough to allow me to believe I was safe. Apart from common sense, my instinct told me that, after what had happened to those other three women, whoever was interested in me would not abandon whatever they intended so easily.

The rest of the afternoon I devoted to working in my room, typing up notes from my meeting with Dani, answering emails, and poring over my case file yet again in the hope some previously overlooked clue might leap out and wallop me. No joy with the latter but, by the time I was once again wondering what to do next, I heard noises in Room 6. A few moments later, I heard the familiar gentle knock on the adjoining door. Ben came in carrying a couple of beers.

"I have spent the whole day making like a tourist, and there is only so much of that to do in this place," he announced as he popped open the beers. We clinked – no, 'thunked' more like -- ice-cold cans and settled in the not so comfortable chairs in my room. "...So, tell me how you gainfully filled your day," he asked.

"As planned, I met with Dani McLeod, the reporter who wrote that article I showed you."

"Okay; how did that go?"

"Good... very good actually; I'll tell you about it, but there was one really interesting thing about that meeting."

"I'm almost not game to ask what it was. Who did you manage to piss off this time?"

"Do you mind? I didn't piss anyone off. Only because they disappeared before I could. No, that's not it. There is something funny going on at that newspaper office. I don't know what it is, and I can't sort out in my mind what it's all about." I spent the next few minutes discussing that time I spent in the newspaper office before I finally met Dani.

"Hmm, I'll grant you it was strange but, like I said, you probably pissed off the receptionist the moment you walked in – and you did interrupt her manicure. Anyway, tell me about the meeting with Dani."

"I didn't get much more from Dani other than what was in the article. However, she did confirm a sneaking suspicion I had about the detective in charge of the case. Her opinion of him is not too high and she suggested that on occasions, he is not too careful with the truth."

"What's your next move, now that you haven't come up with anything new or enlightening?"

"Ah, that's what I wanted to talk to you about. I've wanted to get a look at what that bush track area is like at night, so I decided to take myself for a walk along there tonight. I'll leave it until about 7:30 so that I'll be seeing it at about the same time as those women were on the track. I didn't want you hanging around in the restaurant or occupying the bartender while you waited for me to come in for dinner."

"Given the tail you picked up yesterday, are you sure this is in your best interest? I'm not convinced it's the wisest decision you've ever made. It would definitely be better if we went for a moonlight stroll together."

"Don't go there. That's not going to happen. This is my case, and I need you at arm's length and not involved... just in case something does go wrong at some point."

Ben was not happy and made it clear that he wasn't, but I was adamant he wasn't coming with me – for all sorts of reasons, I told myself. We finished our drinks and Ben read my notes on my meeting with Dani McLeod before he returned to his own room. I mulled over his comments about my safety tonight and decided it probably was no more dangerous than the situations I find myself in as part of any investigation. With some time to kill, I stretched out on the bed, closed my eyes, only to wake with a start and shocked to see that it was already 7:45pm.

The night had grown cool and there was a distinct chill in the air. No doubt, dew would accompany that chill. Discretion said I needed my duffel coat, which wasn't a bad thing as it came with lots of roomy pockets. I didn't want to load my pockets up too much, but I definitely needed a good flashlight of some sort, and I had the choice of two in my kit. I chose the smaller LED version as it was less cumbersome than its larger model and provided a cleaner brighter light. A pocket packet of tissues, my small digital camera, and a notebook and pen completed the cargo for this trip.

I swapped my Nike 'day shoes' for sturdy hiking boots, slapped a cap on my head and tucked my hair up under it before heading out the door. Nobody in the hallway as I left and nobody in the carpark area. The light mounted high up on the rear wall of the motel lit up the parked cars, but it didn't extend nearly so well to the button that unlocks the gate. I found the button by feel rather than sight and slipped through when the gate had opened only about a quarter of the way.

As I strode off towards the track, I wondered about how much moon there was over the Easter weekend. Tonight looked as though it was only two or three days away from full moon, so there was plenty of light out here in the open. When I entered the track, I realised how inconsequential that observation was. Small patches of pale moonlight filtered through the dense overhead canopy here and there. I stood still for a minute or so to let my eyes adjust to the darker environment that surrounded me. It didn't make much difference. The track, shrouded in darkness, didn't present as the most inviting place to be at this hour of the night.

Darkness doesn't worry me. On some occasions, it can be a sleuth's best friend. Somehow, tonight was different. I hadn't gone too far down the track when I became aware of the hairs on the back of my neck starting to rise. Instinct was telling me something, but I had no idea what. Just up ahead, two small patches of light, a couple of metres apart, fell on the track. I skirted around the first patch of light by walking close to the edge of the other side of the track, and then stopped.

I stepped off the edge of the track and stood on the grassy verge in the darkness between the two patches of light. Ears straining for any sound, I stood swivelling my head from side to side for any sign of movement up or down the track. Nothing… no sound and nothing moving. Yet, I knew something – or someone -- was out there. My gut told me so in no uncertain terms. Staying off the track, I skirted the second patch of light and continued a few metres beyond it before stepping back onto the firmer, less slippery surface of the track. The hairs on the back of my neck refused to lie down.

Somewhere up ahead – I couldn't be sure of the distance in the darkness – a large shadow seemed darker than its surroundings. It seemed sensible to step off the track again and move closer to the bush that lined it. This way, I wouldn't stand out as a darker shadow on the track. Decision time: which side of the track to step off? There were only two options. I would have plenty of time to rue my choice.

My foot tangled with a dead branch on the ground. I stumbled. Only just managing to avoid hitting the dirt, I struggled to become upright again and avoid any further contact with the branch. That is almost the last thing I remember. Although foggy, my last memory of my stroll along the track was rough hands grabbing me, and being dragged me along on my heels. Then, blackness descended for an indeterminable length of time.

CHAPTER 12

My head throbbed fiercely. In a bid to open, my eyelids gave half-hearted flutters a couple of times as I fought to reacquaint myself with consciousness. That only made the pounding in my head worse. Extricating myself from the black void, was like trying to swim through treacle. There appeared no painless hurrying of my return to the real world. Various aches and throbs joined the concert of pain that had my head as the lead performer.

The ache in my right hip screamed at me. I tried to reach down to investigate the cause. My right arm felt numb and unresponsive. A cold shaft of fear shot through me. What had happened to me? Why did my arm refuse to move? I swallowed hard to quell the rising fear. A revolting stench crawled into my nostrils and made itself at home there. Questions paraded through my mind. Where was I? What happened? No ready answers lurked in my memory banks. I tried remembering, but there was nothing beyond a recollection of spiralling into a black void. Time to look for answers.

Let your senses tell you something about where you are, I counselled myself. What can you hear, feel, smell…? All I can feel is the hardness beneath me. This wasn't one of those mattresses featured in TV commercials. The stench remained. There was either a blocked toilet somewhere close by… or something worse. A sound drifted over to me: distant and non-threatening, a faint metallic scrape. Only a visual assessment might provide some answers.

What can I see? To answer that, I need to open my eyes. I opened them wide. Arrrggh; that was a mistake. Pain exploded behind my eyes and encouraged the pounding in my head to new height. Don't do that again. I clamped my eyes firmly closed until I felt the throbbing start to ease. Okay, now it's time to be brave again. I let my eyes drift open to narrow slits. It was dark – but not 'night time' dark. My eyes slowly adjusted to the light and foggy images swam into view. A dark grimy brick wall stretched up in front of me, only a few inches from my nose. I closed my eyes again. So far, my sensual assessment of my current location only served to add to my confusion. I found nothing even vaguely familiar.

About then, the pain in my right hip drowned out all other thought, and the source of the pain – coupled with what I had just seen -- became obvious. I was lying on my right side on something hard – very hard – and facing an unfamiliar brick wall. My hip objected to all of my weight resting on it. I tried to move slightly to ease the weight off it. It worked, but not as intended. The weight came off the hip, but I found myself flat on my back. Although I believed it impossible earlier, the pounding in my head worsened. I broke out in a cold sweat and my stomach heaved dangerously. The best approach to adopt: don't try anything quite so rash again for a while.

After a minute or two of lying perfectly still, and with the moisture on my top lip drying, I felt brave enough to try something else… nothing too adventurous though. I tried to move the fingers of my right hand. No response at first, but persistence paid off. I felt them begin to move and become responsive. Next, I tried flexing my wrist. It went through stages of nothing, followed by pins and needles, and then stiff movement. By applying the same gradual approach, I regained ownership of my right arm. Some of the aches and pains began to diminish. My head let me know it wasn't going away any time soon.

There is that noise again – but different. Louder, more persistent; it seems closer. Can't identify it. Lie still. Don't move. Keep your eyes closed. Then the voice… just a whisper. Female I think; too soft to be sure. I sense a presence close to me – very close.

"Are you awake? Hello… hello, can you hear me? Are you awake?" Then a touch on my arm – gentle and tentative. Don't move, Sonny, I tell myself and somehow manage to avoid flinching. The voice persists, "Please, please, speak to me."

What do I do? I can't lie here pretending forever, and besides, I need information – like, where am I and what happened? I let my eyes drift open a fraction and then pause for a moment to allow them to adjust to my surroundings. Then, so very carefully -- and *slowly*, I turn my head towards the presence. A violent jolt of pain halts that manoeuvre. The cold sweat is back and congregates on my upper lip once more.

The voice speaks quietly again but, so concentrated am I on getting my breathing back under control, I don't hear what it says. Some time elapses as I lay there unmoving … seconds, a minute or so, or longer, I have no idea. At last, everything seems normal once more. I pluck up courage and try moving my head again.

"No, don't try to move," the voice commands. "You've got a nasty wound on the side of your head." It's definitely female … and sounds non-threatening.

So many questions need answers; I try to speak. Only a rasping croak escapes. I try swallowing. My mouth is as dry as a desert sandstorm. I try again, and this time, manage to croak, "Water … water please."

"There's only a bit left but, lie still while I work out how you are going to drink it." There was a few moments' pause during which I heard shuffling and something metallic clank close to my ear. "It's no good. You're going to have to try to lift up a bit so you can drink."

Really…? You want me to sit up…? Just turning my head was sheer agony. I pondered the situation for a couple of heartbeats. The voice was right, of course. Short of having a long flexible straw, it was impossible for me to drink while lying flat on my back. Given my current condition, I'd probably drown trying. I tried levering myself off the floor with my elbow. After only a few centimetres, the world started spinning.

Before I could collapse again, strong arms grabbed me from behind. I felt a firm body pressed in hard behind my shoulders. It held me there for a few seconds until I regained control of the world. With 'the body' supporting my weight, I no longer struggled to remain elevated, and relaxed a little. 'The body' started to ease me up further. I closed my eyes and went as limp as possible to give her every assistance.

"There… let's try that. Oh boy, this is awkward, but we will make it work. Okay, how's that? See if you can sip a little when I tip it up."

I managed a couple of sips before the tide rushed in and too much water gushed out into my mouth. Gagging and coughing, and with the front of my shirt drenched, I had to sit up properly. Between us, we got me upright. I leant against the wall. It felt like forever, but eventually I stopped feeling in danger of passing out. The pounding in my head eased a little. Perhaps I'm game enough to try opening my eyes again. I tried – gently and only a fraction. Well, that didn't precipitate any major reaction. Over the next few seconds, I opened my eyes fully. I'm not sure that was such a good idea. Did I really need to see the sight that greeted me?

The world continued to swim before me, but slowly my eyes began to work properly. I let them drift around my surroundings as far as my field of vision allowed without having to turn my head. What the hell was this place? It was not in any way a reassuring sight.

The voice -- which I now realise belongs to 'the body' -- spoke quietly. "I want to clean your wound a bit. Is it okay if I use a corner of your shirt? It's cleaner than mine."

I tried nodding… bad move! I flapped my hand in invitation to help herself to my shirt. A few moments later, a soggy piece of my shirt reached the side of my head. She was gentle, softly wiping the left side of my head, then down over my ear and onto my temple area.

"It's still a nasty gash, but the whole thing doesn't look nearly so bad now I've cleaned off most of the blood. That's more than I can say for your shirt now that I've finished with it."

With my head leant back against the wall and my eyes closed, I realise I am starting to feel as though I might survive the hammering in my head. It's still a monster of a headache, but the throbbing has eased somewhat … and my couple of sips of water appear to have lubricated my vocal cords. I gently open one eye to look at the owner of the voice and the body.

Although there is still an all-pervasive darkness, I can see the woman in front of me quite clearly. I stare at her. A one-eyed stare for a couple of heartbeats as my befuddled brain tries to kick into action. It's trying to tell me something about that person. It keeps nudging my memory bank trying to bring it to life. I open the other eye for a better look and feel a frown develop as I try to place the face in front of me. The gash on the side of my head lets me know frowning is off the agenda for a while yet. I close both eyes again, and slowly an image swims to the front of my mind, a vague memory of a photograph. My eyes snap open again.

"Sarah. Sarah Sinclair, is that you?"

"Yes, I'm Sarah Sinclair. How come you know who I am?"

"It's a long story. One I'll share with you at some other time. Suffice now to say your mother engaged me to find you … but I'm not sure this is what any of us had in mind. Where are we and what is this place?"

"Prison… there's no other way to describe it. We're being held prisoners here, but I have no idea where 'here' is."

"Are there any others?"

"Being held as prisoners, you mean?" I nodded once then thought better of it, but Sarah got the message. "There were two others – maybe three. I'm not sure about that."

"Where are they… what happened to them?" I almost regretted the question the moment I asked it. My mind immediately suggested it might not be good news.

"I don't know … and I'm not sure I want to know. One – a young girl whose name I don't think I ever knew – disappeared not long after I woke up in here. Olivia –the other one who was here – she disappeared maybe a couple of days ago. I think I was here alone maybe for about a day before you arrived."

"Tell me about Olivia. What did she look like?"

"Uhmm … well, she was a bit older than me; probably in her thirties, with shoulder length reddish hair and beautiful skin. Even under all the dirt we accumulate in here, you could see it was fine and very pale –

almost white."

"The other young girl, was she about seventeen and with long blonde hair?

"Yeah, that sounds about right. She was blonde and did look quite young. Were you looking for her too?"

"Difficult question to answer. Let's just say I am interested in both of those other women. What do you remember about how you came to be here?"

"Huh, not much; it's all pretty much a blur. I was at the Easter festival at Minden Hill. On the last night – Sunday night that was – I went to the end of festival big music concert. I remember it was good but loud. I sort of mated up with another girl during the day and we met up again at the concert. At some point during the concert, I decided I was going back to the motel. She was going to come with me but, just as we were picking up our things to leave, a guy came over and started chatting her up. He asked to go for a drink with him. She had been trying to catch his eye all day, so she reneged on going back to the motel and went off to the drinks tent with the bloke."

"S-o-o, you went back to the motel alone… or were there others going back at the same time?"

"No, it starts to get a bit fuzzy about then. I know I started walking back alone. Others might have been on the track at the time but I don't remember. After that, it's all a blank until I came to in here. I don't know what caused it, but I was so sick – couldn't stop throwing up whenever I was conscious. I'm still not good."

"You have no memory at all of what happened on the way back to the motel?"

"No, there's nothing. I think I remember picking up my bag and starting to walk back, and then nothing until I was here."

There were no surprises in that. I can't remember anything after starting to walk down that track to the festival field, and yet here I am too. "I obviously got clobbered somewhere along the line. Were you – or Olivia for that matter -- injured in any way?"

"N-o-o, well not like you were. When I started having the odd lucid moment, I noticed part of my face felt swollen or numb somehow. Olivia said it probably was from when they pressed the pad over my face."

"Pad…? What's that all about?"

"In an earlier life, Olivia was a nurse and then a paramedic. She suffered a bruised face as well, and thought they used a pad soaked with something like chloroform to knock us out." I noted no mention of the haymaker Olivia reputedly received.

It appeared they used a more direct approach with me: a hefty whack to the side of the head. A strong idea about these abductions occurred to me soon after I started investigating Sarah's disappearance. What happened to me strengthened my thinking. All the other abductions I knew about were of fair young women. Olivia, although a bit older and a redhead, still met the criteria. I do not. If my hunch proves right, they – whoever they are – would not want their captives damaged. 'Damaged merchandise' would not sit well with their end game. I am now reasonably confident they have a different end game in mind for me and, therefore, it doesn't matter if I sustain some damage. I think I might try not to dwell on what their intentions for me might be. I don't think it's something I will enjoy. Time for my brain to get back into gear and take stock of the situation. I need more information. As I sat framing my next question to ask, Sarah interrupted my thought processes.

"I don't think we should talk anymore." That's not helpful, but she appeared to be listening for something so I simply raised my eyebrows at her … and that was a mistake. Remember in future: eyebrow is close to the gash on my head and any eyebrow gymnastics is painful. However, Sarah got the message and continued.

"We should get back into our original positions. They bring food twice a day, and they should be along with our evening meal shortly. It would be best if they thought you were still unconscious. I will go back over there and resume my Oscar-winning performance of someone who remains extremely ill."

Okay, I know a good plan when I hear it. I measured my length on the floor again, carefully arranging my appendages as I remembered they were when I re-entered the real world. The main problem was that there was no longer blood on the side of my face. I felt my hair near the gash -- stiff and crusted with dried blood. That will have to do. I pulled the hair forward and arranged it as best I could across the side of my face. Then there was nothing to do but squint at the grimy brick wall through half open eyes and listen for any extraneous sounds.

Sometime during the few minutes I lay like that, I realised it was dark. It was a different darkness from earlier on. A darkness suggesting night had arrived. Any further thought of differing kinds of darkness disappeared at the sound of approaching footsteps; two pairs of feet by the sound of it. Then the jangle of keys and the scrape of a bolt drawn back. Time to be unconscious again.

The heavy wooden door swung open with something more akin to a groan than a squeak. Footsteps grew louder and nearer, then stopped. The dull thunk of metal placed down heavily on the concrete floor seemed loud in our brick enclosure. Footsteps started in my direction. Only a couple, and then they stopped. I heard a male voice announce, "No change," and the footsteps retreated again.

Another voice – male again –"Don't bother checking that one. Smell the stink. It's disgusting." The sound of both lots of footsteps receded; then the groan of the door, followed by the sound of it slamming home. The rasp of the bolt rammed home again, and the jangle of keys once more. Contrary to my expectation, the footsteps didn't head off once the door was locked.

A soft shuffle of feet on concrete mixed with the occasional jangle of keys overlaid conversation barely audible from where I lay. By straining my ears and shallow breathing, I managed to pick up brief snatches of the discussion outside our door. There were two voices. One sounded young, while the other was older and had a distinct growl to it.

"… Going to do with those two?" the young one asked. I got interested. It has to be the future of we two in here he is enquiring about.

"… Short on quota now …Promised a full delivery this time… won't be happy … can't afford to again … try for a few more." There was a coughing fit. This older speaker sounds like a heavy smoker.

"… Have to move quick … end of the week … what about those two?" The young one finally had asked the BIG question – the most important question from my point of view. The response was not encouraging.

"…Until we get back … our losses … dig a couple more holes, eh?" Then the footsteps tramped off into the distance. I had heard enough to spur me into action – especially the bit about digging 'a couple more holes'.

I assumed 'room service' just delivered our evening meals. The question of how long we need to maintain our charades occupies my mind. Sarah is the old hand at this game, so there is nothing for it, but to follow her lead. Come on, Sarah; time is marching on. How much longer do we keep this up? Ah, I think I hear movement. Now what happens?

"It's okay to relax now. They won't be back again tonight," Sarah whispered.

"That's a relief. I was beginning to stiffen up again. Is it okay to talk now?"

"It's okay to talk, but we should keep it very quiet or whisper --- just in case someone is close by outside." I returned to my mental list of questions to ask, and added a few new ones generated by my eavesdropping exercise. I rolled over and eased myself upright again.

A couple of tin bowls lay on the floor in the centre of the room. How appropriate and in keeping with our current situation: our meals arrived in metal dog bowls. By craning my neck up a bit I could see the bowls contained some grey-looking slop. Sarah noticed my long-range inspection of our dinner. She swivelled her head to look at the bowls and whispered, "I think it's supposed to be stew. It's always the same and always grey – especially the meat. Even if I were perfectly healthy and starving, I don't think I could bring myself to eat it."

Even from this distance, I felt inclined agree with her. She shuffled across the floor, stopping when she was about a metre away from me. Good move; conversation will be easier now. I moved straight to my list of questions. After all, who knew when they would 'get back' and decide to start digging those 'couple of extra holes'. There is no time to lose if we are to save them the trouble of digging them … and save ourselves from ending up in them.

"Why was it important for them to think we were ill or unconscious?"

"To avoid…uhmm… they used to take the others away one at a time every so often. Olivia said they did things to them – terrible things. We might avoid finding out what those things are if they continue to find us disgusting and useless." She shrugged, indicating it was a tenuous assumption.

"By 'terrible things', I assume you mean rape -- with any associated whims and fancies attached."

"Yes, rape. Once when they took the young girl away, I heard her screaming. Somewhere in the building I think. When they brought her back, she was so traumatised, she just curled up in the corner moaning and shaking until they came and took her again. She fought and struggled, and started screaming from the moment they started dragging her out. The screaming continued… and then we heard a couple of blood-curdling shrieks. After that time, we never saw her again. She never came back."

"Obviously Olivia also had first-hand experience of these 'terrible things'. How did she cope with what they dished out?"

"She was distraught – traumatised – but she tried to control it. When she came back, she was shaking. She just leant up against the wall and shook … not violently like the young girl, but I saw her hands shaking. She said … I suppose she was giving me a piece of advice: *If rape is inevitable, close your eyes and think of something else. Don't fight it and you are less likely to get badly hurt.* I can't imagine that works with his lot – or that I could do that anyway."

Our future prospects haven't improved by anything I've heard so far. "What happened to Olivia… is she still being held here?"

"No. After they took her away the last time, she never came back, and I was on my own here until you arrived."

Definitely time to devise a strategy for our survival! I spent the next while gathering information on the routines that were in place: how often people came, delivery of food and water … and when did they empty that bucket in the corner that passed for our latrine? In the case of the latter, the smell suggested it wasn't often.

There appeared to be only three people involved with the place: two men and a woman. The men usually did everything. However, on occasions when they were away or whatever, the woman brought the food and water. Sarah's assessment of her was that she was youngish but looked as though she had experienced a hard life. She never spoke and seemed unhappy about having anything to do with what goes on in here. After a couple of minutes pause and a couple of sips of water, Sarah thought of other information worth passing on to me. She was right.

"There's no light in here, and the sun doesn't shine in through that little window." I looked up to where she indicated. I hadn't noticed the window – small and barred, and too high up to see out through. Sarah continued. "It does let in a bit of indirect light and fresh air. I can tell by it whether it's day or night. I try to keep track of the days by scratching marks close to the floor on the wall over there."

"Have you any idea where this place might be? Do you hear any sounds that might suggest what's going on around the place? You know the sort of things: a tractor, traffic, trucks or even animal sounds."

She shook her head. "No, there's nothing to help identify where we are. In fact, it's strangely quiet. The only sounds are the cars occasionally coming and going. You hear them crunching on the gravel driveway and the car doors slamming. They park down there in a clear area near the building."

"Cars… they could be useful. Tell me about the cars and their use."

"I've only ever seen two: a small dark blue van and a white small sedan. If you move those bricks and blocks of wood scattered about on the floor over there and stack them up, you can stand on them to look out of the window. You can't see much, mainly just trees. …But, if stand to one side and look down on an angle, you can see where they park the cars. From what I've seen, the men drive the van. The woman seems to be the only one who drives the sedan."

"Is there any apparent routine or schedule about when the cars come and go?"

"Not really, except… well, I think I worked out that when the van goes away, it is usually gone for more than one day. There are occasions when it does leave early in the morning and it comes back quite late that night, but that's not common."

"I have a feeling they might be going somewhere tomorrow. If I'm right, we need to have a plan in place. It might be our only chance. Tell me more about what the woman is like. Does she show any interest in her 'guests' when she comes in here? For example, if you were lying there writhing in agony, would she come over to investigate?"

"On most occasions, her only interest is in getting in and out of here as quickly as possible. However, having said that, if something appears to be wrong – like one of us is seriously ill – she does come a bit closer to check on them. She doesn't come over real close though."

"Okay, unless you need to go to sleep immediately, I think we should take some time now to work out how we might get out of this stinking mess, and preferably as soon as possible. It sounds like our best bet might be when the men have gone off somewhere and the woman brings our food."

Sarah nodded and shuffled a little closer. So far, all I had seen her do was shuffle backwards and forwards across the floor. It occurred to me that might introduce a major problem from a planning perspective. "Sarah, can you walk? You only ever shuffle across the floor on your backside. Is there a problem with your legs?"

"A problem...? No, of course there's nothing wrong with my legs. I can walk. I don't know why I shuffle. Somehow, it seemed like I should move that way in here rather than walking around."

"Regardless of what plan we come up with, we need to be sure our legs are working okay when the time comes. Later, once we have our plan, I will try to get my head under control and my legs working. You should do the same. If you have been carrying on like this for a while, they will be quite weak by now."

Time slipped by as we formulated our potential escape plan. I don't know how long it took, but it seemed to take a lot longer than if I simply developed it in my own head just for me. I needed to be sure Sarah knew exactly what to do and could pull it off when the time came. By the time we both felt confident we could make it work, the sky beyond the little window showed the first signs of the approaching dawn. We had done all we could.

Sarah stood unsteadily on wobbly legs and walked back to her usual place on the other side of the room. Realising her legs were not as strong as they should be, she walked up and down beside the wall a few times. Then, confident her legs would respond when needed, she again sank down onto her customary place on the floor. I followed her example and eased myself up onto my legs. My head didn't entirely agree with the move, but I ignored it and slowly walked all around the room. After inspecting all the walls and floor and the door, I tried out my designated place in the room should we have opportunity to implement our escape plan. The only problem now was when that opportunity might present. I returned to my original place against the wall opposite Sarah.

In spite of my best endeavours, I felt myself starting to doze off. I shook my head and glanced across at Sarah. Her head has dropped onto her chest and her eyes are closed. Should I try to keep her awake or let her snooze? The sound of car doors brings me completely awake. As I make my way across to the wall with the small window, I call Sarah's name until she responds.

"Car…," I hiss, and start piling up the bricks and blocks of wood so I can see out of the window. Sarah hurries across to help, and then holds things steady as I climb up. The car is not inclined to start this morning. The ignition gets a good work out and it winds for a bit before finally firing. A special thanks to the Gods as the delay has allowed me to be in position in time to see the blue van drive away from its parking spot and disappear. Although lost from view, I remain at the window and listen to the sound of the car receding into the distance.

Back on the floor again, I help Sarah scatter the bricks and wood about as before. When we finish, Sarah stands looking at me. I don't need ESP to read her mind. "It was the van that drove out. If things go as you described them, the woman should deliver our breakfast this morning. We should get into position now and be ready to make the best of it."

No need for words; Sarah nodded and took up her usual position against the wall. I moved to my new position. A few minutes later, there are footsteps coming towards us… soft and muffled, possibly made by rubber-soled shoes. Sarah looks at me and we exchange a nod. She collapses onto her back and starts moaning and rolling from side to side.

Then the jangle of keys and the scape of the bolt… Show time!

CHAPTER 13

The door opens cautiously. Metal bowls clunk against the heavy wooden door as a figure tries to manage the door and the two bowls she is carrying. Sarah's moaning has increased in volume and she is now thrashing about as imagined pains wrack her body. The woman drops the bowls not too far inside the door and rushes over towards Sarah. Instinct brings her to an abrupt halt a short distance from Sarah. Sarah turns on her Oscar-winning performance and croaks at the woman, "Help please. The pains… please help me. I need a doctor." There's a loud scream from Sarah as she clutches her stomach and rolls into the foetal position… that's my cue.

I watched the tableau play out from my new position on the floor alongside the wall in which the door is set. Flanking either side of the doorway is a sturdy brick column about 300 millimetres square. Their purpose is a mystery to me. Nevertheless, I'm please the builders put them there. On my haunches against the wall, the column on the left hand side of the doorway hides me from anyone entering the room.

Everything happens in the space of a few heartbeats. The woman enters the room and rushes towards Sarah, stopping a metre or so away from Sarah. There's a moment of hesitation before she bends over for a closer look at her prisoner writhing on the floor in agony.

I leap up, race across the floor. Just as the woman senses me behind her and starts to turn her head towards me, I clobber her on the back of the head with a piece of brick. She goes down like the proverbial sack of spuds and Sarah springs to her feet. A keyring is hanging from a belt loop of the woman's jeans. Sarah is already standing in the doorway checking outside the room as I relieve the woman of her keys.

It all takes only a matter of seconds before we are both outside throwing the bolt and locking the door. A mad dash down the corridor brings us to a short flight of stone steps. A bit more cautiously, we climb the steps and pause for a moment, straining our ears for any sounds of life in the building. Only the gentle purring of a fridge drifts towards us.

On this level, the corridor appears to carry on to an external door. It might seem impossible to run on tiptoes, but that's what we did towards the door. Just prior to the door, a room branched off from either side of the corridor. "Go in there and see if you can find anything useful – food or water – but don't waste any time," I told Sarah, indicating she should investigate the kitchen on the left-hand side of the corridor.

I heard the fridge door open as I charged into the room of the right side of the corridor. It appeared to be an office. A computer sat on a desk in the corner of the room, and another cheap looking desk sat in the middle of the room buried under papers and other rubbish. Oh, lookee here, someone has kindly screwed a key rack to the wall, and there's a whole host of keys hanging on it.

A woman's tote bag lay on top of a two-drawer filing cabinet immediately below the key rack. I took a quick peek in the tote bag. At a quick glance, it looked like all the stuff you'd expect to find in a woman's bag. I yanked all the keys of the key rack and threw them in the tote bag – with the exception of one. One was a car key, and I hoped the emblem on the key tag match the badge on the sedan parked out front.

Sarah still rattled around in the kitchen, so I explored a little further in the office. The first draw I opened on the desk in the middle of the room contained a number of passports. In one quick move, I scooped them all up and threw them in the tote bag. A quick look in the remainder of the drawers produced a few things that I also thought might come in handy, so they went into the tote bag as well. The bag was now just about full and had become quite heavy. As I glanced quickly around the room for anything else that might be useful, Sarah called quietly from the doorway.

"I thought you didn't want to hang around. Come on, let's get out of here."

She's right of course; hanging around here is not in our best interest. I gestured for her to go, and followed her to the door. A quick peek outside the door didn't produce anything frightening, so we bolted out the door and across to the sedan parked about five metres away. So far, our luck was holding. The car key I still held in my hand matched the sedan.

There was nothing orchestrated about it; it was just the angle that we ran to the car. Sarah was slightly ahead of me and arrived at the passenger side a couple of strides before I reached the driver's side door. Sarah flung open her door and jumped in. Well, that answered that question. The car wasn't locked. I jumped in the driver's seat and had the key in the ignition before I closed the door. As I fiddled trying to slide the key into the ignition, I murmured to Sarah, "Pray this is the right key and we can get this thing started. I've never tried hot wiring one of these modern cars."

The motor turned over and fired on the first turn of the key. I slammed the door quickly, shoved the gearshift into drive, planted my foot and rocketed out of the courtyard fishtailing slightly as I turned onto the driveway leading away from the house. "Buckle up; this could be a wild ride as I have no idea where we going." Sarah was doing up her seatbelt as I struggled one-handed to get mine done up and control the car at the same time.

I really didn't have much of a chance to take in the building or its surroundings. A vague impression of a large old-style brick building surrounded by woodland lingered in my mind as we sped down a rough gravel driveway. I risked taking my eyes off the road for a quick glance at the fuel gauge. It registered full. As I didn't know how long the van would be gone, I wanted to be as far away from that house as soon as possible. The long driveway wound its way through the woods until, a short distance up ahead it ended at a bitumen road. "This track would be about half as long if they laid it straight instead of having it wander around through the bush," I muttered through clenched teeth as I held the steering wheel tightly while the car bounced its way over one last major pothole.

Time for the first decision in our dash for freedom: which way do we head when we hit the bitumen road? It turned out not to require much thought. The track met the road at such an angle that turning right would have been difficult and required driving across a short expanse of rough country. We turned left and smoothly onto the road. The bitumen allowed for a little more speed. A little more speed heading where, was the question. Neither of us had any idea of where we were or where we were heading.

Farmland flanks both sides of the road, dotted here and there with paddocks of grazing animals. Farmhouses and outbuildings flash past, some close to the road and others set well back and surrounded by trees. I think my breathing is starting to return to normal. That probably means it's a good time to take stock of our situation. I glanced across at Sarah. She gazes out at the farmlands flashing past beside us.

"Were you able to extract anything worthwhile from the kitchen?"

Sarah reached round onto the back seat and hauled over plastic shopping bag. "… Some cheese, piece of salami, couple of tomatoes, half a crusty loaf and a couple of bottles of water… oh, and a rather vicious looking knife."

"The knife was good thinking. We should be able to go some distance on your hunter-gatherer efforts. I think it's time we found out exactly what was in that tote bag that I 'borrowed'. I threw a lot of stuff in on top – keys, passports and other stuff – but I want to know what was in there before I began throwing other stuff on top of it."

I heard her grunt as she hauled the tote bag off the back seat and dragged it around onto her lap. After seeing how much was in the bag, she decided to place it on the floor and proceeded to drop everything she removed from the bag into her lap. After a few moments, she broke the silence. "I think I've got to the bottom of everything you threw in the bag. Let's see what other goodies are in here."

It seems we had scored rather well. Amongst the lipsticks and combs and other female paraphernalia were a mobile phone, money purse and a separate wallet containing credit cards and a couple of other cards that were a mystery to me -- probably some sort of store loyalty cards.

Sarah remained strangely silent. She seemed restless. "Something bothering you…?" I asked quietly.

She shrugged and looked out the window, then looked down at her hands resting on the mess of material in her lap. I waited. I almost could hear her mind wrestling with whatever bothered her. At last, she drew a deep breath and blurted out, "Do you think she's dead? Did we kill her?"

"Who? …The woman back at the house?" I risked a sideways glance at Sarah. She sat there biting her bottom lip. "No, we didn't kill her. She is probably conscious again by now, with a terrible headache and yelling the house down – but she is not dead."

"I wouldn't like to think we killed her. I know she was one of them, but somehow she seemed a little more human than the two blokes." I managed a grunt in reply. I didn't share her Pollyanna outlook on life. Perhaps my line of work resulted in the loss of such generosity of spirit. I could live with that. Time to change the subject I think.

"I don't suppose you have any idea of where we are or where this road might lead." Sarah shook her head slowly as she scanned the area around us. "Okay, keep an eye out for any signs that suggest we are approaching a town. Some places have those big 'welcome' boards at their approaches."

"There's a map in the pocket on the door." She waved it at me to prove her point. "It's been folded open to show a particular area. There are no marks or anything helpful anywhere on the map but, if I see any sign that mentions the name of a place, I might be able to make sense of where we are."

"Although it was quite light when we took off, the sun is up a fair way now. I've been watching it come up and from that, I think I've worked out that we are travelling south-east… possibly more east than south."

"Does that mean we have to head north again to get back to Minden Hill?"

"No, not necessarily; it depends on whether Minden Hill is to the north or the south of where we are."

Although we encountered little traffic, we appear to be on a major regional road, but not a main highway. I was pondering our situation when

Sarah startled me with a strangled squeak. "What...? What happened? Are you okay – are *we* okay?" I checked all mirrors but couldn't see any cause for alarm. She didn't answer. When I glanced at her, she was struggling to hold the map still while she concentrated on it.

A response came eventually. "There's a town coming up in ten kilometres... no, less than that now. Slow down a bit; it should be close now. I can't see it marked on the map."

I eased back on the accelerator, and signs of civilisation appeared around the next bend. We cruised through 'town' at the mandatory speed. The 'town' consisted of about half a dozen small cottages, a service station/ auto repairs garage, a café, butcher shop, and what looked like a general store. On the right hand side of the road was an Ambulance station, next to a Police station, and a park with a number of swings and things for children to play on.

"Well, that was interesting," Sarah commented as we exited the town limits and climbed back up to the open road speed limited. "But I'm still no wiser about where we are."

We sped on in silence. About ten minutes later, a sign announced the next town was fifteen kilometres ahead of us. Just as we approached a large sign welcoming us and boasting that the town supported a Rotary Club as well as a Lions Club, and a Chamber of Commerce, Sarah let out a yelp.

"I've found it! Hmm, I don't know how big it is. On the map, it doesn't look like a major centre."

A blue sign up ahead indicated there was a lay-bye area for truckies a few hundred metres up ahead on our left. I made a snap decision and drove off the road and pulled up in the clearing – but kept the motor running. The area was unoccupied. It would be a good place for long-distance drivers to camp for the night. The large level area with a bitumen surface had a dense planting of pencil pines screening it from the road and deadening traffic noise.

Sarah looked alarmed. "Why are we stopping? Shouldn't we keep going? I thought you wanted to get as far away as possible."

"That's true but, now that we know where we are, we need to take a moment to work out what we need to do to get back to Minden Hill. We can't keep careering along this road without a plan. We could end up in Melbourne, or Coober Pedy or somewhere. Let's look at the map for a moment."

I leant over to look at the map as she continued to run her finger along the line representing our road. "That next town after this one we are about to go through looks like it might be a major centre. You said you wanted to keep topping up with small amounts of fuel wherever we could. Will you stop at that next big place?"

"I'm not sure. Let's look at what this town has to offer first, and then work out what happens next." Sarah looked ready to ask a question. I cut her off. "In case you were about to ask, no we are not going to get fuel at this town. How far away is that big town?"

After turning the map in every direction and mumbling to herself, she announced, "If these little numbers are distances – and you can believe them – that big centre is almost forty kilometres from the place we are about to drive through." The fuel gauge told me the distance wasn't a problem. I took the map, opened it up and spread it out across the steering wheel. The big centre we looked at was close to the edge of the open section of the map.

With the map opened out, it was clear we were heading southeast. I found where our road joined a major highway and saw the name of a place along that highway that I recognised. We were way south of Minden Hill. Between here and the highway, any number of roads branched off in various directions. Those that appeared to head in a northerly direction drew my attention, but none of them suggested they headed towards anywhere I recognised. I needed to give it more thought … or get another map. The latter might be an option the first time we stop for fuel. In the meantime, there was something else needing attention.

"Do you think we might sacrifice some of that water you liberated from the house this morning?" Sarah looked confused by my question. "We both need a bit of a clean-up before we go wandering into any service station. I don't know how much good we will do, but we should be able to make ourselves at least look a bit better."

"Good thinking; there's a packet of tissues in the glove compartment and a mirror and comb in the tote bag. I don't think using someone else's comb will worry us today. There's something on the floor behind your seat. It looks like a jacket or shirt of some sort. It might help us look a bit more presentable."

Sarah got out and scrambled into the back of the car. After much grunting and rummaging around, she declared, "It's a positive treasure trove back here. There's a long-sleeved shirt and a pair of runners – might almost be the right size – and there is a towel – oh, and a pair of bathers – stuffed under my seat. She spread everything out on the back seat within easy grabbing distance.

The towel proved useful as Sarah scrubber her face and hands with wet tissues. Then it was my turn. While I did my best to clean my face and remove some of the dried blood from my hair, Sarah opened the boot.

"What are you looking for?"

"I'm not looking for anything, just seeing what might be in here. I'm pleased I did," she added triumphantly. There was a small first aid kit and a gym bag containing a couple of tee shirts, a pair of shorts and a pair of sandals. "Well, at least one of us might be able to look well-dressed when we stop for fuel," she said.

I got back into the car while Sarah changed into the shorts and a tee shirt from the bag. They were a bit baggy on her but looked much better than her own clothes. She came around to the driver's side, opened the door, and told me to turn my head around for her. The gash on my head soon sported antiseptic cream and a plaster – which I could just about hide under my hair.

There was a sheet of analgesic tablets in the first aid kit. I popped two and washed them down with a swig of water. While my head had improved considerably, I still had a dull headache. A few moments were spent sorting things out and placing everything we didn't want immediately into the gym bag. The tote bag now contained only what you might expect to find in a woman's bag. Sarah slammed the boot closed and climbed back into her seat. After checking mirrors and snapping on seatbelts, I drove out of the parking area and headed into town at a sedate pace.

Larger than the previous town we drove through, this one spread down both sides of the road and had a shopping centre tucked away in the block behind the row of dingy buildings fronting the right hand side of the road.

"We could fuel up there," Sarah said and pointed to the large sign that announced the location of a service station.

"No, I don't want to stop here. It's too close to where we were. It's possible the woman filled her car here on a regular basis. I don't want to risk someone at the servo recognising the car – or maybe someone becoming curious about strangers in her friend's car. We'll have a look at getting fuel at the big town up ahead."

We passed cattle yards on the way out of town, and almost immediately found ourselves on the open road again. It was the best part of half hour later before I pulled into a service station. We were making good time in spite of our brief stop at the rest area, but I wanted to get fuel and head off as soon as possible. I didn't pull up at the pumps but drove down the side to where air and water were available.

"I'm going to check the tyres. You take the purse and see if you can buy us a coffee. Check their card reader machines – especially the one where they deal with fuel sales – to see if they have those 'tap and go' type machines."

"Why is that important?"

"If they have that type of machine, and you stay under the limit, you don't need a PIN; just tap the card and the transaction is paid for. I want to make sure we keep the tank full because I don't know how long it will be before someone calls this in as a stolen card and cancels it. Then we will only have the cash in the purse to fall back on… and I don't know how much further we still have to travel."

After making a show of checking the tyres, I spotted the entrance to the ladies' restroom in the wall opposite me. I washed more grime off and tried to make my hair behave before wandering back out to the car. Sarah came back at the same time. She carried two coffees and reported that they used 'tap and go' type credit card machines. We placed the coffees in the holders in the centre console and I drove around to the pumps.

Although I kept a close eye on the litres and dollars involved, I filled the tank for well under the cost limit requiring a PIN. Sarah grabbed the card and disappeared inside. She re-emerged smiling broadly. I breathed a sigh of relief, climbed back into the car and started it ready to go as soon as she joined me.

"A road goes off to the left not too far up ahead, if the map is correct. See if you can see something that says where it might be heading. I want to find one that takes us in a general northerly direction, but it would be good to find one that goes to Ballina or Alstonville, or somewhere in that area."

The first one we came to had a bush track look to it and Sarah said the sign indicated it led to saleyards. The next one looked more promising. A bitumen road, not unlike the one we were on, it was well signposted. Near the turn off, I pulled off onto the shoulder. Sarah checked the name she read on the sign and followed the road through to the edge of the map. We still didn't know how far or where it went, but it was heading in the right direction, and there were a number of both large and small towns dotted along it.

I turned off onto this new road, hoping all the while that this was not a road frequently used by a certain blue van. We swigged at our water supply as we drove along and we were now down to less than half a small bottle. Sarah's stomach growled reminding me it was a long time since we last ate any food. "I'll stop at the next place that looks half decent so we can get some food and more water." I didn't know that it would be about an hour later before we came to a reasonably sized town.

We repeated our previous routine, buying sandwiches, coffee and water and checking out the credit card machines at a sprawling service station complex with a diner attached. I didn't really need fuel again so soon, but I topped up the tank anyway and bought a couple of other maps when I went to pay for it. A short distance further along the road, we came to a roadside rest area with a couple of motorhomes and a campervan still parked in it. It also provided a free toilet and shower block for campers to use.

I drove in and continued around behind the other vehicles. We had lunch on one of the picnic tables with our new maps spread out between us. Sarah managed to find the road we were on near the bottom edge of one of the maps. Many small roads branched off along its many kilometres. However, a major intersection still some distance ahead caught our attention. Where the road reached the top edge of the map, an arrow and the words 'to Ballina' appeared in small print. Damn! I had bought two maps but only one of them was any use. I needed the map that adjoined the top edge of this one and I didn't have it.

"We will have to stop at the next likely looking place to see if we can buy that next map. It has to be before we reach that intersection so we know what to do when we get there. The road we are on continues past that junction but we don't know where it will take us."

Sarah nodded in response but seemed to be preoccupied with the map. After a few moments she spoke. "I think we could be at least 200 kilometres from where that road to Ballina branches off. The way they show these distances makes it hard to work it out exactly. Surely, we'll find somewhere to buy the map we want before then."

Perhaps she was right, but I wasn't so confident and was prepared to stop at anywhere that looked like it might sell maps. Such a place appeared about half an hour later. A newsagent's caught my eye as we drove through a smallish village. I drove into the parking lot out front and dashed into the shop. At first, I couldn't find the map I wanted in the rack. After a bit of digging through the display, I found what I wanted tucked in behind a bundle of other maps.

Back in the car, I risked remaining parked in such an exposed position while we quickly checked the new map. The road we were on continued to some place that meant nothing to either of us. However, some distance past the Ballina turn off, another road branched off to the left. I knew where that would take us. I tossed the map to Sarah to fold and we hit the road again. Without having done the maths, it looked like we still had a long way to go. I decided it was worth risking filling the tank using the credit card once more this afternoon.

We got fuel at a place about halfway between the Ballina turnoff and the one we were heading for. Using the card again didn't raise any alarms, a fact I commented on as we drove off again.

Sarah said she wasn't surprised. "When the van goes away, it is usually gone all day and comes back well after dark. I know we don't know where it has gone, but there's an even chance it won't be back at the house for a few hours yet. They won't know anything has happened – and therefore won't do anything – until they get back and find the woman locked up."

I hoped she was right as, by then, I was counting on being back at Minden Hill.

Our turnoff came up sooner than I expected. I turned onto a wide and well-sealed new road and continued to sit on the speed limit. Once we started on what I hoped was the last leg of our journey, Sarah became interested in the map. She studied it intently as she traced something on it with her finger, before announcing, "Less than 250 kilometres to go now."

That was music to my ears. I had driven all day on adrenaline but it was starting to run out. My shoulders ached and my neck hurt. I knew I was tired but, if the worst happens and the Police pull us over, I didn't want it to be Sarah driving the stolen car. …250kilometres to go … at least another two and a half hours … somehow, it seems so close but so far at the same time. Sarah kept up a chirpy running commentary as we hurtled along the road.

"What was that town? Okay, I see it. Only 200 kilometres to go now… Ah yes, there's that place; 150 to go now…," and she kept it up until we were about a hundred kilometres from Minden Hill. The commentary stopped abruptly when I turned off the road and onto a lesser backroad. "What are you doing? Where are you going? We were so close to Minden Hill…"

"Check that phone that's in the tote bag. See if it needs a PIN to unlock it."

It took her only a few seconds to fish the phone out of the bag and turn it on. "It's not locked."

"Great; okay, please key in this number…" I recited Ben's number and told her Ben was the name of the person who would answer.

"It's ringing… Oh, hello, is this Ben? Hold on a moment please, someone wants to talk to you."

By the time she handed the phone to me, I had pulled up on the shoulder of the road. "Ben, this is Sonny. I need you to meet me somewhere. Are you able to come and meet me in about half an hour or so – you would need to leave now? Okay, I'll give you directions …." I gave him the address of the book/coffee shop where I met with reporter, Dani McLeod.

CHAPTER 14

Today's flight to freedom and everything that happened over the last couple of weeks caught up with Sarah. She started to whine: why aren't we going to Minden Hill? … Who is the bloke you called … Why are we meeting him in a bookshop? I could understand how she felt and empathised with her as I tried to navigate through the maze that was the back streets of Rookwood. …But I was tired and cranky too.

"A-r-g-h, for goodness sake, shut up Sarah." I regretted it the moment I snapped at her. "Instead of sitting there whining, you could help me find a large supermarket that's somewhere around here." A sideways glance at my passenger showed her staring at me with her mouth hanging open. "Look around, please. See if you can spot a supermarket sign somewhere." That produced a result a second or two later.

"There's a Woolworths sign over there, if that's what you are looking for?"

At last, I was beginning to think I had imagined a supermarket in a modern shopping complex around here some place. I drove into the parking lot in front of the supermarket and wove my way through lines of parked cars, working my way closer to the supermarket. In the third row back from the store, a car vacated a parking bay. I sped up and swung into it. Killing the engine and unclipping my seatbelt, I told Sarah to gather up everything in the car. "Everything that's loose needs to go into either the tote bag or the gym bag. We will take the bags with us to the bookshop."

Sarah gave me a look that suggested she thought I had lost the plot, but complied without argument. With the car locked and the key safely in my pocket, we walked out of the parking lot and around onto the footpath along the main street. "It should be just up here," I said as I scanned the signs above the shop entrances. "Yes, there it is."

With the gym bag hefted over my shoulder, I led the way through the bookshop and down the stairs to its coffee shop. We selected a table in a far corner and threw our bags on the floor under it. A waiter headed in our direction. "Feel free to order whatever you feel like. We don't have to wait," I told Sarah.

Our coffees had not yet arrived when I noticed Sarah catch her breath and sit bolt upright. I turned to follow her gaze. A seemingly huge body halfway down the stairs paused and scanned the place through the gloom created by the low lighting. I stood up and waved. Ben had arrived.

The waiter instantly reappeared at our table with our coffees and took Ben's order for a short black. As soon as the waiter left to get the coffee, I got things underway. "Ben, this is Sarah Sinclair, whose parents you might remember engaged me to find out what happened to her." Ben nodded and extended his hand to Sarah. I continued. "Sarah, this Ben Richards, whom I spoke to on the phone earlier." Smiles all round… that's a good sign. As I made the introductions, a sudden thought suggested I shouldn't mention that Ben was a Queensland detective, so I didn't. Although anxious for information, Ben managed to control himself until after his coffee arrived. I knew the interrogation was about to begin, so I tried jumping in first to forestall it. I didn't quite manage it.

"Right, Sonny; where the hell have you been? Was it too much to expect some sort of message from you to let us know what was going on? The last I knew you were going for a short stroll along that path through the bush." Okay, I get it. Ben is not happy. I took a deep breath and prepared to choose my words carefully to diffuse the situation and avoid any further discomfort for Sarah. Again, I was too slow and Sarah jumped in ahead of me.

"Yeah, that's what she did. She took a short stroll … into oblivion…" Sarah said and gave Ben a wry look.

Definitely time for me to rescue the situation. "The story is long and involved, Ben, and I don't want to start here and now. We will talk about it later, after you drive us back to the motel. Can you live with that?" He agreed. "Apart from dozing for a few moments, neither of us slept last night and we have been travelling since before sun up this morning. My head is full of cotton wool and I don't doubt Sarah isn't feeling much better." Ben laid both his hands palm down on the table and studied his fingers for a few moments before speaking.

"At the risk of incurring the wrath, I asked a colleague to join us. No, don't react – just wait and see. I thought he would be here by now."

As he finished speaking, a man came down the stairs and looked around. "Is this your invited 'colleague'?" I asked, nodding in the direction of the recent arrival.

I noted the use of 'colleague' rather than 'friend', or some other term. I assumed he was giving me a heads-up that the new arrival was a fellow police officer. In response to a wave from Ben, the man took a seat at our table, but he declined to order coffee. Ben did the introductions. "Ladies, this is Gerry. We go back a long way, although we haven't had much contact lately." Handshakes all round and plenty of smiles. Then, Ben stood up abruptly and announced, "Sarah and I are going to check out the merchandise upstairs in the bookshop."

Sarah looked stunned but didn't make any move to leave until Ben grabbed her under the arm and hauled her to her feet. Sheer alarm masked her face. "It's okay, Sarah, there's nothing to worry about. I think Ben wants me to talk to Gerry alone for a few minutes." She moved off with Ben, but threw me a meaningful look as they climbed the stairs. Yes, I know you're not happy, I thought as I turned my attention to Gerry.

"I assume Ben's reference to you as a colleague means you are also a copper…" He nodded and gave me a sheepish grin.

"He said you would be prickly about my being here. I won't hang around now, I just need to find out if there is anything I need to know or act on immediately. We will talk at length later."

"Uhmm … yes, perhaps there is. There's a car in the supermarket carpark that might -- or might not -- be reported as stolen. It might be worth keeping an eye on the car in case someone tries to reclaim it." I gave him the key and recited the registration number, which he wrote on the back of his hand. "Oh, and we borrowed a few of a woman's personal items – cash, cards, phone – but more about that when we talk later."

I picked up the bags, dumped them on the table and fished out the purse. "I think it's time we joined the others," I told Gerry. My magnanimous gesture as we exited the coffee shop: I settled the bill for all the coffees with some of that 'acquired' cash.

The four of us stood on the footpath beside Ben's car. I told Ben what I wanted to do before heading to the motel. He looked at Gerry and they both nodded. I climbed into the front passenger seat, while Sarah occupied the back seat along with our two bags. Within moments, we were driving along the line of cars towards our abandoned sedan. Following my instructions, Ben stopped immediately behind the sedan, lowered his window and pointed towards the car. Gerry, stopped about a metre or so behind us, flashed his lights in response. Then, we were on the road and cruising towards a hot shower and sleep.

As we drove along Minden Hill's main street, Ben asked, "How do you want to play this?"

"Nothing fancy; just take us into the motel's parking area and then we will follow you into your room. As I no longer have my room's keycard, I'll use the connecting door from your room to access my room." By the time I finished speaking, we were paused at the security gate to the motel's carpark waiting for the dashboard gadget to do its thing and open the gate.

Not a soul about when we entered the motel through the back door, and we quickly followed Ben into his room. I cracked the connecting door open part way and visually checked my room. Everything looked as I left it. "First things first, Ben. It would be good if you took Sarah to reception to retrieve her belongings the motel has in storage… maybe organise a room for her while you are there."

"That's not a problem, but what do we say if they start asking questions about where she has been all this time?"

"I gave that some thought while I was driving. Many of the locals went down with some new exotic strain of flu around Easter time. I think the story should be that she caught that flu bug and has been ill for the duration. Those clothes she is wearing aren't hers. They are a couple of sizes too large. They make her look as though she has lost a fair bit of weight, and that helps give the story credibility."

While they went to do battle with reception, I went to my room and indulged in a long, hot shower, followed by the luxury of clean clothes. As I gently towelled my hair dry, I heard them in the corridor. They didn't come into Ben's room, but there were sounds from the room on the other side of Ben's. A couple of minutes later, the three of us once more gathered in Ben's room. The gathering was short. Sarah wanted a shower and to sleep before dinner, and went back to her own room. I spent only a few minutes explaining how Sarah was ill and had not eaten much since her abduction, that neither of us slept last night, and how I spent time unconscious and concussed since my disappearance. Then, after Ben promised to wake me at about 6.30pm, I escaped to my room and collapsed into bed.

We entered the restaurant a few minutes after seven o'clock and found Gerry already there. Ben confessed, "I asked Gerry to join us for dinner. Afterwards, we can go to my room and discuss what happened to you two ladies." A waiter materialised beside our table almost the moment we sat down. Sarah and I opted for non-alcoholic, while the other two ordered Scotch. The waiter delivering the drinks bent and whispered something to Ben, who promptly excused himself saying he would be back in minute.

He returned with another man in tow. Wait staff scurried about moving cutlery around on the table, while we shuffled our chairs closer together to accommodate the extra diner. Before taking their seats, Ben announced, "I hope you don't mind, but I took the liberty of inviting one more to dinner. This is Neil Richards. He flew to Ballina this afternoon and has just driven from there."

The usual introductions and getting acquainted stuff happened in a blur for me. I was busy trawling my memory banks for anything relating to a Neil Richards. The trawl produced nothing, but my gut told me Neil Richards probably was Ben Richards' brother. That brought an instant recall. Ben became involved with a previous case I worked in Ralston some while back. At one point, his brother, who was with the Federal Police, provided information and then became involved in closing the case. I never heard the brother's name mentioned, but I would bet my socks it was the same Neil Richards now sitting opposite me at dinner. Having come to that conclusion, I glanced over at Ben. Damn the man! I'm sure he reads my mind. A wide grin split his face and he dropped me a conspiratorial wink.

I chose something small and light from the menu, and cautioned Sarah about trying to eat too much of anything too heavy after having gone without food for so long. A little light chatter accompanied our meal as we ate quickly and soon congregated in Ben's room – after having brought in the extra chairs from my room.

Although Sarah came in with the rest of us, she didn't stay long. While everyone was still fussing over where to sit, she came over and spoke quietly to me. "I need to call Mum. I don't have a phone any more. I don't know what they did with it. Is it all right to use that phone in the tote bag?"

"No, I think it best not to use it anymore." Her face dropped. "It's not a problem. My phone has been on charge the whole time, so it should be working okay – unless it has cooked itself in the meantime." She seemed reluctant to use my phone, so I fetched it from my room, found her mother's number in my contacts list and brought it up. The phone seemed to be working okay. I thrust it into her hand and said, "Just press 'TALK' and it should start dialling." She held it to her ear and I saw her face light up as it started dialling the number. With a signal to me that she was going outside, she left the room to talk to her mother in private.

With everyone else finally seated and coffee delivered by room service the mood in the room became serious. I realised both Sarah and I have starring roles in the night's anticipated program. However, with Sarah out of the room, I decided the time was right for some straight answers before anything else occurred.

"No, hang on, Ben. Before we go any further, I want to know who these two are." I gestured towards Neil and Gerry who sat side by side beside the queen-sized bed.

"What are you on about, Sonny? You know who they are. I introduced you…"

"Maybe I should rephrase the question. I know who they are -- Neil and Gerry. What I should have asked is: *what* are they, and more importantly, why are they here?" Ben squirmed uncomfortably in his chair and looked at the other two men. As if by some unspoked agreement, Neil answered.

"Well, I'd like to say how pleased I am to finally meet you after the help you gave us with busting that drugs trafficking network."

"…So my assumption that you are Ben's Fed Officer brother is correct?" Neil nodded. I turned my attention to Gerry. "…And Gerry, you are …?" Gerry nervously looked at Ben.

Ben shrugged and cleared his throat. "Gerry is the lead detective for this region." I shook my head but, before I could point out that was not the case, Ben continued. "The detective you took such an instant dislike to has a complaint filed against him… nothing too serious. More of a misdemeanour, but he has been suspended pending the outcome of an investigation of the matter. In his absence, Gerry is on transfer from another district to fill the position."

I nodded again. Okay, I could accept all that, but the next question in my mind was why they became involved in something no one seemed to know anything about when I arrived – and nobody had any interest in as far as I could see. I put the question to the gathering. Gerry became the spokesman.

"What Ben didn't mention is that he is now an honorary constable in the New South Wales Police Service." I raised an eyebrow at Ben who was preoccupied with removing some invisible piece of fluff from his trousers. It was clear he hadn't intended sharing that information with me. Neil continued the explanation.

"Ben contacted both of us when you disappeared... me, because of our connection, and Gerry because it all happened in his area. Ben and Gerry go back a long way. They were at the academy together."

"What we want to do tonight is start the process of piecing together everything we can about the abductions," Ben said, leaning forward to rest his elbows on his thighs. We need to trawl both Sarah's and your memories of everything that happen before you start to lose important details."

"I know how post-incident interviews work," I snapped. "…Speaking of Sarah, she seems to have been gone a long time."

"She and her mother have a lot to talk about." Ben was right; there was no arguing with that. Still, it seemed too long for even that sort of phone call. Over the top of Ben's voice, I thought I heard noise in the corridor outside the room. I stopped and turned my head to listen before racing to the door.

I don't know whether Ben heard the sound too, or whether it was my move to open the door that launched him into action. He pushed me out of the way, flung the door open and rushed out into the corridor, closely followed by Gerry and Neil. I found myself relegated to last to leave the room. Ben shouted 'hey you' as he entered the corridor, and I heard plenty of commotion in the corridor immediately afterwards. I rushed out of the room and stopped abruptly. The scene playing out in the corridor sent my stomach into a tight ball.

Sarah was lying on the carpet with Neil kneeling beside her. My phone lay up against the wall with its back cover a short distance away on the floor. A man was face down on the floor. Gerry struggled to snap on handcuffs while Ben knelt with one knee in the man's back.

By the time I reached Sarah, the handcuffs were secure and Gerry was barking into his phone. Neil gently slapped both sides of Sarah's face in an effort to coax her back to consciousness. I knelt beside Sarah. The chemical smell was strong. The main source of the smell seemed to be the folded fabric table napkin on the carpet beside Sarah. Not again; Christ, I didn't rescue her to have her snatched again.

Gerry's phone rang. He spoke only a couple of words before he and Ben hoisted their captive to his feet and propelled him out into the motel's carpark. I sprang up and raced after them. I wanted to get a look at the man. He came as a shock. "You…!" was all I could manage to shout before the two men threw him up against the back wall of the motel. Ben ran and pressed the button and the security gate silently slid open. The large white van-like vehicle waiting on the outside drove in and stopped beside where Gerry continued to hold the man up against the wall.

Two men got out and flung open the van's rear doors. Ben helped these two toss the man into the back of the van. The van's doors slammed closed. Gerry, no longer interested in the prisoner, turned his attention to something in the backseat area of the van. He withdrew something, slammed the car door closed and ran back into the motel. I followed. From what I could make out, Gerry carried something that looked like the small oxygen cylinders carried in ambulance and other rescue vehicles.

When I reached Sarah, Gerry already had the mask over her face. The hiss from the oxygen cylinder provided a backdrop to Sarah's return to consciousness. Neil gently restrained her as she thrashed about and tried to pull the mask from her face. Within a minute or so, she no longer needed restraint. Her eyes fluttered open a couple of time. I spoke quietly to her. She opened her eyes groggily and found my face. Gerry kept the mask in place for another minute or so, by which time she seemed fully conscious but confused.

"Do you think you can sit up?" I asked. She blinked her eyes a couple of times in affirmation. The two men helped ease her into the sitting position and supported her for a few moments. I became aware of someone standing close behind me and spun around to investigate. My nose almost crashed into Ben's knees. "Oh, sorry Ben; I didn't hear you join us. Do you think we could take Sarah to her room so she can lie down for a while?"

"Hmm… no, I think it would be better if she went to my room. We will discuss why later." In a tangle of well-intentioned bodies as we all tried to help, we eased her to her feet. By the time she was standing, the bodies had sorted out their individual roles. Ben rushed ahead to open the door to his room while Gerry and Neil, half-carrying Sarah, followed him. Before joining the others in Ben's room, I stopped to pick up my phone. I checked the battery remained in situ, snapped the battery cover back in place, and tested the phone. The bounce off the wall didn't appear to have damaged it. It seemed okay, except for maybe a tiny piece of plastic missing from the edge of one corner.

In Ben's room, the others gathered around Sarah, now propped up with pillows on the bed. When I arrived, they hadn't progressed beyond asking how she felt and if she were comfortable. Everyone except me seemed oblivious to Sarah's mounting exasperation at all the fussed. "Listen up everybody; if we all accept that Sarah is okay, can we move on to finding out what happened out there?" I was a little brusque and, by the end of my speech, found all eyes focused on me.

Ben chuckled. "It's good to see your absence hasn't changed you in any way. Sonny is right though. If Sarah is up to it, we should look at what happened to her." Murmured agreement all round augmented by nodding heads. "Sarah, tell us what you can about what happened after you left here to call your mother."

Sarah lowered her head and appeared to be studying her hands in her lap. I had seen that look before. I knew she was replaying events in her mind before answering. After a moment or two, she swallowed hard a couple of times and gazed off at some indeterminate spot in the distance. She spoke slowly, picking her words carefully as she walked the memory of the event.

"The phone was dialling as I walked out of here. Mum took a while to answer. I was back at my door by the time she did. She just about became hysterical when she heard my voice, and I only managed a couple of words as I unlocked my door with my keycard. It was an emotional call. Both of us were crying. I sat on the edge of my bed while we talked. The door was partly ajar. I hadn't closed it completely when I went in, but I wasn't worried as there doesn't appear to be anyone else in the motel."

Gerry interrupted. "Did you see or hear anything out in the corridor while you were on the phone?"

"No, nothing; although I wasn't particularly paying attention, I think I'm still twitchy enough after what happened to be aware of anything going on out there. Anyway, we talked quite a while – mainly Mum repeatedly asking if I was okay. It quietened her down a bit when I told her that Sonny had said she hoped to put me on a plane tomorrow or the next day. She wanted to know everything that happened, but I told her it would take too long and it would be better to wait until I got home. We reached the end of the conversation and were doing the goodbyes bit at the end, so I got up and went to the door. I ended the call as I walked out into the corridor. The last thing I remember is closing the door with my left hand – I had the phone in my right – and then turning back and trying the door handle to check it had locked properly."

"Think about when you checked the door was locked, were you aware of any noises or smells, or anything at all unusual around you?" Sarah looked at Ben and went to answer immediately, then stopped. Complete silence filled the room for at least a minute. The Sarah turned to face Ben again, a strange look on her face – mild surprise or shock, perhaps. Again, she went to speak but stopped and shook her head as if dismissing a thought.

Ben encouraged her. "Something occurred to you just then. Tell us what that was. It doesn't matter how ridiculous or trivial you think it is, it might prove important." She shrugged and took a moment to compose what she would say.

"I can't be sure, but I think I heard something. I don't know what… the sound was very soft. Maybe I sensed it rather than heard it. I don't know, but I started to turn around … to look in that direction … yes, that's it. I think something told me there was someone else in the corridor … someone behind me. A little bit more is coming back as I'm thinking about it."

"You're doing great. Don't try to force it… just let it come to you. Sometimes, even talking about the smallest detail will trigger other memories," Ben said.

"I think that's what is happening. I just remembered a bit more." She took another deep breath and ran her tongue over her lips to moisten them. I poured a glass of water and handed it to her. "Thanks; I remember that, as I was turning to check out the noise or whatever, I was grabbed from behind – an arm around my neck. Then he was trying to push something over my face. I'd been there once already. I wasn't going to have all that happen again. I tried to fight him off … I think I bit his arm or his hand."

There was another lengthy pause. Everyone sat still and silent. Sarah appeared to be searching for more memories. Then, she looked up and shrugged as she swept her eyes across us gathered around her. "He must have been too strong for me …but I do remember the smell. It was the same as the one I remember from the bush track the night they took me."

Ben raised his eyebrows at me. I nodded. Yes, the stuff I smelt out in the corridor was the same as was used on me that night along the bush track. Ben sat upright and looked around the room.

"I think the women should be allowed to get some sleep. Perhaps we could leave any other questions until the morning…? Everyone rose and made moves to leave. Ben retained charge of the situation. He grabbed my arm and held me back. "Before everyone leaves, I'd like to put forward a suggestion." Everyone returned to their seats. Ben's plan received the unanimous support of the men present. Sarah and I vetoed it, but it was as though we hadn't even spoken. Everyone vacated the chairs again.

Neil went to his room. Gerry escorted Sarah to her room to fetch a few things. Ben once more grabbed my arm to prevent me escaping and held me until we remained the only two in the room.

"You recognised the bloke they took away." It was a question and a statement rolled into one. I'd known Ben long enough to know that the tone used demanded a straight and immediate answer.

CHAPTER 15

Did I know the bloke…? Had I misjudged the bloke might be a more relevant question… because, yes, I did. "I wouldn't say I knew him, but I did speak to him a couple of times – once in the restaurant and once outside in the carpark area."

"He was a guest?"

"No, he works here… worked in the restaurant and sometimes filled in on reception. I'm now wondering if he didn't have another interesting sideline going on at the same time." Ben's impatience with me began to show, so I got on with explaining my current thinking about the young bloke. "The evening I disappeared, I spoke to him as I was heading off to that track through the bush. There was nothing much involved. I simply asked if he had spoken to Sarah while she was staying here. He said he had – a couple of times in passing, thought she was nice, and it was a shame she disappeared. He quizzed me about where I was going and whether I would be dining in the restaurant that night. That was just before I set off down the track and disappeared."

"…So what are you telling me?"

"Nobody else knew where I was going that evening, yet the 'right people' happened to be in position to nab me as I walked the track."

"He knew you were asking questions about Sarah before you spoke to him outside that evening. …You think he might have tipped off the people involved in Sarah's disappearance about your interest?"

"It takes no time to walk from the motel to the track. I remember having walked some distance along it before everything went blank. No vehicles entered the area after I started on the track. It is so quiet once you are in that bush, you would notice the sound of a vehicle. Therefore, I can only assume my abductors were already stationed somewhere along that track before I started on it. My suspicion now is that our friendly staff member tipped them off about my pending approach."

"Are you suggesting he was a 'scout' for the other mob?"

"My suspicions do suggest that. When he is out there smoking, he sees everyone coming or going on the track and is in an ideal position to relay that information to his associates, who lie in wait for anyone our bloke identifies as a likely target."

"I like your thinking. Although the other two who went missing were not guests of the motel, he would see them start down the track on their way back to the festival site."

"I just remembered something… He said he didn't mind working the extra shifts over Easter as the penalty rates helped meet the payments on his new apartment. It might be worth a look at that apartment to see whether it was affordable on a hospitality worker's wages."

Our conversation came to an abrupt end when Gerry returned with Sarah. Ben's grand plan was for Sarah and me to sleep in Ben's room. Gerry would take Sarah's room and Ben would sleep in my room. Neil would sleep in his own room. 'Sleep' is a bit misleading. The three men would take turns at being 'on guard' over Sarah and me throughout the night. Neither Sarah nor I felt happy about someone watching over us all night as we slept, but it was getting late and we both were fading fast. It had been a long and trying day.

There were two beds in the room, a queen and a single. Faced with the usual polite but often protracted process of deciding who would sleep where, I chose to avoid the problem by announcing I would sleep in the single bed. I noted the fleeting pleased look that flashed across Sarah's features. Beyond that, I don't remember a thing until I opened my eyes again.

"Good morning," Ben chirped from his perch in one of the lounge chairs as I swung my legs over the side of the bed. "I see you haven't changed your habits. I didn't expect to see any movement in here before at least seven o'clock, but I forgot about your practice of early starts."

Maybe I'm not a morning person. I only managed a grunt in reply until I reached the interconnecting door. "I'm going back to my own room to shower and dress. You may continue your vigil… in here preferably."

By the time I felt relatively human again and wandered back into Ben's room, the world seemed to have come to life. Sarah was awake and about to go back her own room to get ready to face the day, and Gerry and Ben were talking quietly in one corner of the room. Sarah opened the door to leave, and stepped aside to allow Neil to enter. It was too early in the morning to be around so much testosterone. I went back to my room.

The previous night hadn't provided opportunity to check whether all of my things were still in my room. After a few moments devoted to checking everything was still there and hadn't been tampered with, I slipped a few things into my bag ready for whatever the day had in store, and then sat down to write up my notes on everything that had happened.

Ben strolled through the connecting doorway and found me staring off into space while my hands hovered above my keyboard. Unfocused, I turned towards him. "I think I was AWOL for four days. Am I right?" He nodded. "Of that time, I remember what happened yesterday and a bit of the last part of the day before. Now I'm trying to dredge up anything from possible half-conscious moments. That's not going too well."

"We could try playing that game we used to play when one of us had a particularly stubborn case."

"Hmm… it might work. Let's give it a try after breakfast."

While the others entertained themselves in one of the rooms, Ben and I retreated to my room. With the drapes pulled and the lights off, just enough lighted filtered in from outside to rendered it pleasantly dark. Time to test a 'special' old technique. Its origin belongs to a time a long way back in our past, to a time when we tried to work out if we wanted to be more than just good friends. Life decided we remain friends … but friends who almost became something else when together.

Back then, Ben had a difficult case. He knew he was missing something that allowed a serial killer to remain free. The more he tried to recall whatever it was, the more it eluded him – and the more frustrated he became. In a bid to release some of his tension, one evening I started massaging his shoulders, moved up his neck to his temples and scalp. It is the most relaxing thing I know, and that night I discovered it also worked for Ben. It's a subliminal feeling that extends to just short of sleep. In such a state, things you were unaware existed in your subconscious float to the surface if encouraged with soft appropriate questioning ... much like being hypnotised without the hypnosis.

I sat in one of the comfortable chairs with my feet up on another. Ben started massaging my shoulders. "If this is going to work, you have to relax. Loosen your shoulders," he demanded. I focused on my shoulders, mentally commanding them -- drop down … flex …relax … loosen up … that's it, very relaxed now. Ben's magic took over. Then, as if somewhere in the distance, his voice softly floats to me and leads me on that walk along the track through the bush again.

"You are at the start of the track … is there anyone around … are there any vehicles … what do you hear … how dark is it … what smells are there … how far along are you …? The questions continued and elicited a running commentary from within the deepest recesses of my memory. I became vaguely aware of my own voice – barely above a whisper and sometimes hesitantly – providing feedback in response to his prompts. I was telling him about the patches of moonlight filtering through the canopy to form pools of light here and there on the track; about the tyre tracks buried under a blanket of leaves; about rustling in the undergrowth; about wondering if it was an animal and my growing unease at its sound.

Then I was telling Ben about a particularly dark part of the track. How an area of even deeper blackness up ahead looked as though it could be a small clearing off to one side of the road. Ben's voice drifted back to fill the void when I stopped speaking.

"Keep walking slowly along the track towards the clearing. Can you see anything … any familiar shapes … can you hear anything … any noises at all …?" I felt myself stiffen and my pulse quicken. Then Ben's quiet insistent voice, "Relax; what do you hear?" A pause when I don't answer immediately, then more insistent, "What's happening … have you stopped walking?" I murmur that I am standing still, listening. "Why have you stopped? What are you listening for … what made you stop and listen…?"

"…Rustling in the bushes – quite close … too close! … I feel a presence … there's someone here! … I know there is someone here." I sat up, tense and tightly gripping the arms of my chair. Ben tried telling me to relax and increased his efforts to bring me back down again.

"Stop it. Stop, Ben; I remember. I heard a noise in the bushed quite close to me – faint but not natural somehow – and I stopped suddenly to listen. I didn't hear anything more, so I started to move on again. After I took a step or two, I was aware of something – someone – right behind me. I spun around to see what it was and was hit on the side of the head."

"Did the blow knock you out?"

"No. I think it made me a bit groggy. Hands grab my arm and try forcing it up behind my back. He tries forcing me down onto the ground. Instinct kicks in. I fight back. Then there are two of them. One of them has his hand hard on the back of my head as he pushes something over my nose and mouth. I feel everything starting to swim and go dark. I lash out with all I have left. My foot makes contact with something soft. There is a grunt and then a stream of swearing. No hands touch my head any longer, but I am falling. I think I remember my face burying in the leaves, then nothing but blackness."

"Your face in the leaves, was that when you hit the ground as you passed out?"

"Yes, I think so … at least, that's the impression I get now when I replay it. There is only one other vague recollection of just before I lost consciousness completely: I felt something dig into my arm that was free. It might have been a stick or something jabbing me as I hit the ground, but I don't think so. What do you think it looks like?" I heard Ben catch his breath and move from behind me around to the side of my chair. I hitched up the one leg of my shorts to reveal an angry looking mark on my thigh. "It looks like a needle stick mark to me," I said, "And I don't think it was a particularly clean needle."

"You need to get that looked at – and some blood tests done," was all he said, but that was all the confirmation of my suspicions I needed.

Our conversation moved on to when I finally regained consciousness in that prison-like room. I relayed the information Sarah supplied about the place and what she knew went on there. We agreed Sarah would need to be questioned in depth – and soon. Until that could happen, Ben suggested we focus on identifying the likely location of that house where they held us. I went in search of the maps we used during our escape and found them in the stolen gym bag.

We spread the maps out on the bed and, starting from the Rookwood end of the journey, I started tracing back along our escape route. Sarah came in with Gerry when I had reached the point at which I had her call Ben's number. All four of us clustered around the maps, and Sarah and I worked our way back past towns and landmarks in the reverse order to the way we came to them yesterday. It took but a couple of minutes to trace the route on the maps back to the first sealed road we encountered after leaving the house. That's where the problem arose.

There was nothing to indicate where we joined that road. I continued running my finger along the road until it came to a town. I knew I had gone past the turn off to the house. Sarah and I slowly worked our way back along the road from the town, checking every millimetre of land bordering the right hand side of the road for any sign of a turn off or a track winding through the countryside. It was pointless. The map's scale was too small to provide the detail we required. We were about to give up when I had an idea.

While my computer booted up, I went back to the map and checked the names of two towns: the one beyond where I believed the house was located and the first one we came to after leaving the house. With Google maps up, I typed in the name of the latter one of the two. Google struggled for a while to come up with anything – not surprising since it was not much more than a small village – but it eventually put a marker in the middle of nowhere. A few clicks brought up much finer detail. There was our sealed road and there was the tiny village.

I worked across the map until I encountered a town beyond the route of our escape… still not enough detail. A couple more clicks for more detail, and I began running the cursor back along the road towards the small village. Now, all the small side roads and tracks coming off the sealed road were visible… but which one was our track. Sarah indicated one that looked promising. I tried following it to see where it led. It ended at a small sawmill, but I felt from the outset that it wasn't the correct one. It didn't wander around enough through the surrounding countryside.

After a couple of half-hearted attempts at following other tracks, I let out a yelp. "I think this is it. Hang on a minute, while I see if I can bring up a bit more detail. There was a brief pause while Google Maps did its thing and I repositioned the cursor on the track. I let the cursor follow its squiggly path away from the road to what appeared to be a clearing occupied by a number of buildings. Sarah and I studied the clearing in silence for a few moments before discussing it.

"I remember seeing two small buildings – sheds probably – as we ran for the car. I think they might be those there," Sarah said as she pointed to a spot on the screen, "And that thing there might be the big building where we were held."

Everyone bunched in closer for a better look at the screen. I clicked again in the hope of a bit more detail and was successful. Although the scene started to pixilate, details of the buildings became clearer. We counted four outbuildings scattered around a large central main building. I looked up at Ben who looked at me intently and raised his eyebrows in silent question. "Yes, I think that might be the place where they held us," I answered. Sarah and I moved away from the laptop to allow the two coppers to move in and make notes.

Neil knocked and joined us while Ben and Gerry were intent on scribbling details of the location of the house. We explained what had transpired in his absence. Then, with the computer abandoned and everyone perched wherever they could, Sarah and I gave them as much information as we knew about the place.

"Interesting…" Neil said, and sat back with his hands linked behind his head. He stared at some obscure point on the ceiling while the rest of us sat in silence and waited to be enlightened. When it began to appear as though enlightenment might not be forthcoming, Ben cleared his throat in the hope of bringing Neil's attention back to the group. It didn't work.

"Oh, for God's sake, Neil, what's interesting?"

"Eh? Oh…, I was thinking about something else that I've had people working on for a while. Some of the scuttlebutt that we picked up leads back to that area. It got me wondering about a possible connection."

"And…?" Ben encouraged him again.

"…And I think that might be the case." Everyone turned towards Neil and waited for him to explain further. At first, he seemed oblivious of our anticipation but, after more prompting from Ben, Neil began to speak hesitantly as he organised his thoughts. "Ladies, I think we need you to tell us everything you can remember about that place, anyone who was there, what happened… everything and anything. Just hang on a moment though, if you wouldn't mind."

With that, Neil got up and went to the computer, checked something and then left the room. We all exchanged glances, but there was nothing to do except wait for him to return. The two men became restless and kept glancing at the door. It was quite a few minutes before Neil returned. Then it was straight down to business again. "Right, where were we? Oh yes, the ladies were going to give us everything they knew about that place. Okay, don't be shy, ladies, what can you tell us?"

Neil seemed a bit more upbeat since returning from his brief absence. His gaze alternated between Sarah and me a couple of times while waiting for one of us to start speaking. I explained that I knew very little and that I already had debriefed with Ben. All eyes swivelled to Sarah. What felt like a long rambling debrief began.

Sarah apologised in advance for any inaccuracies that might occur as she admitted to being unable to distinguish between what happened and what she imagined. That brought an avalanche of questions before she progressed any further.

"I was unconscious and semi-conscious for quite a while – and extremely sick. I think some of what I can tell comes from my own memories, but some of it is second hand. It's what Olivia told me about the place and what went on there."

"Olivia…? Who is Olivia and how does she fit in?" Gerry interrupted. Sarah looked pleadingly at me and I interpreted the look as a plea for help to answer Gerry.

"On the Thursday night before Easter, an early stallholder for the Easter festival, a thirty-something year old redhead was abducted from along that track through the bush. Her name was Olivia."

"…Surname?" Neil demanded.

I shrugged and he looked at Sarah. "I've no idea. I don't think she mentioned it."

"Right, we will come back to her later," Gerry replied. "Okay, we accept that some of it might be hearsay. Tell us what you know, but please start with why you were unconscious or whatever for so long."

"I was unconscious when I arrived. That's how everyone was when they arrived. As I started to regain consciousness, apparently I became aggressive and fought and shouted and carried on. They knocked me out again. This time, as I started to come to, I hallucinated. It frightened them when, in order to get away from the beasts chasing me, I tried to 'fly' off the only chair we had– that was after I tried climbing the wall and a few other interesting things. They knocked me out again. Everything seemed normal when I came to after that last lot except for being so sick. I couldn't stop vomiting. Olivia looked after me as much as she could. Somewhere along the line, she had been a paramedic."

"…So, they kept chloroforming you until you finally were normal when you became conscious…?" Ben asked in confirmation of her story thus far.

"No, that's not what it was. I've tried to remember everything that happened on the track the night they grabbed me. When that man tried to seize me out there in the corridor, the smell of what he used reminded me of what I smelled on the track that night. But, when they knocked me out those couple of times after I was at the house, they used something else." Sarah pushed up her sleeve. They injected me with something – twice; once in the arm and, the first time, in the thigh."

Ben and I locked eyes for a moment. Sarah's needle stick sites looked as angry as mine did. It looks like someone else will need a series of blood tests over the next few months. After the other two coppers took a closer look at Sarah's injection marks, she resumed her story. She told of the daily routines for food, etc., and of Olivia's comments about the 'terrible things' they did to the women. Then she moved on to a part of the story I hadn't heard before.

"I sort of vaguely remember another woman – a young girl really – who was there for a while. I think I saw her the first time I started to regain consciousness. She was curled up in the corner, sort of humming and shaking constantly. Later, when I was starting to enter reality again… it's all a bit foggy, but I remember they came to get her. She screamed and fought like a wild thing. I remember seeing one of them punch her. She went quiet and they dragged her out. Once she was outside the room, she started screaming again. It went on for a while and then stopped abruptly. A little while later – a couple of minutes maybe – she screamed once, one long blood-chilling scream and then nothing. She never came back."

"What can you tell us about that girl," Gerry asked.

"In my memory, Belinda was young and had long blonde hair. I don't know or remember anything else."

"Her name was Belinda, you think?" Gerry checked. All three men turned to face me as Gerry posed the question.

"A young girl, a stallholder's daughter, disappeared on Easter Saturday night. She was still a schoolgirl, had long blonde hair and her name was Belinda," I chanted in response to their enquiring looks. There were nods all round in response to my information before their attention returned to

Sarah and Neil asked her what else she could tell them.

Sarah told them of Olivia's disappearance from their cell, and that she was alone for about a day before I arrived. Then she related details of us hastily devising an escape plan after something I overheard caused me concern. That brought the focus of attention back to me. I shrugged, drew a deep breath and tried mentally to put together the details as succinctly as possible before I spoke.

"I was closer to the door, so I could overhear snatches of the two men's conversation that took place immediately outside our room. My interpretation of the bits I heard goes something like this: they thought Sarah and I received permanent damaged in some way from their treatment of us, and that we were likely to become a problem for them. There was talk about 'quotas'. I don't know what that was about really, but I formed the assumption it had something to do with the number of abductions. Yeah, I know, it's a wild assumption! There were two bits of their conversation that spurred me into action: they would make a decision when they 'came back' and that they 'might be digging more holes in the bush'. After that, although they continued talking, they were too far away for me to hear."

"Do you think that's what might have happened to those other two women... that they ended up buried in the bush?" Neil asked.

"I don't know. It's possible I suppose, but it could have been something else entirely they were talking about... or simply a turn of phrase with no real intent behind it."

Ben chuckled. "If you believed that, you wouldn't have engineered your escape as quickly as you did." That was true, but I was pleased when no one chose to pursue it further.

Things went quiet. Nobody spoke for a few moments until Ben broke the silence. "I don't know about anyone else, but I'm in need of coffee."

The morning had been a hard slog. We all jumped at the chance to take a coffee break. As I wandered over to the door to let in room service with a pot of coffee, I checked the time. Most of the morning had disappeared... and I still hadn't organised Sarah's flight home.

CHAPTER 16

As if by some universal decree, we all stood to drink our coffees. We spent most of the morning sitting, in some cases, quite uncomfortably. With my mug emptied, I decided to check on a flight for Sarah before proceedings resumed … if in fact there was anything more to discuss. Engaged in some private conversation, the two brothers, Ben and Neil, occupied space next to the bench where my computer sat. They looked up and made to move away as I approached. Ben hesitated and watched as I wriggled the mouse to wake up the machine.

"What are you looking up … has something else occurred to you?" he asked, and moved closer to stand behind and look over my shoulder.

"No, it's not that. I need to book a flight to get Sarah home. I want one that doesn't leave her hanging around Brisbane airport for any length of time waiting for a connecting flight to Moxton."

"Oh, don't worry about that. When it's time for her to leave, two of my officers will fly directly to Moxton with her in a private plane," Neil said. "I think it might be a day or two yet before that happens."

Ben nodded and explained. "There's still a bit more we need you both for here." He glanced at Neil and raised an eyebrow at him. Neil confirmed it with an almost imperceptible nod and then continued. "If they locate the house where you were kept, there might be some benefit in having you and Sarah return to the place with Neil's officers."

"Yes okay, but what is that likely to achieve? I am happy to go back as I'm going to hang around for a bit longer anyway, but I don't know that I want to put Sarah through something that is likely to prove stressful if it's not necessary."

"We will play it by ear but, at this stage, I think it is something we need to do. We'll talk to her about it later today and see how she reacts to it." Neil's tone suggested there was no room to manoeuvre, so I signified my agreement and secretly thought that his idea might be the best approach anyway. I didn't want her becoming miffed at some stage later on because of her omission from the investigation.

After more discussion mostly of ground already covered, it was lunchtime. Gerry rang someone at his station to organise lunch for us all and deliver it. It was nearly one o'clock by the time it arrived, and the speed at which it disappeared suggested everyone was as hungry as I was. The gathering dispersed after lunch. Neil went back to his room, his phone already firmly attached to his ear as I let him out of my room. Sarah escaped to her own room to freshen up… and 'have a nap' she whispered to me as she left.

Gerry and Ben, deep in conversation, slowly ambled towards the interconnecting door on their way to Ben's room. Ben opened the door and stepped aside to let Gerry through but, as he went to follow Gerry, he stopped abruptly. "Hang on a minute, Gerry, I've just remembered something." Deep in thought, Ben wandered back towards where I still sat on the edge of the bed. Gerry followed him. "Yesterday, when Sarah wanted to ring her mother, you said something about a phone and then gave her yours to use. I think you said something about not using that other phone. What was that about? What phone didn't you want her to use?"

"As we ran out of the house, I managed to liberate a woman's handbag from the office area. Later, we found a phone in it. Presumably, it belonged to the woman, as did that car we commandeered."

"When you rang me, I didn't recognise the phone number that came up. Did you use that phone to ring me?" Ben asked.

"Yes, we found it wasn't PIN locked and, as it was the only phone we had, that's what Sarah used to call you."

"Where is that phone now?" Gerry asked, suddenly taking an excited interest in the conversation.

I smacked my forehead. Of course, why hadn't I thought of it? That phone can tell us who the woman was and the numbers called also might tell us who her associates are. Off the bed in one movement and over to the wardrobe in two strides, I dragged the tote bag from the bottom of the cupboard. A quick rummage in the bag, and I handed over the fluorescent pink phone to Gerry. My mention of the car we stole brought something to mind. "Did you get anything useful from a registration check on that car we left in the supermarket carpark?"

Gerry considered my question for a moment before answering. "Why would you think we did that?" I gave him an 'aw, come on' look and heard Ben chuckle. "Well, yes, we did check the registration. It is registered to some company or corporation of some sort. I have people digging into the registered owner to see if that sheds any light on the abductors' identities. …And before you ask, they're also looking for any other vehicles with the same registered owner." He walked away a couple of paces signifying I had all the answer I was going to get. I watched him attempting to key something into the phone. Then he swore softly before speaking to Ben and me. "Bloody thing must be flat."

"Geez, I forgot…" I spluttered as I rummaged in the bag once more. "I removed the battery after I spoke to Ben." Gerry was less than pleased. Ben thought it hilarious. With the phone – battery installed – safely in their possession, the two coppers retreated to Ben's room. Alone at last, I sat in one of the comfortable chairs for a few minutes just soaking up the solitude and the silence. I shouldn't have closed my eyes. I dozed off.

A noise brought me back to the real world. Quiet but intrusive, it had me on high alert instantly. I kept my eyes closed and feigned sleep as soft footfalls on the carpet drew nearer. Was that someone's breath I felt? Maybe not, but whoever it was had stopped very close to me. Time to react … I flipped myself out of the chair and into a crouch down beside it on the opposite side from which the sound had approached. A weapon would be handy about now. Something was not right. No further sounds came from the other side of the chair. Whoever it was hadn't moved since my acrobatic exit from the chair. Then I heard him.

"Sonny, Sonny what are you doing? Are you all right?"

"Christ, Ben, you just about scared the bejesus out of me. What are you doing sneaking about like that?"

"I didn't want to wake you if you were asleep … which it seems you were, and I did. Anyway, that aside, the reason I wanted to see if you were awake was to tell you the others want to have a look at that track through the patch of bush between here and the festival field. Do you want to come with us?"

A glance at the time told me I seemed to have lost about two hours since lunch. I wasn't just dozing, I had been asleep … and my neck confirmed it. Having spent so long with my head back at such an angle in the chair resulted in a stiff and sore neck. "Of course I'm going to look at the track with you," I snarled. My neck wasn't the only thing that was sore. I had a headache to go with it. "What about Sarah, is she coming?"

"She's still asleep…" I interrupted Ben to say I should stay to keep an eye on Sarah, but he cut me off. "Gerry has organised a female officer to stay with Sarah. Get your boots on if you are coming. The others are waiting to go."

We headed off to the track with me trailing a short way behind as I struggled to work my stiff body up to full mobility again. Neil called out, making me hurry to catch up to the others. "As we go, point out anything you noticed that night, or anything that you think might be important.

Don't worry about whether you think it might be insignificant or what assumptions you made about it," Neil instructed me.

Ben must have seen my hackles rise … I certainly felt them. "He's gone into 'work mode', just ignore him. Next thing you know, he'll be telling me to mind where I put my feet and to avoid contaminating the crime scene," Ben said. "Neil forgets he is not the only one who knows a bit about investigating a crime scene." I bit my tongue and smiled sweetly at Neil. I think I smiled; might have been a grimace. …But, I knew if he continued to treat me like some vacuous lookee-loo member of the public, I was likely to spit venom in his direction.

As I strode off down the track ahead of the others, out the corner of my eye, I saw what I thought was Ben sending Neil a signal. If that's what it was, it worked. Everyone was quiet and Neil refrained from any further comments to ruffle my feathers. Like a tour guide in full swing, I gave them commentary as we went: there's a shack in there; the woman living there grows vegetables and does crafty things … An old fellow lives in that shack you can just make out back there in the scrub. He's the one who saw a woman being bundled into the van. I think it was Olivia. …Just up here a bit is the clearing where I found tyre tracks under the leaf litter.

While we strode along, I included what I considered unimportant information, such as where patches of moonlight penetrated the canopy lighting the track and where there was no light and I needed to use my torch, where I crossed to the other side of the road after hearing noises in the bushes, and so on. Then I stopped abruptly. Ben bumped into me but the others avoided crashing into each other. "What's up … why did you stop?" Ben asked as he and the others looked around. Bewildered by the fact that nothing significant was obvious, they gathered around me as they swivelled their heads in all directions looking for whatever brought us to standstill.

"This is the last bit of the track I remember seeing that night – I think. Yes, see up there; there's a small clearing off on the left hand side of the track. It was dark – pitch black -- along here but I think there was a darker shape up there a bit further. I remember wondering if it was a van parked there. The others started to walk off to investigate the clearing I indicated, but I remained in the same spot and kept talking. They took only a few steps before my words took effect and they returned.

"I think this is where I was attacked. We struggled and I remember that we ended up off the side of the road over there. Then I was struck on the head and everything went black." I wandered over to the edge of the track, paying careful attention to where I placed my feet. There was nothing obvious until I reached the very edge of the track's hard surface.

While there was nothing immediately in front of me, about a metre or so further along there was evidence suggesting something happened there. I indicated the place. Gerry and Ben surveyed the ground as they walked up to that area.

Neil had his phone out and photographed the area from every imaginable angle before any of us stepped off the track and onto its verge. The narrow sparsely grassed verge gave way to a bare earth shoulder that wasn't quite big enough to be a small clearing. Although recently muddy, it was now dry, but it probably would dampen again in tonight's dew. The three men seemed to be silently checking with each other that it was okay to move beyond the verge. Such niceties held no interest for me. I could see what looked like drag marks in the ground.

I stepped across the verge and onto the dirt. Careful to avoid placing my feet where they might damage any vital evidence, I circumnavigated the area. A struggle happened here. My gut was sure that's what the marks were from and it did a good job of convincing me as well. I looked up to see that the other three were now at various points around the periphery of the patch of soil in question.

Something caught my eye. It made me gasp. I looked around for a stick or dead branch of some sort. I found what I wanted in the undergrowth behind me: part of a branch as thick as my thumb and about a metre and a half long. When I turned back to the marks in the ground, Ben was standing beside me. He cautioned about disturbing the evidence. I ignored him. With the aid of my newly found tool, I carefully lifted and scraped away an area of leaf litter.

"Ah hah," I exclaimed a little too loudly. "I'll bet my socks that's a blood stain. Any takers…?"

Ben giggled. "No one is going to bet when they know they're on a hiding to nothing. I'd reckon that's blood… and I wager forensics will prove it's yours. So, it looks to me like this is where they clobbered you." There was murmured agreement from the other two, although Gerry already had his phone pressed to his ear. I watched him fish around in his trouser pocket with his free hand as he spoke on the phone.

His phone call ended and with his search successful, Gerry triumphantly brandished in the air a length of something brightly coloured. It was twine – or thin rope, depending on your point of view – consisting of red, blue and yellow strands twisted together with the more usual neutral coloured ones. After finding an appropriate stick, he pushed it into the grassy verge in front of our site and tied the coloured string to it. As he stepped back onto the track to admire his handiwork he said, "I picked that up off the squad room floor as I was leaving yesterday. I couldn't throw it away. I just knew it would come in handy." We all had a laugh at his comment, but knew it wasn't because of the comment. Somehow, finding this site had lifted all our spirits in a way that wasn't easy to define.

Now, with the attack site marked, Ben started towards the clearing up ahead. Neil fell into step beside him. I trailed along a couple of paces behind them. Gerry remained at the spot he marked as the attack site. He was talking on his phone and waving his arms in the air giving directions to somebody who couldn't see him. A few moments later, he joined us as we stood along the edge of the track studying the ground in the clearing.

Although a new layer of leaf litter had fallen, evidence of a vehicle having been there remained obvious. The tyre marks and crushed leaves and twigs were visible through the thin new covering. We all stood there, lined up along the track like silent sentinels. I decided to break the silence. "It's obvious a vehicle was here, but there is nothing to indicate why it was here, or that it had anything to do with the abductions… although why anyone would want to bring a vehicle along this track defeats me."

As I finished speaking, the sound of an approaching vehicle drew our attention away from the clearing. Gerry strode off back towards the attack site. He gestured to the vehicle to come to where he indicated. The driver eased the vehicle along the track, trashing low branches protruding over the track. Sometime in the future, someone would have a hard time polishing those scratches off the hood of the car.

We watched the car pull up adjacent to Gerry's marker before we ambled back to see what was happening. It only took us a few paces before we realised Gerry's forensic team had arrived. Three people emerged from the vehicle and went around behind it. By the time we joined them, the forensic officers were climbing into their disposable suits. Gerry waved his arms around as he gave his crew orders about what he wanted done. We stood off to one side and watched until the pantomime finished and Gerry walked over to join us. Then, as if by some unspoken unanimous agreement, we all turned and continued along the track towards the festival field.

I hadn't seen this part of the track at close range before, not having gotten this far before being clobbered and bundled into a van. As we neared the field, clear tyre ruts scored the surface of the track. The bush seemed thinner here. At the end of the track, where it opened onto the field, more moisture was able to penetrate the first ten metres or so of the track… enough moisture for quite clear tyre tracks. More than one vehicle had come this way – or, perhaps more correctly, one vehicle had used the track more than once. Neil's phone came into service again and he photographed the tyre marks. Gerry spoke on his phone. It was a safe assumption he was directing his forensic team to move to this area when they finished their current task.

Our patrol of the festival field produced nothing of interest apart from a couple of used syringes. As we walked beside the bush on our way back to the start of the track, I noticed a couple of narrow, indistinct pathways leading off into the scrub. Somewhere between seeing the first one and the second path, I remembered what the two young lads I encountered here told me about using one of those paths. I decided to take a walk down the second path to satisfy some strange curiosity triggered by the memory of that conversation.

It was narrow -- only a footpath – and quite overgrown by the surrounding scrub. I heard crunching behind me and turned sharply to find Ben only a couple of paces further back. "Tell me please; why are we battling our way along this path?" he asked.

"Remember, I told you about the two lads who saw a van parked along the track. One of those lads was the local detective's son." I saw Ben's face light up as he recalled our conversation and he nodded. "They talked about using a track something like this one as a shortcut and then hiding in here. I wanted to see where this one led and what it was like once you were on it." After a few more metres, the overhanging branches disappeared and walking became easier. A more open area became apparent some distance ahead. We strode on.

"Well, look at that," Ben exclaimed as we came to the end of the path. "I think we made the acquaintance of this small clearing earlier this afternoon." At its end, the path opened into the clearing where a vehicle had parked.

"Should we turn around and go back?" I asked. "The others might be concerned about us suddenly disappearing like we did."

"Nah, they'll assume we are capable of looking after ourselves," Ben replied, but he took out his phone and I heard him tell someone that we would meet them back on track. Rather than sully the evidence in the clearing, we fought our way through the undergrowth around the clearing to emerge further along the track. Ben led the way back towards the field end of the track to join the others.

When we reached the clearing again, Ben showed Gerry and Neil the path we took from the field. I told them of my conversation with the two lads, and made sure Gerry knew the identity of 'busted ankle,' the lad with the detective father. While that happened, the forensic team arrived at the clearing and started doing their thing. We left them to it and started back for the motel.

An agitated Sarah met us in the corridor. She heard us coming and bolted out of her room to greet us with a barrage of questions, her tone both angry and accusatory: where had we been ... why hadn't we taken her ... what had I done about booking her flight home ... why was she being kept in the dark...?

Gerry seemed to have heard nothing of Sarah's tirade and simply asked, "Anyone feel like a coffee?" Everyone was enthusiastic except Sarah who, nevertheless, chose to join us as we gathered in Ben's room. By the time the usual fuss and bother about finding somewhere to sit was over, coffee arrived and Sarah started to get answers to some of her questions. Ben tried placating her by explain that she wasn't being kept in the dark, and that we all thought sleep was more important for her at this time. It didn't have much effect. Neil was more direct.

It was obvious he was unimpressed with Sarah's prima donna performance and his reply made that clear. "You will not be flying anywhere until such time as our investigation has reached a point where your departure will not be detrimental to the ongoing investigation. As for being kept in the dark, that's rubbish. We need you fit and rested for what we have to do tomorrow." Everyone else in the room, apart from the two directly involved in the conversation, shuffled uncomfortably as Neil said his piece.

He had more success than Ben. Sarah looked crestfallen and gnawed her lower lip as Neil snarled at her. When he finished speaking, she looked around the room and apologised for her behaviour. That his words had been a strategic ploy and not malicious was obvious the minute Sarah finished apologising. "Right, what's the hold up? Who is pouring the coffee? Come on, we could all die of thirst at this rate," he said.

We were the only ones in the restaurant that night. "Gerry, do they know about the staff bloke your mob carted away?" I asked once everyone had ordered drinks.

"Oh, Gary... I had forgotten about him. No, I doubt they know what happened. My men took him quietly out the back. There didn't seem to be anyone around at the time and nobody felt it necessary to inform management. They probably are a bit curious about why he hasn't showed up for work without notifying them."

Talk drifted off onto past cases the men had investigated. Sarah was interested and asked questions. I just wanted to shut the door for a while on cases and investigations. I tuned out and found myself assessing the two brothers sitting side by side opposite me. Ben and Neil were not quite mirror images.

Both stood over 190cm tall, were taut and fit. Apart from that similarity, they reminded me of positive and negative of the same image. Neil's hair, although in the same style as Ben's, was a good bit darker, and Ben's incredible blue eyes were replaced by a dark, dark brown pair. Both men sported good tans, but Neil's natural complexion was slightly darker than Ben's. A firm jaw and square chin were common to both, and both faces consisted of lots of planes and angles. If they were out of sight when I heard one of them laugh, I wouldn't be able to tell which one. I had heard the same rumbling chuckle come from both of them on occasion. Sometime in the past, I learned that Ben was the elder brother by about three years, but the age difference wasn't obvious. Although I had known Neil for only a matter of hours, and both men seemed much alike, I thought Ben had the nicer nature. I found myself wondering about what sort of parents it took to produce such good-looking sons.

Someone calling my name brought me back from my fanciful reverie. I blinked a couple of times and swung my eyes around the table, bringing them to rest on Gerry. "We were discussing plans for tomorrow. Are you going to be joining us?" Of course I was I assured him… although I had no idea what he was talking about. I glanced at Ben. He was trying hard not to laugh. Damn the man; he can read me like a book.

After dinner, we all returned to our respective rooms. Gerry scheduled female officers to watch over Sarah. I wondered briefly about the lack of anyone watching over me and, for a moment, felt relieved. Then I heard as part of someone else's conversation that Ben would be 'keeping an eye' on me. My relief disappeared. How Ben intended to do that made me nervous. I had awoken on other occasions to find Ben at rather close quarters 'watching over me'. However, I was alone in my room when I turned off the light. My afternoon nap did nothing to delay the onset of sleep.

CHAPTER 17

It was still dark when I awoke to the aroma of coffee this morning. The days were shortening as we moved towards winter and the chain of low hills that Minden Hill was part of helped delay sunrise even further. After a couple of stretches, I groaned and levered myself out of bed to go and investigate the source of the coffee that now dominated my thinking. I am a morning person, but coffee does help get the system going. On my way to the bathroom, I stopped dead in my tracks. My eyes focused on the dishevelled spare single bed on the other side of the room. An involuntary, "What the …?" received no response from the empty room.

Now appropriately dressed, I marched towards the interconnecting door, the coffee aroma increasingly strong at every step. As I reached for the doorknob, the door opened and a grinning Ben confronted me. "I thought I heard you up and about. Coffee's ready if you are interested." I leant to one side and looked around him. A small capsule-type coffee machine sat on what was intended as a desk. Two mugs waited beside it.

"Where did that come from?" I asked, temporarily forgetting the matter of the rumpled bed.

"While some people snoozed yesterday afternoon, I decided it worked better if we could make our own coffee whenever the urge arose. I slipped down the High Street and picked this up on sale. So, shall I pour yours now?"

"Not so quick, Sunshine, what about the spare bed in my room?"

"What's wrong with it?" So nonchalantly asked, and he didn't even bother to look up from fiddling with the coffee.

"It's been slept in, that's what is wrong with it. Who and why are the questions." I was barking a tad too loudly – and I knew it – but I was none too happy about what I thought happened last night. Like I said, I am a morning person and can do almost anything the moment I'm out of bed… but I am not big on being sociable while I'm about it. It takes about an hour or so for civility to kick in.

"Geez, you are no fun first thing in the morning. Who do you think slept in it and why do you think that occurred?" The rest of that conversation is best left unrecorded, but it appears Ben has allocated himself a 'watching brief' over me to prevent my disappearing again.

We sat and sipped our coffee in silence. It worked its miracles and I felt the real Sonny replacing the shrew who had entered the room in search of coffee. There were things I wanted to ask Ben about, but I wasn't sure I would get any answers. I vacantly gazed at Ben across the top of my mug as I considered how to initiate that conversation. He looked up and saw me watching him. There was that grin again.

"I thought the coffee might help bring you to life ...*also* ... I thought you might want to know what was planned for today, and was what you agreed to be involved in last night..."

See, I told you he reads my mind. That was the main thing I wanted to ask him about.

"...A-n-d, if I may continue, I thought you might want to know what happened last night."

"Last night...? Something happened last night ... when ... what happened?" He now had my undivided attention.

"After we all called it a night, Neil went for a bit of a walk around the place. As he came back to let himself in the security gate, he saw someone in that big old Camphor Laurel tree that hangs over part of the carpark. He decided to wait and watch. The person dropped into the carpark and entered the motel through the back door. Neil let himself in and interrupted the bloke trying to enter Neil's room ... claimed he was the motel's handyman. It seems the bloke didn't know it was Neil's room, and claimed the room's *female* occupant reported a leaking tap."

"He was trying to break into a *woman's* room on a pretty weak pretext... what happened next?"

"Ah well, Gerry was still up and heard voices in the corridor. He took charge of the situation and the cells had another occupant last night."

"Whose room was this bloke looking for?"

"Probably yours... or maybe Sarah's ... but it is irrelevant now. He won't be coming back any time soon. I think Neil's men have taken over 'looking after' him."

"It seems that somehow he had enough information to come to the right part of the motel, but didn't know which room. ...Someone inside feeding information, do you think?"

"Dunno ... but I think Neil's men might be asking a similar question. Anyway, nothing more to do about that for the moment. Now, do you want to know about today's plans that you agreed to participate in?"

I tried to be offhand about my ignorance of the situation. "Doesn't matter what it is, if it has anything to do with my case or my abduction,

I'm up for it."

"So, you don't need me to tell you about it then?"

The shrew hadn't completely disappeared. "Oh, for God's sake, what is the plan – knowing what, when and where might prove useful."

Neil's men believe they located the property where we were held. No one has gone in to investigate yet. That's our mission for today. It seems the surrounding bushland will receive attention as well – for evidence of 'holes' dug there any time in the recent past. I am keen to return for a look around under more favourable conditions than when we left, but I am worried about the effect if might have on Sarah – particularly if they do find evidence of digging in the bush. "Is Sarah involved in today's expedition?"

"Yeah, we were mindful of your concerns about her being involved, but she insisted she needs to be involved. I think she sees it as an opportunity to put the memories to rest – something akin to closure for her." I shrugged. She might be right. I hoped so for everyone's' sakes.

It was about then that I realised I hadn't completed my normal morning ablutions routine or dressed for the day. Now that I know what today's plan is, I need to rethink my outfit. …And I need to think about doing some laundry when we get back here this evening. Jeans and sturdy boots predominated around the table at breakfast.

After a quick breakfast and an even quicker trip to our rooms to gather any essential gear, we gathered in the carpark. Sarah would travel with Neil and Gerry in Gerry's vehicle, while Ben and I travelled in Neil's car. Neil's car replaced Ben's hire car because it was fitted with a radio and would allow us to keep in contact with the others. It wasn't yet eight o'clock when our short cavalcade left the motel. As we drove out of Minden Hill, I idly wondered how the trip would pan out. It took Sarah and me all day to drive from our prison to Rookwood. Granted, we didn't know where we were going, but it occurred to me that today's expedition was likely to involve more than one day. It was as we reached the first of the farmlands that I shared this thinking with Ben.

"You're right. I think everyone is of the opinion that it will take two or three days, depending on what we find when we get there. I think Neil and Gerry have organised at least one night's accommodation somewhere in the vicinity of where we will be working."

"That would have been good to know before we left. An overnight bag would be useful."

Soon, we turned off and headed down an unfamiliar road. It wound its way through rural areas and past small towns and villages that were new to me. About two hours after we left the motel, the other car pulled into a service station with a diner. We followed Gerry's car and parked alongside a couple of semi-trailers in a gravelled area to one side of the building. It was a short stop, just long enough for a coffee. We hadn't travelled too far after our coffee stop before a vague familiarity with the country flashing past my window caught my attention. I sat upright and stared at the road junction ahead. That building on the corner of the junction somehow looked familiar.

We turned right at the tee junction. I stared at the building as we passed. It was that quaint looking craft and second-hand store that caught my attention on our trip back to Minden Hill. My mind went into overdrive. How long after we fled the house was it when I saw that store? As I tried to replay that journey in my mind, a small town appeared in the distance. Yes, I remember this bit of the road – and this town. I felt my pulse step up a notch as I realised we were not far from the turn-off to the house.

The radio crackled and Ben responded. An unknown voice announced that the area seemed deserted. As the call ended, we turned off the sealed road and followed Gerry's vehicle along the winding track. It didn't seem as rough as the last time I travelled it… maybe because this time we travelled slowly and carefully. Gerry's vehicle slowed to a crawl and Ben did likewise as we came to an area of loose gravel. I caught my breath; looming up in front of us was that house. I wondered how Sarah felt at seeing it again.

Two men emerged from the scrub as our two cars pulled up. It occurred to me that Ben had parked in the same spot as where the car we commandeered had been. Neil and Gerry were out of their car and Neil held the rear door open for Sarah to alight. She swung her legs out and then stopped. She just sat there gazing at the main building. Neil stepped around, took her by the arm and eased her out of the car. I think I know what she was feeling. Ben jumped out of our vehicle as soon as it was stationary. Something seemed to hold me back. I took my time unbuckling the seat belt and exiting the vehicle.

Sarah stood beside Gerry's vehicle. Neil still held her arm. I rush over to her. "Are you okay? Would you rather stay in the car? I will stay with you if you want me to."

She shook off Neil and pulled herself up to her full height. "No, I want to do this." Then, with a straight back and determined strides, she marched toward the front door where the three coppers waited. I walked beside her and nodded in reply to the enquiring looks from Ben and Gerry. Yes, I think Sarah will handle it okay – but I will stick close to her.

Those two men who miraculously emerged from the bush when we arrived disappeared again. I was informed they were Neil's officers and would remain outside. Whether the front door was locked when we arrived or not remained a mystery, but it now swung open with a creak when Gerry applied his shoulder to it. Gerry and Neil led the way in followed by Ben, leaving Sarah and I last to step across the threshold. Sarah gripped my hand tightly as we moved up onto the doorstep and maintained her grip as we entered the place.

The three men stopped and waited at what we knew to be the entrance to the kitchen. "Okay ladies," Neil began, "Take us on a tour of what you know about the place." We pointed out the kitchen behind them and the office across the hall from it. Then it was time to take them to the only other part of the house we knew anything about.

"This way…," was all I could manage before Sarah pushed me aside.

"I'll lead the way; it's down here," she said, and set off ahead of the rest of us who fell into line behind her. This was a good sign: Sarah forcing herself to face her demons.

Nothing stood out in my mind from our dash along this hallway. Even now, it seemed ordinary; bare brick walls and concrete floor. Up ahead, Sarah stopped suddenly and the three men concertinaed up against her. I knew instinctively what had happened. She had reached the door to our cell. Her most terrifying demon lay beyond.

I wormed my way through the pack to stand beside Sarah. Although the padlocks had disappeared, the bolt still held the door closed. As I stepped aside to let one of the men draw the bolt and open the door, I almost went over on my ankle. Something hard and lumpy lay on the floor in the darkness a little further along from the door. It rolled a bit under my foot and I yelped. Ben rushed over and put an arm around my waist to steady me. I carefully lifted my foot. Gerry shone a small torch at my feet. The discarded padlock lay open against the wall.

Why bolt the door but discard the padlock? Maybe throwing the bolt on the way out was an automatic action, while fiddling with a recalcitrant padlock wasted time escaping from the place. By now, I was sure the room beyond that door was empty. There was the familiar sound of the bolt and the door opening. That well-remembered stench greeted us, but it now seemed intensified. In an unrehearsed move, Sarah and I hung back to let the men enter the room ahead of us.

The three men coughed to clear their throats. Sarah gagged. I held a tissue firmly over my mouth and nose and fought down the bile that rose in my throat. It didn't take too much to work out that the bucket in the corner – our makeshift toilet – hadn't been emptied in some time. Of more concern was the bloated and decomposing corpse on the floor below the small window.

Sarah began retching. Neil spun her around and pushed her out of the room. I heard them clattering along the hallway as he rushed her outside. Although that familiar iron small associated with blood remained, a cocktail of odours almost completely smothered it. Ben asked with his eyes and a slight flick of his head whether I was up to taking a closer look at the corpse. I nodded weakly and swallowed hard before convincing my feet to move. My hand pressed the tissue even more firmly against my face as I moved a couple of paces closer to the now grotesque figure on the floor. "It's the woman who lived here. The one who brought breakfast the day we escaped." I gave her nothing more than a moment before turning away. I had all I needed to know.

Gerry had his phone out and was on his way to the door. Ben and I followed. As we trailed Gerry down the hall, we heard his side of a phone call: "Mac, it's Gerry … if your forensic boys are coming, they will need a body bag … A couple of extra blokes would be good if you can spare them … no, just for a bit of a tramp in the woods…"

We found Sarah sitting on the doorstep and Neil leaning against the wall beside the entrance. Sarah looked up as we arrived and fixed her eyes on me. "Did we do that? Did we kill her?" she asked. Her face contorted with anguish was pale but her eyes were steady.

"No, Sarah, we did not. Think about …" Gerry interrupted before I could continue.

"…You sure about that?" he snarled.

"Quite sure…" I turned my attention back to Sarah and continued with what I intended to say before the interruption. "Think about what happened that morning, and where it happened. The woman …"

"Rosie…"

"What…?"

"Her name was Rosie – or so Olivia told me."

"Okay … *Rosie* moved about after we left. Think about where she is now and where she was when we left her." I watched Sarah's brow furrow as she dredged up the memory of that morning. When she looked back up at me, she was more relaxed. No one spoke for a few moments.

Ben broke the silence. "Time is getting away from us. Perhaps we should make a start on checking out the rest of the house."

"You're right," Gerry agreed. "We should get as much as possible done before Mac's boys arrive. It will save everyone time in the long run if we do a preliminary run through the place now." There was no argument. Neil levered himself off the wall and mounted the single step in readiness to move inside. Sarah remained seated on the doorstep.

I was torn; I should stay with Sarah, but I wanted to see the rest of the house. Duty overrode desire. "I'll stay with Sarah while you look around."

Sarah sprang to her feet almost knocking me over. "No, I want to see what this place is really like. I'm coming with you." …And then in a quieter more unsure voice, "But we're not going back to that room are we?" Reassured by all the shaking of heads around her, she moved to join the rest of us just inside the doorway.

"Okay, we start from here," Gerry announced. "Note anything that looks wrong, unusual, or catches your eye for any other reason. Sonny, lead off and tell us what you know."

We moved to the office doorway. Ben and Gerry followed me in. The other two remained in the doorway but craned their necks to take in the whole of the room. I pointed out the key rack on the wall, where I found the tote bag, and how I started throwing everything into it before I remembered getting as far away from the place as soon as possible was our objective.

Next, we moved across the hallway to the kitchen area and Sarah took over tour guide duties. She pointed to a drinks fridge similar to those in stores selling bottled drinks. It looked old and the worse for wear. "This held bottled water – a couple of dozen bottles at least -- milk, a few bottles of wine and an unopened carton of beer." Only a few bottles of water and part of a bottle of milk remained.

Then Sarah gestured towards the newer double-door fridge and explained how she took only a few bits of food in her hurry to get out of the place. "I looked around for something to carry it all in. There were some plastic bags from a supermarket scattered on the bench over there. I went to get a couple and saw some bread in that bread bin thing at the other end of the bench, so I took the bread as well. I didn't see anything else or go any further along this room."

All of us stood and slowly surveyed the area. After a couple of seconds, Ben shared his thoughts. "I don't think this was a kitchen originally. Sometime, probably quite recently, the room was adapted for that purpose. In big houses like this, the kitchen was somewhere down the back of the house out of sight. This room – right at the front door – would be some sort of sitting room… somewhere you showed visitors into when they arrived."

"Yeah, it almost looks like a temporary arrangement," Neil added. "That line of cupboards over there isn't attached to the wall properly and there is no splashback – not even behind the sink. …And the sink has only one tap – cold water I presume. Even the tap doesn't belong in a kitchen. It's a hose cock. The sort of thing you find out in the garden with a hose attached to it." I agreed with his assessment, and drew the group's attention to the stove. I didn't know what this state's regulations required, but the way that stove was connected would never pass inspection in Queensland.

With nothing more of interest in the kitchen, we moved down to the other end of the room. It was a long room with high ceiling adorned with an intricate plaster rose that matched the fancy cornice. It was apparent that this end of the room was not in use. It lacked any real furniture, and the few bits and pieces stored there harboured a thick coating of dust. The most recent tenants found that end of the room a convenient place to discard rubbish, including a number of empty beer cartons, a few old newspapers and a mound of plastic garbage bags. A door in the far back corner of the room looked interesting. How inconsiderate of them to leave it locked.

While I rummaged through some old newspapers and Sarah peered over my shoulder, the three men held an impromptu conference about the locked door: should they force it, or call a locksmith and wait for them to deal with it? Although I only half listened to their discussion, I proposed a third option. "Why not try one of the keys?"

"You didn't pay much attention back there in the office," Neil commented. "The key rack was empty."

"Yes, I know," I said, and tried not to sound to triumphant when I added, "I took them."

"You… have… them!" Gerry exclaimed. "Where are they now?"

"In the back of Neil's car; I threw the bag containing the keys into the car before we left the motel … in case they might prove useful." Ben turned on his heel and strode out of the room. He returned soon after with the tote bag.

While Ben was away, Neil asked, "Is there likely to be a key for that front door amongst them?" I remember wondering how we got in, but I assumed it was unlocked. Neil's question suggests that was not the case.

After considering the question for a moment, I answered confidently, "No. The lock on the front door is a big old-fashioned thing that requires a large key. There was nothing like that on the rack."

Ben handed me the tote bag and I ferreted out all the keys I had so unceremoniously dumped into it. There were many, but only a few looked promising. A trial and error process began. As is often the case, it was the last one they tried that opened the door. Although unlocked, the door refused to budge. It appeared grown to the doorjamb. A bit of pushing and shoving -- accompanied by much grunting – by the two burly brothers finally worked it loose. With one final heave, the door swung open, disturbing a cloud of dust.

When the dust settled again, and we all stopped coughing and spluttering, we moved to the doorway and peered down what appeared to be a long dark corridor. Ben's comments on the probable original use of the room we were in came floating back to me. It made sense that, if originally used for entertaining visitors, staff serving refreshments here needed to come and go unobtrusively. I thought the kitchen probably lay at the end of this corridor. In the house's glory days, staff would use this corridor rather than be seen traipsing through the main part of the house with their loaded trays.

Why are we standing here peering into the gloom? We need to investigate this corridor just as we do any other part of the house. I stepped into the corridor and ran my left hand over an area of the wall. Nothing. I tried the other side of the corridor, and found what I wanted. For a moment after I flicked the switch, nothing happened. A couple of heartbeats later, two low wattage globes offered a dim view of what lay ahead of us. I strode off down the corridor, assuming the rest of the group would fall in behind me. After a few paces, I stopped in front of a door set in the internal wall on my left.

The door was unlocked. I opened it and walked in… and realised I was alone. I poked my head out and looked down the corridor. Nobody had moved to join me. "If any of you are thinking of venturing along here, I suggest you bring all those keys in case we come across other doors that are not quite so as accommodating as this one." Almost immediately, I heard footsteps echoing along the corridor.

A couple of bits of old furniture remained in this room, but it was obvious it hadn't been in use for quite some time. After a quick look around, we were off down the corridor again. We passed an alcove containing a staircase leading up to the next floor. With the intention of coming back to the staircase, we continued our exploration of the corridor. The next door we came to, also unlocked, opened into what I thought might be a butler's pantry. Again, no sign this small room was in use in recent times. A short distance beyond the butler's pantry, the corridor ended at a wall with a double door at its centre. This door let us into the original kitchen. While some modifications had occurred in the previous few decades, nothing had happened in this room for many years.

Satisfied that the corridor, and the rooms along it had nothing to do with the recent tenants, we retraced our steps to the alcove and it staircase. In the house's long history since its construction, this staircase had seen plenty of use. Although it still displayed much of the polish lavished on it over the years, the worn stair treads were testimony to the many feet that had used it. A tentative test of the first few treads suggested the staircase remained sound. Ben chose to lead the way up, with me at his heels.

Although I had located a light switch in the alcove, it failed to produce any light. The only thing I had on me was a small penlight torch in my jacket pocket, but it provided enough light to ensure we arrived safely on the next floor.

CHAPTER 18

Yet another corridor awaited us. It was long and at least twice as wide as the previous one we explored. I shone my torch along both walls of the corridor. A number of doors opened off both sides of it. With the light of my small torch, I searched the walls near where we stood and located a light switch. The result was dim but welcome. I counted four doors off the left side of the corridor, and six off the opposite wall.

Ben walked to the first door on the left while Gerry went to the one on the opposite side of the corridor. Both doors were locked. I moved over to Ben and shone my torch on the lock to get an idea of what its key might look like. No need to ask who had the collection of keys, I heard them jangling behind me. Sarah held out a small ancient looking cardboard box towards us. It now held all the keys. I shone my torch on the keys while Ben rifled through them in search of ones that matched the lock. After getting down on his knees to take a closer look at the lock on his door, Gerry came over and conducted his own rummage through the keys.

I followed Ben into the first of the rooms on the left, the others preferring to accompany Gerry on his investigation of the rooms down the right hand side of the corridor. Ben and I exchanged a look. This room was in use – or had been until recently. It was a woman's bedroom, probably that of the woman -- Rosie -- now lying dead down below. The solidly built timber wardrobe in one corner still contained women's clothes, and the bits and pieces on the matching dressing table screamed female occupant.

Another door was in the wall opposite where we entered the room. This required no key so, after a good look through everything in the bedroom, we opened this second door and exited into yet another corridor. This corridor, running the length of the floor, had windows set in at regular intervals along what was an external wall of the building. A couple of old squatter's chairs that had seen better days were the only furniture in that space. After a brief look out through a grimy window, we came back to the next door along from the woman's bedroom. It wasn't fitted with a lock, so we went in. A bathroom, dingy and desperately in need of updating to the current century, it was a depressing sight. So grimy and horrible looking were all the fittings and fixtures, I avoided touching anything.

It comprised an old chipped claw-footed bathtub with a rubber hand-held shower gadget attached to one of its taps. A doorway, with no door, led through to a toilet. I didn't feel inclined to enter and risk whatever bacteria might lurk in that small cubicle. We both avoiding touching anything, Ben reported that the medicine chest above the old-fashioned hand basin contained 'a woman's stuff'.

The next two doors opened into a bedroom. Although nothing remained in the wardrobes, odd bits of kit left lying around indicated their recent occupants were males. Another bathroom lay beyond the next door along the corridor and, again, although little evidence remained, what they left behind indicated this was the men's bathroom. That left only one more door along this corridor.

Unlocked like the others but unlike the others, plenty of evidence remained in this room. Ben opened the door. We strode in and stopped dead. This room's purpose was obvious. It had a particular smell and I felt my nose wrinkle in response… not big on washing bed linen this lot. "Play Room…," Ben commented as he looked around the room.

"What…?" I wasn't sure I heard correctly or that I was meant to hear.

"Remember those 'terrible things' that woman… Olivia was it … told Sarah they did to the women they held here. This is where it happened. This was their 'play room'." Oh yes, that was the smell that hung in the room. A couple of boxes of condom, their contents splayed out around them, were on the floor beside a grubby mattress that also lay directly on the floor. Bits of rope hung from a railing running along the wall behind the mattress. I could see the end of the handles of a couple of tools on the floor on the other side of the mattress (possibly pairs of pliers), along with a couple of empty wine bottles and a broom handle. I didn't need to investigate that room any further. I took myself back out to the corridor and Ben followed me out a minute or so later. My stomach had become unsettled. I had a quiet mental word with myself about it as I walked to the end of the corridor.

Well, the corridor didn't end. Instead, it offered two options: turn the corner around that last room and follow a narrow passage back to that first wide corridor we encountered on this floor … or continue straight ahead and down a flight of stairs to the ground floor again. Ben and I were about to descend the stairs when the rest of the group came along the narrow passage to join us. We delayed our descent.

Gerry reported their findings. "All locked and not in use for a long time: five bedrooms and one bathroom, and nothing much in the way of furniture in any of them.”

"Plenty of dust and cobwebs everywhere,” Sarah added.

Neil shrugged at his brother and commented, “Long undisturbed…”

"Hmm, it seems they used only the rooms they needed. All the rooms along this corridor were unlocked and in use until recently.” I was pleased Ben didn’t go on to mention the ‘play room’ in front of Sarah.

“…Seems they didn’t bother unlocking any doors they didn’t need to access,” Neil added. “Along that central corridor, all the doors to the rooms inspected were locked.”

Any further discussion ended when the sound of people downstairs drifted up the stairwell. I saw Sarah tense at the sound of the voices. I put my arm around her and held her tight. “That will be Mac’s boys,” Gerry said. “I thought they would be here sooner than this. We better go and tell them what we’ve found.” We all started down the stairs.

"I don’t know where these stairs lead,” I thought aloud as I stood on the top step.

"What do you mean?” Neil demanded.

"Well, I mean I don’t know where they come out on the ground floor. We didn’t see any staircases anywhere else we’ve been today other than the one off that back corridor that took us up to the top floor.”

Ben and Neil exchanged a surprised look. “It seems we still have surprises ahead of us,” Ben quipped. With that thought in mind, we all quickened our pace and soon found ourselves on the ground floor and in a small room that seemed to serve no other purpose than to provide access to the staircase.

"Argh, this is all starting to wear a bit thin,” Neil growled. “It’s become a bit like a treasure hunt: ‘where to next?’. How do we get out of this room... and if we find a way out, where will we end up?”

"The ‘how’ is easy – I think,” Gerry said as he walked towards a door in the wall behind the staircase. “We will find out where it leads when we are on the other side of this door.” He tried the door and it opened easily and without as much as a squeak.

Another gloomy passage way led off to who knows where. I watched the others head off along the passage for a while to see where they went. I did not intend following them – not yet anyway. I walked back into the room and fought to stifle a scream when I caught sight of someone sitting on the bottom step. I heard the deep rumbling chuckle. “What the hell do you think you’re doing?” I snapped.

"Probably the same as you,” Ben replied. “I want to have a better look at this room.”

"Yeah, I want to look at those marks on the floor, and on that wall over there. It's clear that the recent tenants used this staircase to access their bedrooms. If they used the other stairs, we wouldn't have encountered so many locked doors."

None of the others came rushing back, so we assumed they weren't worried about us and they safely negotiated the maze to find their way out to the front of the house. After crawling around on our hands and knees inspecting the marks on the floor, we turned our attention to the marks on the wall. None of it was in anyway enlightening.

"It looks as though something was dragged across the floor and it banged into the wall in the process. What's your take on it?" I asked Ben.

"I agree. It's a pity the marks aren't a bit more indicative of what it was. All we have is that something at some time made these marks… not very helpful and probably not significant in the overall scale of things."

"Yeah, it could have happened when they took furniture up to the bedrooms… or it might be from decades ago and made by other long gone tenants. I think I've seen enough. I'm going to find the others." Ben followed me to the door and out into what turned out to be a short passage – with yet another door at the end of it.

The door opened easily and we found ourselves out in the main entrance hallway. Noises came from the direction of our cell and I saw the door was open. Mac's forensic people had arrived. I felt an overwhelming need for fresh air. It outweighed any desire to locate the rest of our group but, when I reached the front door, I saw them perched on some rocks under a tree over near where we parked our cars. I stood on the doorstep and sucked in a few lungsful of fresh air.

Warm sun and fresh air seemed to breathe life back into me after what I found to be a depressing tour of the house. I shook my head to clear my mind. I don't know why the place affected me that way, but it certainly had an effect. I think Ben might be experiencing a similar frame of mind as he remained on the doorstep with me and hadn't made any move to join the others. After a few moments, I felt revitalised enough to join the others and indicated to Ben with a jerk of my head that's where I was going. We stepped down from the doorstep together.

As we strolled over to join them, Gerry called out, "What took you so long? Lunch is waiting. Mac's blokes brought food and coffee. At least, I think there's still some coffee."

The rolls were fresh, crusty and good, the coffee barely lukewarm. They were a decidedly subdued group. I raised an eyebrow at Ben to see if he noticed it as well. He indicated he had, and gently tried initiating conversation.

"I know you lot probably have debriefed already on our tour of inspection, but how about sharing your thoughts with us now we're here?"

"Not much to tell," Neil said without shifting his gaze from some point in the distance.

Gerry nodded. "Yeah, it wasn't particularly informative. As these two told us, it appears there were three of them living here – two men, one woman – and they only occupied the few rooms they needed. At this stage, it appears the men did away with the woman and then took off out of here."

"I've got my people chasing up details of current ownership of the place and any recent rentals, Neil informed us. "Has there been any interest in that sedan these two escaped in," he asked Gerry whose men still monitored the vehicle in the supermarket carpark.

"No, and it doesn't look like there will be. This morning I told them to take it to the Police compound. Now the men from here have decamped and are running scared, they won't be interested in that car."

Conversation lapsed again. I was only half-attentive anyway. My mind was dealing with its own questions about the house. After a couple of minutes of silence, I decided to voice some of my thoughts. "I'm intrigued by the layout of that house… all those passageways. I understand that away back when, the owners probably wanted servants to remain invisible and passageways kept them out of the main part of the house, but something about this layout doesn't make sense."

"Hmm, I know what you're saying," Ben agreed. "There's evidence of quite a few renovations, or modifications if you like. Perhaps subsequent owners attempted to sort it out and make the place more suited to their needs."

"There's still a big area of the house we didn't see," I suggested.

"Eh… where…? We tramped all through the place." Gerry looked bewildered and shook his head as he spoke.

"There's a fair area on the ground floor we didn't go into. I accept that the recent tenants probably didn't go in there either but, if we are to claim we have investigated the house, someone should inspect those other areas as well." I don't know why I felt it necessary to hammer the point but my gut told me it was important … and that it was about something more than just knowing we did a thorough job. There didn't appear to be any support for my suggestion, so I changed the topic. "…So, now that the forensic people are here, what's our next move? What do we do for the rest of the day?"

"I think we should go into the woods," Gerry replied.

"What, all of us or just you two?" Neil asked. "We wouldn't want to spoil your fun by all of us tagging along." Neil's feeble attempt at injecting humour into the mix met with some success. There were giggles all round… with the exception of Gerry who glared at Neil and continued with what he intended to say.

"Neil has two men searching the woods and Mac sent four uniforms to help with that. It probably would be best if we stayed out of the way until forensics are finished with the house… so we could help search the woods for a while." Everyone was in favour of the suggestion. The only point of disagreement was whether we should form one team or two. The argument seemed to be that a team of two was a waste of resources. As the woods were being line searched in a grid pattern, a team of five would work better. That argument finally won out and we got ourselves organised for a couple of hours of tramping through the trees.

After pegging out our first strip with a couple of pegs and crime scene tape from Gerry's car, we set off – arms outstretched fingertip to fingertip – ducking under low branches and scrambling through undergrowth on occasions. We opted to go around to the back of the house and work the area on that side, while the other men worked in the area of the woods at the front of the house.

By the end of about an hour of searching, the operation was fast losing its charm. The ankle I tweaked when I stood on the padlock this morning started complaining in earnest after a rock I stood on rolled under my foot. Not wanting appear a wimp, I soldiered on although I became increasingly grumpy. Some relief came in the form of an injury to Sarah. Something thorny ripped her arm as she pushed her way through a patch of undergrowth.

We sat down while Sarah received makeshift first aid. The wound wasn't bad but bled profusely. I doused it with some of my bottle of water and Gerry produced a clean handkerchief we used as a bandage. Ben also offered a handkerchief. I took a few tissues from a pocket pack I carried in my jacket and formed them into a pad between the two folded handkerchiefs. It's as well Sarah has a thin forearm. The handkerchiefs just managed to go around it with barely enough left to tie a knot.

By the time we were on our feet again, it was approaching four o'clock. We agreed to continue our search until five o'clock and then work out what to do after that. I hoped that would involve going back to the motel, even though it would be late when we got back. Although it was a pleasant day with a lovely cool breeze blowing, it is a different world when you are tramping through the woods. There was no breeze and I worked up quite a sweat. The thought of having to wear these clothes again tomorrow did not thrill me, but that's what we all would have to do if we stayed somewhere overnight.

I surreptitiously checked the time on my phone: 4.40pm, only another twenty minutes of this to endure. Then, all hopes of going back to the motel tonight seemed dashed. Neil, on our far left flank, called a halt and announced he thought he had found something. We stopped and stood where we were while he checked his suspicion. I peered ahead of me through the trees. Up ahead, I could make out a rock formation rising up almost vertically from the ground. That was our boundary. If we hadn't stopped, we would have made it by five o'clock. I almost prayed Neil had imagined whatever he thought he found. That wasn't to be.

A few moments later, he was waving his arms excitedly and calling us over to where he was down on his haunches beside a disturbed patch of ground. "There's been digging here," he said, and we followed his arm as he indicated an area in front of him.

I exchanged a look with Ben. "…Just about grave size," he said. I moved to stand beside Sarah. She does not need to see this I told myself, without knowing how to achieve that. "Sarah, why don't you and I go and tell the forensic boys about this? They'll need to investigate whether an animal made this or if it is something else." I caught her by the arm before she could answer and started leading her away from the group. She didn't resist but kept looking back over her shoulder.

Ben understood what I was doing and joined us. "I'll come with you. I'll be able to lead the blokes back here while you deal properly with Sarah's arm." Because we no longer searched the ground as we went, it took us no time to exit the woods. When we emerged from the bush, Ben handed me his car key. "There's a small first aid kit in the boot you can use." He gave me a look to make sure I understood what he was doing. I understood perfectly. By doing this, Sarah and I wouldn't need to go back into the house or have to take the men back to where Neil and Gerry waited.

It took no more than five minutes to clean and dress Sarah's arm. I had no idea how long it would be before the others returned but I suspected it would be a while. "See that patch of grass under the tree where we had lunch, I think you and I should go and stretch out on it for a rest." Sarah looked over at the grass and shrugged, but came with me and stretched out beside me.

"Will your mother be at work today?" I asked, hoping to work the conversation around to the direction I wanted.

"Uhmm, what's today… no, she has a day off today."

"When you spoke to her when we first arrived back at the motel, what did you tell her about when you were likely to be going home?"

"I said it would probably be a day or two."

"She will be getting anxious about not having heard any more from you by now. Maybe you should give her another call. We still don't know when you will be able to go home, but hearing from you will reassure her that nothing else has happened to you." I pulled out my phone and flicked through my contacts to her mother's entry. "Here, give her a call," I said and thrust the phone at her. She took the phone, shrugged and pressed the appropriate key.

Sarah was slipping increasingly deeper into depression. I had expected it to happen once things became normal again after her ordeal. However, not being able to go home and coming back here again today – and all that entailed – had not helped her recover her equilibrium. Once I knew her mother had answered, I wandered off for a look around the yard, leaving her alone with her call. There were a number of small outbuildings, but none of them looked sufficiently interesting to warrant venturing inside. After working my way around the house, I came back to where Sarah remained under the tree.

"Your phone will need charging again soon," she said as she handed my phone back.

"How is your mother?" An unnecessary question I know but I wanted Sarah to talk… and it worked. Of course her mother remained worried about her daughter, but Sarah seemed much brighter after talking to her. She relayed what her mother told her was happening back at Moxton and a few other bits and pieces but, once that was done, we both stretched out in silence on the grass.

Just as I felt my eyes getting heavy, she startled me by asking, "You think that's a grave we found out there in the woods, don't you?"

"I don't know, Sarah, but it is possible. We have nothing to suggest that it is a burial, but they can't dismiss that possibility without investigating further. Not enough is known about the people who were here or what they were up to – or why – to form any opinion." Before she spoke again, there was another period of silence while she digested what I said.

"I told you about that young girl – Belinda – who never came back after they took her away that day… but there was another disappearance as well."

"Do you mean Olivia?"

"Well, yes, Olivia did disappear as well, but that wasn't who I meant. There was another woman – or girl. I think she was here for only one day before she disappeared."

"What do you know about her?"

"Nothing really; Olivia told me I was the fourth one taken that weekend. Olivia disappeared on the Thursday night, Belinda on the Friday night, and they grabbed me on Sunday night. …But Olivia mentioned another one whom she thought they abducted on the Saturday night. She said that one arrived around midnight and disappeared sometime the next day. The girl was groggy the whole time and Olivia didn't get to speak to her."

"You realise you could be jumping to conclusions about what happened to those that disappeared, and about what that might be out there in the woods. It would be best if we all keep an open mind until we know something definite." Her scepticism was obvious, but she nodded and closed her eyes. I took a quick look at my phone: almost six o'clock. That probably explains why daylight is fading fast.

I wondered about what I should do next: should we continue to sit here and wait for the others to reappear, or should I go back into the woods to find out what was happening. The latter option had a few drawbacks. Someone needs to be with Sarah at all times in case there was another attempt to abduct her -- unlikely but still a possibility to consider. The alternative was to take Sarah back into the woods with me. That had no appeal whatsoever. I didn't know what they found, and she didn't need any more stress. That left only one real option: stay put and wait. I had only just reconciled myself to that fact when I heard voices coming in our direction.

Gerry led the others around the corner of the building, and the three men came directly to where we waited. I noted they all looked grim. A forced smile crossed Gerry's face as he approached. "There's nothing more for us to do here, so we should head back to the motel for dinner and a hot shower." I shot Ben a quizzical look. It missed its mark. He was too busy watching the toe of his boot scuff up a clump of grass.

Nobody needed a second invitation. We all moved off towards our vehicles. Gerry and Sarah led the group. It seemed an automatic thing for us all to return to the car we arrived in. I hung back until Neil caught up with me. I caught his arm and held him back until the others were a little ahead of us. "It appears Sarah is going back to the motel in the vehicle with you and Gerry. She is very fragile right now. Please be careful what you say in front of her," I cautioned. He signified he understood before stepping up his pace to reach the car at the same time as Gerry and Sarah. I stood beside Ben's vehicle and watched the others climb into their car and set off before climbing into the passenger's seat beside Ben.

Somehow, I managed to control myself as we negotiated the track that snaked out to the road but, once we were on the sealed road, the floodgates opened. "Okay, Ben, what happened out there in the woods after we left?" He looked set to evade the question, so I charged on. "Blind Freddie could see whatever happened wasn't good news. I saw it written all over your faces when you reappeared. I'm guessing it was a grave." He nodded. "For God's sake, Ben, talk to me. I think we all knew from the outset that it was a grave – even Sarah convinced herself it was – so, what's this tight-lipped performance all about?"

His voice was thick and seemed to come from a place far away when he spoke. "Yes, it was a grave. There were two bodies. One was a female – late teens to early twenties. The other was female: a child, maybe twelve or thirteen years old. Decay had not progressed too far yet. There was clear evidence of brutal treatment peri mortem." He didn't take his eyes off the road as he delivered the details.

I expected a horror story and thought I could handle it. I was wrong. Confirmation of my darkest fears about this place and its people still came as a shock. "Sarah will want to know what was found. She already thinks it was a grave, so it should be safe enough to admit that. Any details beyond that are likely to be more than she can handle right now. Today has not been good for her. I want her out of here and back in Moxton ASAP, and I'll be telling Neil and Gerry that tonight. They will have a rugged fight on their hands if they disagree."

"It's a serious case, Sonny. They have to carry out their investigations as thoroughly as possible. They might …"

"I don't want to hear any more, Ben. You can either support me in this, or stay right out of it. There isn't any more she can tell them – or that I can't tell them for her – and I will not stand by and see her damaged further. As I said, you have a choice how you proceed."

"Sonny, I know how strongly you feel about this, and I value our friendship but …"

"If you don't care enough about that young woman to stand up for her, then our so called friendship isn't worth the breath it takes to mention it. There's nothing more to be said."

…And nothing more was said as the kilometres rolled by. The only thing to break the silence was a call on the radio from Gerry. He asked whether we were okay to keep going to the motel and have dinner there, or did we want to stop somewhere sooner to eat. Ben looked at me for a response. I glared back. "I think everyone in the vehicle would prefer to eat when we get back to the motel," he told Gerry.

CHAPTER 19

It was late when we arrived back but a call earlier from Gerry ensured the kitchen would still feed us. After a quick detour to our rooms to wash hands and faces, we ordered meals and drinks in the restaurant within minutes of our arrival back at the Wisteria Inn. Even after our drinks arrived, we remained a subdued bunch. It wasn't until after we finished eating that we became ourselves again. While we waited for our coffees to arrive, Gerry requested a meeting as soon as we left the restaurant. Nobody was keen. We all looked forward to a shower and bed, but we agreed to meet in Ben's room.

Gerry apologised for imposing the meeting on us, but felt it important to discuss the day and gather our thoughts on what we saw. He didn't get much response outside what we discussed at lunchtime. A few minutes into the meeting, Sarah excused herself to go to the toilet. In her absence, I took the opportunity to share with the others what she told me about yet another girl allegedly abducted that Easter weekend. "Might be Belinda or this other unknown one that's in the grave with the child," Gerry commented.

"You always thought it strange that nobody disappeared on the Saturday night," Ben reminded me. "Whoever the abductors were, they had a busy time that weekend."

"Having my suspicions confirmed doesn't mean much. I'm more interested in why and what became of the women. Are there more as yet undiscovered graves in those woods, or were they destined for something else?"

"What are you suggesting, Sonny? Would you care to elaborate?" Gerry's questions had a sarcastic edge and I felt my hackles rise in response.

"No, not really; I don't have any well-formed ideas to share. However, I do want Sarah out of here and on a plane to Moxton tomorrow." I fixed my gaze on Neil as I spoke. I saw him shake his head almost imperceptibly and I knew he was going to argue. I continued before he had the chance. "Let's cut to the chase, shall we? Is Sarah under arrest?"

"No, of course not," Neil snapped. The other two men echoed his answer.

"Good; then, you can organise the private plane and her minders for tomorrow… right?"

"Oh well, no I don't think I …"

"That's okay. There's really no need for that anyway. I think this meeting has run its course. I'm going back to my room. …So, if you'll excuse me…"

"Hang on a minute, Sonny. Perhaps we could discuss this further, unless you have something important to do." Gerry said.

"As a matter of fact, I do have things to do. I have to book flights for tomorrow. I will be driving Sarah to Ballina and flying home with her. … So, I'll say goodnight gentlemen." I strode to the interconnecting door, and heard someone throw their chair back and swear as I entered my own room. However, the last thing I heard as the interconnecting door clicked shut was Ben telling someone to sit down.

Back in my room, I booted up my computer and, with surprising speed and ease tonight, booked us both on a flight to Moxton the next day. Then I rang Sarah on her room phone. …Strange that going to the toilet had taken her so long … She apologised for not returning to Ben's room and claimed she had enough of the day without having to discuss it any longer. I knew exactly how she felt.

"Good for you; I've just walked out as well. Please get packed up tonight. We will be leaving for Ballina early in the morning, and flying to Moxton on tomorrow's flight." I heard the catch in her voice as she thanked me repeatedly. The only thing left to do was to ring reception to find out how early we could settle our accounts in the morning. The time they gave me was early enough for us to get away on time. I pulled out my bag and started packing. Only a couple of things had found their way into my bag when a knock on the door interrupted proceedings.

Neil stood there looking extremely uncomfortable with a grinning Ben beside him. "May we come in, please?" How odd for Ben to use that door and not the interconnecting one. As I took a moment to ponder the request, Ben lowered his eyelids in a signal that it was okay. I reluctantly stood aside and gestured for them to enter.

"Look guys, I don't think there is anything more for us to discuss, and I am busy. Say whatever it is you came here for. Get on with it so I can get back to things I have to do."

"Can we have a few minutes to talk to you? I know we got off on the wrong foot tonight, but I think we can fix that." Neil smiled encouragingly as he finished what obviously was an uncomfortable speech for him.

"Come on, Sonny; truce. Just give us – Neil -- a couple of minutes. Hear him out, please," Ben asked. What could I do? A couple of minutes wouldn't make much difference to what time I got to bed tonight. I gestured for them to sit down.

Neil focused on the carpet, cleared his throat and began hesitantly. "Have you booked flights for tomorrow?" I nodded. "Can you cancel them – without too much penalty, I mean?"

"Why would I want to? Have you decided to arrest us both on some trumped up charge so we can't leave?"

"I could have you detailed as … as material witnesses."

"No you couldn't … and we both know you couldn't… so, if you have come to insult my intelligence, you can leave now."

Ben jumped up and began pacing the room. "Come on -- both of you – this is not doing anyone any good and is wasting valuable sleep time. Call a truce and get on with it," Ben demanded.

"I'm sorry; this isn't going as I hoped," Neil said. I bit my tongue and let Neil work out how to take the conversation forward. "If you are adamant Sarah should go home tomorrow, the private plane and two minders we discussed before will be available. My two officers would collect her from here at about 8.30am tomorrow. They will fly direct to Moxton and be there at about one o'clock. Can you agree to that?"

"Uhmm … yes -- maybe … NO! …no, that arrangement doesn't work for me."

"What…you want to go too?"

"No, of course not, I still have work to do here. I don't think it's a good idea for your officers to be picking her up here at the motel."

"What's wrong with that? They would just drive up to the back gate, we would let them in, throw Sarah and her gear into the vehicle, and they would be off again on their way to the airfield."

"I'm not confident about how secure this place is. We know Gary is no longer a problem here, but we don't know if any of the others are associated with the abductors, particularly the manager here. He seems to be something of a mystery man – who doesn't have much to do with the motel – but who manages to afford to drive a very nice expensive car I've noticed. Is this motel doing so well that he and his wife can employ enough staff that they don't even have to work in the place? He might be okay, but I'm not confident of that. I need Sarah's departure from here to be more covert than you're suggesting."

Ben tried to stifle a chuckle and ended up coughing a bit before he found his voice again. "I can see your point. Have you any better suggestion?"

"I'm thinking it might be better if we took her somewhere to meet your vehicle. Yes… we could roll up to the police station – go around the back if possible – and Sarah could transfer to your vehicle quietly and out of sight while we hung around for a while."

"…You're still so concerned about her safety?" Neil asked.

"Maybe unnecessarily so, but she is my responsibility. I do not want anything to go wrong at this stage of the game."

"I do like that plan better," Ben said, "However, I think there is a slight 'modification' that would make it even better." He had both Neil's and my attention. "I think she should leave here with Neil and Gerry in Gerry's car … just like she did today. Sonny and I will follow in Neil's car – or my car, whichever – and we will park around the back of the station as well."

I could see what his thinking was… and I was sure he knew I wanted to follow Sarah to the airfield and see her safely on her way home. "I like that plan," I announced, "But something about it niggles me. It probably will become clearer by morning. We can make any changes we need to then."

With Sarah's departure plan in place, there was nothing more for the three of us to do. I needed to tell Sarah about the change of plan, I needed to cancel flights and she needed to let her mother know the plane's anticipated arrival time at Moxton. I was ringing Sarah's room phone as the two brothers entered Ben's room via the interconnecting door.

Although I assured Sarah I would settle her account at the Wisteria Inn after she was back in Moxton, she remained anxious about it. Apart from that, everything else went according to plan. Ben suggested one minor change over breakfast. It received unanimous support. …So, shortly after eight o'clock, Gerry's car drove out of the motel's carpark with Sarah on board. The changeover went without a hitch and an unmarked van with its 'special' passenger drove out of the back entrance to the police station at 8.30am as planned.

Ben's change of plan meant we didn't follow the other car to the police station. In accordance with Neil's directions on how to get to the airfield, Ben and I left the motel first in Neil's car and drove to Rookwood. We parked at a diner just outside town and sat sipping coffee until we saw the van drive past and a call on the radio confirmed it as the one with Sarah as a passenger.

We waited a few minutes before easing out into morning traffic and following the van through town. Once we were on the open road again, we hung back, keeping a couple of cars between our two vehicles.

Most of the traffic dropped away as we went through Rookwood and the remainder turned off into an industrial area. Apart from a couple of trucks in the distance ahead of the van, ours were the only two vehicles in sight. It was a fresh, bright morning. What could be nicer than a quiet drive in the country? Like all good things that end, our relaxed state didn't last long.

What looked like a reafforestation area with trees of varying ages all planted in nice neat rows caught my attention. As we drove past, I noticed a narrow side road running back through the plantation to a more densely wooded area some distance from the main road. A few moments after we passed the plantation, a black sporty looking hatchback roared out of that side road and was riding our tail within seconds.

I saw Ben reach down between his legs and scratch around under his seat before sitting upright again with his hand dangling down between his thighs. It didn't take too much to work out what he was doing. I was copying his lead when I saw him lay a weapon on his lap and reach for the radio's microphone. Static filled the cabin. He adjusted the squelch and tried again; better this time. A few crisp sentences alerted the van driver of the potential problem now appearing glued to our rear bumper.

My weapon was a Glock 17. Ben's looked like some Smith & Wesson model. I delved under my seat again and came up with a spare magazine. Ben hadn't shared what his strategy would be, but I lowered my window. The smell of freshly tilled soil wafted in. My side of the car didn't offer a good vantage point, so I slid the sunroof cover back, unclipped the sunroof and slid it open about a centimetre to ensure it would open easily if needed in a hurry. A sunroof always seemed ridiculous to me in our climate, but this one could prove useful if I had to do something creative about stopping that black car. I had second thoughts about the wisdom of leaving the sunroof ajar as the air rushing in as we tore along at high speed filled the car with an almost deafening whistle.

Ben was doing a good impersonation of those infuriating drivers on our roads today, the sort whose attention in on the radio, their music, or the passing scenery, and not on their driving. You encounter them in situations where there is no opportunity to overtake, and find yourself dealing with mounting frustration as you remain stuck behind them for kilometres. Ben sped up, almost tailgating the van, before gradually reducing speed and allowing the van to increase the distance between us. When I least expected it, Ben indicated and pulled sharply off onto the wide shoulder of the road.

The driver of the black car planted his foot, screamed past us and ate up the distance to the van. As soon as the car passed us, Ben pulled sharply back onto the road and sped up until we were only a few metres behind the black car. "Did you see inside the car as it went past?" he asked.

"Not much; male driver – I think – wearing a baseball cap… passenger slumped down in the seat with feet up on the dash."

He called the van, "How far to the turnoff?" A disembodied voice said it was now only about three kilometres ahead. "Okay, better go for it…" Ben replied. The van sped up immediately, showing remarkable speed and power for something so cumbersome looking.

Now a different voice floated through the ether – female this time. "Armed and implementing strategy in five… The voice counted backwards from five and then shouted, "Now!"

I watched the van, while still at full speed, veer off the road and slow almost to a stop. The sleek looking black car wasn't fitted with ABS braking system. Its brakes locked, tyres squealed and smoked as the driver jumped on the brake pedal to avoid rear-ending the van. Full marks to its driver though; he managed to steer the car out into the oncoming lane and around the van, while his passenger – a female with long dark hair whipped back by the wind – hung out of the passenger's window to give the van driver a two-fingered salute and a mouthful of abuse.

The black car continued at speed and soon became a dark spot in the far distance before disappearing around a bend in the road. Ben reduced our speed to a very sedate pace by employing a careful braking regime. As soon as the black car passed the van without displaying any ill intent and the van was back on the road, everything returned to normal. I raised my window and closed the sunroof. The wind no longer shrieked in through the slim sunroof opening. The silence that followed was wonderful. By the time I finished returning things to normal – except for the Glock that now lay on the floor at my feet – we were turning off the main road onto a quiet country track.

After a few kilometres along the track, an airfield came into view. The van, already on the tarmac beside a small jet plane, disgorged its cargo. A female officer stood holding the van's back door open. Sarah scrambled out and the officer helped her with her luggage. A man standing beside the rear section of the plane -- the pilot perhaps -- opened a hatch and loaded the luggage. As soon as Sarah and her luggage were out of the van, the driver circled around and parked the vehicle between the hangar and a small admin building.

The pilot was in the cockpit and Sarah and the female officer somewhere in the cabin by the time the other officer sprinted from the van, across the tarmac and up the stairs. With the turbines already warmed up, they howled and revved up to top speed as the second officer retracted the stairs and locked the door. It took only moments for the plane to be moving at speed down the runway. Ben and I stood waving at the plane's dark faceless windows until it left the runway and headed for the clouds. Silence and the smell of aviation fuel filled the air as Ben and I maintained our position until the plane disappeared from sight.

"Feeling a little more relieved now?" Ben asked as he turned and gestured towards the car.

"A bit; I will feel a lot better when Maggie rings to say Sarah is safely at home." I fell into step beside him and was silent for a few paces. "What now?" I asked. It seems the question caught him unaware.

"What do you mean … what now? Are you asking what we do next?"

"Y-e-s, getting Sarah on that plane was the only thing on the agenda for today that I'm aware of … So what else is happening today, assuming something else is planned?"

"We are all going back to that house. I'm not sure how long we will be there today, but it should be the last time we go there."

"Good; I would have gone back there on my own if nothing was planned."

"What…? You would go back there on your own after what happened to you…? There is no guarantee that any of Mac's or Neil's officers are still around."

"There's something gnawing at me … something I missed … something I didn't do. I don't know what, but my gut is telling me to go back to look at something."

Ben, having been through this sort of thing with me a number of times before, knew better than to question my gut instinct. Instead, as we buckled up, he said, "Gerry and Neil are on their way there. They should be there by the time we arrive."

Our trip took us along a different road for some time before joining with what was becoming a familiar road. The sun, now high enough not to shine in my eyes, flooded through the windscreen warming my torso and legs. Drowsiness descended and I was drifting off when we reached the house.

Gerry and Neil sat under the tree where we had lunch yesterday. They stopped at the last town they passed through and bought us all coffees and doughnuts. I didn't think I was hungry, but the heady aroma of sugar and cinnamon escaping the box of doughnuts changed my mind. Gerry and Neil wanted to check on officers still combing the woods. That left Ben and I to our own devices. "…So, what do you want to do? Have you worked out what it is that's gnawing at you?" Ben asked.

"Not really, but I know I want to go back to that rubbish at the far end of the kitchen. I had a perfunctory flick through some of those old newspapers while we waited to open that door. The earliest one I saw was from about three years ago. A proper look might provide a better idea of how long the last tenants were here."

The smell of garbage assaulted out nostrils as we entered the front door. "They've left food scraps behind in here somewhere," I said as I started opening cupboard doors … and immediately wished I hadn't. An open rubbish bin under the sink was crawling with life. I gagged and stepped back. Ben grabbed the bin liner and twisted it closed before taking bin and contents outside.

A phone call to Gerry confirmed that the forensic crew were finished with the house and it was okay for us to touch things. While Ben dealt with the bin, I wandered down to the other end of the kitchen. As I left the main kitchen area of the room, the garbage smell diminished, the earthy smell of dust and musty smell of old newspapers replacing it. I hadn't noticed these smells yesterday. Perhaps the sight and smell of what we found in our former cell deadened my senses to all else.

After spending a few moments working out how to attack the pile of rubbish, I started rounding up all the newspapers scattered through it. There was no rationale to what papers they kept. It simply appeared that, on some occasions, it was easier to throw the paper here on this pile than dispose of it in some other way. A search of the newspapers now dumped together in one corner, confirmed that the earliest copy was from about two and a half years ago.

While I fussed over the newspapers, Ben occupied himself gathering all the empty beer cartons – and a few empty bottles – into a discrete pile. We stood back to look at the remaining rubbish littering the floor. Our efforts so far made it surprisingly easy to assess what remained. The pile now comprised mainly a jumble of black plastic garbage bags with a few other items visible here and there amongst them. None of the garbage bags looks full. There is no smell of garbage at this end of the room, so it is probably safe to assume they don't contain kitchen waste. We stood contemplating the rubbish as we considered what to do next. "Let's do what we have been doing. Let's move all the garbage bags into a separate pile so we can see what else might be mixed in with them," Ben suggested. It seemed as good an approach as any ideas I had, so we made a start on it. We had each moved only a couple of bags when something caught my eye.

"Ah-hah," I yelped. "That's what it was; that's what has been nagging at me." Startled by my outburst, Ben stood up and followed my line of sight to a particular bag in the pile of rubbish. The confused look remained plastered on his face. He followed me over to one edge of the pile of rubbish. "Look... see that there; see where I'm pointing," I said.

Some way into the pile, one of the bags had a tear at one corner. Part of its contents had escaped. The buckle end of an embossed leather belt snaked out through the tear. The corner of something else protruded… something large and squarish. I waded into the pile, pushing bags out of my way until I reached the one with the torn corner. This is what subconsciously registered in my memory banks yesterday: a mere glimpse in passing of what protruded from that bag. It wasn't the belt that caught the attention of my subconscious yesterday. It lay buried under other bags and hidden from sight. It was the small part of the other object visible through the tear in the bag that kept calling to me.

"Look, look at this bag. This is the one" I snatched up the bag and held it up like a victor brandishing his trophy. Something fell out and landed somewhere between other bags near my feet. I promptly held the garbage bag out from me at arm's length. Good knows what else might escape through the hole in it… and I didn't want it spilling all over me. Ben found the whole thing hilarious. "What …" I snapped. "What's so funny?"

"I wish you could have seen your face when that thing fell out. Bring the bag over here and let's have a look at what else is in there." I refused. I wasn't carrying this bag anywhere. What I was going to do was place it on the floor right where it was. After kicking a few more bags out of the way to create a clear space on the floor, I gingerly set the bag down and encouraged it to remain upright to keep the loosely twisted opening at the top closed.

"The way you put that down looked as though you half expected it to explode," Ben chortled. Now standing beside me, he asked, "Are we going to stand here wondering, or are we going to open it and dare to look inside?" He had a point. I was acting like a prize wimp.

Ben opened the top and I peered into what resembled a black hole. "That's not going to work," I said and took the bag from him. A slow upend of the bag resulted in an avalanche of objects that landed at my feet. The belt slithered out, along with a watch, a couple of pieces of jewellery, lipstick, small folding brush with a mirror in the handle, and a magnetic card. As the last item fluttered to the floor, Ben whipped out his handkerchief and used it to grab the card the moment it hit the floor. "Looks a bit like a door keycard," I observed.

Careful to avoid adding his fingerprints to the card, Ben turned it over. "Wisteria Inn! Not a door keycard, it's for that back gate," we exclaimed in unison. Ben retrieved his phone with his free hand. "Gerry, I think you better get Mac to bring his forensic boys back here," he said quietly, and then to me, "They want us to wait. They are only a couple of minutes away from the house."

The garbage bag hadn't emptied when I upended it. It still felt heavy and the object poking out through the tear remained firmly in place. I upended it again and shook it vigorously. Out tumbled a tan leather handbag. It looked handmade and featured an intricately tooled panel on its front side. We both stared at it for a few moments. "…Safe to assume they are a woman's belongings, don't you think?" I asked, tongue in cheek. Ben shot me one of *those* looks as we both bent down for a closer look at the handbag. I desperately wanted to rifle through the stuff, but there are protocols to follow.

"I want to bag this stuff up again, but we need a new bag – and gloves. Did you see anything in that cupboard under the sink?" I asked.

A rummage in the cupboard produced a roll of kitchen bin liners – white not black, but they would do. I found a half-empty box of disposable gloves. "Bring the roll with you," I told Ben. "We might need more liners if we find other bags that are torn," I suggested as I strode back to the pile of black garbage bags with the box of gloves. Ben tore off one of the bin liners. With gloved hands, we gathered everything that fell out of the torn bag and placed it in the bin liner, including the torn bag itself. "Hang on a minute; I want to find whatever it was that fell out and landed over here somewhere." I had a reasonable idea of where I saw it land, and started moving more bags in an effort to find it. The only loose thing I found was a phone.

I went to add it to the bag with all the other gear. "No, don't put it in there," Ben said. "We don't know for sure that phone came out of this bag. It might have been lying there the whole time." I was almost confident it was what fell out of the bag, but I understood the rules of evidence. We hadn't *actually* found the phone in the bag with the other stuff. I slipped the phone into a spare disposable glove and tied it closed before adding the glove, complete with phone, to the bin liner.

"Ben, where are you?" Gerry called from the front door.

"Kitchen,"

"I hope you found something interesting. Mac wasn't too happy about pulling some of his guys off another crime scene." Gerry went on to tell us that Mac's forensic team intended to come back to collect bits and pieces, including this pile of rubbish when they finished with their new crime scene. They were of the opinion the rubbish wasn't important and, at best, would only repeat fingerprints already found throughout the house.

"Well, we thought it interesting," Ben started slowly. "The evidence in that bag ties it to the Wisteria Inn and possibly one of the missing women."

"What sort of evidence?"

I dropped Ben a sly wink before answering Gerry. "Oh, you know, the usual gear: phone, watch, magnetic card and stuff."

"Could belong to anyone – from anywhere… even a male…"

"Not when the magnetic card is a Wisteria Inn card and there are a few feminine hygiene products amongst it," Ben assured Gerry.

"I have the feeling they don't belong to the body we found yesterday. Somehow, they don't look like her style," I offered in the hope of avoiding the next obvious question.

"Look, now that we are all here, I thought we might start going through the rest of those garbage bags," Ben suggested. We can sort the one containing possessions from those that contain genuine rubbish to make the job easier for the forensic crew." It seemed like a sound idea. Neil tore off several bin liners and covered the kitchen table with them while Ben retrieved another of the garbage bags.

More than half of the garbage bags had undergone the same cursory scrutiny by the time the (considerably diminished) forensic crew arrived. Gerry took charge, indicating the bags containing personal possession, and pointing out the only bag found so far containing genuine rubbish.

We continued working our way through the garbage bags while the forensic team relocated to their van those already checked and now contained in white bin liners. With the four of us working on it, we completed the remainder of the pile in about ten minutes. When the forensic boys finished loading everything into their van, they waved goodbye and headed back to their lab. We helped ourselves to bottled water from the battered drinks fridge and wandered out to our usual tree.

It was way past lunchtime and our stomachs rumbled. There was consensus we should buy food along the way as we head back to the motel for the rest of the afternoon. I felt mixed emotions as I watched the house glide out of sight when we drove away from the place for the last time. Soon after we hit the main road again, I checked my phone. I had missed the text from Maggie when it came in: *Sarah safely home. Thank you.*

I reclined my seat a tad, settled back and took in the scenery flying past. I was relieved to end the case that brought me to Minden Hill. Now I could concentrate on the situation I had walked into at Minden Hill.

CHAPTER 20

"You're a bit quiet; everything all right?" Ben asked after about half an hour on the road back to Minden Hill. "I'm not sure whether you planned to snooze all the way or if you are quiet because something is wrong."

"No nothing is wrong; quite the contrary. Message from Maggie said Sarah is safely home. That was the whole object of coming to this area so, strictly speaking, the case is closed … and I now have a mass of notes to write up and an account to pay for Sarah's room at the motel."

"So, you'll be heading back home now?"

"No. The case is closed but the story is not over. I still don't know what was behind the abductions. There has to be some end game and I still don't know what that is. Sarah's case is closed, but what happened to me isn't."

"That's what Gerry and Neil will continue to work on for some time I imagine. Knowing that pair, they will eventually get to the bottom of it and then we both will know as well."

"Hmm, yes I suppose that's true, but I became part of whatever their operation was and I'm not entirely comfortable about leaving what happened to me to others to investigate. Speaking of Neil, why was he involved in all this?"

"What do you mean? He's a copper…"

"Yes, he's a copper, but he is a Fed. I can understand Gerry's involvement because it all happened on his patch, but the question is: what has it to do with the Federal Police … or was Neil's involvement simply because he happened to be in town to spend time with his brother?" Silence oozed from the driver's side of the car. After a few moments of no response, I looked across at Ben to see if something was wrong. Perhaps I had upset him somehow.

It was as if he could feel my eyes on him. He removed his eyes from the road briefly to glance in my direction before speaking. "That's a really good question… a-n-d one I don't have an answer to. Neil and I were going to meet up at Ballina, so I had to ring and cancel because I came to Minden Hill. As you would expect of Neil, he wanted to know all about what happened here. About half an hour later, he called to say we would catch up at Minden Hill instead of Ballina… and then he arrived."

"He got involved in the case as soon as he arrived and even called in federal resources to help out. I don't think that was all about doing a good turn to help out Gerry."

One thing led to another as random conversations often do and we were soon sharing our thoughts on what happened to those young women and why. What nobody had mentioned, although I'm sure it occurred to all of us, was the number of black garbage bags containing women's possessions abandoned in that kitchen area.

"Did you count those garbage bags – the important ones, I mean?" I asked quietly as I replayed the sight of that pile of rubbish through my mind.

"Twenty, or maybe nineteen; I think I miscounted near the end."

"Yeah, I was the same, but I think there were twenty. I'm almost not game to think about what that means. Up until now, I thought we were looking at the abduction of four women – and me of course. A part of me hoped it was something driven by the opportunity the festival provided. Now, it's obvious this was a long-term operation. There had to be more involved than simply the rape and abuse of abducted women who never resumed their former lives."

Ben nodded and grunted his agreement. I waited for some comment but, when none was forthcoming, I continued with my hypothesis. "They only found the one grave in those woods, so what happened to the rest of the women whose possessions we found? I suppose they could be buried somewhere else – anywhere else. It makes sense that they wouldn't bury that many people in the one area and hope to get away with it. So, if murder was their end game, logically they would use a number of sites and, preferably, further away from that property."

"Your reasoning is probably right. They wouldn't want too many bodies too close to home, although the likelihood of someone discovering graves in those woods is slim. There wasn't any evidence of any human intrusion in those woods – apart from the grave; no evidence of ramblers or shooters."

"I don't think this was about rape and murder. I think there was a more sinister game plan operating here." Punctuated by long pauses from time to time, our discussion occupied most of the remainder of the trip to the motel. Although we talked about the abductions from every angle, neither of us voiced any firm opinions regarding what it was all about. At least, I hadn't noted any, and I knew I carefully avoided voicing the firm opinion I was developing. For the last few kilometres of the trip from Rookwood, I decided a change of subject would help lighten the mood. "Is Neil likely to hang around now that the Sarah thing is finished, or are you still planning to spend time together before you head back home? I imagine Gerry will go back to sleeping in his own bed."

"I've no idea what the other two are planning to do. All I know is that Neil didn't come to Minden Hill to spend time with his brother. That being the case, there's a fair chance he might disappear now that the investigation has reached this point."

I had seen what I thought was their car parked out front of some shops at one of the towns we went through and, when they arrived back at the motel shortly after us, they brought food for a very belated lunch. As seemed the accepted practice, we gathered in Ben's room for food and coffee. Well, he had the coffee machine, so it had to be his room.

We bunkered down for the rest of the afternoon and made good use of Ben's coffee machine. It wasn't until darkness descended that we dispersed to our own rooms to clean up before dinner. We agreed to meet in the restaurant at seven o'clock. I wanted to settle Sarah's account today, so I left my room little earlier than the others and went to reception. The young lass manning the desk that evening was new, and it seemed to take her an inordinate amount of time and fluster to deal with Sarah's account. As a result, by the time I paid it, the others already had drinks when I arrived at the restaurant.

Conversation at dinner was in short light snatches about nothing in particular. It struck me as odd. The only other diners left the restaurant shortly after we sat down at our customary table in the far corner. There was no one around us to overhear if we talked 'shop', but it appeared nobody felt so inclined. We didn't dally in the restaurant, leaving immediately after we finished our meals. Once more, we gravitated to Ben's room … and everyone loosened up.

Once we were back in the room, Gerry announced he would be checking out in the morning. I queried whether that meant they were convinced there was no further connection to explore between the Wisteria Inn and its staff and the abductions. It seems my assumption was correct. The police believed Gary, now safely behind bars, was the only connection. After dealing with a few comments from the others, Gerry turned his attention to Ben and me.

"What about you two, are you heading off too?"

I shook my head. "No, I think I might hang around for a couple more days." Gerry looked at Ben and raised his eyebrows in question.

"Me…? No, I don't think so. I think I'll hang around for a few more days. I have plenty of time before I need to take up my new posting.

Anyway…" Ben added as an afterthought, "I'd like to know what came out of all those garbage bags. I mean, I know what we saw as we checked each one, but what do their contents tell us?"

"That's what has us all intrigued," Neil mumbled from over at the coffee machine.

"Forensics say they will finish with them late tomorrow at the latest and we should be able to have them the day after… might be another day or two before we get their report though," Gerry said.

It wasn't too much later when Gerry claimed he had calls to make and left us. Neil followed his lead soon after, leaving Ben and I alone with our half-drunk mugs of coffee. "Was it something we said?" I quipped as Neil closed the door behind him.

"We certainly know how to clear a room. Maybe they just wanted to leave us alone together," Ben said, and gave me a lecherous grin. I shot him a hard look across the top of my coffee mug.

"Is it just my suspicious mind, Ben, or does it strike you that Gerry and Neil appear to have another agenda that we know nothing about?" Ben looked at me for a couple of seconds as he considered the question. I continued while he thought about it. "How come Gerry didn't ask Neil what he was going to do? I suppose he might know already as they did travel together today and probably talked about any number of things along the way."

"That's possible, but I suspect you might be right about us being kept in the dark about something, although I have no idea what that is. So far, Neil hasn't said anything to me about what he's doing, or whether we should spend some time together before I head back up north." If there were some secret secondary agenda, I wanted to work out what it was.

Ben appeared mellow tonight. I decided to test my luck by pushing him for his thoughts on this whole abduction operation. After being hesitant to answer initially, he chose his words so carefully his response told me nothing... that is, nothing other than he thought there was a much bigger story to uncover. I wasn't overjoyed when he claimed he wouldn't be able to squeeze information that we didn't already have out of Neil. "Neil is funny like that. He never did get the concept of sharing, even when he was little. I think his idea of sharing is that others should give him everything and he should enjoy receiving it."

Funny that. Ben just described exactly my assessment of Neil, but it's probably not wise to tell him so. I tried a few more probing questions in a bid to have Ben share his thoughts with me, but they failed. I decided to call it a night before I succumbed to utter frustration. I made noises to that effect.

"Feel like a scotch before bed?" He waved the bottle of single malt at me.

Why not… what harm could a few more minutes do? I could always take it back to my room with me. "Yeah, that's sounds good."

Ben scrunched down in his chair and put his fee up on the built in desk. I sat in the other comfortable chair with my feet up on the end of the spare bed. Each of us alone with our own thoughts, we sipped our drinks in silence. Ben startled me back to reality when he asked, "What do you think?"

"Eh…? What do I think about what?"

"Oh. Come on, Sonny. I've known you long enough and well enough to know you have a theory about these abductions. I'm asking you to share it with me."

"I've spent half the night trying to get you to do the same thing. You're right though, I have a theory of sorts but I've no confidence in it. It's a bit like a jigsaw puzzle that I don't have all the pieces for, and therefore can't see the whole picture clearly."

"Okay, but tell me anyway. Give me your glass. I'll refresh your drink while you marshal your thoughts."

Where to start…? I waited until he had his feet up again, and then just let it all roll out as though I was in automatic report back mode. However, the process of organising my thoughts and then voicing them gave clarity to what started out as a hazy idea. I didn't have a bottom line to share with him when I started speaking. Instead, I concentrated on delivering a series of what I considered the important facts as I knew them.

"Here's what I know – or think I know. Three women went missing over Easter but now we know there were four. The abductors have a penchant for fair skinned with blonde or light ginger hair. They prefer young – teenage or early-twenties; Olivia was an exception – redheaded and a bit older – and they were worried about her 'suitability'. With the exception of Sarah, none ever turned up again. I wasn't part of the same story. They took me because I was nosey about Sarah's disappearance, not because I matched their 'criteria'. How's that for a start? What have I left out?"

"I don't know that you have left anything out, but what do you make of all that?"

"There are a few more things to look into before we can draw any definite conclusions … and there are a few major unanswered questions that keep nudging me to find answers to them."

"I knew this conversation wouldn't be simple, so tell me… what more information do you need before you're prepared to share your ideas with me?"

"Well, some of it should be straightforward research: the surnames of Olivia and Belinda, and if there is any record of the one that disappeared on the Saturday night and her name."

"Yes, it would be good to know all that, but I don't see how it helps formulate your hypothesis."

"It doesn't but it would eliminate some of the questions that keep clogging my thinking. In my mind there is a huge question mark hanging over that lead detective who Gerry came to replace. When I first spoke to him, he didn't want to know anything about Sarah's disappearance. He gave me the same line as he gave her mother: that Sarah probably was off somewhere enjoying herself. There were already two other women reported missing from his patch on that weekend. Don't you think he might have shown a little more interest in the report of another?"

Ben nodded but continued scribbling in his notebook without looking up. I noticed him whip out his notebook at some point during this conversation and start scribbling something as I kept talking. I'm not sure that's a good sign that he is taking me seriously, or a bad sign that he is busy dealing with other things on his mind. With nothing to lose after having gone this far, I pushed on with articulation – more like 'development' -- of my hypothesis.

"Whose belongings were in those garbage bags? Were the belongings of the three whose names we know in those bags? There were about twenty bags. If each bag represents an abducted woman, is there an equivalent number of missing person reports? Are you still attached to the local police service? Those belongings could tell us volumes about their owners… if we could access them."

Now I had his attention. Ben stared off into the distance for a moment or two, blinked a couple of times and then focused his amazing blue eyes on me. "As far as I know, I am still attached to the New South Wales Police Service. You make a valid point about accessing the information those garbage bags might contain. Gerry said forensics wouldn't be finished with them until the day after tomorrow. That gives me enough time to work on whomever to ensure we get access. Now, time's up. It's getting late, what's your bottom line?"

"I've been trying to explain why I don't have a 'bottom line' yet."

"Yes, you do. Stop mucking about and tell me what you think."

This was not how I planned for this to go. I didn't want to look like I had departed from reality. Nevertheless, I sighed, took a deep breath and launched into it. "At the risk of sounding totally off the planet, my thinking tends towards people trafficking. It appears a certain type of woman is taken, and never returns. What do you do with all those women… if each garbage bag represents one woman? The abductors would need to be of an energetic disposition if they were to bury each woman when they finished with her. I think they are being shipped off to some place overseas."

"At last, the bottom line…" Ben's chuckle didn't make me feel any better about having voiced my thinking while it remained nothing more than a half-baked notion. I waited while he seemed engrossed in the contents of his notebook, flicking through the pages and only occasionally slowing to scan a bit here and there. I was fast approaching the point where I would get up and walk out when he snapped the notebook closed and tossed it up onto the desk beside his feet. Then, with his hands clasped behind his head and his eyes fixed on the ceiling, he started speaking slowly, considering each word as he went.

"Yes … I … think … you … could …be … right. Yeah, that fits with what we know so far, but…" He stopped speaking abruptly and appeared to disappear into the deeper recesses of his mind again. I waited impatiently for as long as I could – probably about two heartbeats – before deciding he wasn't going to continue with whatever he left unfinished. A couple of other thoughts I'd held for a while, but hadn't shared, were now banging to be let out… so, I obliged.

"If my thinking is correct, it might explain Neil's interest in the case. However, a more troubling aspect of all this is how the scheme operates. Although I only managed a sneak peek at the two abductors, they looked like the hired muscle, not the brain. There has to be someone somewhere driving an operation like the one I envisage."

"You are right on the money again, Sonny, but it is getting late. I think we should call it a night. We should try to have a think tank session tomorrow – just the two of us. Tomorrow will be a good time to quiz Neil about his involvement – although I probably won't get a straight answer – and to talk to Gerry about access to the stuff in the garbage bags."

It had been slow and painful – a bit like pulling teeth – but, by the time we said goodnight, I felt good about the position we achieved. However, it wasn't sleep conducive. My mind insisted on working flat out for a long time after I turned off the light. The process of talking through everything allowed the big picture to become clearer. After tossing and turning for what felt like hours, I crawled out of bed and got to work.

I started by bringing my notes up to date. That brought to mind a couple of things I had mentioned earlier to Ben. Once that was done, I dug a rather tattered large sheet of butcher's paper out of my bag and started a mind-mapping exercise. By the time I had added all the information I had, I discovered I had created several more questions to follow up.

By the time I crawled back into bed, it was after 3.00AM. Sleep was no longer a problem. Now that I had documented everything I had tried to hold in my memory banks, I drifted into a sleep untroubled by dreams of any kind.

Hammering on a door woke me. I forced one eye open a fraction and squinted at the bedside clock. God, it was after seven o'clock. My inbuilt biological alarm clock failed to wake me at my usual time. "What…?" I bellowed at what could only be Ben banging on the interconnecting door.

"…You're not dead then? I got worried when there was no response from your room. …Was just about to come in to check you hadn't been snatched during the night." I wasn't buying that for one minute. If he were concerned something happened, he would have been through that door to check before this. "Should I wait for you for breakfast?" he asked.

"Give me five minutes and I'll join you."

With the speed of a gazelle, I galloped around the room throwing on clothes, splashing water on my face and combing my hair. Then I strode through to Ben's room still feeling as grumpy as when he woke me. "I'm here. Are you right to go?"

"…And good morning to you to; I see the late night worked wonders for your disposition." As I led him out of his room, Neil stepped out to join us in the corridor. Gerry sat alone at a table and waved us over as we entered the restaurant for breakfast. There were the usual few minutes of confusion and messing about as we selected our individual breakfast choices from the breakfast buffet line-up before we all settled at the table with Gerry. Not surprisingly perhaps, the first topic of discussion was what everybody's plans were for the day.

Gerry confirmed he would checkout straight after breakfast and would spend the day in his office at the precinct. Neil was a bit noncommittal about his plans for the day but, if I read between the lines correctly, his day somehow would involve Gerry. I saw Ben shoot Neil a meaningful look. The only problem was, I didn't know what the look meant. Ben managed to be sufficiently vague about his plans for the day without giving the impression he was ducking the question. His response suggested he would be spending the day looking around the area a bit more as he didn't know if he'd ever be back this way again. Then all eyes were on me.

My mouth dried up as I tried to kick my brain into a higher gear. The truth was I didn't have any plans for today. Well, nothing you could call plans… more like vague ideas at best. Since my conversation with Ben last night, the notion that I should talk to Dani McLeod again haunted me. I had nothing specific in mind to ask her. It was just that I felt that now I knew a little bit more about the abductions, she might be able to provide some further information or insights that previously neither of us was aware were relevant.

We returned to our rooms and I had a quick shower to wake myself up properly before booting up my computer. My hope was that a trawl through all the notes and comments in Sarah's case file might produce a Eureka moment that would bring me a little closer to understanding the full extent of what went on here. I barely started reading the file when Ben knocked on the interconnecting door and came in.

"The others have absconded. We two are all that remains of our once much larger group. S-o-o, what shall we do today? I'm afraid I'm a bit light on ideas, so I'm open to suggestions."

"I don't know that I'm in a much better situation, but I was thinking of trying to catch up with Dani McLeod again. Want to tag along?" What a waste of a question; of course he wanted to tag along. I'm almost sorry I invited him. He is liable to go into 'policeman mode' and start interrogating her, when all I want to do is chat and explore ideas and possibilities. I continued to wrestle with my conscience about the intelligence – or lack thereof -- behind the invitation as I keyed in Dani's number. I hadn't thought through what I would say, as I didn't expect her to answer. As a result, when she answered immediately, I stumbled around getting the conversation started and eventually resorted to saying there were some developments with my case I'd like to discuss with her.

Dani already had her coffee when I joined her at ten o'clock in our now favourite coffee place in Rookwood. Ben stopped to look at something on his way through the bookshop and arrived a little after me. Dani shot me a nervous look as Ben approached our table. "Relax, he's one of the good guys," I said, and gave her an abridged version of my connection with Ben. I hadn't bothered with the bit about his being a copper. It seemed to work. Dani relaxed, we ordered coffee, and I led into the reason for our meeting as soon as our coffees arrived.

For somewhere better to start, I told her we now knew of four abductions over the Easter weekend, and five if you included mine a week later. After the initial look of disbelief crossed her face, I watched her go into 'deep thought' mode. Dani sat gazing at the tabletop. I wanted to move things along, so I talked over whatever churned in her mind. "Are you aware of anything like this happening around here previously… maybe last year or even around the time of some other festival?"

"I'm trying to remember something. I think it happened around the time of that big fair they held at Minden Hill around the end of November. It was their Christmas fair for the locals to offer their handmade goods as potential Christmas presents. They hold a Christmas fair every year. It draws people from miles around, not only for the bits and pieces they can pick up for presents, but also for the fresh produce, and jams and preserves that are really good quality. They are a bit like a farmers' market and a craft market rolled into one, and they usually have a line-up of local musicians playing throughout the day."

"Sounds like the right kind of event. What happened?"

"Sonny, I'm struggling to recall the details. I know that's a strange admission from a journo, but I remember there was something received a few lines in the paper at the time. Whatever the incident was, it wasn't anything major, but it's calling to me. I didn't cover the fair, as there were other things happened that weekend. There was a bit about the Christmas fair in the social column, but I didn't take much notice at the time." After shaking her head in frustration, she whipped out her phone and started flicking through screens. "Damn, this is so slow it's useless. I need a computer."

"We have a couple of those over at Minden Hill," Ben said. "You could use them, if you have the time to come to Minden Hill with us. From our point of view, it might be preferable to use ours than trying to work on something at your office." I was somewhat surprised when Dani agreed the Minden Hill option was best.

"I'll follow you over in my car," Dani said. "That way, you won't have to worry about bringing me back here when we finish. I suspect this story has a long way to go and I think it might be just the opportunity I have been waiting for." Ben and I exchanged glances, before Ben had all three of us on our feet and heading for our cars.

CHAPTER 21

The fact that Dani didn't travel with us gave Ben and I the opportunity to discuss exactly what we would and would not share with Dani at this time. When we arrived back at the Wisteria Inn, I got out of the car as soon as we entered the motel's carpark and waited by the security gate for Dani who was a couple of minutes behind us. I opened the gate to let her drive into the parking lot. Although we didn't discuss it, neither Ben nor I wanted anyone aware of Dani's presence at the motel. We didn't want her parking in the street and wandering through the front door and the reception area.

Dani parked in the bay next to Ben's car, and the three of us wasted no time making our way to Ben's room. I suggested Dani use my computer. There was no argument. It might have been an unnecessary precaution, but I wasn't sure whether Ben's machine was his personal laptop or Police Service issue. Although I doubted it was the latter, I didn't want its use monitored, or any evidence of what we were doing left in its history. We relocated to my room and Dani got busy on my computer, mumbling to herself the whole time.

"Ah-hah, I knew I'd seen something. What's the date on this … yes, that ties in with the Christmas festival."

She had my undivided attention. "What did you find … does it tie in with what happened at Easter?" I almost was not game to ask the question. Could we be so lucky as to find another piece of the puzzle so soon? Dani ignored my question. I watched images rolling on and off the screen as she searched online copies of the local newspaper. That kept her preoccupied for several minutes, during which time Ben and I tried desperately to follow what was happening by what little we could see from over her shoulders. With a couple of emphatic stabs at the keyboard, the screen returned to my search engine's homepage and Dani stared at her hands poised but unmoving above the keyboard.

Then, as if suddenly remembering there were others present, she spun around in her chair to face her audience.

"Sorry… I wasn't ignoring you. I was trying to get my head around a couple of things." She smiled apologetically. I encouraged her to go on. "I found the bit I was looking for in the social column but there was no subsequent mention of the matter. One of the stallholders caused something of disappointment for many when she suddenly upped sticks and disappeared before the fair opened the next day."

"Was she a local?" Ben asked.

"No, I don't think so. At least there was nothing to suggest she was. In fact, I drew clear inference that she wasn't from around here, but that could be because of the way it was written up."

Aw, do come on, I thought. The suspense is killing me. I held out my hands, palms up to her, and raised my eyebrows at her, imploring her to tell more.

"Yes, of course…" she began. "I notice it is almost lunchtime. Do you guys want to go for lunch or something before we get stuck into this thing? I need to call someone before we try to look too much further at what happened."

"No…" Ben answered a tad too loudly, and then amended his demeanour. "We don't need to go out. I'll order room service. Is there anything special anyone wants?" He was gone as soon as he finished speaking. Dani already had her phone to her ear as I followed Ben to his room. "Why did you follow me?" he asked when he realised I was standing behind him. "I thought you would stay and listen to what was going on in there." He gestured towards my room.

"I have the feeling she would make sure anything I overheard wouldn't tell me anything. I got the distinct feeling she is herding together all of the information available before sharing it with us. I think I understand her motivation. Anyway, I'm confident she will tell us all she knows. She wants to know what we know and I think she is aware that she will get nothing if she doesn't give us something first."

"Okay, okay. I just don't want to find that she is running a separate agenda."

"Oh, I'm sure her agenda differs from ours, but I am confident she is smart enough to realise that her agenda will be best served my helping us with our agenda." Ben looked confused. I told him to trust my instincts. He seemed to accept that and picked up the phone to order lunch. I quietly moved to stand beside the interconnecting door. With a bit of effort, I could just about make the conversation in the next room. Then it stopped. I waited a moment, and then indicated to Ben I was going back to my own room, and rattled the door loudly as I opened it and strode in.

Dani had her notebook out and I assumed she was recording the salient points gleaned from her phone call. She welcomed me back with a smile that briefly interrupted her notetaking. Not wanting to interrupt her, I didn't speak. While she continued writing, I moved chairs over to the small round table that was part of my room's furnishings. A few moments after I finished fussing with the chairs, Ben returned and announced that lunch would arrive in about fifteen minutes. "So, while we are waiting, please can we at least go through what you know about what happened at the Christmas fair?"

"Okay. A stallholder, who was a regular at all the market-type events held here at Minden Hill, arrived in town the day before the fair… as was her usual practice. She had an old kombi van she travelled and slept in, and she would set up next to the van a portable gazebo thing from which she sold her wares. Felt items … she hand-felted various articles including hats, bags, vests and other clothing. It was well-made and good quality. There were many disappointed people around when she didn't open for business the next day. The story …"

The arrival of lunch brought Dani's story to an abrupt but brief halt. Ben had ordered club sandwiches for three, a jug of orange juice, and a pot of coffee. We sat around the small table with lunch spread out in its centre and occupying most of the tabletop. It took no time for everyone to organise their own plate of food and drinks. After pausing for a few bites of her lunch, Dani yielded to our encouragement and carried on with her story.

"There isn't much else to tell. Other stallholders arriving the evening before the fair and some of the locals who passed through the field that afternoon recalled seeing the familiar van already parked there, and she had had set her stall up already by the time other out of town stallholders started arriving later that evening. However, next morning, her van was gone and she didn't return. Her stall structure remained in situ, so people assumed she simply went off to get something she needed and would return in time for the start of the fair. She didn't… and she didn't return to collect her stall. When the organisers returned to clean up the place the next day, the thing was still there. They packed it up and one of the organisers took it home for safekeeping."

"What actually was left behind? Did it include her stock and everything, or just the gazebo thing?" I asked.

"No, I don't think there was anything else, only the gazebo and one of those plastic tables that folds in half and the two halves lock together so you can carry it by a handle attached to one end of it."

"Has she been back to any of the fairs or festivals since then," I asked, although I knew what the response would be.

"Apparently not, although only the organisers would know for sure."

"I wonder if the Kombi van ever turned up anywhere," Ben mused aloud. "We would need the registration number – or at least her name – before we could initiate a search."

"It looks like our next port of call might be the fair organisers," I said. Ben and Dani nodded in unison.

"I've got a couple of names. I'll see if one of them might be available this afternoon," Dani volunteered and started flicking through her notebook. About fifteen minutes later, we were pulling in to a driveway leading to a low set brick farmhouse.

The visit was like uncovering the mother lode. The man we came to see meticulously maintained a database of what seemed like every imaginable bit of information relating to Minden Hill's fairs and festivals. It provided us with the woman's name and her van's registration number – stallholders, at the time of booking a space, had to identify any vehicle they would park on their plot. He could also tell us about the products she produced and sold, and from where she sourced her fleece. We discovered he genuinely was interested in his stallholders, so found out all he could about them and their wares and recorded it all on his database. …And he confirmed the woman hadn't been back for the Valentine's Day fair or the Easter festival, both of which she regularly attended.

As soon as we had all there was to know about the woman, Dani seemed to vanish, leaving Ben and I alone with the man we came to see. We spent a few minutes discussing the Easter festival and quizzing him about anything unusual he was aware of that happened over that weekend. There were a few things. They were annoying, inconvenient or frustrating from an organisational point of view, but not of interest to us. Our meeting at an end, we thanked him and made our way back to the car.

Dani leant up against the car, her phone to her ear and speaking earnestly to whoever was on the other end of the call. Rather than intrude, Ben and I slowed our pace and ambled up to the car to arrive in time to hear her ending her call. She looked like she had received word she won Lotto. Her face was in danger of splitting, she was smiling so widely, and her eyes positively sparkled.

"That was amazing…," she greeted us with, and then rushed on with the details. "I rang that place where the woman supposedly got her fleece from. The bloke I spoke to was her father. He owns a big sheep property and his daughter kept a few 'special' sheep there for their fleece. I'll tell you about it on the way back to the motel."

Information gleaned from the father included the fact that his daughter hadn't been to the property in quite a few months, and there was quite a bit of fleece waiting for her. They included her sheep whenever shearing was happening, kept their fleece separate, and stored it for her in a small shed near the farmhouse. He wondered how she managed to produce new stock without collecting the fleece from storage. Although he gave Dani other information about how his daughter treated and dyed the wool herself before using it for felting, Ben and I were interested only in the fact that she hadn't been around for quite a while.

By the time we arrived back at the motel, the afternoon had disappeared. We spent about 45 minutes reviewing information gathered today and making sure we documented it all before Dani left. I walked out to her car with her and arranged to talk to her again tomorrow. It was dark when I opened the security gate and waved her off.

As I walked back inside, Neil drove into the carpark. I stopped to wait for him and we walked in together. Ben heard us talking as we came along the corridor. He opened his door and invited us in. His invitation for us to join him involved waving a bottle of red wine in our direction. Although I didn't really feel like wine, it would be impolite to refuse. With bottle and glasses in hand, we adjourned to the colonnaded area outside our rooms. That's where we were when Ben's phone rang. Gerry had arrived early for dinner and nobody responded when he banged on Ben's door.

Without any pre-planning, Ben and I both chose to play down what we did all day: nothing much; went for coffee, took a drive, spoke to a couple of people. Then, having shared what our day was like – well, that *is* what we did – we began the arduous task of extracting information from the other two. We concentrated on Gerry first. He would go home after dinner, but Neil would still be here. We could work on him later. The process began slowly and reluctantly, but perseverance paid off. It became obvious that Gerry and Neil, although working separately, both worked on the case all day using their individual resources.

Gerry's news caused some excitement. Forensics identified one set of prints from the house. They belonged to one Frank Bellamy, whose name appeared frequently in the system. After a quick search on his phone, Gerry showed us a photo of the gent in question. As much as was possible to tell from the image on the phone's small screen, Bellamy looked a bear of a man who had survived a few rough encounters. "Have they identified any other prints from the house?" Ben asked.

"No, not yet," Gerry said, and gave a resigned shrugged. "We hoped they would identify all the prints straight off. I suppose it was too much to expect, but I felt so sure those involved in this were not amateurs. It is disappointing but it is still early days. Who knows what they might find. They confirmed that they are finished with the stuff in the garbage bags and we can access it tomorrow."

An idea came to me while Gerry was speaking. As soon as everyone finished speculating on how useful the stuff in the garbage bags would be in determining the exact nature of the operation, I asked my question. "Would it be possible to send that image of Bellamy to my email address? I'd like to see if Sarah can identify Bellamy." Gerry appeared to ponder the question for a brief moment. Then, after a couple of quick jabs at his phone, he announced the image was on its way to my inbox.

With nothing more of any import to share, Gerry turned to Neil. "How did your day go? Did you manage to turn up anything useful?" he asked.

"It came as something of a surprise, but we did have one breakthrough. As I suggested yesterday, I had my blokes try to track down that company that came up as the registered owner of that sedan the women commandeered."

"By the way," Gerry interrupted, "There hasn't been as much as a murmur about that vehicle being stolen or missing." That brought a snicker from around the table.

"Anyway…" Neil continued. "The short version of it is that they drew a blank. I was about to tell them to leave it and go on with something else when one of them had a bright idea. He suggested they run a check on the Mossack Fonseca Panama papers stuff that leaked just the other day. It seemed like a longshot but I gave them until the end of the day to see what they could find. They struck gold. Just before knock-off time, I heard this shout go up from where they all sat glued to their screens."

"They found it?" Gerry exclaimed loudly … and then looked around to see how much attention he drew. Apart from those of us around the table, the only other person in the restaurant was a bemused looking barman. He wasn't particularly interested and quickly went back to polishing glasses.

"Yeah, just before I left this afternoon. They were still unravelling all the details but they established it had its origins in the Middle East somewhere. It's a fairly tangled trailed they're working with."

"Arabic connection of some sort…?" Ben asked. Neil nodded and confirmed the company had its roots in that part of the world.

Ben and I locked eyes for a moment. That certainly added strength to our assumption of some form of people trafficking. Added strength but not confirmation… still, it was encouraging and would suffice for the moment. "Something you want to share…?" Neil demanded.

"Eh? No, nothing to share…" I replied as I stalled for time to think of what to say that would deflect attention from Ben and me. "We wondered why we couldn't find anything on that company, but that explains it." It wasn't the truth, but it was an adjusted version of it. I had searched the web for reference to the company without finding even the slightest hint of its existence. Ben completed the task of steering attention away from us.

"How does accessing the contents of those garbage bags work, Gerry? Will you bring the stuff back here or will it remain at the forensics lab?" Ben asked.

"I tried to have it brought back here, but they want to hold on to it. We will have to settle for working at their lab – at least for the immediate future anyway."

"I'm pleased to hear that word 'we' used. Will all four of us be going to look at the stuff tomorrow?" Ben looked deliberately at Neil as he finished speaking. Neil and Gerry exchanged a look before Gerry tried to string together an answer.

His initial effort didn't sound promising but Ben's set jaw and steely glare forced him to rethink his original response. "Uhmm… I will go, and Neil needs … aah, yes … I suppose all four of us could spend the day going through the stuff." I suspect Gerry's hesitancy was because of my inclusion. He had assumed correctly. There was no way I wasn't going with them.

There followed a short interlude of planning travel arrangements and activities for tomorrow that brought our time in the restaurant to an end. We three walked out to the motel's carpark with Gerry to see him off, before returning to gather in Ben's room. "I see Gerry still has the motel's dashboard gadget that opens the security gate," I remarked, and scored a giggled from the other two.

"I believe the Police Service might have commandeered it for a while… well, for as long as we continue to stay here," Neil said, as he closed the door and followed Ben and I into the room. Ben asked whether we wanted a drink or coffee, and then discovered he had run out of milk. "I've got an unopened carton in my room. I'll get it," Neil volunteered.

As soon as Neil left the room, I quietly asked Ben if he would prefer to be alone with his brother. I felt he might be able to get more information out of Neil if I weren't around. Ben looked surprised by the question. "No, I don't think it makes any difference. I'm almost convinced he doesn't know much more, but we will see how it goes. If I think he is being cute with us, I'll give you the nod to have some urgent work you need to complete in your own room."

Coffees in hand, we sat around sipping and making small talk briefly before Ben started the serious discussion. "Neil, that offshore company that owns that vehicle, was there anything else over here that it owns?"

"We're still trying to follow up on it and haven't found anything yet… but it's a bit like trying to chase a rabbit back to its burrow. Why do you ask?"

"A thought is bugging me. An offshore registered foreign company would hardly own vehicles here unless they had some sort of operation in this country. It might be that they operate an investment firm, or an agency of some sort… or they might own property. My money is on them owning property. What sort and where, I haven't a clue."

"Yeah, could be property, but it might be held under some subsidiary registered in Australia so it doesn't show in records as foreign ownership."

Since we were sharing nagging thoughts, I shared one that bothered me almost since I arrived at Minden Hill. "I'm a bit intrigued by the fact that Sarah's hire car was found in Brisbane. Why would they take the car to Brisbane when there are so many large towns and cities much closer? They could have abandoned the car anywhere. In fact, it probably would remain undetected for a longer time if it were dumped in some smaller country town."

"I had forgotten about Sarah's car," Ben said. "You're right though, Brisbane is a strange choice … *unless...*" Ben stopped speaking abruptly, but I could tell his mind was working overtime. "…*Unless* … unless they were already heading in that direction for some reason."

"You think they were taking those women to Brisbane?" Neil sounded sceptical.

"No, not necessarily, but it's possible I suppose. I was thinking more along the lines of their destination being somewhere outside of the capital, but somewhere in the southern part of Queensland."

I liked where this was going. All sorts of interesting scenarios generated by it flitted through my mind. I was staring at the pattern in the carpet when I heard my name called. "What…? Sorry, I was thinking about something and I wasn't listening. What did you say?"

"I asked if you had any bright ideas to contribute regarding why the car ended up in Brisbane." The sarcastic edge to Neil's voice raised my hackles. From long association, Ben knew it was likely to cause me to spit venom and become uncooperative. He interceded to smooth my feathers before they became too ruffled.

"Given everything that's happened and the car being found in Brisbane having bothered you for so long, I suspect you have given this whole thing plenty of thought. I sometimes like where your instinct takes us." Good old Ben; he always did know how to get around me.

"It's nothing really. I just thought it unlikely that they would go out of their way – drive all that way to Brisbane – just to dump a car. To my mind, it's more probable they were heading that way, took the car with them, and then dumped it where they thought it least likely to be found… well, not for some time anyway."

"...And in this fantasy of yours, is there a reason why they might be heading towards Brisbane? What is it that would drag them so far from what appears to be their home base here?"

Ben caught my arm as I turned on my heel and was about to flounce off. With his eyes and a slight flick of his head in Neil's direction, he gave me what I interpreted as the go-ahead to blast Neil with the mouthful I was carefully trying to bottle up. S-o-o, I did – and Neil looked suitable stunned when I finished. A mumbled apology followed, before Ben stepped into the breach again. "Do you have any thoughts on what would lure them north?" he asked quietly and smiled encouragingly.

"What do they do with the women they abduct? I don't really see them bumping them off when they finished having fun with them and then burying them at various locations. There had to be something more than a bit of fun for them involved... and I'm confident that 'something' was money. Why were they going to Brisbane? I don't think that was their destination. More likely, it was somewhere in south-east Queensland but outside of the capital... but it was a stop-over place and not the final destination."

"Hmm... yes, over the border and then somewhere to the west of Brisbane. Make a detour to dump the car in the city and then continue to the original destination. Yes, I can go along with that, but what's the attraction about that part of the world? Why go there?" Neil spoke without lifting his eyes from the toes of his boots, which he had been studying throughout the conversation. It was a valid question, and one for which I didn't have a well-defined answer, but I outlined a possible scenario.

"If we assume that those women are on their way to somewhere else – for whatever purpose -- it is likely the preferred method of delivering them is by plane, a light aircraft maybe. If that is the case, there are plenty of private airstrips and private planes on properties in that south-western area of Queensland."

"Are you suggesting the women are simply moved to another location somewhere and passed on to others to 'enjoy'?" Ben asked.

"Yes and yes ... I think."

"Where would they take them?" Neil looked sceptical and shook his head as he spoke. "A bevvy of strange women suddenly arriving in town would raise the odd eyebrow or two. Not only would it cause a bit of a flurry, but the local cops might be a bit interested as well."

"Come on, Sonny. Share your thoughts. This is a think tank session. In case you have forgotten, that's where you throw everything into the mix – no matter how ridiculous it sounds – to see where it leads," Ben reminded me.

"That's the problem. I don't actually have a clear thought to contribute yet. Just give me a minute to see if Gerry's photo of Frank Bellamy has arrived. I want to forward it to Sarah tonight so we can get her reaction as soon as possible. It will only take a minute." I left Ben making more coffee for himself and Neil, having declined another cup for myself. I was going to have trouble sleeping as it was after one cup at this late hour.

It took longer to boot up the computer than it did to forward Gerry's emailed image. However, the whole process did provide a few moments of solitude to devote to my as yet half-arsed idea of what the endgame was for the abducted women. By the time I returned to Ben's room, some clarity had crept in to my thinking, but not a lot. As expected, the moment I returned to Ben's room, the inquisition resumed.

"All done…?" Ben asked. I nodded. "Good. Now elaborate on what you think happens to those women."

Neil looked a bit sheepish and echoed Ben's request. "After all, at this point in time, you are the only one of us who seems to have any ideas on what it's all about."

I began hesitantly. "W-e-l-l, as I suggested before, I think they take the women – in small batches – to some location reasonably distant from here and load them onto a small plane to fly them to another location. I don't think that new location is the end of their journey."

"So, what are you suggesting…? From that new location, they are taken somewhere else, and then what… the ladies find themselves in business when a new brothel opens up in yet another location?" Neil was making what he thought of my idea quite clear, and even went so far as to add a sneer to help me get the message.

Ben stepped into the breach once more. "I suppose what you are suggesting is a possibility, Neil, but we gave Sonny the floor to share her thoughts before we started jumping to our own conclusions. Sonny, is what Neil is suggesting in line with your thinking?"

"Yes… and no; that's not exactly how I see it happening. I don't think there are any new brothels suddenly springing up around Australia."

"They could hardly take them offshore," Neil exclaimed. I bit my tongue, but gave him an exaggerated 'do tell me more' look – and he took the hint. "I mean, they couldn't fly them out of the country. They would never get them through all the checks and controls. It looks like there are about twenty women involved. It might be possible to get one small group of, say, four or five out without attracting too much interest, but not twenty – even if the departures were spread over an extended period of time."

To my way of thinking, he was right about them moving the women to their final destination in small groups. In fact, it was likely all of their movements from place to place were in small groups. I glanced at Ben. There was an air of excitement about him and I almost could hear his mind's cogs spinning at supersonic speed. "I think I see where you are going with this. Keep going; I want to hear the next bit of your theory," he said.

"I do think their final destination might be overseas somewhere, but I don't think their departure involves all the checks and controls that the rest of us encounter when heading overseas. I see this as a well-planned and executed operation. They would work out how to get around any such hurdles early in their planning."

"The Gulf again! They get them out somehow – possibly from somewhere on Cape York – via the Gulf of Carpentaria." Ben looked hard at me as he spoke, and then he gave me a grin and a nod. "It's the drug smuggling operation all over again, only in reverse this time."

Out of the corner of my eye, I saw Neil sit up sharply at Ben's comment about the drug smuggling. A few years ago, his men brought down a drug trafficking network bringing drugs in through the Gulf, but it was the work Ben and I did in Ralston that was instrumental in busting the ring and its supply network.

"Hmm … similar, but not necessarily the same as before. Your thoughts about Cape York might be right, but it could be from anywhere along the northern coastline, even remote parts of the northern Western Australian coastline." It was the best I could come up with at short notice, but I had to admit to favouring Cape York as well.

"You both talk about the coast and/or the ocean. I take it, you don't think they fly the women offshore somewhere," Neil asked.

"It's possible they do fly them somewhere… maybe one of the islands in the Torres Strait or the Gulf, or even the islands off the top end of the Northern Territory. But, if they do fly them anywhere, it is to somewhere on Australian soil with easy access to the sea." A vague idea of how it happened started to gather in the murky depths of my mind. Ben was right. This think tank approach might just work.

I played with the embryonic idea, gradually coaxing it to take form and make its way to the front of my mind. My feeling that the women's last contact with Australian soil being somewhere on the mainland was winning out over the suggestion of island options. What did I know about those northern waters? I found myself slowly developing the conviction that they left Australia by sea. All further wrestling with the problem ended when I heard my phone ring in the next room. I remembered leaving it next to my computer when I emailed Sarah.

It was Sarah. The image confronting her when she opened my email rattled her a bit. "Yes… yes, he was one of the two men I saw at the house. I think he was the offsider, or the assistant or something. The other bloke seemed to be in charge. He was even bigger than the bloke in the picture. That one – the boss -- had a raised angry-looking scar running down and across a cheek… uhmm, his right cheek, I think." Sarah gushed on for a few moments: who was he … what had we found out … had we caught Bellamy...? I let her spit out all her questions before giving her the one brief answer that dampened her enthusiasm: we hadn't made any real progress. There was no point in telling her about the contents of the garbage bags until I could add to it other more positive information. The call ended shortly after I promised to keep a disappointed Sarah informed of any progress as it happened.

The others had drifted onto other topics when I returned to Ben's room. It seemed the brothers were reminiscing over past shared times, times and events I knew nothing about. After relaying the key points of Sarah's phone call, I made my excuses and took my leave after agreeing to meet up again at breakfast.

CHAPTER 22

Although it was late when I left Ben's room and I already had felt my eyes getting heavy much earlier, sleep did not come easily. All the talk of what might have happened to the abducted women – particularly the how and where -- had my mind working overtime. I turned the lights off, sat in one of the comfortable chairs and put my feet up on the end of the bed. Blackness didn't envelope the room. Light from the corridor crept in under the door, and the so-called 'block-out' curtains on the window were something of a misnomer. At best, my room was a twilight zone. At worst, it was too light for sleep if that commodity were proving difficult to come by.

My head dropped with a sudden jerk jarring my neck. Sleep had found me. I don't know how long I was asleep in the chair but, judging by the stiffness in my neck and shoulders, it was much longer than was good for me. I scrambled out of the chair, and stumbled a few steps to fall into bed. In those intervening few moments between being semi-awake and sleep, I felt the glow of self-satisfaction. I knew what became to those women and how it happened. With no further impediment, sleep descended swiftly and soundly.

In those last few moments between sleep and awakening, those last few moments when the ends of your lashes remain firmly clamped together, I knew I had to get out of bed and record the outcome of my late night – more like early morning – deliberations on the fate of the women. Should I share my thoughts with my colleagues, or wait for some appropriate moment? Perhaps I should wait until there is some evidence to verify my thinking. Breakfast passed without having to make a decision on the matter. The nostalgic journey the two brothers embarked on last night continued into the wee hours, and resulted in little conversation at breakfast this morning. Gerry arrived while we were still in the dining room. He raised his eyebrows questioningly at me when his attempts at conversation failed to ignite discussion.

The only thing I learned at breakfast was that we were going to examine

184

the contents of those garbage bags again this morning. Why we would do that was a mystery to me, but I chose not to question it. It appears that, when they discussed and agreed it yesterday, I either was missing or tuned out. Another revelation was that we would not go to the forensic laboratory as originally thought. Gerry arranged for the bags to be in his evidence room by this morning. While I felt our previous time with those bags was too short, I didn't have anything specific to follow-up on today.

At nine o'clock, we left the motel in our now familiar convoy on our way to Police headquarters. We followed Gerry directly to the room set aside for examining the contents of the bags. Everyone seemed a bit slow warming to the task but soon all were engrossed in something of their own choosing. On my way to the far end of the long, wide table on which the bags awaited us, I saw the bag containing Sarah's belongings. I took it with me to the far end of the table.

As I passed a small table pushed to one side of the room, a stack of photocopies caught my eye. Each document, comprised of a number of sheets stapled together, provided a complete inventory of the contents of each of the garbage bags. The document was a list of all the information gathered so far for each bag, including list of contents, any known owner's details, and anything noteworthy gained from their phones. I held a copy in front of me and perused it as I started to walk away. After only a couple of paces, I stopped and changed my mind. I wasn't sure why these documents were there, whether they were restricted in any way, or if I could have a copy. I wanted one to use now and to keep for my files, but I could think of someone else who might make good use of a copy as well. I retraced my steps and quickly snatched up a second copy.

I dumped Sarah's garbage bag in the clear space at the far end of the table and bent down to place my own tote bag on the floor under the table. While down there, I slipped the second copy of the document into my bag. If I wasn't supposed to have a copy of the document, I could plead ignorance… but I could have problems explaining why I needed two copies.

With Sarah's belongings spread out on the table in front of me, I dredged my memory for the conversation with Sarah when she told me what she had with her the night she disappeared. After mentally ticking off each item against my memory of the conversation, only one thing appeared to be missing. She said she always wore a gold zodiac sign medallion on a fine gold chain around her neck. I wasn't on the table.

One by one, I examined each object. Her coin purse was empty. Credit cards remained in her wallet. The phone was flat. Various bits and pieces usually found in a woman's handbag were all there: pens, small notebook, a couple of credit card slips, comb, lip balm… nothing of any import amongst that lot. I expected the leather handbag to be empty. I was wrong. A quick look inside initially confirmed my expectation. Then, I turned it upside down and shook it, not for any reason other than it seemed like the right thing to do. The zodiac medallion fell out of the bag and hung there, held by the chain that tangled around the zip on one of the bag's pockets. I flicked through the document to the list of Sarah's garbage bag contents... no mention of the necklace. The forensic boys hadn't found it. A certain feeling of 'one-upmanship' flooded over me.

For a while, I stood looking at the objects without seeing them. My mind assessed the way in which the abductors went about their business. It appears that any money was up for grabs. No notes or coins were amongst Sarah's belongings. However, everything else, including credit cards and the phone, seemed off limits. Perhaps they were smart enough to realise use of these things could be traced. It appears we aren't dealing with rank amateurs.

After shoving all of Sarah's belongings back into the garbage bag, I randomly selected another bag from those closest to me, found its listing on the document and tipped its contents out onto the table. Nothing surprising discovered from that exercise. The contents were true to the list but again there was no cash amongst the contents. I repeated the process with another couple of bags, generally with the same result. In the case of the last bag I checked, a pair of earrings caught in the lining of the handbag were not on the bag's list of contents. In all cases, the abductors appear to take only cash while ignoring anything identifiable or traceable. After the third randomly selected bag, I lost interest and made my way back to the other end of the table to see what the others were doing.

I found them doing much the same as I had, and wondered how long they intended to continue with what I saw as a pointless pursuit. "Are you guys looking for anything in particular … and do you need a hand?" I asked. Gerry straightened up from leaning over the table and stretched his back. He shook his head.

"We're not looking for anything in particular – just looking at what's here."

"It doesn't seem like you need me to help with that, so I'm off to look for a coffee."

"Wait for me," Ben said as he stuffed the contents he was examining back into their bag. "Coffee is a lot more attractive than whatever we are doing here." It appears that was a common belief. All four of us wandered down the street to a coffee shop, Gerry having warned us off the coffee in the police canteen.

We agreed there was nothing more to gain from the garbage bags and we should return to whatever other plans we had for the rest of the day. That was fine for Gerry and Neil who had men to check on and other matters to pursue. I had no plans and, as far as I knew, Ben had none either. That could prove tricky. I did want to get away from the motel for a while, but I needed to be alone. I did not want Ben tagging along because he had nothing better to do. It came as something of a relief when, over coffee, I heard the brothers planning for Ben to go with Neil to look over his operation and the evidence they had uncovered so far.

Travel arrangements needed adjusting to accommodate this new arrangement. Gerry remained at the police precinct. Ben travelled with Neil to wherever he had set up his operation. That left me with Ben's hire car. Although I wasn't listed as a driver on his hire agreement, we agreed that, as long as I didn't bend the car on the way back to the motel, no one would be any the wiser. After waiting until the others left, I made a phone call before driving out of the police precinct carpark. I enjoyed the short trip back to the motel with a station on the radio playing some very nice blues for company.

With a couple of hours to fill in, I sent Sarah an email about the whereabouts of her belongings, how it might be a while yet before they were returned, and how she should talk to her bank about issuing her with new credit cards. It struck me as strange there was no watch amongst Sarah's belongings. Many of the other garbage bags had watches included in their list of contents. I knew Sarah owned one of those expensive modern ones that tell the time purely as incidental to everything else that they do. Sometime during our escape from that house, she complained about having lost it and her necklace. My email shared the news that, while her necklace was with the rest of her stuff, the watch wasn't.

There wasn't much else I could do at Minden Hill. I had remained here not because of Sarah's case – that closed the moment she arrived home safely – but because of wanting to investigate my own abduction. I was determined not to leave until I had solved the mystery of what was going on and there was a good chance of seeing key players brought to justice. Honestly, what did I *really* hope to achieve by sticking around? It wasn't my case. I was only a bystander to this investigation… albeit one given quite a deal of leeway. It wasn't Ben's case either, but he continued to be involved. I'd like to think it was because of me. Logic said it was more to do with being around the other two cops and their teams.

Time slipped away. I had other clients to consider. Fate intervened on my behalf with two clients I was to begin work for this week. I rang to apologise and postpone, but in both cases, before I had a chance to say my piece, they requested a delay. Circumstances at their end rendered a start impossible until about the end of next week. Hooray, sometimes the Gods do come to the party. However, there were two enquiries from potential new clients on my answering machine. With still a little time to fill in before I left the motel, I gave both enquirers a quick call – nothing impossible in what they wanted – and emailed them my brochure and fees schedule.

It felt strange as I drove away from the motel alone and in what constituted my own car while I was at Minden Hill. It sat idle for so long, but started at the first turn of the key. Traffic was light as I drove down Rookwood's High Street to a vacant parking space right in front of my regular coffee shop. As I exited the car, I saw Dani McLeod coming along the footpath. I waited and we walked in together to take our place at what appeared to our favourite table. Aware of how busy Dani was, as soon as we ordered coffees, I got straight down to business.

"Thanks for finding some time to meet. I don't know if what I have will help with your story or not." I handed over one of the lists of the garbage contents and explained what it was. Her eyes lit up as she flipped through the pages.

"It certainly will help. Thank you. When I hadn't heard from you for a while, I began to wonder if you were still here and how the investigation was going. I held off ringing you because I wasn't sure if that might cause a problem."

"I don't know if it would or not, but I feel a bit the same way. That's why the others don't know about this meeting or that you now have that list. Have you been working on the story at all?"

Dani had been busy over the last couple of days. …And so had some of her 'friends' – or should that be 'contacts'? I gave her the registration number of the car we commandeered from the house for our escape. She used 'a friend' to get the owner's details. Then, another 'friend' checked company records for any connections with the owner, while yet another 'friend' checked land records for any connections. It seems her 'friends' are able to work a lot faster than Neil's team. She started outlining the outcome of her friends' work and had me diving into my bag for notebook and pen.

"They found an Australian registered subsidiary company – or shelf company or whatever they are called – and followed it through. It bought a couple of small parcels of land in Sydney initially, but might have since sold them. However, it owns a huge parcel of land on the western side of Cape York, right up near the tip. Its holding doesn't quite stretch across to the east coast of the Cape."

I could hardly control my excitement and struggled to keep my voice neutral when I asked questions about that holding. "Do we know anything about what they do with it? It seems a long way north to be running cattle, but I don't suppose there is much else they could do so far from developed areas. If it is cattle they are into, they would have to get them to an abattoir somewhere – or a port for live cattle trade shipment."

"Yeah, I did some digging. It seems like cattle is the main interest. Although, I found something that suggests there might be some connection with either the prawning or fishing industry in the Gulf. In spite of my best efforts so far, I haven't been able to dig up any more on that side of operations. However, a rural reporter I know says the property ships cattle to abattoirs and to Darwin for the live cattle trade. I don't know where they load them, whether it's from the property itself or if they have to take them to some other loading place."

Once she finished relaying all her newly found information, I took a gamble and asked a question that bothered me from the start of our relationship. "What's with the people in your office…?" I saw her confused look and she shook her head to indicate she didn't know what I was asking about. I explained about my original attempt to meet her, and how I had to resort to sheer cunning to speak to her that first day I called at newspaper office. "Have you pissed off the receptionist – as well as various other staff – over something?"

She shrugged. "…Internal politics, that's all."

That might be true, but she looked less than convincing when she said it. "Are you sure that's all it is? It isn't likely to have anything to do with this case is it?"

"N-o-o… No, of course not. I've had a bit of success lately and the golden-haired boy and his supporters are right offside about it. Ye-a-h…, I'm sure that's all it would have been about."

"If you say so, Dani, but please take care just the same. Don't go into any dark places alone… and it might be best if nobody knows what we have been talking about." She nodded and I was confident she knew what I was talking about.

With the sheet of paper with the company's details she gave me and my notebook safely stashed in my bag, I lingered in the store's front bookshop to watch Dani walk back to her office until she was out of sight. She hadn't attracted any interest. I scanned the street and its surrounds as far as I could for anything suspicious before hurrying across the footpath to my car. By the time I arrived back at the motel, I had just about worn out the car's mirrors by constantly checking for a tail or any other worrying activity. Ben's car was where I left it but Neil's vehicle hadn't returned.

As I reached the rear entrance to the motel, the security gate slid open and a short blast from a horn made me stop and look. It was Neil and Ben returning. I waited and we walked to our rooms together. After wrestling with my conscience since leaving Dani, I had reached a decision. As we approached Ben's room, I stopped and spoke to the two men. "You probably had a big day and I'm not sure what you've come up with, but I think I need to talk to you both as soon as you are free."

Ben knows me too well. "You've discovered something. What have you been up to while we were away?" He held his door open and ushered Neil and I inside. I declined coffee. I'd drunk more than enough for one day. While the other two helped themselves to cold beers from Ben's fridge, I fetched a bottle of water from my room. I barely re-entered the room when Ben demanded, "Right, come on, spill … what have you discovered?"

Was I being a touch too dramatic? Did I really have something to tell them that they didn't already know? It was only a fleeting moment of self-doubt. The other two made sure I didn't dwell on it and pressed me to tell them what I knew. I started cautiously, not wanting to make a big thing out of something they might already know.

"Have you found anything more to indicate where they might take the women they abduct?"

Neil shook his head. "No, and it might take a while. We all agree that it is probably somewhere just inland from some place along the northern coastline. The problem is that from, say, Townsville around to Broome is a long strip of coastline."

"…Anything more on that Panamanian-registered company?" They both shook their heads. I could see frustration written all over Ben.

"Come on, Sonny. I thought you were going to tell us something, not grill us for information."

"Okay, okay. I wanted to be sure that I had something you didn't already know. Notebooks and pens at the ready, please, to take down the following information." I rattled off details Dani gave me of the subsidiary company, its property on Cape York and its operations. "I haven't had a chance to follow-up on any of that information but, Neil, I'm sure your team will be able to uncover more fairly quickly."

Both men sat bolt upright in the chairs and looked at me, faces expressionless. They both had been heads-down, scribbling furiously as I spoke. Now, they sat digesting the information received. Then Ben's eyes lit up with excitement. "We were right. It's all there: isolated area, ocean access, boats, everything needed to move them out of the country."

I nodded. "Only one missing piece of the puzzle now: how do they get them to Cape York?" Ben nodded gently, more to himself than anyone else, as he pondered the question.

"Might one ask how you came by all this information?" Neil asked. His tone had an edge to it that I didn't much fancy.

Ben chuckled and spoke before I could answer. "You can ask, but you're not likely to get the sort of answer you want. Take it from me, save yourself the bother of asking."

My phone chirped for attention. I recognised Dani's number and excused myself to take the call in my room. "Just as a quick footnote to today's meeting," she began, "My contact has found another small property owned by that subsidiary company. It's in southwest Queensland, only about 150 kilometres from Brisbane by the look of it and not as big as the one on the Cape. What would they do there… cattle?"

"…Maybe, or more likely sheep. It sounds like it might be in that crossover region where it could be either." There wasn't opportunity to ask questions. Dani said she was emailing details of the property and ended the call. If she only just found out about the place, she probably couldn't tell me more about it anyway.

I was still holding my phone when Ben tapped lightly on the interconnecting door. "We are going to the restaurant for a drink before dinner. Will you be joining us?" I flicked a corner of the curtain aside. It was already dark outside. A check of my watch told me it was our usual hour to head to the restaurant. With my phone back in my pocket, I joined the brothers on their walk to the restaurant. Gerry waited at the bar. I guess that answers my unasked question. Yes, Gerry would be joining us for dinner again this evening.

It seemed like a good idea to leave it to Neil and Ben to decide whether to share my information with Gerry or not, so I said nothing and waited to see what happened. There wasn't much to see. Nothing happened while we sat at the bar. Later, as we went through the motions of taking our seats at our table, I noticed Ben trying to give me a signal with his face and eyes. It went over the top. I didn't have a clue what he was trying to tell me, but I nodded anyway to signify I understood and would comply. It left me not very communicative for the whole meal, as I wasn't game to say anything in case it was what I wasn't supposed to say.

I did have something I needed to ask Gerry. "The manager here seems a man of mystery. Do you know anything about him at all? I can't help wondering whether he was working with the abductors, and if Gary and the other bloke that came in via the Camphor Laurel tree worked for him."

"Nah… we checked him out but he's clean. It seems he's a trader – you know, shares and the money market and the likes. That's what he does on his computer upstairs all day and is successful at it. It seems the couple are quite well heeled. The only interesting thing we discovered was that he's not the manager of the place… well, in name only apparently. That dragon on reception is his sister and she is the real manager. But the chain that owns the motel hold the antiquated view that there needs to be a couple living on the premises, so her brother and his wife live upstairs. The wife keeps up the charade by coming downstairs occasionally. The couple live upstairs free and rent out their substantial seaside home. The sister lives in a penthouse apartment not too far away."

"Okay, it looks my villain-detecting radar malfunctioned in his case. I assume Gary gave the 'tree man' information on what part of the motel we stayed in." He shrugged to indicate that was possible. I was surprised Ben and Neil did not comment, preferring to study the contents of their plates instead.

Gerry left as soon as we finished eating. In spite of our discussion, he seemed a little disgruntled throughout the meal. Either his day had proved disappointing, or he was disappointed Neil had nothing new to contribute on the investigation. I still couldn't figure out why, but neither Ben nor Neil even hinted at uncovering any new information.

Not having spoken much during dinner gave me time to think a few things through and make a couple of decisions. I needed to talk to Ben as soon as we were alone tonight. That proved earlier than I expected. As we walked the corridor to our rooms, Neil took a phone call. He said he needed to take it in his room and had urgent work stuff to do afterwards. Ben and I sat in Ben's room, Ben with a scotch and me with a mineral water. I took the opportunity to tell him I would leave Minden Hill in the next day or so. He looked surprised.

"It's not like you to disappear before we completely unravel something. What's going on? Oh… hang on a minute… you have some other information you're going to follow-up on haven't you? It was that phone call just before dinner, wasn't it?"

He does read me too well. I laughed. "Actually, I was going to book my flight home this evening but still haven't done it. I have clients expecting me to start work on their cases in a few days, and I still have to return to Moxton to finalise all Sarah's stuff before finally going home to Millhaven. …But, okay, you guessed right. I did get another bit of info from that phone call." I relayed Dani's information about the second property not far out from Brisbane. He didn't question the source of the info, just asked if I trusted it.

After a couple of sips of scotch, he asked casually, "Am I right in assuming that, when you leave here, you won't be flying to Moxton?"

See, he does know me too well! "That's a fair assumption. I thought

I might take a scenic drive for part of the way and then maybe fly from Brisbane."

"I can't see much sense in us taking two cars. Are we taking yours or mine?" He didn't bother asking how I felt about us travelling together. After some discussion, we decided to take his vehicle. It was the bigger, more powerful of the two. By the time we said goodnight, all that remained to do, was decide when we would leave Minden Hill.

CHAPTER 23

Neil hadn't emerged from his room when Ben and I made our way to breakfast. In the short time we had alone together, we decided to leave Minden Hill the next day and planned how that should happen. We also agreed how to acquaint Neil with the fact that we were both leaving tomorrow. Neil was part way through his bacon and scrambled eggs when Ben introduced the subject.

"Sonny tells me she is leaving tomorrow; going home at last."

I thought I glimpsed a look of relief flit across Neil's face. He said nothing but asked the question by raising his eyebrows at me. I shrugged and stalled as I put together a response. "Yeah, I've taken more time off than I should. Luck has been on my side with a few things that happened with clients, but I can't put them off any longer. I need to get back to work."

Neil took a sip of coffee and looked over his mug at me. "I wouldn't have thought that mattered much. As the only one of your kind in town, what else are they going to do but wait for your return?"

"You're right. As the only Private Investigator in town now, they don't have too many options. …But it doesn't do my reputation or my professional profile much good if I treat clients like that… and they can always decide not to proceed with the investigation. The wife and the errant husband might have patched things up. Anyway, I thought you would be sick of me tagging along by now." Neil didn't rise to the bait and ignored my last comment.

"You should put your skills – talents, if you will – to proper use instead of chasing after errant husbands and cheating wives."

"What … join one of the Police Services, like yours for instance?"

"Why not? The work is interesting and varied; good pay and conditions…"

Ben snorted with laughter. "Sonny wouldn't last five minutes in a regulated environment like the Services. She tried being in the Public Service once before. Don't be ridiculous, Neil. I thought you had gotten to know her better than that."

Although I did my best indignation performance, Ben was right. I probably would find myself chucked out in quick time. I don't work well in those sorts of situations. My previous life in the Public Service is evidence of that. No doubt in an effort to diffuse the situation, the brothers then concentrated on planning their day. I sat through a couple minutes of their discussion before taking my leave and heading back to my room alone.

There was nothing I needed to do today other than to catch up with Dani McLeod. I wanted to have one last chat with her and say goodbye before leaving. It was still early, but it probably was a good time to ring Dani before she got too involved in other things. She was already at work covering a story on an overnight ram raid on an electrical warehouse. We agreed a time and place to meet. Our call was ending as Ben tapped lightly on the interconnecting door. I gestured for him to come in.

"Breaking the news of your departure to Neil went well I thought. Your performance was Oscar nomination material." My response is best left unrecorded.

Everybody's plans for at least the first half of the day now were in place. Ben would follow Neil into work to spend some of the morning looking over progress on their investigation. Later, the brothers intended to call on Gerry to see if he had anything new to contribute. I agreed to meet Ben at a bistro in Minden Hill for lunch. I didn't mention my planned meeting with Dani, instead vaguely gestured towards my files scattered over the table. Perhaps I would tell him about my meetings with Dani later … much later … like, in a few months' time.

Somehow, the drive to Rookwood that morning seemed shorter and more pleasant than previously. I allowed myself plenty of time as we were meeting at a different coffee shop today and I wasn't sure I knew where it was. As it turned out, the Caffeine Heaven coffee shop was only a block away from the bookstore where we usually met. From my table towards the back of the place, I idly watched the world go by the plate glass windows until Dani arrived. Breathless and red-faced from rushing down the street, she arrived about five minutes late. "I can't stay too long after all," she said after ordering a latte. "I've a chance at an editorial on today's story. I've got to get back and get it filed on time."

She gave me an overview of her story. I told her of my intended departure tomorrow. Dani genuinely seemed disappointed by my news. Back out on the street, we were about to say our goodbyes, when I dropped my bombshell … after checking there was no one within earshot. "Ben and I are heading up to Queensland with the intention of visiting that property outside Brisbane. I'll email you anything new that happens." She thanked me and we hugged and said our goodbyes before starting to walk off in our separate directions. After a few steps, I stopped and called Dani back. "I know you're in a hurry, but I just remembered something I don't think I told you about." I gave her an abridged version of the theory Ben and I shared about what happened to the abducted women and the connection with both the properties Dani had located.

After twiddling the knob a bit, I gave up trying to find a radio station playing some good blues music. Although a blues addict, the likes of Charlie Parker and Thelonious Monk were good company on the drive back to Minden Hill.

With not much time to fill in before meeting Ben for lunch, I couldn't do much more than tidy my files and stack them neatly to at least make it look as though I was in my room doing paperwork all morning. Allowing myself plenty of time, I set off on foot for the bistro and a lunch I was really looking forward to enjoying. I didn't take a jacket. The sun failed to conquer the bite in the air. Rather than go back for a coat, I wrapped my arms about my chest and stepped up my pace. I soon warmed up and arrived at the bistro a few minutes early. Ben was already waiting at a table by the window.

Lunch was good -- very good. Good food, good wine, good conversation, all accompanied by surprises. The plan was for Ben to tell Neil sometime during the morning that he thought he might follow Sonny's lead and head back home tomorrow. He didn't have to do that. Soon after he arrived at Neil's makeshift headquarters, Neil broke *his* news instead.

"It looks like things are starting to happen on Neil's side of things. When we left Gerry, Neil was going back to the motel to check out. He and his team are packing up their operation here this afternoon before going home to pack and be ready to fly to North Queensland early tomorrow morning. It seems someone's 'friend of a friend' has arranged for them to stay incognito at a place about halfway between Kurumba and the target property up on Cape York."

"Any clues as to what prompted the sudden move... has some new evidence come to light?"

"No-o-o, he didn't say so. I think it is more a case of those in authority having to get everything in place first. I'm sure everyone wanted to head up there as soon as they discovered the ownership of that property, but planning and arrangements always delay things."

"Well, if Neil is not around this afternoon, we might hand my vehicle in today instead of having to do it in the morning. That will give us a clear getaway without having to detour to drop off my car." Rather than have

Gerry and Neil become suspicious about what we were up to, our plan was for me to leave the motel first tomorrow morning, drive to the hire car place and complete the paperwork while waiting for Ben to follow along a while later. After that, we would travel together to the Brisbane area. Now, there was no need for the subterfuge.

Dinner that evening was a subdued affair with just the two of us, although Gerry did drop in for a drink on his way home. He too seemed disappointed everybody was leaving town. He didn't think he would have much more to do with the investigation as the focus was now on places outside his area. In one last bid to clear up one last lingering question, I surprised both Gerry and Ben when I asked it. "Gerry, what's happening with that detective you replaced… you know, the one who was suspended over some complaint or something."

"Ah, yes… well, not much I can say on that matter." I looked at him reproachfully. After a slight hesitation, he continued – carefully. "There appears to be another matter – which you would not be unfamiliar with I think – that will have more serious consequences for the man than the original issue." In spite of his carefully chosen words and his deadpan look, it didn't require too much thought to work out that Gerry referred to the abductions case. Damn, I wish he were more forthcoming. I want to know what the bloke's role was in all of this. His parting comment as he shook hands with us surprised me. "Looks like I'll be staying where I am for some time to come. It would be nice to keep in touch… not only about this case and however it pans out." We agreed, although I'm not sure whether we had our fingers crossed behind our backs at the time.

Our plan was to be away before reception's normal opening time, so we settled our accounts before returning to our rooms after dinner. We saw Gerry off and as soon as we finished eating, went back to our rooms to pack and be ready for an early start. I made up the account and emailed it to Maggie Sinclair. If I am meeting the client again later, I prefer them to have the account beforehand rather than handing it to them at the time. That way, they can work out what they want to quibble about when we next meet. Then, after about half an hour of packing, showering and washing hair, above the roar of the hairdryer I heard Ben call out an offer of a coffee or nightcap. Over a scotch, we agreed to forego breakfast at the motel in the morning in favour of hitting the road by six o'clock. The scotch helped, but it was still a restless night. It was amid mixed feelings about leaving Minden Hill that sleep finally came.

A definite chill greeted us as we made our way to Ben's car and dumped the last of our stuff into the boot. The sun started to peep over the distant hills as I stood in the morning dew and pressed the button to open the security gate for Ben. He relinquished his dashboard gadget for opening the gate when he settled his account last night. Soon, we were out of the town and heading up the highway in that cold half-light before dawn.

Neither of us spoke for quite a while, each occupied with their own thoughts. About half an hour into the drive, Ben announced that the next reasonable diner we passed was where we would have breakfast. It was about an hour later before a service station appeared. We ate more out of habit than to enjoy the food or ward off starvation. With no time wasted, armed with muesli bars and bottled water, we were back on the road and the kilometres were slipping by.

By mid-morning, we reached the outskirts of Brisbane and headed for an auto repair shop owned by a mate of Ben's. His private vehicle was due for some expensive maintenance, so he chose to leave it with his mate to work on while he flew to Ballina and hired a car. After settling his account, Ben drove away from the auto shop in the hire car and I followed in his vehicle. The big boxy diesel 4x4 felt like driving a tank. I'm okay in the centre of Brisbane, but I don't know my way around the suburbs, so I stuck close to his tail all the way to the next suburb. An office of the appropriate car hire firm was located in a huge shopping complex. It was where Ben planned to drop off the hire car.

Although there appeared to be acres of carpark, it was full and it was paid parking…and expensive. Ben pulled into a loading zone a few doors down from the hire firm and I nosed in behind him. He spoke to me through the passenger's window. "Don't bother trying to find a park. Just drive out of the shopping centre and spend some time driving around the suburb before cruising past here again to see if I've finished inside." With no idea where I was going I drove off and soon found myself weaving my way through a maze of tree lined suburban streets.

I came across a corner store and a newsagent on a back street, and stopped to replenish our bottled water supply and bought a map of the surrounding district. Then, back to the shopping complex. No sign of Ben, so I drove around through the parking area to eat up more time before cruising past the pick-up place again. He was there on my second pass, climbed in quickly, and I drove out onto the street again. At the first place where I could pull over, we swapped places and Ben took over the driving. He steered us out into the rural countryside and, about an hour later, we stopped at a café in a small town.

The dyed blonde leathery looking woman behind the counter wasn't exactly rushed off her feet. We were her only customers. Ben's blue eyes worked their magic and she was on for a chat … with Ben that is. I was either invisible or she chose to ignore me. He did the interested - tourist - from - the - city thing and she was happy to tell him all about the town, its district, the surrounding properties and the social event of the year happening over the coming weekend. At about that point, I gave up being polite and wandered outside for a look at what else the town had to offer… not much as it turns out.

As I made my way back to the vehicle, something further along the street caught my eye. Ben unlocked the car. I climbed in without taking my eyes off a blue van parked in front of a stock and station agent's premises. "Blue van…" I said, and indicated where with a jerk of my head.

"Yeah, it's definitely a blue van. So what?"

"It's the blue van I saw drive away from that house before we escaped that morning."

"It's not a very distinctive van -- no markings on it anywhere that I can see. What makes you think it's the same van."

"I'm sure it is… no, I know it is. Look how incongruous it is with the rest of the vehicles in the place. The rest of them are all farm type vehicles; Land Rovers, utilities and light trucks and things with stock crates on the back." Ben shook his head in disbelief and flapped open the map I bought earlier. He spread it out across the steering wheel and mumbled to himself as he traced various roads with his forefinger. I ignored him and kept my attention focused on the blue van.

A man carrying two cartons stacked one on top of the other came out of the store. After placing the cartons on the curb, he walked around and opened the van's rear doors. About then, the thunder of four big black Harleys came down the street. The motorbikes were still some way off when one by one the man loaded his cartons into the van. Then, as he slammed the rear doors shut, the bikes roared past him. He stood and watched, pivoting from the waist to follow their progress as they continued on their way up the street towards where we sat.

I whacked Ben on the arm. "Look! Look at the bloke," I hissed, as I hauled out my phone and frantically scrolled through my emails.

"Yes, I can see a bloke watching the bikes. I'm sure that's not illegal."

"Look at this," I said as I shoved my phone in front of him. "Look at the image Gerry sent me."

Ben glanced at the image, then back at the man for a split second before the man turned and disappeared from view around to the passenger's side of the van. "Yeah, I'd say that was Frank Bellamy," Ben conceded. "You might be right about that being the same blue van. I think this town just gained a whole lot of fresh attraction."

The van drove off. A large truck loaded with portable toilets and other gear, and a utility with a stock crate followed it out of town. Ben eased out onto the street and fell in behind the other three vehicles but kept well back from the utility until it turned into a property after about ten minutes. We followed the truck for another half an hour, slowly allowing a little more distance to develop between us. Out of nowhere came an unexpected complication. What looked like some sort of hay baling rig drove out onto the road in front of us. We weren't in any danger of hitting it, but we did have to stop while it crossed the road to enter the property on the opposite side.

When the road was clear again, the truck was some distance ahead and indicating it was turning into a property off to the right. It slowed to a crawl as it negotiated the cattle grid at the entrance to the property. We waited for it to clear the road before continuing. The blue van was now a long way ahead. As we got closer, we watched the passenger – Bellamy, we had agreed – get back into the van after opening and closing the gate for the van to enter a property on the left side of the road. Then the van threw up a cloud of dust as it sped along a track towards a cluster of building some distance from the road.

We drove past the gate. A twenty-litre drum mounted on a post close to the gate served as the property's mailbox. They conveniently displayed the name of the property along the side of the drum. This was the place Dani's contact had identified. A short distance further along the fence line from the gate, a thin patch of scrub grew in the ditch beside the road. Ben pulled onto the shoulder of the road. We spent a few minutes looking across at the cluster of buildings through the curtain of scrub.

"That's a long airstrip… and it looks well made," I commented aloud. The airstrip ran all the way up to one of the buildings that stood with its doors wide open. Its doors formed the entire end wall. "I think that might be a hangar building. Yes, I think I can just about make out the nose of a plane inside."

"That's interesting." That was and unusual response from Ben, although I don't know what I expected.

"Y-e-s, it is interesting, but it is what we expected … isn't it?"

There was no reply. I spun around to look at Ben. He wasn't looking at the building. He was looking over towards the other side of the road. Then I saw it: a long banner tied to the opposite property's fence. Ben pointed to the banner. "That's the social event of the year the woman at the café told me about: a racing carnival on Saturday afternoon, a B&S (bachelors & spinsters) ball, on Saturday night, and a 'recovery breakfast' available all Sunday morning. I think it would be remiss of us to leave without experiencing what the place has to offer."

"Eh? Do we qualify as bachelor and spinster?"

"Neither of us is married. Of course we do."

"Nothing happens until tomorrow afternoon. We need to find somewhere to stay tonight."

The decision about where to stay didn't prove much of a problem. There was only one motel, a not particularly exciting looking place amongst a few cottages at the eastern approaches to the town. However, when we arrived there was a problem. They had only one room available. Ben assured the receptionist that wouldn't be a problem. I made to protest, but caught his steely-eyed stare and bit my tongue. The room contained two beds: a queen sized and a single. Guess who drew the short straw for the single bed. At least I fitted. Ben was a few inches too long for it anyway.

Last thing before the shops closed, we revisited the main street. We had no camping gear with us and the nights were cold. Ben parked in front of the stock & station agent's store and disappeared inside. A second-hand shop back along the street a few doors interested me. I bought a cheap pair of jeans, a polo shirt and a heavy duty denim shirt before returning to the agency to join Ben. I found him hunkered down in the back corner with and enthusiastic salesman who was extolling at length the virtues of the various brands of swags.

I discovered that what appeared to be a closed-up store next door was in fact a part of the agency. Removal of much of the dividing wall provided internal access to the area, which held the store's various clothing lines. Everything from work wear, through boots, hats to belts and buckles enticed me in to fill in time while I waited for Ben.

While rifling through the racks of clothing, I spotted a coat similar to one I almost bought last winter. Somehow, I managed to resist it then, probably because winter last year consisted of only a couple of cool days… and I didn't have any night surveillance happening at the time. My resistance failed me this time. A flat-topped Akubra hat and the coat joined my earlier purchases. Those purchases were justified. The limited wardrobe I took to Minden Hill would stand out like the proverbial in this place and was definitely not suited to camping out. Ben added two swags to my purchases. We threw everything into the back of the vehicle before heading over to the local pub for a drink and indulging in whatever was on offer in the way of counter meals. It turned out the food, while simple, was good.

Our motel maintained the practice of delivering breakfast on a tray to the rooms if requested. As we had nothing to do until around lunchtime when we hoped to set up camp at the social event of the year, we asked for a late breakfast. Even so, the mandatory ten o'clock check out deadline still left us with a couple of hours to kill. While Ben settled our account, I checked the room for anything we left behind before going out to the car. The cleaners, busy in one of the already vacated rooms, had their trolley parked in the hallway. As I walked past, I grabbed a couple of towels off the pile of clean ones in a stack on one end of the trolley and stuffed them in my tote bag.

"It's unlikely to be the establishment's silverware, so what have you got stuffed in that thing?" Ben asked as I flung the bulging tote bag on the back seat.

"Towels… now, let's get away from here before anyone comes looking for them."

"You do remember that I am a police officer and nicking stuff won't look good on my CV… or do my career any good?"

"Relax; I intend to return them before we leave town – without being seen preferably – but I had this strange idea that towels might be handy when we had our showers tonight."

We drove around for an hour or so just checking out the lay of the land until a few light aircrafts coming into land suggested it was time to find ourselves a camping site. A site adjacent to the fence and opposite the place where we pulled off the road yesterday seemed ideal for our purposes. I checked under the vehicle. "What are you doing?" Ben asked.

I looked up find him standing hands on hips checking out my rear end. "I was checking how much clearance there was under the car. We will need to sleep in our swags under there tonight if we don't want to be soaked by the dew."

"We could drop the back seats and sleep in the back of the vehicle. It would mean shifting everything out of the car… and I only would fit diagonally across it. On the other hand, we could rig up that ubiquitous blue poly tarpauling I have in the luggage compartment so that it keeps the elements off us." Okay, so I hadn't noticed the tarpaulin… probably because its case looked like a computer bag. It took only a few minutes to string it up between adjacent trees so that it covered about half of the vehicle and extended cover for some distance behind it.

With our camp set up, there wasn't much else to do for the rest of the afternoon except mingle with the other attendees, with occasional return visits to our vehicle to peer over the fence to check anything happening on the property across the way. As the afternoon progressed, the number of light aircraft coming into land increased until they resembled a swarm of flies. By dark, all was quiet. The place came to life again around eight o'clock when people began to converge on the area allocated to food stalls. We joined them in search of an evening meal. There were no tables to sit at, just hay bales for diners to sit on spread around three stalls selling food.

One offered burgers – or all of the burger fillings on a disposable plate. The second one sold take-way containers of Chinese food, while the third stall struggled to meet demand with its undersized portable pizza oven. Having decided trying to balance a plate of food on your knees was likely to be messy, Ben settled for a proper burger, while I bought fried rice. After watching the crowd for a while, I commented to a bloke on the next hay bale, "I haven't seen any ball gowns anywhere in the crowd. Don't people dress for the occasion?"

"Eh? Oh, just you wait and see. The crowd will thin out soon as they all go off to get their glad rags on for the ball. That wool shed over there is where the ball happens, but not until after about ten o'clock. What did you think of the races this afternoon? Didn't do your money, did you? Weren't there some exciting finishes?"

"No. No, we didn't make any bookies rich today." I excused myself and walked to the nearest bin to get rid of my plastic container. Ben followed me.

"What happened back there? You got up and left a little abruptly."

"He was starting to talk about this afternoon's horse races. I didn't want to admit we hadn't watched any of the races and weren't interested in them." I passed on the bloke's information about timings for the rest of the evening's events. We decided to slip away to our campsite along with the rest of the crowd heading off to get dressed for the ball.

We sat in the dark on the tailgate of Ben's vehicle while we waited for the crowd go dancing. There were no other campers within about a fifty metres radius of us, so we didn't have to worry about attracting too much attention. That suited us, as did the weather outlook. The weather report forecast a cold night without frost. I decided that wouldn't be a bad thing and crawled into my swag after removing only my boots.

CHAPTER 24

My inbuilt alarm woke me at my usual time. Ben slept on. I wriggled my top half out of the swag, sat upright… and reached for my new coat. It was freezing. Parts of me I didn't know I owned complained about having spent the night on the ground, albeit in a nice warm swag. I must be getting old. It certainly felt like it as I struggled to my feet. I spent the next couple of minutes stretching, and wriggling anything that moved in an effort to become mobile again.

Somewhere amongst all that, Ben woke up, and grunted and groaned as he too tried to regain the human race. The weatherman was right. There was no frost. Dew blanketed everything, and a thick mist clung to the tops of the trees and in the patches of scrub.

Careful to avoid touching the dripping top rail of the fence, I tried to peer through the scrub on the other side of the road. This repeated the last thing I did before crawling into my swag last night. In the clear night air, the lights of the distant buildings were clearly visible through the scrub. Off some distance to the west from the cluster of buildings at the airstrip was a large building I figured was a homestead. No lights showed from the building I thought was a hangar, but the smaller shed next door to it showed signs of life. Light escaped through the narrow gap around its door. This morning, although I could make out the cluster of buildings, the mist through the scrub prevented a clear view.

I toyed with the idea of crossing the road to get closer to the line of scrub for a better view, but decided against it. "Binoculars would be handy," I told the world in general and no one in particular. I heard Ben slam the car door and come to stand beside me.

"These might help." He held out a pair about the size of opera glasses.

I let out a loud guffaw at the sight of them. Then I saw the magnification information inscribed on their side and, refraining from comment, I smiled at him and held out my hand. Wow, they really are good. I could see the cluster of buildings clearly. As I made fine adjustments to the glasses, the hangar doors swung open. With the glasses, I had a clear view of the nose of an aircraft. Something was happening over there and, if I was going to watch it, I might be standing here for some time... and holding the binoculars to my eyes for any length of time would be a challenge.

The top railing of the fence was dripping with dew. I was reluctant to get my new coat wet... and it was too cold to take it off. I ran my hand along the rail but it only spread the moisture around instead of removing it. Ben shoved me out of the way and wiped the railing with one of the motel's towels. I planted my elbows firmly on the top rail, put the glasses to my eyes and made myself comfortable for what I thought would be a long vigil. I was wrong.

As I steadied and refocused the glasses on the buildings at the end of the airstrip, an aircraft nosed its way out of the hangar. It was a small jet. I didn't recognise the make. What surprised me was the lack of activity about the place. There was no one about anywhere near those buildings, not even a dog wandering around.

My attention returned to the plane. It taxied out of the hangar and down the runway a short distance before describing a wide arc and heading back towards the hangar. On the return trip, it travelled right out on the far edge of the strip. When it was close to the buildings again, it passed by the hangar, turned towards me, and parked in front of and parallel to the small shed next to the hangar. It was in close to the shed and I couldn't see what was happening on the other side of the plane but, by looking below the plane, I could see that the stairs were down.

Without taking my eyes off the plane, I yelled at Ben and waved him over to me. "Quickly, write this down..." I read off the tail numbers, and then read them out again... not because I thought Ben had missed them, but to imprint them on my own memory. "They are on the move I think. Yes, I just saw feet and legs on the stairs." I chanced a quick glance at Ben. He wasn't there beside me where he had been a moment ago.

Then the turbines stepped up from an idle. Their high-pitched scream filled the heavy morning air. After a bit of careful manoeuvring to line the aircraft up on the runway, the turbines went to full power and the jet screamed off down the runway and into the air. At last, there was activity on the ground. Two men appeared to lock the small shed before one of them disappeared around to the back of the building. The other walked across to the hangar and began closing its huge doors.

That now familiar blue van came around the corner of the hangar and stopped in front of it. The man struggling to close the hangar doors walked to the van driver's window. After only a brief conversation, he turned to walk back to the doors and, in doing so, faced me for the briefest moment. Frank Bellamy! ...and why not, I suppose. It shouldn't be a surprise. After all, he was with the van in town yesterday.

The driver of the van seemed to be doing something – undoing his seatbelt maybe. I yelled for Ben to bring the digital camera from my tote bag. I held the glasses to my eyes with one hand, held out the other hand and Ben plonked the camera into it. Then, quickly switching from the glasses to the camera, I had just finished adjusting the focus when the driver stepped out of the van. In the few moments it took him, to shut the van door and turn to walk over to his mate, I had the telephoto lens zoomed in on his face. I checked the image; a lovely clear shot. Now, to whom should I send it… Neil or Gerry?

I looked around for Ben. He was leaning on the bonnet of the car with his phone to his ear. Once the plane became visible above the trees, he stood beside me at the fence and swivelled around on the spot to track it as it streaked across the sky. He was still beside me when I asked for the camera, but then moved away to make his phone call. I wandered over to show him the image of the van driver. He stood up as I approached and shoved the camera in front of him. Although he continued speaking into the phone, his attention switched to the image I showed him. I wandered away and left him to get on with his call. It ended a few moments later.

By then, the plane was nothing more than a spot in the distant sky. I walked over to him and gestured with my chin to the phone still in his hand. “…Anything important happening?”

“…Thought Neil might find those tail numbers useful. They are on that property way up north… you know, the property next to the one we think is involved with the abductions. Their accommodation is in a bunkhouse some distance away from the property's homestead. I don't know much more than that, but he would like you to send him that image so he can have his mob work on identifying Bellamy's colleague.”

I hauled out my computer and set up to transfer the image from camera to computer. I did some thinking aloud as I did so. “They definitely loaded people onto that plane, and it seems to be heading on a northerly course. Could it get to the property on Cape York in one hop?” I really had been talking to myself and it came as a surprise when Ben answered.

“Yeah, I think the range of that jet is more than enough to take it to that property in one hop. There is an airstrip on the property. Where to land won't be a problem.” While Ben spoke, I downloaded the image of the van driver to my computer and sent a copy to Neil.

It seemed like a good idea to check again on what might be happening on the opposite place. With the binoculars to my eyes once more, I leaned on the fence and scanned the area around the cluster of buildings at the end of the airstrip. No sign of life there, and the blue van had disappeared.

I widened my scan area and caught a glimpse of the van through the trees, parked near what I assumed to be the property's homestead. Well hidden by the dense stand of trees, I wouldn't know the building was there if I hadn't seen it lit up last night. In spite of the cover provided by the trees, the blue of the van stood out from its surroundings.

Nothing much seemed to be happening over yonder, so I lowered the glasses and turned to lean my back up against the fence. "What do we do now?" I asked.

"Well, we pack up our camp, and then I thought we might go and indulge in some of that Recovery Breakfast that's teased my tastebuds ever since I woke up. We can talk about what happens after that while we are having breakfast." If it hadn't been for the wet tarpaulin, packing up would have taken only a couple of minutes.

By the time we had the soggy uncooperative blue poly mass folded and back in its plastic bag, we both sported many wet patches and much grass and mud. I gathered what water I could off the fence railings to clean my hands. Nevertheless, the once pristine white motel towel was a sad sight when I finished. Since I was standing at the fence, I decided it was worth another look to see if anything more had happened across the road. I didn't need the binoculars to see the blue van on the track. It approached the property's gate at a fair speed, even managing to raise a little dust in spite of last night's heavy dew.

I called Ben over to watch with me. The van stopped a short distance back from the gate and Bellamy climbed out to do the honours with the gate. After the van rattled across the cattle grid set into the entrance, it stopped and waited for Bellamy to lock up and climb in again before driving out and onto the road. It headed back towards town. A feeling of frustration surged through me; a feeling of having let them slip away.

Ben was on his phone again. This time he barked instructions at whoever was on the other end of the call. He got into the car as he spoke. Then he ended the call. "Get in," he yelled at me. I raced over and dived into the passenger's seat. I was still closing the car door as he roared away from our campsite.

"What's happened… where are we going?"

"To help the local copper; I think he might be faced with more than he can handle. Reach under your seat…" I did as requested. My hand closed on a familiar shape. With my head still down on my knees, I looked up and Ben and raised my eyebrows in question. "…Just yank it, it should come out easily." Why didn't I think of that? I took a firm grip and yanked hard. My hand flew out from under the seat, slamming my knuckles into the underside of the dashboard. I didn't bother checking my knuckles. I was too busy checking out the police service weapon in my hand. Ben didn't look at me.

Without taking his eyes off the road, he simply said, "There should be ammunition under there too. See if you can find that as well." I would be happier if he didn't take his eyes off the road – or his hands off the wheel – at the speed we were travelling. I still didn't know where we were going -- or why – but I felt the adrenalin rush that accompanies a tight situation. Whatever this mad dash was all about, I knew instinctively it involved some degree of danger. I checked the weapon and loaded it as best I could in the moving vehicle. I'm sure there is something in Workplace Health and Safety manuals about not doing this.

Ben fiddled with the knobs on the radio. I thought, for God's sake, Ben, don't do that when we are travelling at this speed, but I avoided verbalising my thoughts. We barrelled along. The weapon was on the floor by my feet. My knuckles were white from hanging on for dear life. The crackle of the radio suddenly filled the cabin. A voice I didn't recognise said he was in position but hadn't sighted the target yet. The voice also gave Ben instructions on what road to take. I interpreted it as being a backroad that skirted the town.

We turned off sharply onto what I assumed was the backroad that bypassed the town's main street. Ben did not ease off the accelerator. The big powerful vehicle cornered like the box on four wheels that it was, throwing me wildly against the seatbelt at every change of direction. For their own safety, I hoped the good citizens of the area stayed off the roads. Then I saw the reflection in the shiny paintwork of the car's bonnet: alternating read and blue flashing lights. There was no siren accompanying our wild dash, but the police warning lights Ben had fitted to this private vehicle were doing their thing … and, with any luck, keeping the road clear ahead of us.

We came around a final corner. Ben eased off the pace – a bit – as we headed towards a tee junction with the main highway through the place. Two police had two vehicles stationed at the intersection. In a cloud of dust, we skidded to a stop behind one of the police vehicles. Thrown forward hard against the seatbelt, I grunted and rubbed my shoulder as I struggled to regain an upright position. In the midst of this, Ben yelled at me, "Weapon…"

I undid the seatbelt and reached for the weapon I had placed on the floor. He made an impatient 'give-it-me' motion with his hand and, having located the weapon now half under my seat. I slammed it into his outstretched hand. "There's another one under my seat. You probably should get it – just in case you need it." I didn't need a second invitation;

although I still had no idea what was happening. I reached over and felt around under the driver's seat. Aahh, that's better; a fully loaded Glock … my weapon of choice.

No point hoping Ben would enlighten me. He had sprinted off to join the cops from the other vehicles. Whatever Ben expected didn't seem like it would be a friendly affair. In that case, being inside the vehicle wasn't a good thing. With the Glock buried in the cavernous pocket of my coat, I eased out of the vehicle and gently pushed the door closed. I looked around. No one issued me an invitation to join the others. That's okay… up there is where all the action is likely to be. I'm perfectly happy to stay back here. …But where exactly 'back here' do I want to be if things go pear-shaped and bullets start flying?

About five metres back along the way we had come and a short distance off the side of the road, a patch of scrub and vines almost subsumed what remained of a small corrugated iron shack or shed of some sort. It struck me as being the right place to be, rather than out here on the road. At a run, I crossed the spoon drain alongside the road and continued around the end of the patch of scrub and onto the derelict building. I moved around until I found a vantage point that allowed a view of anything moving from either direction along the road … and it even came with a seat, the stump of a tree felled long ago. I was still settling down in my 'hide' when I heard it. A vehicle travelling at speed came along the road from the same direction as we had. It didn't have the same gutsy growl of a powerful engine as Ben's vehicle. I guessed it to be a light four-cylinder model, probably pushed to its limit by the sound of it. I eased forward on my stump for a better look back along the road.

A small blue van approached at speed. Even at such distance, I made out something strange about the shape of it. It only took a couple of seconds for it to come close enough for me to see what was wrong with it. Head and shoulders out of the passenger's window, Frank Bellamy aimed some sort of semi-automatic weapon towards the vehicles and the cops at the intersection. No time to think; the vehicle is travelling too fast for the luxury of thought. Just act…

I raised the Glock, worked the slider, took aim and started counting heartbeats. After four beats, I judged the vehicle to be within range. I waited another heartbeat, let out my breath and fired. Yes…! From my position in the scrub, I watched it all happen in what seemed like slow motion. My shot found its target. The van slewed violently. A short burst of automatic fire from Bellamy's weapon described an arc skyward. Bellamy no longer hung out of the window as the driver struggled to regain control of the van. A volley of shots rang out. Without bothering to check from whom or where the shots came, I scrunched down and rolled off my stump onto the damp leaf litter surrounding it.

The van made a few strange sounds and died. Then, the once quiet country road echoed to the thunder of boots and shouted commands. The cops had arrived. Although I couldn't see what was happening, I guessed the shots I heard had disabled the vehicle. Amid the cacophony of slammed doors, shouted commands and other thumps and bangs, I crept out of my hiding place and along to the end of the of scrub. Foliage was thin here, providing a clear view of the scene playing out on the road.

Everything happened at warp speed after that. One of the cops ran and brought back a police vehicle. The van driver was bundled into it. Radios crackled and squelched. An ambulance turned up a few minutes later and left with Bellamy in the back. One of the cops photographed everything. A tow truck arrived. The van went onto a trailer and disappeared. A police paddy wagon arrived and took the van driver away. Ben took a couple of phone calls and looked pleased. …And then silence descended again, except for the crunch of Ben's boots on gravel as he came towards me.

"I think it's probably safe enough for you to come out now," he suggested. I strode out, trying to look nonchalant about the whole episode. The two local coppers did not attempt to hide their curiosity as I joined them on the roadway. One of them shuffled his feet and cleared his throat in readiness to say something. Both Ben and I read him well, and Ben jumped in before the bloke could say anything. "Don't worry about her," he said, waving his hand in my direction. "She's not one of us, but she is licensed to wave that thing around." He said, referring to the Glock, but didn't bother to explain why that was.

"Judging by the accuracy of that shot, I'd say she's spent quite a bit of time 'waving it around'," one of the others commented. Ben introduced the speaker as Harry, the local cop. Harry then introduced his colleague as Ray, the copper from the neighbouring area.

While I waited in the car, Ben spent some time talking to the other two cops about procedures, protocols, statements, internal investigations, and whatever else cops need to take care of in these situations. Then, one after the other, the two police vehicles drove off, and Ben slid into the driver's seat of his own vehicle. I had to ask the question I had avoided thus far. "How bad…? It was Bellamy, wasn't it?" Ben nodded. "How badly was he hit?" I swallowed hard and asked the real question. "Fatal…?"

"No, not quite … well, not yet, but that might change." I groaned at the thought of all that might follow if it did prove fatal. "Relax; it won't be a problem for you. Trust me, it won't be." I don't know if I like the sound of that or not, but I'll accept it as a good thing for now.

CHAPTER 25

It was time to make a few decisions. We had nothing more to do about the blue van incident – or so Ben assured me – and we were still in need of breakfast. Our first decision: where to eat and how soon. It was still early and the motel we stayed at on Friday night offered breakfast in a small dining room for anyone who dropped in off the street. That suited me, and we soon pulled into a parking lot out front of the motel. I slipped around to the guests' entrance while Ben went to the dining room.

The cleaners' trolley was in the hallway but so were the cleaners. I dawdled around outside for a few moments until they disappeared into one of the rooms before hurrying down the hallway. The motel's two towels came out of my tote bag and went into the soiled linen bin on the trolley in one deft move and I continued on to the dining room.

We started getting pointed looks from the dining room staff. It took us an inordinately long time to finish our breakfasts. Ben had a lot to tell me about how this morning's operation to apprehend the blue van was set up so quickly, and I wanted to know every minute detail. The story started back on Friday afternoon when I went into the second hand shop while Ben went to discover all about swags at the stock and station agency.

Harry, the local copper was in uniform when Ben met him in the agency. They introduced themselves and Ben had the foresight to ask for Harry's card with all his contact details. This morning, when things started happening on that property opposite our campsite, Ben rang Neil first and then, when the blue van started moving, Ben rang Harry about the possibility of setting up a roadblock. On the off chance he might need back up, Harry rang Ray, the copper from the next area. Ray, out on patrol at the time, was only a couple of minutes away from the boundary between the two police districts. It took no time for the two cops with their stingers at the ready to be in place. The only problem was, everyone expected the van to use the main highway and not the backroad as Ben had done.

I seemed to be having difficulty remembering we were back in Queensland, where Ben is a member of the state's police service and a high-ranking officer at that. It is much easier for him to make thing happen up here than it was for him in New South Wales. He assured me that apprehending the van was only a small part of the story. The big story would play out elsewhere – probably on a property on Cape York.

It occurred to me that a big part of the story was that property outside town where they held the women before loading them onto the plane. I voiced my concerns. "What about that property opposite where we camped last night? Surely, that is a major part of the network. The people living there must be involved up to their necks in what happens to the women."

"I think you will find Neil has arranged for another bunch of Federal Police officers to pay the place a visit."

We finally heeded the looks the staff gave us and left the dining room. As we walked to the car, I asked yet again the question that was becoming all too familiar. "What happens now?"

"Well, we both need to go home, so how about we head for the A1 Highway and head north, unless you have other plans?"

"I haven't made other plans but I intended flying from Brisbane to Moxton on the first available flight. I only need to spend about a day there to finalise Sarah's case before flying home to Millhaven."

"Do you want to fly? If we get moving now, we could be in Moxton by tonight or, alternatively, we could take our time, spend tonight somewhere along the way and arrive in Moxton tomorrow morning early."

The availability of the people I needed to see at Moxton depended on their current work rosters. "How about we head for the A1 and head north while I make a couple of phone calls? That way I'll know if there is anything critical about when I arrive in Moxton."

After my phone calls, we agreed to stop overnight at a beach along the coast, leaving us only a three-hour run into Moxton the next morning. The arrangement was for Ben to drop me at Emily's place before going on to Ralston to pack up his belongings for his move to Millhaven. Emily would be home and insisted I stay with her. I would fly home to Millhaven when my business in Moxton was completed.

Everything fell into place. Ben dropped me at Emily's at 9.30 on Monday morning. At ten o'clock, I met with Maggie and Sarah at the Moxton coffee shop where I first talked with Maggie about Sarah's disappearance. That meeting took longer than expected as they both wanted to know what we found out about the abductions and all that occurred after Sarah flew home. Nobody questioned the account, which Maggie had already paid. They drove me back to Emily's in time for lunch. In the afternoon, I went through a repeat performance with Emily, who wanted to know 'all about everything'. In amongst it all, I managed to book my flight home for first thing next morning.

Emily and I spent a quiet Monday night at home. I caught up with paperwork and phoned clients to set up appointments for the next day. Emily rang her mother, which turned into a very long chat – mainly about me and how the case had ended. I look forward to being in my own bed tomorrow night.

My flight to Millhaven left at seven o'clock and landed a few minutes ahead of time at 9.17am at Millhaven. The cab rank was empty. I waited twenty minutes for the first one to appear and, in spite of morning peak-hour traffic, arrived at my front door on the dot of ten o'clock. My first appointment wasn't until one o'clock, so I had the luxury of a couple of hours to unpack and relax before heading into my office in the city centre. I hit my workload head on. There were four clients' appointments booked for the afternoon, three more enquiries on the answering machine to deal with, and I would spend tonight in surveillance of and allegedly unfaithful husband.

The hectic pace continued all week until Sunday, when I finally felt the worst of it was behind me. Sunday evening, as I sat on the deck to watch the sunset light the clouds in unbelievable colours, my mind drifted back to Minden Hill. I thought about my time there and all that happened both there and afterwards. The frustration of not having any real closure to that episode washed over me. My mind began dwelling on the fate of all those other abducted women, that property on Cape York and whether there was a connection between the two. The longer I sat there, the more depressed I felt. My phone startled me back to reality, saving me from myself. It was Ben.

"What are you doing, have I interrupted anything important?"

"Not a thing; just sitting watching the sun set."

"Good, I'll be over in about half an hour with Chinese for dinner."

He had settled into his new place in Millhaven. Although officially he still had the next week off, he would be spending time at the police precinct familiarising himself with everything before starting in his new position the following week. It developed into a late night as he brought me up to date on everything that happened after we parted at Moxton. I wasn't the only one who had a busy week.

Neil and his team intercepted the jet when it landed at the Cape York property and rescued the five women on board. They also rescued another four held captive on the property awaiting the next stage of their journey. The wife of one of the men running the Cape York end of things decided she had enough of what was going on – and enough of her husband as it turns out – and filled in a few gaps in the story for Neil. Her information caused a flurry of activity.

After the women arrive at the property, they stay there until arrangements for the rest of their journey is in place. Then, in a small group of up to eight – sometimes as many as ten -- they board a fishing boat or trawler for a trip across the Gulf and out to the edge of Australian waters. The boat anchors or hangs around out there, to all intents and purposes engaged in its lawful business of long-line fishing. That is, until one night when another boat arrives. Under the cover of darkness, using dinghies, they transfer the women from the fishing boat to the luxury cruiser. The transfer occurs somewhere out of the way at the start of international waters and takes no more than an hour.

Once the women are on board the cruiser, it heads for an isolated small island in Indonesia. They hold the women prisoner at a remote location on the island until a private jet arrives. It collects maybe ten or twelve women each trip. The jet heads back to its home base in the Middle East – exact location unknown – and the sale begins. The buyers select and purchase their acquisitions from the batch of new arrivals, and the women disappear off to all points of the compass within that region.

Armed with the information provided by the disgruntled wife, the Federal Police intercepted the fishing boat, removed six women and took charge of the boat. They moved the boat further into Australian waters and set up the sting. Border patrol's drones alerted them when the luxury cruiser approached the area. By anchoring well inside Australian waters, the cruiser had to leave the safety of international waters. That night, the transfer didn't involve women. Armed Special Forces members took the place of the women in the dinghies and took command of the cruiser… after all, it was in Australian waters.

By the time Ben relayed this much of the story, we had despatched the Chinese food he brought and a nice bottle of white wine. I fetched mineral water from the fridge and replaced the empty wine bottle in the ice bucket with it. Ben continued with the story.

"Apparently, the Feds arranged with the Indonesian police, or military or whoever, to be kept informed as taking down the network progressed. Once the Aussies captured the cruiser, the Indonesians raided the remote compound on that island and rescued another group of women scheduled soon for despatch to the Middle East. Two of them were Australians and their names appeared on the list of belonging in those garbage bags."

"Uhmm… all that is great news but, if my calculations are correct, the total of those rescued falls a long way short of the twenty names on that list."

"Yeah, two of the women on the list remain unaccounted for."

"No, there are more than two."

"Eh? Oh yeah, I forgot to mention the additional two graves Gerry's team located. That now gives us four burials. Those four, plus Sarah and the thirteen rescued by Neil's operation, makes a total of eighteen we know about. Therefore, only two remain unaccounted for."

"What about those two… do they think there is any hope of rescuing them too?

"Er, well, current thinking is that there still might be another couple of undiscovered graves somewhere."

That was not a great note on which to end the story. I found it unsettling and sat in silence for a few minutes as I tried to digest all Ben told me. Ben let me sit with my thoughts until eventually becoming concerned for me. "Are you okay? I thought you wanted to know…"

"Yes, I did want to know. Thanks for telling me. I'm just finding it unsettling – and frustrating – that, what was nothing more than a money-making operation for those two blokes in the blue van, resulted in the deaths of possibly six women. Even those rescued are never likely to be the same again after what they experienced at the hands of those two men."

We eventually put that conversation to bed. However, I knew it would haunt me later when I was alone and in bed. I made coffee and we moved onto discussing other topics, including his move to Millhaven and his new job. We chatted on until after midnight. After he left, I cleared away the remnants of our meal and did anything else I could find to delay going to bed. Almost as an afterthought, I send Sarah an email to tell her Olivia's name was on the list of those rescued. Unfortunately, I knew nothing of Belinda's fate … at least, that's what I told Sarah. It was easier than telling her that Belinda probably occupied one of those graves. No doubt, there will be many long conversations with Sarah in the coming days. With my mind still in turmoil, I took myself off to bed when it was close to two o'clock.

After a restless night, I was slow off the mark this morning. At some time during the night, I heeded Ben's parting comment about focusing on the good, rather than the bad. Somehow, I managed to reconcile saving fourteen of the women from a life that wasn't in their plans for the future with the loss of four – and potentially six – lives.

With nothing requiring me at my office in town until after lunch, I spent the morning at home catching up on paperwork and domestic chores. An image of Dani McLeod swam into my mind. I sent her a long email. I didn't have the sort of accurate information she would want about how the abductions operation ended, but I suggested the sort of questions she should ask and directed her to the most likely people for answers to them. I liked Dani and she played a vital role in breaking the abductions network. I wanted to stay in her good books in case I found myself in need of a friend in future.

When I stopped mid-morning for coffee, my mind found something more frightening to worry about. Ben now was in Millhaven, working around the corner from my town office and living not all that far away. Was that a good thing or not? We were good friends from way back, and almost more than that at one time. After not seeing each other for some years, a case brought us together again a couple of years ago. …And now he was here in Millhaven again – where our friendship first began. What did that really mean for the future?

I wasn't sure there was any question to ask other than of myself … and I managed to do that in spades. What did I think might happen? Did I want him in my life … on some regular basis or otherwise? Did he *expect* to become a part of my life… to just show up and be around whenever he felt inclined? How did the prospect of that make me feel?

Too many questions and no real answers. Part of me was happy to have him around, while part of me dreaded the fact. I continued to wrestle with those questions as I drove into my office, and finally decided the angst was pointless. Whatever might come of it, only the future would determine what that was.

In the meantime, I have a busy afternoon with clients to contend with … and I have to shop for something to take with me when I go to check out Ben's new apartment this evening. Perhaps this will be the start of the future. Let's see where it leads.

The End

Missing!

ABOUT THE AUTHOR

Neive Denis is the creator of the series featuring the Private Investigator, Sonoma Whittington. Neive Denis is the pen name of a writer who was lured from her usual genre to focus on the mystery and excitement that are a part of Sonoma Whittington's world. Neive came into being specifically for this series and, for the moment at least, intends remaining faithful to only Sonny's stories.

This series of stories tells of the intrigue and scrapes – some on occasion life threatening – that are part of the life of Sonoma Whittington, an Australian Private Investigator based in a Central Queensland coastal city. However, Sonny doesn't confine her escapades to Australia, and that provides Neive with an opportunity to weave some of her other areas of interest into Sonny's hair-raising adventures.

See more about Neive Denis and her work at

www.neivedenis.com